Chaos

By David Meyer

Chaos Copyright © 2011 by David Meyer

Guerrilla Explorer Publishing

Publishers Note:
This book is a work of fiction. Names, places, characters, and incidents either are the product of the author's imagination or are used fictitiously, and any resemblance to actual persons, living or dead, business establishments, events, locales, is entirely coincidental.

All rights reserved.

No part of this book may be reproduced or transmitted in any form or by any means, electronic or mechanical, including photocopying, scanning, uploading, recording, or by information storage and retrieval system, or the Internet without prior written permission of the Publisher, copyright owner except where permitted by law. Your support of the author's rights is greatly appreciated.

First Edition – September 2011
ISBN -13: 978-0-6155503-1-2
ISBN-10: 0-6155503-1-2

Manufactured/Printed in the United States of America

Dedication

*This book is for Julie, my wife and the love of my life.
Without your support, none of this would've been possible.
Thank you for everything.*

PROLOGUE

THE OMEGA

March 6, 1976

The long, twisting tunnel should've been empty.

Fred Jenson's heart skipped a beat as he examined the gigantic black shadow that rose menacingly out of the darkness. What was a subway car still doing in the tunnel? Had it been damaged by the fire?

Sweat poured from his forehead, soaking his grimy face. With shaking hands, he lifted the bottle of Evan Williams, unscrewed the top, and tipped a few ounces down his throat.

It didn't burn. It never burned. Not anymore.

He stared at the car through bleary eyes. Must be fire-damaged. That was the only explanation that made sense. Yet, at least from his vantage point, it looked perfectly normal.

Jenson inched forward. He didn't want trouble. He merely wanted to see the destruction. The old guy, the one in the checked blue coat who slept in the maintenance shack, had told him all about it.

The old-timer said it was the worst disaster he'd ever seen. Maybe even the worst disaster in the history of New York's subway system.

Earlier that evening, a mysterious fire had ravaged the Times Square station, destroying a five-car length strip of the terminal. The 42nd Street Shuttle ceased operations immediately. Shortly after, the Metropolitan Transportation Authority shut down the entire route. Maintenance workers converged on the station, eager to complete repairs before the morning rush.

Three R36 ML subway cars were crippled by the blaze and all had supposedly been evacuated from the area. Scores of people suffered burns, with at least four confirmed fatalities. While the cause remained unknown, the old guy swore he overheard police officers chatting about it.

And they thought it was arson.

Abruptly, Jenson stumbled to his knees. His teeth clenched as a thousand knives pierced his skull. His vision crumpled from the corners and blackness enveloped him.

A roar of pain screeched out of his belly. Slamming his mouth shut, he cut it off, just like he'd done thousands of times before.

Breathe, damn it. Breathe.

No one's going to hurt you down here. The war is over.

Jenson began to count to sixty, slowly and methodically.

One. Two. Three…

The excruciating pain continued.

Twenty-four. Twenty-five. Twenty-six…

Gradually, lines and shapes began to poke out of the darkness. He saw the concrete trough. The dull running rails. The rotten wood ties. His pulse slowed. His nerves relaxed. Finally, the knives exited his skull and he exhaled with relief.

It was over. Sixty seconds had passed since he'd first felt the pain. Just sixty seconds. And yet, it felt much closer to sixty days instead.

His fist still held the half-full bottle of Evan Williams. Rising unsteadily to his feet, he raised it back to his lips and poured more bourbon into his stomach. His heavy breathing eased.

He took another swig.

Then another.

And then another.

He stared at the bottle, wavering slightly in his hand. Cheapest medical treatment he'd ever known. And far safer than those damn Veterans Affairs hospitals. He had that thing that was all the rage these days...what did the papers call it? Post-traumatic stress disorder?

Jenson bent over, fished through the dirt, and retrieved the cap to the bottle. Slowly, he screwed it back into place, protecting the precious liquid.

Sixty seconds. That's all it took. Sixty seconds to normalcy. Sixty seconds for his body to forget that other sixty seconds in Iwo Jima, the ones that had destroyed his life. That day, a bomb exploded in his soul, shattering it into a billion pieces.

Within sixty seconds of hitting that hellhole, enemy fire cut down his four closest friends. The five of them had jumped off the boat together and stormed the beach. But it was no ordinary beach. It was volcanic ash. As they ran forward, they quickly found themselves buried waist deep in it.

And then the shooting began.

Jenson didn't know how he survived the battle. The last thing he remembered was seeing his friends bent over at the waist, their arms splayed to the side, their faces lying in ash, their bodies riddled with holes.

After the war ended, he returned to his family. He went back to work at Brooklyn Gas & Electric. And for weeks on end, he sat in his chair, hunched over his desk, checking transactions for eight hours a day. He tried to live a normal life. And it worked.

For a little while.

Admittedly, he hadn't tried that hard. What was the point? He wasn't the same person, not anymore. So, how could he be expected to return to the same life?

Sure, living with the other bums in the subway tunnels wasn't exactly paradise. But at least they didn't expect anything from him. At least they didn't give him funny looks.

Jenson took a deep breath and walked forward, determined to conquer his fears. Fuzzy lines gradually firmed up and he began to see the subway car and its surroundings clearly. His aged, cauliflower ears caught something. He cocked his head and listened for a second. An uncomfortable feeling crept over him and he felt his blood pressure rise.

The noises arose from the general direction of the subway car. Noises he recognized. Noises that told him one indisputable, yet disturbing fact.

He wasn't alone.

Jenson felt a pinprick in his skull. He clamped down on his emotions, struggling to get them under control.

Eventually, his breathing slowed. He forced himself to look at the car and put it into context. It was one of the ruined R36 MLs. It had to be. And the noises probably came from subway workers. They were preparing to tow the car back to one of the yards for repairs. Yes, that explained everything.

And yet, it didn't.

He could see shadowy figures now, moving back and forth from a gaping hole in the south wall to the subway car. Two figures climbed out of the hole, carrying a massive bell-shaped object between them. It looked like it weighed a thousand pounds. And yet, the two figures held it aloft with little apparent effort.

Jenson's brain told him to turn and run. But the strange object piqued his curiosity. Against his better judgment, he crouched down and moved toward the center of the tracks, hoping for a better look.

The two men carried the object to the side of the subway car. They stood tall, unbending, as if the object in their hands weighed nothing at all. They disappeared into the car and then reappeared a few seconds later.

They walked away but Jenson barely noticed them. Instead, his eyes remained fixed on the car, trying to catch another glimpse of the strange, bell-like object.

But before he could do so, the men returned. This time, they carried a long, cylindrical burlap bag between them. Jenson stared at it.

His heart skipped another beat.

The bag was moving.

He'd seen enough to understand the danger he faced. If the shadows saw him, they'd kill him. Spinning around, Jenson ran.

Twin lights surged from behind him, casting a bright glow across the tunnel. Cursing, he slipped to the side of the track, opposite the third rail, and put on a burst of speed.

The single, non-pedestrian track under his feet connected the 42nd Street Shuttle Line to the Lexington Avenue Line. Ordinarily, it allowed shuttles to be taken in and out of service. But now, it served another purpose. It was his way out. His freedom.

His salvation.

Twenty yards to go.

He felt the ground tremble slightly. Digging deep, he picked up the pace.

Ten yards.

He stumbled. His hand reached out and touched the wall. Lurching forward, he tried to maintain his footing.

Five yards.

The light grew brighter and brighter. With one last long step, Jenson flew into another tunnel. Ducking to the side, he plastered himself against the wall. His heart slammed against his chest.

The subway car breached the pedestrian tunnel. It moved slowly and quietly, almost as if it were sneaking away from something.

As it passed by, Jenson couldn't help but stare at it. In addition to its strange contents, the railcar itself was highly unusual. Unlike the dull, faded grey that covered most subway cars, it exhibited a rich coat of silver paint. Instead of graffiti scrawls, a single word, written in black foot-size lettering, adorned the low alloy high tensile steel siding.

Omega.

The *Omega* paused and Jenson pressed his body as hard as he could against the concrete. Someone had seen him. He was sure of it.

But then, with a sullen, mechanical groan, the car completed its turn and pressed forward, heading south.

Jenson slid down, his back scraping against the wall. His haunches came to a rest just above his worn shoes.

Relief swept over him.

A loud high-pitched shriek reverberated across the tunnel, ping-ponging from wall to wall. Jenson glanced to his right. The *Omega* stood quietly in the semi-darkness.

Now what?

Metal rasped against metal. Then, three shadows hopped out of the subway car's side and ventured to the front.

"Running rails," one of the figures announced. "How the hell…?"

Jenson squinted. Long metal slabs lay perpendicular across the tracks. He didn't remember seeing them earlier.

Gunfire erupted from the south. One of the shadows jerked backward and fell. The other two retreated to the safety of the *Omega*.

Knives sliced back into Jenson's skull, sending waves of debilitating pain down his spine. He crumpled to the ground.

New shadows, too many to count, swarmed the subway car. The ear-piercing barrage continued for another forty seconds. As the tunnel fell quiet, Jenson felt more screams barreling their way toward his throat. Desperately, he tried to stop them. Any noise would give away his position.

And he wasn't ready to die. Not yet.

Blackness reappeared at the corners of his vision, eating its way toward the center. He blinked. The *Omega*'s doors remained open, providing some visibility to its interior. During the battle, the objects inside had shifted.

He sensed the new shadows surrounding the *Omega*. But he ignored them, keeping his attention focused solely on the bell-shaped object.

He now understood its secret.

And it scared the shit out of him.

Darkness swept across his eyes, consuming his sight. He felt himself falling, falling, into a deep abyss. And then, nothing.

Nothing but blackness.

PART I

VANISHED

Chapter 1

August 21, Present Day

Javier Kolen held his breath as he descended into the ground. It was a totally useless gesture, yet he found it comforting. The longer he kept the odors below from penetrating his nostrils, the better.

His hiking boots emitted soft scraping sounds as he worked his way down the rungs. His palms, encased in cheap leather gloves, held an iron grip on the rust-ridden bars.

He could've let go like the Braggart. He could've just dropped into the maintenance tunnel. After all, just ten feet separated his short, stocky frame from the concrete below. But that wasn't his style. Safety remained his top priority, no matter how much the Braggart needled him for it.

Kolen clambered down the rest of the ladder and stepped off into the old stone-block tunnel. As his boots sank into the inch-thick grime, he finally allowed himself to breathe. The odor, an unsettling combination of stale air and decaying trash, sickened him.

He looked up. The lamp strapped to his protective headgear shone on the closed manhole one hundred feet above him. The sight made him dizzy.

Two thousand dollars. Two thousand dollars.

Kolen repeated the mantra a few more times until his head began to clear. He didn't like the job. It didn't feel right. Yet, two thousand dollars cash was impossible for him to resist.

Reaching to his belt, he unclipped a handheld transceiver and raised it to his mouth. "Team Eagle is in the pot. We're ready to cook. See you on the other side."

The radio vibrated in his hand. "Roger that."

As he returned the transceiver to his belt, Kolen sensed movement. Turning to the side, he noticed the Braggart clawing frantically at the back of his neck.

Kolen tilted his head, confused. Suddenly, he felt skittering tiny touches on his shoulder. He swept his hand through the air, brushing off some sort of bug. He started to shudder but stopped cold instead.

Cockroaches.

The tunnel was crawling with them. He swiveled in a tight circle, horrified yet awed. The nasty little bugs covered practically every inch of the walls and ceiling. They shifted constantly, always in motion, a never-ending showcase of creepiness.

"Damn it, Javier," the Braggart said. "Stop standing there like an idiot and help me out."

Kolen didn't respond right away. He didn't like the Braggart, didn't like him one bit.

The Braggart's real name was Dan Adcock. He was just a kid, a ridiculous looking kid. His long black hair, tied into a ponytail, looked silly. His soft, hefty frame was laughable. Heck, even his gait, which was far too short for his lanky body, seemed absurd.

Kolen didn't know much about him, just that he was some kind of amateur treasure hunter. A treasure hunter who liked to talk about himself. A lot.

As he looked into Adcock's contorted face, Kolen found himself feeling the familiar doubts all over again. He was a respected urban archaeologist for God's sake. So what the hell was he doing in the middle of New York's subway system with a joker like Adcock?

Two thousand dollars. Two thousand dollars.

Kolen needed the money, needed it badly. He cleared his throat. "Why didn't you wear a turtleneck?"

"Do I look like I've been down here before? How was I supposed to know this was cockroach central?"

Reluctantly, Kolen walked over, peeled back Adcock's shirt, and flicked away a couple of large cockroaches. "Next time come prepared. And don't ask me to do this again. You're on your own from here."

"What's your problem?"

Kolen felt his temper building. "Nothing."

"You're full of it. You've been on my ass ever since we met."

"No I haven't."

"You think you're better than me don't you?"

"Of course not."

Adcock made a face. "You're a liar. You think you're better than me. But you know what? You're wrong. You might have a fancy degree. You probably get quoted in obscure magazines every now and then. But since you're here, I'm guessing your profession doesn't pay shit. And in a capitalist world like ours, that means your work is worthless."

Kolen knew he shouldn't respond. But he couldn't help himself. "There's more to life than money, you little bastard."

"Than why are you here?"

"I have my reasons. What about you?"

Adcock shrugged. "I like money."

"You're a treasure hunter right?"

"That's right."

"Ever find anything?"

"All the time."

Kolen laughed. "I doubt that. But regardless, do you know how to properly excavate a site? Do you know how to remove artifacts without damaging them? Do you keep every single thing you find, no matter how small, and painstakingly record it for future analysis?"

"Well…"

"Of course not. Because you don't care that you're destroying history. In fact, I bet you don't care about anyone but yourself."

Kolen sensed a weight lifting off his chest. It felt good to speak his mind. But one look at Adcock's sneering, obnoxious face caused the weight to come crashing back down again.

"You talk a good game," Adcock said. "But it's just talk. Otherwise you wouldn't be here."

"This is different."

"Yeah? How so?"

Kolen fell quiet. Not because he couldn't answer the question but because he didn't want to give Adcock the satisfaction.

Two thousand dollars. Two thousand dollars.

Kolen felt sick to his stomach. He was violating his principles, selling his soul for two thousand measly dollars. But he didn't have a choice. He needed money to pay off his gambling debts. Either he did the job or he'd lose his life. It was that simple.

That complicated.

Adopting a quick pace, Kolen strode through the tunnel. After a few moments, Adcock fell in behind him. Together, they walked through a couple of maintenance tunnels before finally arriving at the IRT Lexington Avenue Line.

The four-track line stretched from 125th Street in Harlem to downtown Brooklyn. It served more passengers than any other subway line in the United States. In fact, it served more passengers on a daily basis than both Boston's and San Francisco's rapid transit systems put together.

Adcock reached into his pocket and removed a wadded up piece of paper. Unfolding it, he stuck it against the closest wall. "We're here." He jabbed a finger at the paper. "And we're going here."

Kolen watched Adcock's finger trace a winding path that encompassed Grand Central Terminal, Union Square, and Penn Station. "How many miles is that?"

"How should I know?"

"Guess."

Adcock folded up the map and placed it back into his pocket. "We're covering a couple of lines here so maybe ten to fifteen miles. Of course, that doesn't include non-revenue tracks."

"That's a lot of walking."

He smirked. "Are you giving up already?"

"No, I'm just saying that we've got a lot of ground to cover."

"It could be much larger you know. There's about six hundred and sixty miles of passenger tracks under New York. Adding in non-revenue tracks, that number rises to eight hundred and forty."

"What's our strategy for staying safe down here?"

Adcock shrugged. "I wouldn't touch the third rail if I were you. Other than that, we should be fine. Whoever's pulling the strings on this little operation managed to temporarily shut down service in this area. So, we won't have to worry about running into any trains."

Kolen followed Adcock into the tunnel. They walked south for a short while and eventually reached the 42nd Street station. Two girls, young and drunk, milled about the area in their skimpiest clothes, waiting for the next train. When they saw Kolen and Adcock, their jaws dropped open. Kolen felt like telling them that they had a long wait ahead of them. But instead, he kept his mouth shut.

As he entered the next section of tunnel, Kolen felt a pebble work its way into his boot. "Hold up. I need a second."

Adcock sighed loudly but pulled to a stop. Then he began to look around, studying the walls with his light.

Kolen knelt down and untied his laces. "You know, this job would be a lot easier if there were video cameras down here."

"There are cameras down here. They just don't work very well."

"Sounds useful."

Adcock shrugged. "Your taxpayer dollars at work."

"I'm surprised Jack Chase hasn't tried to modernize it. He's got the dough."

"He's not going to spend his own money fixing up a public system. And besides, he's just the acting MTA Chairman. He won't be around forever."

"How does one become an acting Chairman anyway?"

"In his case, someone had to die."

"Forget I asked."

Adcock clucked impatiently. "Are you almost done?"

"Just a second."

"We're on a pretty tight time schedule. If it's all the same to you, I'm going to go on ahead."

"Fine."

Adcock started to walk south, the light from his headlamp diminishing with each step. Soon he was nothing more than a speck in the eerie darkness. As Kolen watched him leave, he continued to wrestle with his feelings. He wasn't sure what he disliked more...Adcock or the assignment.

Two thousand dollars. Two thousand dollars.

Kolen's hand shook as he took off his boot. He tried to ignore them, but his instincts told him that something was wrong. Shoving the thought from his mind, he removed the pebble, stuck the boot back on his foot, and retied it. Then he focused his eyes on the dim light cast by Adcock's headlamp and began walking again.

He shuffled forward for a block and then another one. Gradually, his mind shifted to other things...the leftovers waiting for him back in his apartment...his little niece's dance recital...next week's poker game.

It promised to be a good week, maybe even a great week. That is, assuming he paid off his debts before it was over.

A loud crashing noise broke his train of thought. The light in front of him vaporized and pure darkness settled over the tunnel. Kolen chuckled. Adcock must've fallen face-first onto the tracks.

Served him right.

He waited a few seconds, listening as more crashing noises followed the first one. A troubled feeling formed in the pit of his stomach. He lifted his head and turned his helmet, but the headlamp didn't detect any movement.

"Hey Dan," Kolen shouted into the darkness. "Are you okay?"

There was no response. Just more noises. They sounded like fleshy material pounding against concrete.

"Dan, can you hear me?"

Kolen heard a strange, tearing noise, like a garment being ripped in two. And then...

"Help me...help..."

Kolen sprinted forward, pumping his arms as he ran. He forgot everything else around him. He forgot his location, forgot his problems. He even forgot his dislike for Adcock.

After no more than a hundred feet, he spotted the man lying on the ground, motionless. His eyes tightened and his body tensed.

Kolen slid to a halt next to Adcock. Reaching down, he grabbed the man by his belt. Adcock seemed light for his size.

"Dan, what happened? Are you okay?" Kolen froze. A helpless, frightening feeling crept over him.

Adcock wasn't okay. He was dead. But that wasn't the worst of it.

Half of his body was missing.

Something had ripped him in half. Something that was, in all likelihood, still in the area.

A rush of movement came from the west.

Kolen whirled toward it. His headlamp caught a frenzy of activity. He tried to move but the sight of the horrible beast shocked him into stillness.

Powerful jaws clamped down on his leg and he felt himself dragged to the ground. He wanted to scream but his throat didn't work.

He tried to move, tried to stand up, tried to fight.

But it was too late.

He felt a wrenching pain in his waist.

Then he felt nothing at all.

Chapter 2

September 5

Hoisting myself up, I grabbed onto another handhold, desperately trying to maintain my concentration. After three years, I knew the warning signs. I knew all too well the headaches, the sensitivity to the sun, the mental haziness, and the sudden rush of intense, conflicting emotions.

The precariousness of the situation didn't escape me. I was nine thousand feet above sea level, surrounded by early morning light, and alone.

Completely, utterly alone.

Now, an episode was coming. It was inevitable, unavoidable.

And unless I reached the plateau in time, it would be lethal as well.

Along with my trusty self-belay device, I'd solo climbed plenty of peaks over the last three years. I knew the routine. It was engrained in my skull.

Set the anchor, lead the pitch, and fix the ropes. Rappel the pitch, clean the pitch, and haul the bags.

Rinse and repeat.

Over and over again.

Ordinarily, I found mountain climbing exhilarating yet mind-numbing. I hardly ever found it stressful. But this was no ordinary climb.

I climbed faster, my hands and feet scrabbling for holds on the schist. And ever so slowly, I moved up the sun-kissed rock face.

I could almost feel the flashback as it hurtled to the surface. The fallout, like always, was impossible to predict. I could black out. I could scream, alerting Standish's people to my presence. I could even rip away my climbing protection in a fit of temporary insanity.

The plateau grew larger, dominating my field of vision. It was so close. Just a few more feet.

Suddenly, violent colors erupted in my eyes. I felt a stinging, debilitating pain in my forehead.

Not now. Please not now.

My brain seemed to separate from my body. I couldn't see anything, couldn't do anything. Vaguely, I felt my arms reach out, stretching across the plateau. Then, my boots kicked to the side, landing on top of the rock.

I stood in lower Manhattan, hands on hips, soaking in the moment. The previous day, I'd made the find of the century. A find that would revolutionize the way historians viewed early Manhattan.

A find that would make my career.

Of course, I wouldn't take all the credit for myself. There was plenty to go around. But deep down, I knew the truth. Without me, none of it would've been possible. I was the one who found it. Me. No one else.

A loud shout caught my attention. Turning my head, I saw someone running toward me.

"Cyclone! Come quick! There's been an accident."

I frowned. "An accident?"

My headache vanished. The colorful sparks in my eyes died. My head cleared. My emotions dissipated.

I breathed heavily, giving myself time to return to normal. I hated the episodes with every ounce of my being. But that was the price I paid for my sins. It struck me that the experience, although shorter than usual, had been unexpectedly intense. I wondered what it meant. Maybe nothing.

Maybe everything.

Lifting my head, I examined myself for wounds. Seeing none, I propped myself up on my elbows. I ran a hand through my tousled hair and looked around. I lay on a patch of thin soil, covered with grass. Glancing to the side, I noticed that I'd rolled twenty yards away from the cliff.

At least I didn't roll the other way.

Noises and voices reached my ears. Twisting around, I saw a small camp about a hundred yards away and at a lower elevation. Large trenches zigzagged across a cleared-out field. More than twenty people, wearing hardhats and carrying hand tools, milled about the trenches performing archaeological work.

At least, that's what they thought they were doing.

Quickly, I stood up and took cover behind a large rock. After removing my climbing gear, I stowed it out of sight. Then, I checked my own tools.

Satchel? Check.

Machete? Check.

M1911A1 pistol? Check.

Reaching to my shoulder holster, I unsnapped the leather strap securing my gun. I wasn't eager to use it. But with what I intended to do, I was certain to attract unwanted attention. And if someone attacked me, well, all bets were off.

I performed reconnaissance for a few minutes. I didn't see Ryan Standish's massive frame anywhere. Nor did I recognize any of the workers. That wasn't terribly surprising though. Standish preferred to use local help for his dirty work. It made it so much easier to screw them over after he found what he wanted.

The workers appeared diligent but unskilled. The former archaeologist in me grimaced every time one of them picked up something from the ground. They were like kids in an antique store.

An antique store filled with irreplaceable artifacts.

Crouching low, I darted down a short slope. As quietly as possible, I penetrated a small tree grove and skirted my way around the edge of a cloud forest until I reached the rear of the dig site.

A dome-like structure, ten feet tall and thirty feet in diameter, stood before me. It was supported by heavy-duty PVC piping and covered with hefty green canvas. Four smaller domes sprouted out of the ground on either side of the main one.

I grabbed my machete from its sheath. Sneaking forward, I cut a small hole into the large dome's canvas and peered inside.

Hundreds of artifacts were scattered about the interior, spread out across dozens of tables. Tags dangled from most of the objects. However, they were noticeably missing from the largest and most impressive finds.

After confirming the dome was empty, I snuck inside. Looking around, I saw potsherds, carved greenstone rocks, flint arrowheads, and broken staffs. My eyes swept to the opposite end of the dome, passing by stacks of empty cardboard boxes and giant piles of various packing materials.

A two-foot tall artifact stood alone on a small table. Its golden edges gleamed in the few rays of light that managed to poke their way into the dome. I strode over to the table and picked up the relic.

My heart pounded as I studied the cacique, or pendant, cast from gold. It was heavy, yet felt light in my hands. It appeared to depict an important man, perhaps a chief. He stood with his hands on his hips and a fierce look across his face. Regardless of his place in the Tairona society, he was clearly a great warrior.

I turned it over, marveling at the craftsmanship. Every inch of the cacique featured rich detailing and underlying meaning. The scope of the work took my breath away. The Tairona people were, beyond a shadow of a doubt, the most spectacular gold workers of pre-Columbian America.

"Hello, Cyclone. Good to see you again."

I whirled around, still clutching the cacique. A tall, broad-shouldered man stood in the middle of the tent. He was clearly athletic, with rippled muscles showing through his tight t-shirt. His hair, wiry and black, was long and tied into a ponytail. His facial features, including a pair of sharp, grey eyes, were strong and distinct.

My muscles tensed. "It's Cy. And I wish I could say the same thing about you, Ryan. But frankly, I don't like you. Never have, never will."

Standish walked forward, taking long strides and swinging his powerful arms. At the same time, three brawny men stepped out from the shadows and formed a loose semicircle around me.

"You have excellent taste." He nodded at the cacique. "That's the prize of the dig. It should fetch at least a quarter of a million at auction."

"It doesn't belong to you."

"I found it, I keep it."

"You didn't find it. You didn't find any of this stuff. You paid off some local officials to let you hijack a pre-existing dig."

He shrugged. "It's business."

"It's theft."

"You should talk. You're not an archaeologist, not anymore. You're just a treasure hunter."

"And you're an asshole."

He held out his hand. "Although I'd love to keep this up, I have work to do. So, if you don't mind, I'd like my cacique back."

I stepped backward toward the canvas. My free hand brushed against something hard and slightly sharp on another table. It felt like an arrowhead and I quickly palmed it. "I found it, I keep it."

"You're on an isolated plateau in the middle of the Sierra Nevada de Santa Marta. You're surrounded by my employees. You have nowhere to go and no one to save you."

"You're right."

He looked at me suspiciously. "Then you're going to give it back?"

I held out the cacique. "I want free passage off this mountain."

"Of course."

I wanted to punch him and his magnanimous smile. He had no intention of letting me live.

Then again, I had no intention of giving him the cacique.

I tossed the artifact over Standish's head. His eyes widened and he dove to the ground to catch it. The other three men, distracted by the action, looked toward him.

Spinning around, I grabbed my machete. Sweeping the flint arrowhead across its back, I sent a shower of sparks flying into a nearby pile of foam peanuts. Small flames formed and grew in size, quickly igniting the canvas tent. Before I knew it, a wall of fire rose high into the air.

I shifted my attention back to Standish. He lay on the ground, holding the cacique, his attention diverted from the ensuing disaster.

"*¡Rápido!*," he shouted. "*Obtener los –*"

I stepped forward and kicked him in the jaw, cutting him off. Then I reached down, grabbed the cacique from his outstretched hands, and darted into the blaze.

Tremendous heat engulfed me. It singed my shirt and burnt my jeans. It leapt at my throat, stealing my oxygen. It was hell, pure and simple.

And then a split-second later, I was free.

I sprinted toward the cliff, passing a series of stunned, frozen workers. Behind me, I heard shouts and orders.

At the bottom of the hill, I glanced over my shoulder. Every single worker, male and female alike, raced after me. It was a strange, disconcerting sight, like being chased by an army of angry lemmings.

I sprinted uphill and grabbed my climbing equipment. As I slipped into the harness and secured my weapons, I snuck another look behind me. The workers were right on my tail. I didn't have much time.

I didn't have any time.

I stuffed the cacique into my satchel and ran forward to where my climbing rope was still anchored to the boulders below. With a savage cry, I leapt off the cliff. As my feet left the ground, a single thought raced through my mind.

What the hell am I doing?

I soared through the air and twisted my body, taking one last look at the workers. They returned my grin with shocked expressions. I shot them a quick salute and then, like a cartoon character, dropped like a rock.

Wind rushed into my face and ruffled my hair. I fell, praying to God that my multi-directional anchors would hold. They had to.

So, why am I still falling?

Abruptly, the rope jerked and my body jolted. I swung to the side, bashing my back against the hard schist. Looking up, I saw that the jutting cliff blocked me from view.

I was safe.

I was alive.

At least for the moment.

Chapter 3

Although exhausted and jittery, I still stopped to check my appearance in the cracked, dusty mirror. My face, covered with dried grime, looked worn and tired. My body sagged and my neck and shoulders sported numerous abrasions.

I tried to wipe away the dirt but merely succeeded in spreading it across my face. Next, I fiddled with my hair, turning it from a mess into an even bigger mess. I breathed rapidly through my nose, highly annoyed at myself.

Calm down, Cy. She's just another girl.

But she wasn't just another girl.

She was Beverly Ginger.

Giving up on my appearance, I walked over to the dilapidated, unmarked door. Lifting my fist, I rapped on the surface.

"The door's open."

Her voice, spicy yet melodic, sent shivers down my spine.

Get a grip on yourself, you idiot.

Twisting the knob, I opened the door. "I got it. I…"

My tongue tied as my eyes fell upon the woman sitting at the small table. With a classic hourglass figure and long, cascading chestnut brown hair that seemed to dance as she moved, Beverly Ginger was a strikingly gorgeous woman. Her tanned facial features were those of a classic beauty and radiated a youthful glow. Her eyes, a deep violet, seemed to peer right into my soul.

She wore a tight blue t-shirt that curved in all the right places. Her khaki pants hugged her hips and tapered downward, accentuating her long, shapely legs. A pair of slender boots completed her eye-popping look.

She was a goddess, an unobtainable, unreachable goddess. It wasn't her face or her body that gave me butterflies. Nor was it her clothes. It was something else, something intangible. She possessed that rare, indefinable quality that turned men's heads and caused women to shrink into their shoes.

She was, for lack of a better way to put it, Beverly Ginger.

Beverly looked up at me, batting those long eyelashes. Her smile vanished, replaced by a concerned look. "Are you okay?"

"Nothing that a cold shower and a hot meal can't fix."

She grinned. "Then you came to the wrong place."

I glanced around the room, surprised to see no bathroom or kitchen. In fact, there wasn't even a bed. There was nothing, except for the table and two chairs. "Do you live here?"

"No. But I wanted to meet someplace private."

I walked over to the table, opened my satchel, and removed the cacique. "As promised."

She took it into her hands, coddling it gently, like a baby. "It's beautiful. I've never seen such workmanship."

"Neither have I."

"Any problems?"

"Nothing I couldn't handle."

She placed the cacique on the table and stared at my bruised face with concern. "I'm sorry. I shouldn't have brought you into this."

"I recovered an artifact for your museum and got to kick Standish in the face. Honestly, I couldn't ask for a better day."

"I'd love to hear all about it. That is, unless you're busy."

"As long as you don't mind hanging out with a human dirt pile, I'm all yours. What did you have in mind?"

"First things first. I owe you money. Five million Colombian pesos right?"

"When you put it that way, it sounds like a huge score."

She smiled. "It converts to about three thousand of your American dollars. Not exactly earth-shattering money."

"I'm not really an American," I replied. "These days, I'm more of a nomad. How'd you raise all that cash anyways?"

"I rustled it up from the locals. They're just as mad as I am about Standish stealing my dig site."

"That's awfully generous of them. I bet they can't wait for you to open your museum."

She stood up and crossed the room. In the corner, she picked up a small shoulder bag. "They're excited all right. When we open next July –"

"Next July? I thought you were opening this year."

Returning to the table, she rifled through the bag. "Did I say July? I meant December."

My nerves began to tingle. "Wasn't it November?"

"I'm sorry, Cy. I really am."

She pulled a metal object from her bag. Startled, I reared up, knocking my chair over.

A crushing, tingling sensation erupted from my chest.

I fell to the ground, writhing in pain. I tried to fight, tried to resist, but my body refused to respond.

As my eyes began to close, I tilted my head upward. Beverly Ginger looked down at me, hands on hips. Flipping her hair over her shoulder, she gave me a saucy smile.

My vision deteriorated. Desperately, I fought to hold on to consciousness but it was a losing battle. Finally, my mind drifted away and I hurtled into darkness.

Hurtled into the unknown.

Chapter 4

As I stumbled forward, handcuffed and blinded by the coarse woolen bag tied around my head, I felt a profound sense of shame. It was the sort of shame that wrenched the gut and extended to every last cell of my body. But for once, it wasn't caused by memories of that fateful day three years prior. No, I felt ashamed for being caught off guard.

Ashamed that I'd fallen into Beverly's trap.

A loud scream reverberated in my ears and I ground to a halt. I didn't recognize the voice, although I was almost certain that it was human. But I could sense its anguish, its despair. It was the cry of sheer terror.

It was the cry of insanity.

As the scream died off, softer sounds began to emerge around me, sounds that had previously escaped my attention. Tiny claws skittered against the concrete floor. A metallic object, a pipe perhaps, hissed and vibrated. Liquid dripped from above, plopping into the tiny lakes that surrounded my feet.

Something hard poked at my spine, its coldness seeping through my sweat-drenched shirt. Taking the hint, I shuffled forward, water splashing under my mud-encrusted boots.

"Where are we?"

Silence followed my question. Again. It was annoying, unnerving. Eight hours had passed since my abduction in Taganga, eight hours without a single shred of conversation. Why wouldn't anyone talk to me? Who were these people?

Abruptly, a thin shaft of light penetrated the woolen fibers that covered my face. Twisting slightly, I aimed myself at the source and walked toward it. With each step, the light intensified, and soon I was forced to shut my eyes. But even that couldn't stop the growing brightness.

A catcher's mitt of a hand grabbed my shoulder. I halted and breathed deeply, inhaling the sickening odors of mildew, rotten meat, and spoiled fruit.

A lock clicked and metal scraped loudly against concrete. The light intensified again and beefy, powerful hands pushed me toward it. Gritting my teeth, I took a few awkward steps forward.

Where am I?

Almost all indications pointed to a prison. And yet, I sensed open space around me, far too much for a typical cell.

The hands grabbed my sore wrists and freed them from the handcuffs. Then, the woolen bag was torn away from my head. Blinding light flooded into my eyes.

Metal scratched against concrete and I heard a door slam behind me. Seconds later, the lock clicked.

"Hello, Mr. Reed. Please have a seat."

The soft, fuzzy words reverberated in my ears. I didn't recognize the voice, but I could sense its coolness, its strength. It was the voice of a leader. It was the voice of someone who wielded power.

Tremendous power.

"Give me a second," I muttered. "It's a tad bright in here."

"Of course. Take your time."

Rubbing my eyes, I racked my brain for a strategy. The man in front of me held my future in his hands. The right words, delivered with the right attitude might save my life. They might even give me back my freedom. But the wrong words or the wrong tone could worsen an already miserable situation.

As my eyes adjusted to the light, I lifted my head and prepared to speak. But the room in front of me took my breath away.

Dark wooden paneling covered the walls while an elaborate oriental carpet adorned the floor. Fine wooden tables, tall bookshelves filled with dusty volumes, and expensive sofas were tastefully positioned throughout the space. Antique lamps cast ridiculously soft light throughout the room, far softer than I'd realized. If I hadn't known better, I'd have thought I was in a mansion.

I lowered my eyes to the polished wooden desk that sat in front of me. A thin muscular man sat behind it, bathed in patches of light and shadow cast by the various lamps throughout the room. His eyes were small and brown, matching the mop of hair that topped his lined, tanned face. He wore an expensive pinstriped suit, complete with a dark red tie and white gloves over his hands. Every inch of him, except for his head, was covered with clothing.

He was a man of obvious wealth and power, a man who knew how to get what he wanted. But I wasn't intimidated.

At least not totally.

"Nice room," I said nonchalantly. "Where are we exactly?"

"A little ostentatious perhaps, but it serves my needs," he replied. "As for our location, well, that's my secret."

"Who are you?"

"It's Cyclone right? Cyclone Reed? Why don't you sit down? We have much to discuss."

I remained standing. "Call me Cy. Who are you?"

"Jack Chase."

"Nice to meet you. Now, can you give me one good reason why I shouldn't march over there and beat the crap out of you?" I watched him carefully, looking for signs of fear or adrenaline. But I saw nothing.

Instead, he leaned over the desk, picked up a crystal tumbler, and sipped it. I'd met some cool customers before, but Chase was in a league of his own.

After a moment, he set the tumbler back on the desk. "My apologies. We were a little disingenuous with you."

"Disingenuous? More like blatantly dishonest. Your girl hired me to retrieve a priceless artifact under false pretenses. Did she even manage the previous dig or was that just a lie?"

"She works for me. However, I'm arranging for the artifact you recovered to be delivered to the real archaeologist."

"That's comforting," I replied scornfully. "Oh, by the way, did she tell you the hell I went through to acquire that thing? And how she rewarded me with a Tasering?"

"Beverly can be a bit of a handful," he shrugged. "But she gets results. I asked her to test your limits, to see how far she could push you. And I must say, I'm extremely impressed."

Chase's icy demeanor frustrated me. At the same time, I couldn't help but feel curious about his motives. I sat down in a hand-carved wooden chair. "What do you want?"

He held up a bottle and a tumbler. "Scotch?"

"Sure."

He poured me a glass and passed it across the desk. Then he opened a file and flipped through it.

"Cyclone Reed," he read aloud. "Approximately thirty years old. Born and raised in New York City. PhD from New York University. Worked as a historical archaeologist, specializing in cities or, if you will, urban archaeology."

"Do you want my autograph?"

He closed the file and stared at me. "Tell me, why did a highly touted urban archaeologist, once viewed as the second-coming of Hiram Bingham III, leave it all behind to become a treasure hunter?"

"Mid-life crisis?"

"I don't think so."

"You've got my file," I replied. "Why don't you tell me?"

"Three years ago, there was an incident. One week later, you were gone."

My expression hardened. "Is that so?"

"Yes. And since then, you've been on the move, traveling from country to country, never staying in one place for more than a few months. You eke out a living by retrieving lost or stolen artifacts. But as far as I can tell, you're extremely discerning about the jobs you take."

"Not discerning enough, apparently."

"You're a treasure hunter," he continued. "Yet you retain the soul of an archaeologist."

I rolled my eyes. "Thanks for the psychoanalysis. Now, it's my turn. You're a wealthy executive who doesn't like to get his hands dirty. People are pawns to you. You think nothing of kidnapping an innocent man and holding him against his will. In short, you're a powerful man. Yet you retain the soul of a coward."

He leaned back in his seat and crossed his legs. "I see that I owe you an explanation. I'm the founder, owner, and CEO of a small security-consulting firm named ShadowFire. We're headquartered out of Manhattan. I'm also the acting Chairman of the Metropolitan Transportation Authority."

I laughed. "The MTA? New York's MTA? You must be joking."

"It's not a joke. The previous chairman passed away less than a month ago. I'm assuming the reins until a more suitable replacement can be found."

"So what do you want from me?"

"I want to hire you."

"Pass."

"That's too bad. Because I think I can help you."

"Help me? You must be out of your mind."

"You have hefty legal charges pending due to the, ah, incident. I can make that disappear and provide you with a generous stipend to boot. In other words, I can give you a blank slate. How does that sound?"

"Too good to be true."

He smiled, a bit too widely for my liking. "I know what you're thinking but I can assure you there's no catch. Upon successful completion of the assignment, my lawyers will negotiate with the necessary parties to clear your legal record. In addition, we will provide you with a substantial dowry. One million dollars to be exact."

One million dollars. That was mouth-watering, life-altering money. But I didn't like the strings attached to it. "Not interested."

"Just hear me out."

Obviously, he wasn't going to give up. And anyway, I wasn't in much of a position to bargain. "Okay," I replied after a moment. "I'm listening. What's the assignment?"

Chase lifted an old color Polaroid from the desk and passed it to me. The faded image depicted a strange-looking fellow, with puffy eyes, a bulbous nose, and misshapen shoulders.

Sort of like the love child of an ostrich and an ape.

"His name is Dr. Karl Hartek," Chase said. "He was a German physicist during the Second World War."

"What happened to him?"

"He emigrated to the United States in 1945, shortly after the surrender of Nazi Germany. He was a part of Operation Paperclip."

"Never heard of it."

"It was a program designed by the Office of Strategic Services. With the war coming to an end, America was already looking ahead to the Cold War. So, they recruited former Nazi scientists to come to America. After several months of interviews in Cape Canaveral, Hartek was relocated to Manhattan. He vanished a few years later."

"So what?"

"My researchers have linked Hartek to the *Organisation der ehemaligen SS-Angehörigen*, or ODESSA. ODESSA was a postwar network designed to help SS members escape the Allies. It also enabled those same SS members to transport Nazi resources out of Germany."

I shrugged. "Does this story have a point?"

"I'm getting to it. Although he was just a scientist, Hartek apparently held influence within the SS. As such, ODESSA entrusted him with a substantial treasure after he was forcibly immigrated to America."

"What happened to it?"

"Nobody knows for certain. However, two months ago, a man walked into a Manhattan pawnshop. He attempted to sell a gold bar, which displayed the markings of the *Deutsche Reichsbank*. Naturally, it raised the proprietor's suspicions. The proprietor called the police, but the man fled before help could arrive. Eventually, the story came across my desk and I was able to confirm that the serial number on the bar matched that of a gold bar distributed by ODESSA to Hartek many years ago."

"Do you have a lead on this man?"

Chase passed me another photograph. The lines were fuzzy and it lacked color, but I could easily make out the picture of an older man. He exhibited good posture. A fierce scowl was etched across his face. His hair looked dark and bushy. Although clearly advanced in years, his eyes maintained a spark of vitality that gave me pause.

I frowned as I passed it back to him. "You didn't answer my question. Do you have a lead on him?"

"Fingerprints at the scene confirmed his identity as Fred Jenson. He served during World War II. After the war, he returned to Brooklyn for a short while before going off-grid. This is the first time he's surfaced in decades."

"Off-grid? Where does he live?"

"Underground," Chase replied with a wily grin. "About one hundred feet under the streets of Manhattan, to be precise."

I tightened involuntarily and then forced myself to relax, cursing myself for being so transparent. "Are you sure?"

"Positive."

"So you want me to find him for you?"

"Obviously, we've done our research on you. In your previous life, you conducted an archaeological study of New York's subway tunnels, did you not?"

"Well, a section of them. But —"

"Then, you're the perfect man for the job." He paused to take a breath. "According to the pawn shop proprietor, Jenson said that he knew where to find more gold bars. He indicated that they were very close to where he lived. I want to hire you to find him as well as Hartek's treasure."

I held up my hand. "I don't think you know what you're asking. New York has hundreds of miles of subway tunnels and thousands of miles of sewers. And that doesn't even include naturally formed underground spaces."

"I know it won't be easy. That's why we're willing to pay you handsomely for your efforts."

"You're crazy if you think I'm going to spend the next few weeks dodging trains just so you can get a little bit richer."

"I'm not going to keep the treasure. On the contrary, I'm planning to return it to its rightful owners."

"Why?"

"Let's just say I have an interest in righting the wrongs of the past."

"You're going to have to do better than that."

He sighed. "My father was an American soldier. He died during World War II when I was just an infant. I think he'd appreciate my tiny effort at obtaining justice."

His face betrayed his steady voice. There was something else driving him, a reason he didn't want to share. I considered pressing him on it but ultimately, decided to forget it. "Aren't you worried I'll steal the treasure?"

"I doubt you could, even if you wanted to. We believe that ODESSA supplied Hartek with nearly half a ton of gold."

The staggering figure swirled in my brain. "How do you plan to conduct a treasure hunt under New York anyways? The moment the news gets out…and it will…you'll have a full-fledged riot on your hands."

"A solution is already in place. Now, will you take the assignment?"

A breeze passed through the room, chilling me to the bone. I tried to return Chase's stare, but the cocky smile that adorned his face was too much to bear. He was pushing all the right buttons with ease, playing me like a stupid keyboard. Instead, I looked over his head and for the first time noticed a window on the opposite side of the room.

A window covered with bars.

I needed the money. And a blank slate would go a long ways toward putting the incident in the past. But something about Chase bothered me, even beyond the fact that he'd kidnapped me. "You don't need me for this kind of work. Why don't you call in some locals? I can give you a few names if you like."

Chase looked uncomfortable. "We already tried that. Unfortunately, there was, well, an accident."

"What kind of accident?"

"Two of the people we hired vanished into thin air. At last contact, they were venturing toward Grand Central Terminal on the Lexington Avenue Line. They never reached the rendezvous point and a subsequent search failed to locate them."

"Did you call the police?"

"They filed a report and conducted a routine examination of the area. But they found nothing."

He folded his hands and placed them on the desk. "We tried an internal manhunt. We tried the police. The only option left remaining to us is to bring in an outsider. Someone who holds a deep knowledge of New York's underworld. Someone like you."

I rose to my feet. "Unfortunately for you, I'm not interested. Now, how the hell do I get out of here?"

"You're free to leave of course." He thrust one more picture into my hands. "But before you do, please take a look at this."

Annoyed, I quickly examined the photograph. Then, my fingers flexed, crumpling the sharp edges of the picture. "That's…"

"Yes," he said sadly. "Javier Kolen is one of the two men who disappeared."

The realization bathed me in its chilling waters. Kolen had worked with me on my final excavation. I didn't know him well, but I'd always considered him a rock-solid friend.

Something changed inside me. For three years, I'd buried my past. Three long, miserable years. Confronting it wouldn't be easy. But I couldn't just turn my back on Kolen. I needed to help him. Even if it meant a return to the one place on earth that I truly feared.

I cleared my throat. "How soon can you get me to Manhattan?"

Chapter 5

Everywhere I looked, I saw historical genocide. The quaint, elegant buildings from my previous life were long gone, replaced by skyscrapers and fancy new high-rises. Stores that I once frequented had shut their doors, making way for new retailers who would soon be replaced as well. The never-ending, so-called progress grated my nerves. In New York City, no one gave a damn about preservation.

"Are you okay, Mr. Reed?" the driver said over his shoulder. "Do you need anything? There should be a bottle of water at your side if you want it."

I looked into the rear view mirror of the Lincoln Town Car. Chase's personal driver, a skinny kid named Jim Walker, stared back at me. His face looked pale and his eyes seemed glassy. He looked like he might pass out at any second.

"I'm fine," I replied for the thousandth time. "Don't worry about me."

Walker nodded. As he turned to face the road, I allowed my mind to drift for a few moments. Many hours had passed since my encounter with Ryan Standish. Since my meeting with Beverly Ginger. Since my agreement with Jack Chase.

Many long hours.

I still felt in the dark. Chase flew me to Manhattan on his corporate jet. However, he spent the entire flight making business calls, shut away in a private compartment. After we landed, I tried to get a few minutes alone with him, to ask him some questions. But he sent me with Walker instead, claiming we'd meet later in the day.

His caginess made me leery. But my apprehension melted away the moment I climbed into the back of the Town Car. First, a ride in a private jet. Now, a ride in a private car, complete with personal driver. I never really yearned for wealth or power, but I found myself enjoying it, much to my dismay.

Something buzzed. Walker reached to his ear and began speaking in a muted tone.

A surge of nervous energy flowed through me. Three years ago, I abandoned my old life. I put it, along with New York City, behind me.

Forever.

But of course, I'd never forgotten it. And as I entered the city limits, I found myself growing increasingly restless.

My eyes drifted to the seat next to me, landing squarely on my beat-up canvas satchel. All my worldly possessions, a few changes of clothes, my holster and gun, my sheathed machete, and some odds and ends, were contained within it. It was remarkably old-fashioned, kind of like me.

I didn't have a laptop. I didn't possess a cell phone. In fact, I didn't own a single piece of electronic equipment. Walker, on the other hand, was more machine than man. He kept a cell phone in his hand, a headset in one ear, an iPod bud in the other, an iPad on his lap, and a GPS device in front of him. As I watched him juggle the devices with ease, I couldn't help but feel a little outdated.

I was an anachronism.

A man out of place.

A man out of time.

Walker coughed. "Sorry about this, Mr. Reed."

I shook my head, freeing myself from my thoughts. "What's that?"

"I was just apologizing for the wait. This traffic's a nightmare."

Leaning to the side, I glanced out the front window. Just ahead of us, cars lined up for blocks on end, noisy yet unmoving. It was the worst traffic jam I'd ever seen. "What's going on?"

"The MTA declared a lockout. Until further notice, all forms of public transportation are closed."

It had to be a coincidence. Chase wouldn't shut down New York's subway system just to conduct a clandestine treasure hunt. Such a blatant misuse of power was unthinkable.

I tried to drum up another explanation. But the truth blazed its way into my mind. Chase had knowingly endangered my life. He'd kidnapped me and manipulated me. There was no telling how far he'd go to get what he wanted.

"When did this happen?"

"Late last night," he replied. "But the conflict's been brewing for weeks now, ever since Mr. Chase took over as acting Chairman."

"Why am I not surprised?"

He shrugged. "The MTA's got a big deficit. Mr. Chase needed to draw the line somewhere. He's asking for cuts across the board, with heavy emphasis on pensions and healthcare benefits."

"Let me guess. They refused to budge?"

He nodded. "Did you know that public workers in this town make more dough than private ones? Mr. Chase just wants to bring them back into line and save the city some money, that's all."

"He's a real altruist."

Walker fell silent. I sat back in my seat, feeling less comfortable by the minute. Chase was prone to abrupt, egocentric action. I didn't like working for him. Only thoughts of Kolen kept me from demanding a ride back to the airport.

Kolen was a grumpy, tough old man. But he'd been a faithful friend to me ever since we met. He was one of the few people who stood by me after the incident. I couldn't turn my back on him, not now, not in the moment of his greatest need.

The minutes ticked by and I grew increasingly stir-crazy. I felt smothered by memories of Kolen, memories of my old life. I needed to move, to experience life. I wanted to leave the safety and comfort of the

Town Car. I wanted – no, I needed – to see Manhattan again, on my own terms. I needed to reconnect with it, to understand it.

Tentatively, my fingers reached for the door.

I jiggled the handle.

Locked.

Walker shot me a disapproving look. "Thinking of going somewhere?"

"I'm just bored. We've only gone five blocks in the last thirty minutes."

"Traffic will pick up soon. Once people get sick of waiting, they'll clear out of here."

"And go where? As far as I can see, every road is packed and every parking space is filled."

"It'll clear out. Just give it time."

"If I give it anymore of my time, I'm going to be filing for Social Security."

"Want me to put on the radio?" he asked. "Or if you like, there's a television set in front of you. Just pull down the panel on the back of my seat."

I pulled down the panel. Sure enough, a television screen appeared before my eyes. For a brief second, I considered turning it on, checking for news on the lockout. But the thought of watching a bunch of talking heads debate its merits made me queasy.

A large sign outside the window, posted at a bus stop, caught my attention. It read, "Last Year, 2,678 New Yorkers Saw Something and Said Something." A line of smaller text read, "If You See Something, Say Something."

Well, at least one thing about Manhattan hadn't changed. It still brimmed with fear. Tiny video cameras poked out of every nook, recording everyone at all times. Parents darted down the sidewalks, holding their children with iron grips, afraid of bogeymen around every corner. And now, even the public service ads were advising people to spy on their neighbors.

But where did all of the fear come from? The terrorist attacks of 9/11? A hyper-vigilant media? Politicians seeking re-election? No, those were just manifestations of a pre-existing emotion. The truth was that fear lived in everyone, at all times, just waiting to emerge.

Fear of pain. Fear of loss. Fear of death.

Fear of the past.

Traffic moved and we drove forward a couple of inches. As we jerked to a stop, I heard tiny splashes of water. Looking up at the sunroof, I noticed raindrops splattering on the glass, growing bigger and increasingly frequent.

A light mist settled over the streets, dimming visibility. With every passing second, the city outside my window grew more and more distant.

I needed to do something. Lifting my hand to my mouth, I coughed loudly. Walker, consumed with his music, didn't raise an eyebrow.

I grabbed my satchel. Then I reached up and unhinged the sunroof. As it opened, large raindrops engulfed me, splashing my shirt and jeans. I couldn't see anything outside, but I longed to be a part of it anyway.

Walker whirled around. "What are you doing?"

His fingers brushed against my ankle as I hoisted myself onto the roof. The cool air and powerful mist contrasted sharply with the car's warm and muggy interior. With one quick move, I leapt onto the street.

My boots touched the hard black pavement and I felt something I hadn't felt in years. A smile curled upon my lips as I darted toward the sidewalk. Many things had changed since I'd left Manhattan. But the energy remained the same. It was still there, pumping overtime.

I knew Walker was furious. Soon, Chase would be just as angry. But that didn't matter, not at the moment.

At long last, I was back in Manhattan.

I was home.

Chapter 6

The tall building didn't belong on the island of Manhattan. It belonged on Mount Olympus.

Thick, ornate columns rose high into the air, creating a false sense of grandeur. Stained glass windows, mounted at uneven intervals, stole the few rays of available light, casting strange color schemes over parts of the white marble exterior. Creepy, colossal faces of famous explorers stared out over the street, their dull eyes forever watching the unworthy.

Most people loved the Explorer's Society's headquarters. But I detested the place.

It was so damn pretentious.

For five minutes, I stared at the towering structure, nearly oblivious to the cold rain attacking my face, knit shirt, and jeans. A fierce wind plugged my ears. I smelled rotten milk, urine, and mothballs wafting from the trash bags piled nearby. But despite my discomfort, I remained rooted to the sidewalk.

Back in my youth, I'd sprinted up the exterior staircase every single day of every single week. I'd slip past the enormous doors and find myself in a whole other world. A world of adventure. A world of danger.

Sometimes, I'd stay past dinnertime. Curling up in the lecture hall, I'd drift off to sleep, dreaming of far off, exotic places. Inevitably, I'd wake up back at home, tucked under the covers. My mother, God bless her soul, never complained. I don't know why. Maybe she just liked seeing a smile on my face.

The building held many fine memories for me. I still felt pride when I recalled the day I finally received one of its exclusive memberships.

But much had changed over the last three years. The Society was different now and so was I. And as I examined every inch of the imposing edifice, it no longer seemed like a second home. Rather, it felt aloof and hostile.

Gritting my teeth, I tossed my satchel around my neck. No one knew where to find me. Not Walker, not anyone. And even if they did, gridlock would slow them down.

Although I felt in sync with the energy around me, I still felt out of place. I wanted to reconnect with my surroundings and there was only one person who could help me do that.

Lowering my head, I marched up the staircase to a pair of heavy oak doors. I traced my finger along the grooves for a moment, trying to recall the magic I felt as a child. But it wasn't the same. Emitting a deep sigh, I shoved the door open and stepped into the building.

My heart soared as I walked into the Great Hall of the Explorer's Society. Tall ornamental columns rose from the ground to the ceiling, forming elevated arches high above. Dark wood paneling covered the walls and floor. Crisp oriental carpets lay in several locations, their unique colors blending together to create a seamless fit. Centuries old stuffed heads hung from the walls, displaying animals that no longer existed.

A little smile crossed my face. Even after three years, the Great Hall still took my breath away.

My gaze swept the room, taking in the familiar wood and glass display cases. The extraordinary objects they held caused excitement to boil within me.

I saw Lewis and Clark's journals. A frozen case of liquor recovered from Ernest Shackleton's Nimrod Expedition. A hat that belonged to Ponce de León.

But the longer I studied the objects, the more my enthusiasm waned. As a kid, they inspired me. Now, they served as painful reminders of a life gone far off the rails.

I turned toward the back of the Great Hall. For the first time, I noticed a crowd of well-dressed men and women standing in tight groups. They laughed and chatted, oblivious to my presence.

I recognized some of the faces. Dale Hearns, the world-renowned anthropologist. Betsy Reese, the mountaineer. Mitch Lander, the ethnographer and writer.

My palms began to sweat. I hadn't talked to a single one of them since the incident. The thought of being surrounded by all of them was disconcerting, to say the least.

I saw a large sign behind the crowd. It advertised the lecture for that day, "Treasure Hunters: The Scourge of Archaeology."

A jolt of annoyance shot through my body.

Can this possibly get any more awkward?

Blocking my face, I forged through the crowd. I felt ashamed of myself and yet annoyed with my shame.

After jostling my way to the back of the room, I turned right and strode down a long hallway. Framed paintings adorned the walls, displaying the annual winners of the prestigious Explorer of the Year award. Once upon a time, I'd imagined that my visage would someday adorn those walls.

A painting came into view and my feet slid to a stop in front of it. Surprise filled me as I stared at the 2010 winner. It depicted a woman standing on a red carpet against a plain brown backdrop. She displayed a pretty face, perfect posture, a beautiful curvy body, and long, luxurious blonde hair. Her blue eyes sparkled with mischief and I found myself momentarily transfixed by them. I knew her.

I knew her well.

Ignoring my bubbling emotions, I continued walking down the corridor. At the end, I turned to face the door on the left. A nameplate, mounted at eye level, read, "Dutch Graham – Chairman."

As I slipped into the room, the stale aroma of musty books greeted my nose. It reminded me of a library. A very old library.

Two-hundred-year-old paintings, part of the Society's Hudson River School collection, hung crooked on the walls. Antique pieces of furniture, drowning under a sea of papers and books, were strewn haphazardly across the floor.

On the far end of the room sat a large oak desk and a fancy office chair. A man sat in the chair, facing the other direction. His legs angled upward and his feet rested on the fifth shelf of a large bookcase. His right hand glimmered and I caught a glimpse of a magnifying glass clenched in his fingers.

I cleared my throat. "Here's to us and those like us."

The man whirled around in his chair. A wicked grin spread across his face. "Damn few of us left," he replied in a harsh, gritty tone.

"You're looking good, Dutch."

"I look like hell and you know it."

Slowly, Dutch Graham rose from his seat and hobbled around his desk. He was from an earlier generation of explorers, more adventurer than scientist. Ever since we'd met, he'd viewed me as a kindred spirit, a sentiment I shared.

A lifetime of adventure had taken its toll on his body and he carried a myriad of battle scars, including a patch over his right eye and a mechanical left leg. Yet, I sensed that his ageless soul remained full of deviousness, exemplified by his timeless love for women, wine, and poker. It was little wonder that the other members used to call him El Diablo behind his back.

I grabbed Graham and bear-hugged him. "How are you?"

He returned the hug with surprising strength. "Same as always. Thanks for drying off before you barged in here."

"It's not my fault. It's raining outside."

"Ever heard of an umbrella?"

"Is this how you greet all your old friends?"

"Old friend, my ass. You haven't visited in years. And if you really were my friend, you wouldn't have left me alone with these pompous windbags."

"Someone has to keep them in their places."

"I'll say. So, when do I get to meet the wife?"

"I'm not married."

"Why not? It's not like you're getting any younger."

"I guess I just haven't found the right girl yet."

He nodded. "So, how long has it been since I last saw you? Two years?"

"More like three."

"Where do you live?"

"A bunch of places," I replied. "I haven't really settled down."

He studied me closely. "Don't get me wrong, I'm thrilled to see you. But what are you doing here?"

"I'm back in town for a week or so. A guy by the name of Jack Chase hired me to do something for him."

"That jerk? Why are you working for him?"

"You know him?"

"Not personally. But he runs an outfit called ShadowFire. Let's just say they're no stranger to controversy."

"He told me it was a security consulting company."

Graham snorted. "That's just corporate speak for a PMC. You know, a private military corporation. They're in the news every other week, fighting in one place, buying weapons in another. I'm surprised you haven't heard of them."

"I don't read much news these days."

"Well, watch your back. Chase is a snake, plain and simple."

"I see you're still judging people you haven't met."

He grinned and clapped me on the back. "Some things never change."

I returned the grin. "I was hoping to treat you to a couple of slices, give us a chance to catch up for a bit. If you want, I can come back later, after the lecture."

"Are you kidding? I hate those things. The other board members tell me I'm supposed to go but they don't really care. Frankly, I think I'm an embarrassment to them. No big deal. They share a shot glass worth of brains between the whole lot of them. No, I'm up for some food. Let's blow this joint."

Graham limped through the door and started walking down the hallway. I followed him out and then fell into step with him.

As we passed by the lecture hall, I happened to glance inside. My eyes were immediately drawn to a young woman with long blonde hair. She stood behind the podium, surrounded by fawning sycophants. An overhead fixture cast a soft glow upon her, lighting her up like an angel. A black dress and black boots covered her slim, curvy body. Her facial features were attractive and well proportioned, highlighted by a cute nose and big blue eyes.

It was Diane Blair, the girl from the painting.

She looked so different, yet so similar. I felt emotions stirring inside of me, emotions I hadn't felt in a long time.

I glanced at Graham. "Change of plans. Let's go to the lecture."

"I thought you wanted to skip the lecture."

"I do. But the lecturer, well, that's another matter altogether."

Chapter 7

"Not only do treasure hunters steal artifacts," Diane announced. "They steal history as well."

She spoke in a cool, clear tone. I hadn't heard her voice in three years. Yet, it sounded so familiar to my ears.

She stood behind a podium at the front of the Lindbergh Auditorium. Although it was a bit on the small side, the Auditorium put more than a few Broadway theatres to shame. Once upon a time, I'd found it magical and awe-inspiring. But now, I viewed it with a measure of distaste instead.

The walls and ceiling that surrounded the stage were painted gold and inlaid with dizzying designs and flamboyant stones. The stage itself, framed by rows of billowing burgundy curtains, practically screamed for attention.

Glass and wood cases, similar to those in the Great Hall, sat at various positions around the stage. The exhibits themselves – a pipe, a tattered book, and dull rocks – seemed innocuous enough until one realized that they came from Christopher Columbus's voyage to the Americas, the Pancho Villa expedition, and the Apollo 11 moon landing, respectively.

I wondered how those famous explorers would feel about their personal belongings being showcased in such a pompous manner. Somehow, I doubted they'd approve.

I shifted uncomfortably in my chair. A couple dozen rows of soft velvet stadium seats stretched between Diane and me. Most of them were filled with haughty, hobnobbing scientists.

It was an impressive turnout, especially considering the traffic issues. I wasn't terribly surprised though. As 2010 Explorer of the Year, Diane was apparently quite the hot ticket.

And the fact that she's beautiful doesn't hurt either.

I looked at Diane. The rows of seats were like a gulf between us, a gulf that grew with every word she said to the audience. She stood on the respectable side of exploration, shoulder-to-shoulder with archaeologists, scientists and other academics. I used to stand with her. But these days, I increasingly found myself on the other side, in solidarity with the treasure hunters, the smugglers, and the black market dealers.

Still, I wanted to talk to her. I wasn't sure if she'd feel the same, not after the way I'd left her all those years ago. But I needed to try anyway. I checked the clock and decided to keep a low profile until the break. Then I'd find a way to get some alone time with her.

Of course, it was one thing to plan a conversation, another thing to actually follow through with it.

"We face an uphill battle," Diane said. "Interpol estimates that the black market antiquities trade is a four billion dollar business on an annual basis. Advances in ground-penetrating radar and other forms of technology have made it easier for treasure hunters to operate. Also, on-line auction sites now provide dealers with a safe and secure method of distribution. The authorities are stretched to the limit and fight an increasingly sophisticated enemy, driven solely by unfettered greed."

My eyes narrowed. One of the common fallacies of archaeology, one that I used to believe, was that archaeologists were selfless public servants. According to this line of thought, they eschew financial rewards and other baubles in order to unearth and understand history.

But archaeologists were just people and as such, subject to the same impulses as everyone else. Every treasure hunter I'd ever known exhibited greed. But so did every archaeologist as well. It was just a different type of greed. Greed for grant money. Greed for fame. Greed for professional respect. And most of all, greed for the power to control history.

Her eyes traced the crowd. Instinctively, I slouched into my seat, avoiding her gaze.

"...and people like us," she said as I returned my full attention to her speech. "The road is a long one. Wealthy collectors in particular must be convinced not to purchase artifacts with uncertain or fabricated provenances. Governments must be convinced to treat artifact smuggling as a serious crime, with punishments that deter would-be offenders. And finally, the media and groups such as ours must educate the public on the line between archaeologists who seek to preserve heritage and treasure hunters who seek to destroy it."

Out of the corner of my eye, I noticed a furtive look in my direction. Twisting my head to the side, I saw a woman whispering to the man next to her. Then they both looked at me. Gritting my teeth, I sank even lower into my seat, until I was practically lying in it.

"...in Egypt," Diane's unwavering voice continued. "It was one of the most resilient rings of black market smugglers that..."

The whispers in the room grew and the stares from the audience became increasingly frequent. I glanced over my shoulder, marking the door's position. It was time to leave before Diane noticed the disturbance. I'd go outside, melt into the shadows, and wait for the break. Placing my palms on the armrests, I started to stand up.

"Ms. Blair?"

I froze as the voice rang out above the crowd. I couldn't believe it. But there was no mistaking that arrogant, cocky tone.

She stopped in mid-sentence and peered into the audience. "Yes?"

Standish stood up and slowly turned to the side, forming an awkward triangle between him, Diane, and me. "It's my understanding that there's a treasure hunter in the audience today. His name is Cyclone Reed. I wonder if he'd be so kind as to provide us with his point of view on the subject?"

The audience shifted their positions to look at me. I sensed their dirty looks, their scornful expressions. My ears heated up until they were piping hot, like a forger's fire. Part of me wanted to look at Diane. The other part of me wanted to hop over a few rows of seats and coldcock Standish.

How the hell did he get back to Manhattan so quickly anyway? And why?

Slowly, I rose in my seat and looked at Diane. She stared back at me with a shocked face. I tried to swallow, but my mouth felt parched. There was no escaping the situation. I had to tough it out. "I'm not the only treasure hunter around here." I turned toward Standish. "Speaking of which, have you appropriated anyone else's dig sites lately?"

He raised an eyebrow. "There's no need to wage false accusations."

"I wasn't."

"I just wanted to hear your opinion on the subject. I'm not trying to bruise your ego."

"Maybe not, but I sure as hell enjoyed bruising your jaw."

His forehead cinched and his fingers curled into fists.

Out of the corner of my eye, I saw the large wall clock. The hands seemed to fly by, moving way too fast. Everything was spinning out of control.

I glanced at the stage. Diane's eyes clouded over and in an instant I felt three years of her anger and pain. I'd expected a little shock, a little surprise. Maybe even a little disgruntlement. But nothing could've prepared me for what I saw in her eyes.

She hates me.

After a long moment, she turned toward the audience. "I'm sorry for the interruption, ladies and gentlemen. However, this is as good a time as any to take a break. Please enjoy the refreshments outside and we'll reconvene in here in ten minutes. Thank you."

A murmur rose from the audience as Diane stepped away from the podium and strolled confidently through the doors to the Great Hall. With a quick nod to Graham, I tried to follow her.

But Standish blocked my path. "It's good to see you again so soon, Cyclone. I thought I'd have to wait months to pummel your face, but it looks like I got lucky."

"Get out of my way."

"Make me."

He was bigger than me, meaner too. I'd gotten the drop on him in Colombia, but this time I lacked the advantage of surprise.

I looked to the stage. Diane was gone. It took me only a second to make up my mind. Swinging to the side, I vaulted over a couple of rows.

"You're a coward, Cyclone," he called out. "You're a damn coward."

Ignoring him, I darted down the stairs and through the double doors. As I slid into the Great Hall, I saw Diane walking toward the exit. I tried to run after her, but the crowd gathered around me, peppering me with questions.

"Diane," I shouted. "Wait."

I pushed through the members, splitting the crowd. Precious seconds passed. Finally, I managed to break free.

"Hold on just a second." The new voice caught me off guard.

Twisting to the side, I saw Walker. His face betrayed his aggravation.

I shoved him out of the way and moved forward. But the crowd expanded, trapping me inside. Straining my neck, I managed to get one final glimpse of the exit.

But she was already gone.

Chapter 8

The small skyscraper at the corner of 52nd Street and 2nd Avenue didn't project importance. Even the light coating of raindrops that covered its exterior couldn't shine its dull granite blocks, its curiously short columns, and its large, unadorned windows. But despite its unimpressive looks, the building somehow managed to command respect.

Walker stopped the Town Car in front of the façade. Twisting around, he stared at me. We hadn't exchanged a single word for almost two hours. Not that I cared. I didn't feel much like talking.

"Do I need to escort you inside?"

I shrugged. "Sorry Jim, I didn't mean to waste your time."

"Don't apologize to me. Apologize to Mr. Chase."

As I stepped onto the sidewalk, rain poured down from above, stinging my face. Quickly, I maneuvered past some large planters and strode into the building.

At first glance, the lobby looked simple and elegant. The walls consisted of large granite blocks. Tall glass windows provided the space with a sense of openness. A stone fountain gurgled pleasantly from the middle of the room, pouring streams of water into a waiting pool below. The pool itself was brightly lit and I could see colorful fish swimming around inside.

But the lobby carried a darker side as well. Multiple cameras, whirring softly, scanned the room. Men and women, sporting hard, lined faces, milled about the area.

Looking around, I spotted a small circular desk. I hoofed my way across the marble floor and stopped in front of it.

A young woman looked up at me with a broad, confident smile. "May I help you?"

"I'm here to see Jack Chase."

Her smile slipped away. Behind her, I saw two heavies straighten up and glance in my direction. Apparently, it wasn't everyday that someone off the street came looking for the boss.

"Do you have an appointment?"

"No."

"I see. Well, if you leave your name and number with me, I'll be sure –"

"He's expecting me. My name's Cy Reed."

The heavies took a few steps forward, positioning themselves on both sides of the desk.

Frowning, the woman checked her screen. "I'm not seeing anything here. Perhaps you have the wrong date?"

"Not a chance."

Her frown deepened. "Well, I'm not seeing…"

I noticed the heavies moving behind me. Suddenly, I had an epiphany. "Maybe he used my full name. Cyclone Reed."

Abruptly, her smile returned. "Ah yes, Mr. Reed. I'm sorry about the confusion. Do you have your driver's license with you?"

"I don't drive. And before you ask, I don't have any other identification either."

The frown returned. She picked up a phone, punched in a number, and spoke softly into the receiver for a moment. Then she gave me a surprised look. "Mr. Chase will see you now."

Slowly, almost reluctantly, the heavies drifted away. As they returned to their original positions, the woman printed out a visitor's nametag and instructed me where to go.

I left the desk and walked through a guarded waist-high turnstile. Instantly, lights flashed and a loud buzzing noise burst into the air.

A third heavy stepped in front of me. "Sir, are you carrying any metal items?"

I looked down at my satchel and realized my gun and machete were inside of it. "Uh, yeah."

"I'll have to take them from you."

"That's not happening."

He started to reach for me and then pulled his hand back. The heavy listened to his earpiece for a moment and then shot me a curious glance. "My mistake, sir. You're free to go."

I walked ahead and entered an elevator. The panel consisted of just two buttons, Up and Down. I pressed Up.

I rode the elevator for a full minute before it eased to a halt. The doors opened silently and I stepped out into a corridor. Following it, I walked through a pair of clouded glass doors and into a small reception area that had all the personality of a dentist's office.

A middle-aged man peered up at me from behind a pair of thick glasses. He appeared to guard access to a single metal door located on the other side of his desk. "Good afternoon, Mr. Reed. Please take a seat. Mr. Chase is just finishing up an appointment."

I noticed plenty of magazines lying about the room. *Small Wars Journal. Jane's Intelligence Review. Soldier of Fortune.*

My eyes shifted to the walls, which were covered with plaques, certificates, and framed newspaper articles. I walked over to the largest of the frames. The piece, a front page article for the Washington Post, was entitled "ShadowFire: Mercenaries or Heroes?"

The accompanying photograph showed Chase standing casually in front of a compound, staring into the sky. I skimmed through the text, skipping the parts about the company's ongoing operations in the Middle East and its efforts to enter the anti-sea piracy market. One section in particular caught my attention and I leaned in for a closer look.

When confronted with their accusations, Mr. Chase laughed heartily. "My critics like to call me a death merchant," he said. "But the truth is I'm just a businessman with a product, no more and no less. I don't create the demand for it. I merely provide a service that attempts to satisfy that demand with as little..."

"I won't give an inch."

The muffled words drifted into the reception area, breaking my concentration. I pretended to keep reading, but the burgeoning fight behind the metal door occupied my full attention.

"We don't need this kind of publicity," replied an unfamiliar feminine voice. "ShadowFire's in enough hot water as it is. Just make a deal with them."

"Not a chance. Those leeches have bled this city dry for too long. I'm not going to stand by and let them continue to rip off the taxpayers."

The metal door flew open and a short, stocky woman strode into the reception area, clenching her fists. Moments later, Chase poked his head out of the door and flashed me a smile. "Come on in."

I stood up and followed him into his office. The room was small and sparsely decorated. Several oil paintings hung from the walls, depicting famous battles of American history. The solid wood floor looked dull and unpolished. A desk, completely lacking in papers of any kind, sat in the middle of the room, its singular prominent feature being an antique lamp. Behind the desk, I saw a bookshelf, a small refrigerator, and an old office chair.

As I sat down in one of the guest chairs, I noticed a securely locked glass case pushed up against the wall. Antique guns of all shapes and sizes rested on velvet pads within it. "I guess I should explain," I began.

"No need. By the way, what do you think of my firearm collection?"

"Pretty impressive. The Colt Army Model 1860 is in particularly fine condition."

"I didn't know you were an enthusiast."

I shrugged. "Chalk it up to coincidence. We used to have that exact same model on the mantle when I was a boy. It belonged to my third great-grandfather. He fought in the Civil War."

"I see bravery runs in your family. My favorite is the Smith & Wesson Victory Model. A remnant of a simpler time, when war was considered a noble, necessary response to a dangerous world."

"Speaking of a dangerous world, have you been outside lately?"

"Walker gave me the traffic report after you, uh, left. I understand it's quite a mess out there."

"It is."

"The union bosses have this city in a death grip. They make far more than their nonunionized counterparts and yet, provide mediocre services. They're protected from layoffs and practically unaccountable. Frankly, I'm sick of it."

"The timing seems fortuitous."

He gave me a shrewd look. "Do you think I planned it to facilitate your search?"

"Did you?"

He chuckled lightly. "So, other than traffic, I trust that your trip was satisfactory?"

I was annoyed at his refusal to answer my question. But that wasn't the only thing that bothered me. Something else gnawed at my brain, something unsettling. "How did Walker find me?"

"What do you mean?"

"Out of all the places in the city to look, why'd he search for me at the Explorer's Society?"

Chase stared at me for a long minute. "We placed a homing beacon in your satchel."

"Are you serious?"

"Please try to understand. I've invested a lot of time and money in this hunt. I can't afford anything happening to you."

"I'm touched."

"If you want, you may remove it. It's attached to your blade."

I reached into the satchel and felt around. At the base of the machete, I felt a small, hard object. Peeling it off, I tossed it onto his desk. "Let's get one thing straight. I'm already wavering on this assignment. If you pull another stunt like this, I walk."

"I understand. You have my word it won't happen again."

I nodded. "Now, before we proceed, I have one more question for you. What do you know about Ryan Standish?"

"Standish? That name sounds familiar."

"It should. Beverly hired me to steal the cacique from him."

"Ah yes, the crooked archaeologist."

"Did you know he's in Manhattan?"

"No, but I suppose I'm to blame. I have many friends within the Colombian government. As such, I was able to arrange for his deportation."

"They moved fast."

"My friends are powerful."

I sat back. "I guess so. Well, I prepared a search plan. Are you ready to get started?"

"In a minute."

"What are we waiting for?"

"Your partner."

My lip curled in annoyance. "I work alone."

"What if something goes wrong? What if you're injured and need help?"

"That won't happen."

"Maybe not, but all the same, I'd like you to have someone watching your back."

"You mean you want someone to spy on me."

He didn't answer. Instead, his eyes shifted. I followed his gaze to the metal door. As it opened, my muscles tightened.

"I know you two met before but let's make it formal," Chase said. "Cyclone Reed, meet your new partner. Beverly Ginger."

Chapter 9

I barely controlled my anger as Beverly glided into the room. The last thing I needed was a partner, especially one who'd already Tasered me.

She sat down next to me. Crossing her legs, she stared directly at Chase. I glanced in her direction and felt my jaw unhinge.

Beverly wore a tight, white collared shirt, popped open at the top, highlighting her ample chest. Her black and white pencil skirt hugged her hips and tapered to her knees, accentuating her legs. A perfect French manicure peeked out of her open-toed high heels, one of which she swung back and forth, over and over, like a hypnotist's swing watch.

First, she'd portrayed a victimized archaeologist. Now, she wore the attire and hungry look of a corporate executive. She was like some kind of sex-charged chameleon, changing her outfit and personality to match her needs.

And to seduce her prey.

I turned toward Chase. "You must be out of your mind."

"I know there are some trust issues here but –"

"She lied to my face. She risked my life." I raised my voice. "Then to top it off, she kidnapped me. Trust issues are the least of our worries."

"I understand your feelings. But this is non-negotiable. You need a partner."

I jerked my thumb at her. "And you think she's the best choice? Does she have any experience conducting a manhunt? Does she know anything about the tunnel system?"

Beverly smiled. "Maybe not. Then again, I'm not an archaeologist either, but I still managed to fool a so-called expert."

My blood boiled as I looked at her. "This isn't some kind of game. I'm going to venture miles into a hostile, closed environment. There are no food sources and few places to access potable water. I can't afford to expend time and energy babysitting you."

"I've experienced every type of weather and terrain known to man. I think I can handle a couple of city tunnels."

"In case it's escaped your attention, the two subjects vanished for a reason," I retorted. "Maybe a little-used tunnel collapsed on them. Maybe it was foul play. Regardless, if something goes wrong, there's nowhere to run to, nowhere to hide. I'm dead and so is anyone unfortunate enough to be with me."

I looked at Chase. "You already tried a manhunt. You already tried the police. You said it yourself back in Colombia…a solo operation might be the last chance you have to find Kolen and Adcock."

Chase smiled.

The bastard. He's actually enjoying this.

"So I did," he replied. "However, Beverly's still travelling with you. But you have my word that she won't get in your way. Her responsibilities are strictly limited to observing your progress and reporting back to me."

His tone indicated that the discussion was over. I leaned back in my seat and crossed my arms.

"Good," he said. "Now, let's get down to business. You mentioned you'd prepared a strategy?"

"According to the briefing I read aboard the plane, after attempting to pawn the gold bar, Fred Jenson disappeared into a subway station near Union Square. An initial investigation revealed that he maintained a permanent residence somewhere in New York's tunnels. Subsequently, you hired several teams to canvas the area."

I leaned forward. "One of those teams consisted of Javier Kolen and Dan Adcock. They entered the subway system shortly after midnight on August 21. They were tasked with searching several miles of tunnels, beginning with the Lexington Avenue Line. Javier reported his position at the start of the search but failed to check in at Union Square. Thanks to an eyewitness…"

"A severely intoxicated eyewitness," Beverly added.

"…we have reason to believe that they successfully passed through the Grand Central Terminal station. Thus, I'll begin my search at that point and trek south to Union Square."

Chase frowned. "I hoped for something more creative. The manhunt and police search exhaustively searched that entire length of tunnel."

"Those efforts were heavily flawed. They were conducted far too quickly and with a greater emphasis on locating people rather than clues. My search will be far more detailed and wider in scope."

Chase looked at me thoughtfully. "What sort of supplies will you need?"

"Access keys. And maps. I need maps of every known underground installation in Manhattan. Subway tunnels, access corridors, sewers, everything."

"Beverly can handle that. She'll load them onto her laptop."

I shook my head. "I don't want to have to worry about recharging a computer. I want hard copies."

"Her laptop is state-of-the-art and can go many hours without a recharge. If you like, I can arrange one for you as well."

"No thanks."

"Are you sure?"

"Positive. I just want maps I can hold."

"Will do. As for accommodation, I think you'll be pleased to know that we've booked a suite for you at the Ritz-Carlton."

"I'm not sleeping in a hotel. Neither is Beverly."

She shot me a glance. "Is that right?"

"Conventional search tactics have failed. As Jack already mentioned, creativity is important at this stage of the game. Therefore, I want to immerse myself completely into the environment."

Chase gave me a strange look. "What are you saying?"

"Just this...once I enter the subway system, I'm not turning back. I'm going to eat, drink, and sleep in those tunnels. I'm not resurfacing until I have answers. Or until I'm in a body bag."

Chapter 10

Someone was following me.

I'd sensed the presence five minutes earlier while crossing 71st Street. At first, I paid it no heed. But by the time I reached 78th Street, an alarm bell rang inside my head.

As I turned the corner at 2nd Avenue, I glanced at the sky. I couldn't see the moon or stars. I couldn't see anything but the boatloads of rain that poured down on me.

Taking cover behind a brick wall, I peered back. Thanks to the late hour, the street was nearly empty.

My eyes swept across the rain-soaked sidewalk, the mist-covered parked cars, the dark storefronts, and the overflowing trashcans.

Nothing moved.

I pressed my head against the cold, wet bricks.

You're hearing things.

I started to pull my body away from the wet wall. Then I halted and stood still for a minute.

Something about the block seemed different.

It wasn't a recent change but rather, a change that had taken place sometime over the last three years. I spun in a circle, examining the block. Was it the landscape? The storefronts? The flowerboxes hanging high above me?

Suddenly, it came rushing back to me.

The odor.

I twisted around to face the intersection. A barbecue restaurant once sat on the opposite corner. In my former life, I'd walk by it and smell the intoxicating aromas of pit smoked barbecue pork ribs, beans, and salt potatoes. I never ate there. I didn't know why. But damn, I loved its smell.

It was a small thing but it bothered me. The apartment halfway down the block once served as my second home. And the odor acted as a welcome mat of sorts. Without it, I felt completely out of place.

Shifting positions, I stared down the street. I needed to meet Beverly in an hour. And then, we would embark on our assignment. It could take days, maybe weeks. I didn't know when I'd get another opportunity to visit that second home.

To visit her.

Water splashed noisily under my boots as I marched ahead. It sounded thunderous to my ears, especially when pitted against the near silence of the vacant, lifeless street. I tried to step more carefully, but I just kept getting louder and louder.

Halfway down the block, I turned to the side. Through the thick mist, I saw the familiar fifteen-story apartment building looming on the opposite side of the street.

Darkness and sheets of rain engulfed the structure, rendering it nearly invisible. Even its bright lights, protected by a concrete overhang, barely made a dent in the night. Although less than a hundred feet separated me from the building, the distance looked and felt more like a mile.

A gust of wind caught hold of me but I stood my ground. As it faded away, my eyes lifted to the fourth floor, second window from the left. Although I couldn't be sure, I thought I saw a tiny light. Did she still live there? Or had she moved on with her life?

Thunder clapped and a bolt of lightning shot across the sky. Its fierce light lit up the block. And in that one brief moment, I saw her.

Diane stood at the window, arms crossed, staring into the rain. Her face looked tight, her expression pensive. In the momentary flash of light, she stood out above everything else, like a dazzling star in a dull sky.

The image blinked away into nothingness. And as darkness returned, I knew I'd never forget it.

My brain wrestled with itself for a few moments. I wanted to see her, talk to her before it was too late. I knew all too well the pitfalls of waiting to deal with something. One day turned into another and then another. Soon, everything got buried under the surface, a tumor waiting to kill you.

But it seemed selfish only to consider my own needs. I'd hurt her badly three years ago, worse than I'd realized. Maybe the best thing I could do for her was walk away and let her forget me all over again.

My hesitation built upon itself and my brain began to churn up more and more excuses. I felt like a teenager at a school dance, one part raring to go and the other part glued to the wall.

A covered bus stop sat on the sidewalk, just a few feet away. Seeking shelter from the stinging rain, I walked into it.

A sign hung on the left wall. "Call Your Representatives," it screamed in bold lettering. "And Tell Them to Sack Jack!"

The accompanying image showed Chase standing in the middle of a destitute, disgusting subway station. His hands were spread wide and his face reflected a mixture of confusion and stupidity. I chuckled. It was actually a pretty decent likeness.

Next to it hung a similar sign, clearly meant as a response. "Call Your Representatives," it read. "And Tell Them to Back Jack!" The image on this poster was different, with a strong, determined Chase sending away a bunch of fat cats, who obviously represented the labor bosses.

My eyes lingered on the bosses. Dollar bills flowed out of their pockets. Back in my former life, I would've favored the labor movement. But three years spent living on the fringes of civilization had caused me to rethink my political views.

That didn't mean I supported Chase. Quite the contrary. Even if his motives were pure, I still wouldn't have supported him. He and the bosses were just different ends of the same government entity. And these days, my opinions on government were well outside the realms of polite thinking.

Thunder clapped again. With a sigh, I stepped out of the shelter. Steeling myself, I walked into the quiet street and began to cross the pavement.

Abruptly, the wind accelerated. It caught me mid-step and I lost my balance.

I smashed into the street, smacking the back of my head against the concrete. For a few seconds, I lay there, trying to blink away the cobwebs, tasting raindrops and blood on my tongue.

I propped myself up on my elbows. The wind intensified, plowing into me like a freight train. Ignoring the pounding in my head, I looked up at the building, searching for Diane's window. I hoped to see a light, hoped to see her face.

But all I saw was darkness.

Slowly, painfully, I rose to my feet. But something kept me from walking forward. I didn't know if it was guilt or something else. All I knew was that I wasn't ready to see her.

I wasn't yet ready to confront that part of my past.

The wind lessened as I turned around and wobbled back to the sidewalk. At the corner, I took one last look over my shoulder, hoping to see another flash of lightning. Hoping to see her building.

Hoping to see her.

But all I saw was darkness.

Chapter 11

Ryan Standish stepped into the shadow of a staircase. His black poncho blended in perfectly with the darkness, rendering him nearly invisible. Silently, he watched as Cyclone Reed strode down the opposite sidewalk.

Standish barely recognized him. Reed appeared distracted, lost in thought. He was but a mere shadow of the fearless, reckless man Standish had confronted back in Colombia. Something must've ripped the wind right out of his sails.

Something recent.

Something at that apartment building.

But what?

After reemerging from behind the staircase, Standish walked down the block. He'd followed Reed for hours, searching for insights into the man's personality.

Standish wanted to know everything about Reed. His interests. His desires.

His weaknesses.

Everyone had weaknesses. There were no exceptions. And if exploited correctly, those failings could turn even the most determined person into nothing more than a simpering fool.

The trick was to find such weaknesses. Most people hid them. But if one kicked over enough stones, they always came to the forefront. Some cared for ailing family members. Others got weak-kneed for fast women. Still others would do anything for power.

Standish found it all rather pathetic. He didn't mind powerful emotions. Not at all. They were an essential part of humanity. And with the right discipline, they could be a source of great power as well. But he had no patience for boundless feelings. Emotions, like so many other things, were best experienced in moderation.

Initially, he'd looked forward to uncovering the chinks in Reed's seemingly impenetrable armor. But as the night wore on, he found himself increasingly agitated. No strip clubs, no drugs, no gambling, no alcohol. At least for the moment, Reed seemed incredibly focused and businesslike.

In other words, boring as shit.

The visit to the Upper East Side represented the first ray of hope in an otherwise bleak night. Clearly, Reed took an intense interest in the tall apartment building on Standish's side of the street. For a minute, it even seemed like he would attempt to enter it. However, a sudden gust of wind apparently changed his mind.

Standish thought about following him, but ultimately chose to stay behind. Something about that building mattered to Reed. Mattered a great deal. And Standish wanted to know what it was.

Stopping outside the structure, he peered up at it. It looked normal enough, albeit a bit dingy for the area. Standish walked a few more steps, taking refuge under a concrete overhang. Then, he examined the list of names mounted on the wall next to a buzzer.

He stopped on D. Blair.

Short for Diane Blair.

A wide smile stretched across his face. He'd been so busy trying to get under Reed's skin at the Explorer's Society that he'd missed the obvious signs. Reed knew Diane. Knew her well. Perhaps even intimately.

Standish turned around and retraced his steps down the block. As he walked, he felt a surge of pleasure. The information was better than he could've imagined.

Standish had met Reed many years ago. And although he didn't know the man very well, he'd always considered Reed exceptionally tough. But in the end, Reed was just another fool, one with a soft spot for a woman.

It was a simple flaw, a common flaw.

A pitiful flaw.

But most importantly, it was a flaw that could be easily exploited. And when the time was right, Standish intended to exploit it to its fullest advantage.

Dance, puppet. Dance.

Chapter 12

"You're late."

Beverly's annoyed tone cut through the pouring rain like a machete through overgrown thicket. I stopped next to a tall black beam. Two cubes were stacked on top of it, one colored green and the other displaying the MTA's logo. "How late?"

"Does it matter?"

"Of course it matters."

"You were supposed to be here an hour ago."

I feigned surprise. "Really? And here I thought I was early."

She looked at me from underneath the hood of a black windbreaker, her angry violet eyes like a pair of lights in the dark. "Let's get one thing straight. You don't like me and I don't like you. But we're stuck with each other. This will go a lot faster if we put our differences aside."

I looked down. A short staircase plunged into the ground and ended at a thick metal grating. Beyond that grating lay the 51st – 53rd Street station complex. From there, we could access multiple sets of subway tracks, including the IRT Lexington Avenue Line.

I looked back at Beverly. "You've got the keys. Lead the way."

As she passed by me, I studied her. True to her chameleon ways, she'd changed outfits yet again. Underneath her unzipped windbreaker, she wore a form-fitting black tank top that wound its way around her curvy body. Olive jeans poured down her legs. Matching boots rose up to meet them, creating an almost seamless fit. Combined with a small over-the-shoulder pack, she looked every bit the fearless adventurer.

I just hoped she could live up to the image.

I followed her down the stairs. At the bottom, she unlocked the gate, and ushered me into the station. As she relocked it, I took my holster and sheath out of my satchel and donned them. Then I pulled out a large flashlight and turned it on. The tiled walls lining the entranceway lit up with a soft glow.

Slowly, I led Beverly down another set of stairs and onto the main landing of the complex. It was quiet and still. I found it almost peaceful, in fact. But the moisture-laden air and irregular creaks and groans coming from all directions kept me on edge.

"How far down are we?" Beverly asked. "Twenty feet?"

"More like twenty-five feet."

"I was close."

I shrugged. "If you say so."

"Why are we here anyway? Shouldn't we start at Grand Central and work our way south?"

"Kolen and Adcock entered the system north of Grand Central. By starting here, we should be able to retrace the vast majority of their path."

She unlocked one of the tall metal turnstiles and pushed her way through it onto the platform. Turning around, she pointed her flashlight at me. "What's taking so long?"

The beam smacked me right in the face. I shielded my eyes. "The fact that I can't see anything isn't helping matters."

She swung the beam toward the ground. As I pushed my way through the turnstile, I saw her lips purse into a sly smile.

This is going to be a long night.

A very long night.

I pointed my beam to the south. It shot down the long, cavernous tunnel before yielding to darkness. Steeling myself, I leapt onto the track bed. Something small and furry yelped and slipped off into a crack. Reaching up,

I offered Beverly a hand. Ignoring it, she jumped onto the bed next to me, landing lightly on her feet.

I turned to look at her. "Follow me and walk single file. And whatever you do, don't touch that."

She followed my beam to the third rail. "Jack told me that the workers turned off the electricity after the lockout."

"Okay, go ahead and touch it then. But before you do, you should know that six hundred and twenty-five volts run through that rail when it's in operation. That's more than enough to push a lethal current of a couple thousand amps through your body. In other words, if Chase was wrong, you'll die before you even know what hit you."

Her eyes widened slightly. "What if the rain gets down here?"

"Don't know for sure," I replied. "But if you see puddles collected around the third rail, steer clear of them."

"I don't like it. I don't mean the third rail either. It's something else. Something just doesn't feel right."

I knew what she meant. For some reason, it felt like someone was watching us. It was just a feeling, of course, but that didn't make it any less unsettling. "That's your nerves talking. Give them time. They'll get used to it."

I began walking south, leading us past the Grand Central Terminal platforms. I moved slowly and cautiously, taking time to examine my surroundings. My initial unease began to slip away, replaced by a sense of fascination.

Most people found subway tunnels uniform and boring, mere carbon copies of each other. But to me, every inch of every tunnel was unique. There was something about the cramped isolation of the underground world that heightened my senses. Sights, sounds, smells, touches, and even tastes differed wildly from one tunnel to the next.

We walked past the 33rd Street station and ventured deeper into the tunnel. Every second I spent in the confined area took my mind further from civilization and more into my surroundings. The subway system was like a mystical, forgotten world. I felt a little like an explorer penetrating a series of unknown connected caves, filled with giant metal monsters, ancient ruins, and lost treasure.

At the same time, the lack of subway trains and other people created an eerie sense of desolation. And although I was confident that I could find Kolen and Adcock, I couldn't escape the thought that something terrible had happened to them.

We strode through three more stations all the way to Union Square. Then, we turned around and retraced our steps. Although I hadn't expected to find anything on the first pass, I couldn't help but feel a little disappointed at my failure.

I knew one thing for certain.

Kolen and Adcock didn't vanish into thin air.

So where the hell were they?

PART II

THE COLONY

Chapter 13

"I lied to you."

Mary Kantz gave Peter Dask a suspicious look. "Oh?"

"There's an ulterior motive for this walk. I wanted to get you alone."

A pit formed in Mary's stomach. Peter was taller than her. Bigger too. She couldn't fight him off, especially not by herself. "I hope you're not thinking…"

"No, it's not that," he replied. "Not at all. I just needed to talk to you about something. Something important."

"So talk."

"I'm planning a coup."

Mary shook her head. "That's not funny. If Ghost heard about this…"

"I'm sick of Ghost. He's a stubborn old bastard whose time has passed."

"You're serious aren't you?"

He sneered. "Damn right I'm serious. Someone needs to take a stand. Our people are dying. The healthy ones are deserting in droves. If we wait any longer, the colony will be extinct."

"We owe Ghost. He saved us. All of us."

"Your loyalty to him is going to get you killed."

Mary spun on her heel. Lost in thought, she marched through the long thin subway tunnel.

A coup.

The very idea made her nervous. She liked Dask. Liked him a lot. But Ghost was like a father to her.

As she walked, she shifted her gaze from left to right, sweeping it across the cool, dank space. Thanks to twelve years spent living underground, her eyes had grown accustomed to darkness. As such, she could see almost everything around her. Scattered trash. A discarded boot. Smashed boxes.

A shopping cart.

Her eyes lingered on the cart. It was a whole lot bigger than the carts she'd seen while begging outside D'Agostino's. But its size wasn't its only unique feature. Through some feat of magic, it stood solely on its hind wheels.

Puzzled, she studied the strange spectacle. It took her only a few seconds to unravel the mystery. A thin metal pole rose out of the ground and sliced through the bars of the cart, impaling it at an awkward angle.

Glancing upward, she noticed that the pole extended all the way through the ceiling. She frowned. How had someone gotten…?

Dask coughed. "Listen Mary, forget I said anything. I'm just blowing off steam, that's all."

Mary wanted to believe him. The colony was the closest thing she ever had to a real family. "I know."

"It's just that Ghost…he doesn't…well…"

His voice trailed off. Mary considered probing him to say more. On one hand, the conversation made her uncomfortable. But on the other, she didn't want to push Dask away by ignoring his feelings. Already, she sensed a wall growing between them. And that terrified her almost as much as losing her family.

Emotionally torn, she pushed on, plunging across the tracks that made up the Lexington Avenue Line. The lockout presented a rare opportunity to enjoy the tunnels that surrounded her home without fear of being run over by subway trains. She did her best to enjoy it. But her heart was no longer in it.

Mary snuck a glimpse at Dask who strode behind her, stress lines etched across his handsome face. He no longer looked like the frightened, bratty, annoying kid she'd met all those years ago. Now, he was a devilish, tough twenty-two-year-old.

He sported rippling muscles. His sullen eyes weakened her knees. She liked everything about him, from his long blonde hair to his permanent stubble to his taste in music. He was the kind of boy...the kind of man...that struck fear in the hearts of parents.

Her thoughts drifted to her own mother. What would she think of Dask?

Mary never knew her mother. She didn't know the woman's dress size, her favorite food, or her hobbies. In fact, she didn't even know the woman's real name. But years of longing and dreaming had answered those questions.

Sort of.

Mary imagined her mother as Penelope Jarvis, a name that she'd picked out randomly from a discarded newspaper. Penelope was a beautiful woman with long blonde hair and curly eyelashes. She fit snugly into a dress, loved spaghetti and meatballs, and read books for fun.

Somehow, Mary and Penelope had been separated at birth. It wasn't Penelope's fault. She would never knowingly abandon her child. In fact, every day she spent hours calling around, searching for her long-lost daughter.

Searching for Mary.

Penelope would love Dask. Penelope loved everyone. The longer Mary thought about Penelope, the better she felt. It was a fantasy to be sure. But in Mary's experience, fantasies were almost always better than real life.

After another few minutes, the tunnel yawned open, revealing a platform. But this one was shaped like an island and stretched longer than the others. She recognized it immediately. It was the platform that divided the two sets of southbound tracks at Grand Central Terminal.

As she walked through the open area, her chest began to hurt. She didn't like the silence. She wanted to talk to Dask, to explain her feelings.

She glanced over her shoulder. "I get it. The past two months have been awful. I've lost too many friends. I don't want to lose anymore. Can't you and Ghost find a way to resolve your differences?"

Dask grabbed her shoulder and spun her around. "People are dying, Mary. And Ghost won't do anything about it."

"Can't you just talk to him?"

"I already tried. He's far too conceited to listen to me."

"Maybe if I tried…"

"Don't waste your time."

He paused for a moment. "You're my girl, Mary. I need you. I need your support."

Mary walked into the next tunnel, furtively wiping her eyes in the process. His words touched her. But they also made her ill at ease. Did he really care about her? Or was he just using her to aid his ambitions?

A single set of tracks ran down the middle of the tunnel, separated by I-beams and walls on either side. The tracks themselves were relatively clean, largely free of trash and debris.

"Mary, take a look at this."

Sensing urgency in his voice, she turned around. Dask knelt a few yards behind her. Despite the blackness, his face looked ghostly white. "What's wrong?"

He pointed at the ground. "Look."

She walked over to the side of the tunnel and saw a couple of half-footprints. "What about them?"

"Not those. Look at the marks."

Leaning back, she noticed something strange. A thick layer of gravel and dirt covered much of the ground. But near the footprints, a large, oddly shaped area had been wiped clean and filled with a pool of slime and sewage.

Dask looked at her. "We need to get out of here. Now."

She worked her mouth but nothing came out.

"Mary…" His voice was louder now, more urgent.

She turned around. And that was when she saw it. It flew across the tunnel, sweeping a wide swath in its wake.

The beast slammed into Dask.

He toppled over, hitting his head on the ground.

His eyes rolled to the back of his skull.

Mary tried to scream as the horrible thing shot toward her. She saw its red eyes, the blood dripping from its pointed teeth.

With tremendous force, it crashed into her. She fell backward and the creature slid over her, pushing her down with its weight.

The gigantic jaws opened wide.

Teeth clamped around her face.

She heard a sickening crunch.

And then, it began to eat.

Chapter 14

Beverly yawned. "Well, that was a couple hours of my life I'll never get back. I hope you've got something better planned for tomorrow."

"Patience is a virtue," I replied. "One you seem to lack."

She walked a little farther and then pointed to the right. "I keep seeing those things everywhere we go. Do they have a purpose?"

I glanced over my shoulder, following her finger to a gigantic steel piling. Dotting the entire area, the pilings looked like a metallic garden, sprouting out of the concrete and growing through the ceiling. I touched one as I passed by it, feeling the cool metal course through my fingertips. "It's definitely not useless," I replied. "That is, unless you've got something against midtown Manhattan."

"How's that?"

"A long time ago, railroad tracks and a large train yard sat above our heads. But the land was far too valuable to be used in that manner. So, in 1903, New York Central started to move everything underground. Then it built a new terminal and constructed Park Avenue on top of the whole mess."

"What's that got to do with the pilings?"

"New York Central sold the air rights to developers, which gave them the right to build in the area, but with no right to the ground itself. So to support their buildings, developers drove steel pilings deep into Manhattan's bedrock. Without them, midtown Manhattan would literally fall right through the earth."

"You make it sound dangerous."

"It's downright deadly if you consider the thousands of trains weaving through here every day, traveling at top speeds. It's a wonder midtown hasn't caved in yet."

"Not that I care, but where'd you learn all that?"

I shrugged. "Back when I was still an archaeologist, I spent a few months studying these tunnels in great depth. Picked up a few things along the way, I guess."

I led Beverly through a few twists and turns until we finally arrived at a large open space, consisting of crumbling maintenance shacks, half-completed structures, unused tracks, and rusty subway cars.

"Where are we?"

"Hidden layup yard. The MTA stores out-of-service trains here."

"This wasn't on Kolen's and Adcock's search grid."

I shone my light around the space, surprised to find the area deserted. Something about it bothered me, but I couldn't quite put my finger on it. "No, but it's quiet and dry. Plus, it gives us easy access to the tunnels."

"Wait, we're not…"

"We sure are."

A disgusted look appeared on her face. "We can't sleep here."

"Why not?"

"Well for starters, there aren't any people around here. I thought you wanted to infiltrate a homeless community in order to gather information."

"A couple of years back, a shanty town existed in this area. Unfortunately, it looks like they cleared out awhile back."

"So, let's go find them."

I shook my head. "We could look all night and not find anyone. Better to get some rest and try again tomorrow."

"So, it's just you and me?"

"Unfortunately, yes."

She made a face. "Where am I supposed to sleep? On the ground?"

"You'll see."

I paced all the way to the rear of the layup yard. As I walked, my eyes passed over various graffiti messages that adorned the walls. Some I remembered. Some I didn't.

One message in particular, which covered a five-foot by ten-foot swath of wall, caught my eye. Its text was written in black paint over a faded yellow background. The top line declared, "Page 134 – July 1, 1997." As I passed by it, I glanced at the message.

This is my home. Our home. Anything but your home. We are the abandoned, the ignored, the hated. Society tossed us away years ago. But don't pity us. Don't you dare. Just leave us alone. Stop rooting us out, stop forcing us to the surface, and for God's sake stop trying to normalize us. You already destroyed our lives. At least let us have our dignity.

The message was tagged with the moniker Ghost in the lower left corner. I'd never met the man, but I knew him by reputation. He was a legend among New York's indigent population, partly due to his subway-based autobiography. The tunnel walls were his parchment. Spray paint was his quill.

During my previous life, I'd read more than one hundred of his entries. But based on the numbering, I knew that was just the tip of the iceberg.

"Where are we going?"

"Over there," I replied. "All of the tracks down here are numbered. We're going to camp right by that platform, at Track 61."

"Wonderful. What could be better than sleeping on a nice, soft slab of concrete?"

I pointed at a rusty old subway car parked at the end of Track 61, just beyond the platform. "Actually, we'll sleep in there. At the very least, it should keep the rats from eating our eyeballs."

She shuddered. "Any other nightmarish facts you want to share about our sleeping quarters?"

"You should be proud. That's FDR's car. According to legend, President Franklin Delano Roosevelt's people used it to transport him and his armor-plated Pierce Arrow car through the tunnels. That way, he could travel directly to his room at the Waldorf-Astoria without exposing his paralyzed legs to the public."

Her eyes brightened. "Really?"

"Nope. It's just a legend. His real subway car is housed in a museum somewhere down in Florida."

"So that subway car isn't important?"

"Not unless you have a fascination with old Pennsylvania Railroad express-baggage cars from the 1940s."

She frowned. "You really know how to make a girl feel special."

"Hey, it's free. And believe me, you're worth every penny of that price."

I walked over to the subway car and opened the rear door. Taking off my satchel, I pulled out two bottles of water and tossed one of them to Beverly.

She caught it easily. After taking a drink, she unzipped her bag and removed two plastic pouches.

I grabbed one from her. "This is supposed to be food?"

"It's an MRE. What kind did you get?"

"Cheese tortellini."

She smirked. "I hope you've got a strong stomach."

I tore open the plastic pouch and dumped a number of packages into my hand. "How's it work?"

"It's not rocket science. That package on the right is a flameless cooker. You just open up the tortellini and dump it in there to warm it up. And in case you can't figure it out, the plastic spoon is used for eating."

I opened the tortellini package and prepared the meal. Then, I leaned against the car's open door and started to eat it.

She adopted a serious expression. "So, what's your story anyway?"

"What do you want to know?"

"Jack told me that you left here because of an incident. What happened?"

"Boy, you don't beat around the bush, do you?"

"Are you surprised?"

I shrugged. "A couple of years ago, I worked as an urban archaeologist. I spent most of my career focused on Manhattan, with particular emphasis on the remains of New Amsterdam."

"Never heard of it."

"It was the first European settlement in Manhattan," I replied. "It was founded by Dutch fur traders in 1614 and built on the southern tip of the island. Anyways, after extensive research of surviving records and old maps, I decided to see if I could find tangible remains of Cornelius van Tienhoven's house."

"He was important?"

"Extremely important. He sparked fights with Native Americans and probably caused the Peach Tree War. He vanished in 1656. Some think he was murdered, others think he fled the city to avoid the wrath of the Dutch West Indies Company."

I took another bite. "To make a long story short, our work proved accurate and my team managed to uncover the house's foundations. At that time, it was the single greatest moment of my life."

"But something bad happened?"

My chest tightened. "As we excavated the walls, we built braces to keep them in place. One night, three diggers were working the site. A wall collapsed, killing them instantly."

"What went wrong?"

"The braces failed. I still don't understand it. I supervised their construction and placement. They should've held."

She raised her eyebrows. "I see."

Memories flashed across my mind. I saw the broken braces, smelled the corpses, felt the overwhelming sadness. My chest started to hurt. "Anyways, everything changed after that. My career was finished. My colleagues at the Explorer's Society started to ignore me. That is, when they weren't whispering behind my back. A few days later, I got an offer to head up a dig of a different sort. A treasure hunting dig. It went against everything I'd ever been taught. But it gave me the opportunity to get away for awhile. An opportunity to clear my head."

"You're an idiot."

"Excuse me?"

"It was a horrible accident. But it was still an accident. It's not like you meant for it to happen. Yet, you shouldered the guilt all by yourself and threw away your entire life in the process. To me, that's idiotic."

"I –"

Cold, stiff fingers wrapped around my neck, choking off my reply. My head flew to the side, bashing into the door.

Foggily, I reached for my belt.

But my machete was missing.

With my head plastered to the door, I twisted my eyes to the side, seeing a murderous gaze staring back at me. My eyes bulged as they caught a glint of light.

It was my machete.

I didn't know the man who held it. But I knew what he wanted.

He wanted to kill me.

And he was going to use my own blade to do it.

Chapter 15

The machete flashed forward, its sharp blade gleaming in the dim light. Desperately, I tried to jerk myself away from the door.

The blade tore through my flesh. Searing pain gripped my shoulder and I tensed up. My mouth tried to scream but the hand over my windpipe cut it off at the pass. Familiar voices rushed into my brain.

"Cyclone! Come quick! There's been an accident."

I frowned. "An accident? But that's impossible."

"A wall fell on them. Tim, Abe, Cody..."

The light dimmed...

Colors, bright and vivid, exploded in my eyes.

No, not now. Please God, not now.

Gritting my teeth, I forced myself to fight two battles, one against myself and one against my attacker. Twisting violently, I struggled to free myself from the iron grip. But my attacker countered every move, thwarted every attempt to breathe.

I snuck another look at him. The attacker smiled, showing off a mouth of cracked yellows. His eyes looked dull yet fiery. His cheeks drew in and out rapidly, like a puffer fish.

Abruptly, he reared back, the tendons on his arm twitching with anticipation. The machete plunged toward me.

I saw nicks in the blade.

Gouges on the spine.

Splotches of deep red blood.

My blood.

I jerked away from the door again. This time the machete missed its mark. I kicked my feet up and bent my knees. My boots soared behind me and touched the subway car. Extending my legs, I pushed as hard as I could in the man's direction.

I flew forward and landed hard, my body smashing into the larger man beneath me. The grip around my throat loosened. Turning my face, I bit down hard on a hairy arm.

The man yelped and suddenly I was free. Rolling forward, I leapt to my feet and spun around.

I looked for Beverly, but before I could locate her, my eyes fell upon the mammoth man.

Slowly, he stood up. I judged his height at an inch or two shy of seven feet. His powerful arms bulged everywhere, as if he were made of baseballs. He clearly was a man who inspired awe, even fear. But I felt no fear. I felt nothing. Nothing but cold, silent rage.

Suddenly, pain erupted in my forehead. Caught by surprise, I flinched. It shot its way through me, invading every inch of my body.

Colors sparkled in my eyes. I couldn't see. I couldn't move.

And then a fist crashed into my skull.

My feet lifted off the ground and I spun through the air like a rolling pin. Air whooshed out of my lungs as my back smashed onto metal tracks. The colors in my brain flashed, sharpening and dulling, sharpening and dulling.

Squinting, I saw the vague outline of the giant standing over me. His mouth twisted into a scowl. His eyes hardened. They looked like the eyes of a dead man, incapable of remorse or feeling.

I shifted my eyes to search for Beverly. But before I could spot her, the man lifted his knee. His boot crashed down, directly at my head.

I rolled out of the way and lifted myself to a sitting position. Grabbing hold of the giant's arm, I yanked. Caught off balance, he lurched toward me.

The man tried to fight me off but I was ready for him. My legs rose up, meeting his crouched frame. I wrapped one around his waist and the other around the front of his neck. Then I yanked my arms and pulled my legs.

He toppled like a redwood, causing the ground to tremble in the process. His head snapped back, bashing against metal tracks. Blood flowed onto the ground. He looked unconscious, but I wasn't about to risk it.

Lying perpendicular to the giant, I draped my legs over his body, pinning his left arm to his side. His right arm, clenched in my hands, was caught in the narrow space between my legs.

Leaning back, I pulled with all my strength. His arm bent awkwardly toward me. My fury increased and I pulled even harder, determined to break it.

Something swished. Out of the corner of my eye, I saw a shadow on the far wall. It flitted back and forth for a moment before vanishing into darkness.

Slowly, I turned my head in a circle. Strange eyes stared at me from the darkness.

They started to move.

Slowly at first, then faster.

And then even faster.

Body odor and dried urine filled my nostrils. Hands grabbed at my shirt, pawed at my arms, scratched at my face.

I released my grip. Rising to my feet, I found myself surrounded by hot, sweaty bodies. Eyes flashed at me. Bruised faces quivered with anticipation.

Punching wildly, I connected hard against a fleshy surface. A face vanished but another one rose to replace it.

They pressed against me and I fell backward, blanketed by the bodies. Amongst the mess of flesh and hair, I saw tiny, revolting details.

Crippled hands with bent, inflamed joints.

Clenched toes lacking nails.

Severely peeled, discolored skin.

Toothless, rotten mouths.

Who are these people?

And what the hell happened to them?

Desperately, I attempted to push my way out of the mess. But my breathing was labored and my strength depleted. It was all I could do to keep from passing out.

I looked around, searching for Beverly. This time, I spotted her. Two men held her in firm grips. She struggled mightily but her efforts were futile.

Thrusting her from my mind, I tried to calm down, to concentrate. I needed a plan. But my brain hurt and I couldn't think.

The air burst. Something popped loudly in my ear.

My vision vaporized into white light. Blinding pain struck my head. The ground swirled underneath me. The bodies vanished, along with everything else.

Panic rose in my chest. "Are they...?"

"They're dead, Cyclone. Oh my God, they're dead."

Chapter 16

The stabbing headache was gone. My eyes saw only darkness. My mind felt clear. My emotions no longer raged underneath the surface.

Stirring, I opened my eyes. Immediately, I recognized my pistol. It was clutched in the arthritic fingers of a withered hand.

And it was pointed directly at my face.

"Don't move."

The voice sounded uneven and scratchy, yet packed with raw emotion. Shifting my gaze, I saw a haggard man kneeling in front of me. From all appearances, Father Time hadn't been kind to him. His posture, even while kneeling, was stooped beyond his age. His face, covered in wrinkles, looked ancient. Only his eyes, which sparkled with an odd sort of energy, retained any vestiges of his lost youth.

Colors flashed around the edges of my gaze. I took a few gulps of oxygen, sucking it in greedily. My lungs quickly filled and after a few seconds, the colors disappeared.

"Who are you?" I asked.

"Call me Ghost."

"Ghost? The real Ghost?"

"The one and only."

"Prove it."

"I don't have to."

Good point. "Okay Ghost." I shrugged. "I'm Cy."

"I know. Your companion told me that."

Swiftly, I scanned the area and spotted Beverly kneeling on the ground. Despite the faint light, I saw long red scratches on her arms and purplish welts on her neck. "Quite the welcoming committee you've got here. I'm guessing you don't get a lot of repeat visitors."

"We don't like visitors."

"And I don't like people attacking me for no reason."

"You trespassed on our property."

"It's city property."

"We live here. That makes it our property."

"You're out of your mind."

He waved the gun at me. "This is our home. We're not vacating it for anyone. I suggest you leave at once and don't come back."

"If you don't get that thing out of my face, we're going to have a problem."

His eyes tightened and he stared at me with quiet anger. I returned the glare. After a minute, he relaxed and lowered the pistol.

I widened my gaze. Off to one corner, I saw the giant sitting on the ground. A brief smile crossed my face as I watched him clutch his arm, grinding his teeth in pain.

Rotating my head, I saw a ring of seven other people surrounding me. Their faces looked gaunt and their bodies showed signs of malnutrition and abuse. "What is this place? Who are you people?"

"This is our home," Ghost repeated. "As for your second question, we're a colony of like-minded individuals. A family if you will. No different than any other family."

"Yeah, you're just like the Joneses."

"I'm sure we seem strange in the eyes of a surface dweller like you. For your kind, normalcy is endless war, consumerism, and perpetual debt."

I stood up and eyed his band of ragtag starving colonists. "This is the best alternative you could manage?"

"Try to understand –"

"Understand what? That you're hiding a zombie colony down here?"

He paused for a few seconds. Then, he gave me a peculiar look. "What do you know about Peter and Mary?"

"Who?"

"Peter Dask. Mary Kantz. What did you do to them?"

"I have no clue what you're talking about."

"Did you kidnap them?"

"Of course not."

"Then why are you here?"

I didn't want to alarm him by talking about people disappearing in the tunnels. Instead, I chose to focus on my secondary objective. "We're looking for a man who lives in these tunnels. His name is Jenson. Fred Jenson. You can see his photo in my satchel."

"I saw the photo when we searched your stuff. What do you want with him?"

"He visited a pawn shop a few weeks back. He tried to sell something that didn't belong to him."

"Well, I've lived in these tunnels for a long time and I've never seen him."

"Would you tell me if you had seen him?"

"Probably not."

"You're a big help. So, who are these two people you mentioned? Peter Dask and Mary…?"

"Mary Kantz. They've lived with us for years. A few hours ago, they took a walk down the Lexington Avenue Line. They never returned."

Lexington Avenue Line? How come I didn't see them?

"Maybe they got sidetracked," I suggested. "Or maybe they went somewhere else altogether."

"I doubt it. We've lost five people in similar fashion over the past few months."

"Maybe they got sick of the crappy existence your colony seems to offer. Seriously, what the hell happened to you people?"

He clenched his fists. "It's just a bug. The worst of it has passed. Maybe the others weren't so lucky, but the rest of us are going to make it."

"Wait, are you saying that people died down here too?"

"That's enough questions. You need to leave."

I tried to read his face but it was a mask of blankness. In my travels, I'd seen other communities with similar characteristics to his colony. Most of them functioned just fine in good times. But when things got tough, they tended to put their faith in the wrong sort of leaders. They chose smooth-talking charlatans who promised easy answers and quick fixes. More often than not, those things led the people into even greater disaster.

Was that the story behind Ghost and his colony? It made sense. Outcast by society and ravaged by disease, the survivors would've been tempted to turn to a charismatic leader. Ghost, with his fame, strong presence, raspy voice, and lively eyes, was a natural choice. As he consolidated his power, some people left on their own volition. The ones who stayed behind lost the capacity to act on their own.

But even as I considered the scenario, I found myself rejecting it. Despite his prickly attitude, I sensed that Ghost wasn't interested in acquiring power. Instead, he seemed legitimately concerned for the welfare of his people.

I decided to extend an olive branch. "Are you sure...?"

"Go. Now. And don't come back."

"I'm not leaving without my stuff."

He considered me for a moment. Then, he shrugged and handed me my gun and machete. After returning them to their rightful places, I retrieved my satchel from the ground.

At Ghost's nod, the two men holding Beverly released her. Slowly, we backed out of the layup yard, keeping a close watch on the colonists.

"You okay?" I asked her.

"A few bruises but I'll manage. You?"

"Nothing a couple of shots won't fix."

"They look sick. What do you make of it?"

"No clue. Let's just hope they aren't contagious."

"Agreed." She glanced at me. "Do you think we should get checked out?"

"Not yet. I want to take another look at the Lexington Avenue Line."

"Now?"

"Especially now. Ghost mentioned that two people recently went missing while walking through the tunnel."

"So what? They probably fled this hellhole."

"Communities like this one are built on longstanding relationships and trust. People don't just leave, even if they are sick. No, I think they vanished. And if we find them, we might just find Kolen and Adcock too."

"Do you think something bad happened to them?"

I thought for a moment. "Yes. Yes, I do."

Chapter 17

Inch by inch, I worked my way through the tunnel system, examining every single crack, cranny, and nook. I knew I was missing something.

But what exactly?

My foot splashed in water. My gaze shot to the ground. Under my boots, I saw a small stream running next to the tracks. It wasn't deep enough to reach the third rail. Still, I didn't feel particularly comfortable standing in it.

Beverly pointed her flashlight to the other side of the tunnel. "It's over there too. Where's it coming from?"

"The storm," I replied. "The rain must've raised the water levels in the Hudson and East Rivers. That overwhelmed the pumps, assuming they're even still operating. Probably parts of the sewer system too."

She edged to the side, as far away from the third rail as space permitted. I followed suit. I didn't know what would happen if I accidentally splashed water onto the third rail. Maybe nothing.

Maybe something.

Stooping down, I examined another section of concrete. I needed to squint to see every detail and it struck me that visibility had diminished within the tunnel. Seeing nothing, I stood up again.

For what seemed like the tenth time, I strode past the Grand Central platform, taking time to examine both the local and express tracks. My nerves tingled and every now and then, I'd check over my shoulder to make sure that we weren't being followed. I wasn't the paranoid type, but a little extra caution seemed in order. Assuming that Ghost told me the truth, seven people had recently vanished from the colony, two within the last few hours. Adding in Kolen and Adcock, that number rose to nine.

Nine disappearances.

All within the same general area.

It was too much of a coincidence to ignore. And unfortunately, only one explanation seemed to fit the facts. An explanation that chilled me to the bone.

Someone killed them.

All of them.

And that someone was most likely nearby.

"What happened back there?" Beverly asked.

"What do you mean?"

"During the fight with that psycho, your face turned purple and you looked like you were in pain. I thought you were going to pass out."

"You must've been seeing things."

"Are you sure? I've seen that sort of reaction before, back in my military days. The doctors call it post-traumatic –"

"Leave it alone."

"But I –"

"I said leave it alone."

"You don't like me very much do you?"

I glanced toward her. Her hands rested defiantly on her cocked hips. Her nose was set, tilted slightly in the air. Her eyes, locked upon mine, blazed with intensity. She looked cool and calm, yet incensed at the same time.

"Did it really take you this long to figure that out?" I asked.

"Everything I did to you, I did under orders."

"Oh, that makes it much better."

"Anyway, Tasers are perfectly acceptable non-lethal weapons. Police officers use them all the time."

"My favorite part was when the electricity actually entered my body. I love foaming at the mouth."

"You weren't in any danger."

My gaze hardened. "That's easy for you to say. You weren't the one getting Tasered."

"You're overreacting. I had orders not to harm you under any circumstances. You were perfectly safe."

I snorted. "That's comforting. Let me ask you this…what if your orders were the opposite? What if Chase told you to shoot me?"

"He wouldn't do that."

"But what if he did?"

"He wouldn't."

Her answer didn't reassure me, not by a long shot. But I decided to let it go. It occurred to me that a little bonding might be in order. So far, our collaboration had proven contentious. And with a possible killer stalking the tunnels, the last thing I needed was a hostile partner.

I cleared my throat. "You said you were in the military?"

Her face, framed in a shifting pattern of multi-colored shadows, contorted. "My dad was in the navy so I was a brat pretty much since birth. While the other girls played dress-up, I read books on military strategy and tactics. I memorized everything I could find on the greats. Sun Tzu. Hannibal. Alexander. Patton. Eventually, I went to West Point and then served in the Marine Corps for a couple of years."

"How'd you get involved with ShadowFire?"

"I met Jack while serving in Baghdad. I was disillusioned with the Marine Corps. He was recruiting new personnel. It didn't take him long to sell me on a career with his company."

"Is he a good boss?"

"He's a brilliant boss, decades ahead of his time."

I nodded. "Okay, your turn. What do you want to know about me?"

"I know more than enough about you already."

"Is that so?"

"Your given name is Cyclone Reed," she replied. "But you prefer to be called Cy for some reason. You were born in this city and lived here pretty much your entire life. Your dad died in rather horrific fashion when you were little and your mom never remarried. When…"

For the next minute, she proceeded to peel off facts about my life as if I were some kind of onion. It was startling, disturbing even. Clearly, my life was an open book.

Even worse, she'd memorized every word of it.

Patiently, I listened for a little longer. But when she started to reel off names of former flings, I had to draw the line.

Raising a hand, I stopped her in mid-sentence. "That's plenty. I never thought I'd say this but I'm bored with myself. Is this what you do all day? Sit around and memorize people's files?"

"Sometimes. But files only take you so far. If you truly want to know a person, you have to walk in their shoes, spend time with them, study their reactions."

"Is that why you're here? To gather intelligence on me?"

She laughed. "Not at all. You heard Jack. I'm here to help, nothing more, nothing less."

I thought about responding but returned my attention to the tunnel instead. I could banter with Beverly later. For the time being, I needed to focus my attention on tracking down Peter and Mary. The trail was hot but it wouldn't stay that way for long. Not with water flooding into the tunnel.

Beverly walked ahead of me, her gaze and flashlight beam firmly attached to the tunnel walls. Although she continued to rub me the wrong way, I was beginning to appreciate her presence.

As she passed farther into the tunnel, her light dimmed. I felt strangely protective of her.

If something happened…

If the killer appeared…

I didn't want to think about that.

Something splashed. My arm swept to the side, casting light on the opposite wall. Nothing. My imagination was playing tricks on me.

"Cy, come look at this!"

I broke into a run, covering fifty yards in less than eight seconds. Not exactly world-class time, but considering the environment, not half-bad either.

I slid to a stop, splashing water onto her boots. "What?"

Silently, she pointed at the ground.

I knelt down and took a closer look. At first, I didn't see anything of interest. Other than a pile of debris, the lower half of the wall appeared no different than any other section.

Then my flashlight beam skipped over some rotten wood and rusty broken tools. It looked like there was something behind them. Something dark. Gently, I brushed the debris aside.

A hole appeared before my eyes.

It was large but well covered by garbage and slime. Its jagged, yet smooth edges indicated that tools hadn't carved it. Rather, it looked like time and pressure were to blame.

Bending over, I saw a partially submerged passage lying behind the hole. It appeared to curve up and to the right and I guessed that it was a natural fissure in the bedrock.

Carefully, I examined the area just inside the passage. It didn't take long for my light to catch a red smear. I brought my eyes right up to the mark and studied it. From up close, it looked more like a splatter than a smear.

I breathed in, inhaling the scent. It smelled sour yet sweet. I also detected a hint of copper. There was no mistaking it.

"It's blood," I said. "Pretty fresh too."

"Are you sure?"

"Positive."

Beverly frowned. "We should get to the surface and find some help."

"Screw that."

"I don't know what's going on around here, but it seems pretty clear that people are dying. I'm not going to allow you to risk your life."

"That's not your decision to make."

"It's protocol to –"

I slammed the side of my fist against the wall. "Screw your protocol. Kolen was a friend. And I'll be damned if I leave this place without finding him."

"Don't be stupid. We have all the evidence we need."

I dropped flat on the wet ground. Shining the beam before me, I crawled into the dark tunnel. "I'm not looking for evidence," I called out grimly. "I'm looking for bodies."

Chapter 18

It didn't take long for me to smell sewage. And the farther I inched through the natural crevice, the stronger the smell.

Or rather, smells.

Numerous odors melded together into one giant noxious aroma. I felt myself getting light-headed. Grimacing, I wrapped my shirt collar over my nose and held my breath. But the stink was inescapable.

I followed the twisting, turning tunnel for what seemed like hundreds of yards. Along the way, I passed several other fissures, which branched off of the main one. But I ignored them and continued on, driven, yet repulsed by the overwhelming stench.

The tunnel began to descend. Eventually, my beam cut through the end of the passage and I saw a perpendicular tunnel. It looked larger than the one that surrounded me but much smaller than the one I'd left behind. Crawling forward, I slid headfirst into it.

And headfirst into a mess of filth and muck.

I scrambled to my feet, bumping my head against the ceiling in the process. I frantically tried to wipe away the sludge. But it was too late. I smelled like garbage and industrial waste. But most of all I smelled like shit.

Tons and tons of shit.

Beverly scraped her way out of the passage and stood up. Her face was white and she looked ready to vomit. Slowly, she bent at the waist and placed her hands on her knees. "Oh my God. This place is revolting. I swear I'll never forgive you for this."

"You didn't have to come."

She gave me a queasy look. "I thought you said these sewers were flooded."

"Some of them probably are flooded. We happened to get lucky. Don't jinx it."

Tightening my grip around the flashlight, I pointed the beam around the tunnel. It stood close to six feet tall and was shaped in a cylindrical fashion.

I heard a soft splash. Twisting swiftly, I pointed my beam down one end of the tunnel.

I saw nothing.

Nothing but more tunnel.

And more sewage.

I switched my attention to the tunnel roof. "I've got more blood. Lots of it, in fact."

She shrugged. "No big surprise there. Someone probably stood up and bumped against the ceiling."

"The splatter is too widespread for that. No, I think something else caused the blood to land up here. Something that struck with tremendous force."

"Then where are the bodies?"

I pointed my flashlight around the sewer tunnel. While both ends looked alike, the blood marks appeared to travel in just one direction. I unsheathed my machete and stepped forward, following the trail of red smears through the tunnel.

"Is it safe in here?" Beverly's voice didn't waver.

"Are you kidding? Don't you see all this blood?"

"I don't mean that. I mean is it safe to breathe the air?"

"We should be fine unless we stumble on a pocket of carbon-monoxide."

"What happens if we do that?"

"We die. Pretty quickly."

Despite the warm tunnel, cold sweat dripped down my face. For the next thirty seconds or so, we tramped through the tunnel in relative silence. It angled slightly, ascending upward. Then it leveled off again. I kept my flashlight moving the entire time, looking for signs of life.

Abruptly, my beam fell upon a couple of lumps.

My fingers tightened around the machete until my knuckles hurt. My other hand drifted to my chest, just above my pistol.

I approached the lumps and studied them.

They were bodies.

Dead bodies.

The sweet, sickly odor of decomposition forced its way into my nostrils. A deep sense of foreboding filled my chest. I knelt down, allowing my knee to sink into the soft sludge. I exhaled as I examined the corpses. They were in horrendous shape. Most of the skin and flesh was gone. The parts that remained were covered with deep, gouging bite marks.

My gaze drifted to what remained of a face.

It was a face I recognized.

It was Javier Kolen's face.

Memories flooded my skull and I fought back an urge to vomit. Colorful lights appeared at the corners of my eyes and it took all my willpower to stave off yet another incident.

As I regained control of my emotions, I shifted my flashlight up and down his body. Bits of clothing and inch-thick grime covered his legs. Reaching out, I flicked away some of the sludge, revealing more bones.

Bones picked clean.

"Good lord," Beverly whispered. "What in the world happened to them?"

I didn't answer. What the hell could I say? The sight was more shocking, more horrifying than anything I'd ever seen in my life.

I closed my eyes and tried to say a prayer for Kolen's soul, for all of their souls. But gruesome images kept shooting through my brain, causing me to forget my words. I glanced at Beverly. "I don't know. But I do know that this skeleton belongs to Kolen. I can't be sure about the others."

"I'm sorry."

"Not your fault."

Her voice turned businesslike. "We need to get out of here. Jack needs to know about this."

"Who could've done this?" I muttered under my breath. "And why?"

"Cy, did you hear me?"

I nodded.

She gave me a long look. I sensed a deep emotional struggle waging within her.

"This is the end of the line," she said after a minute.

"What are you talking about?"

"I'm going to advise Jack that we call off this search."

"But..."

"A Nazi treasure that may not even exist doesn't matter much anymore. We need to focus our efforts on returning these poor folks to the surface and giving them proper burials."

"We also need to bring whoever did this to justice."

"That's not your responsibility."

"I want to help."

"It's a job for the police. As of now, you're released from your obligations."

"I don't want to be released."

"You'll be paid of course," she replied. "In full. But your work is done. You're free to leave."

"But..."

Her face darkened. "But nothing. I don't want to see your face again. If I do, I'll make sure you never get your money."

Turning around, she walked back through the tunnel. I watched her leave, feeling confused and unsatisfied. It was all happening so fast, so abruptly.

It's not supposed to end this way.

Still, a murderer had killed numerous people. That changed everything, at least for the time being.

I wanted to feel relieved. After less than twenty-four hours of work, I'd become wealthy, wealthier than my wildest dreams. I could pay off my debts. I could go anywhere, do anything. My whole life was a book waiting to be written.

But a vague sense of dissatisfaction gave me pause. With a long sigh, I stood up. As I did so, my flashlight tipped and the beam glinted. I stared at Kolen's body for a moment, trying to decide whether to leave well enough alone.

Finally, I leaned down and examined an ivory-colored object. It stuck straight out of Javier's leg bone but didn't seem like it belonged to him. I grabbed the object, wrenching it free.

I brought it to my face. At first glance, it looked long and sharp. As I turned it in my hands, a horrifying realization hit me.

It was a tooth. A giant tooth.

The biggest one I'd ever seen.

Chapter 19

Never before had a building inspired such loathing in my soul.

From the opposite sidewalk, I stared up at the Explorer's Society's headquarters, barely containing my disgust. The more I saw it, the more it served as a stark reminder of simpler, happier times. Times spent laughing with Diane. Living in Manhattan. Working as a respected archaeologist. Living a life free of guilt, free of regrets.

Living a life without the constant reminder of death.

Sheets of rain engulfed the building and the surrounding area. Dark shadows plagued everything. It was early morning and yet it didn't look like it.

I gulped in a few mouthfuls of cold moisture-filled air. Then, I crossed the street and started up the staircase. I kept my eyes low to avoid the rain, deliberately ignoring the stained glass, the white marble, and those creepy statue heads.

At the pair of heavy oak doors, I paused. My instincts told me to trace my fingers along the grooves, just like I did as a boy. But I ignored them. Instead, I shoved the doors open and stepped into the interior.

Despite the relatively early hour, a few people milled around the Great Hall. I didn't look at them although I sensed their eyes on me, staring, wondering, evaluating. Without pausing, I marched forward, barely noticing the dark wood floor, the oriental carpets, or the exhibits. I had no interest in the Society itself, not anymore.

At the rear of the Hall, I angled right and hurried down the long corridor. As I passed Diane's painting, I wanted to stop, to drink it in. But I averted my eyes and continued walking.

The door at the end of the corridor was closed. As soon as I reached it, I grabbed the knob, twisted, and flung it open.

"What the hell?"

The gravely, gritty tone brought a smile to my face. It felt good to smile. I couldn't remember the last time I'd done it. "Long time no see."

Graham spun around in his chair and flashed me a tired grin. "Well, well, look who decided to show his face. After yesterday's little debacle, I thought I'd never see you again."

"What's a little fight between old friends?"

He chuckled. "I wish I'd taped it. One minute you're toe to toe with Standish. The next, you're gone and he's tripping over a seat trying to grab you. The poor bastard fell flat on his face."

"It couldn't have happened to a nicer guy."

"What was that all about anyway? You mentioned Colombia and caciques?"

I sat down in a chair. "He bribed his way into ownership of a dig site and proceeded to clean it out."

Graham frowned. "You should lodge a complaint against him. The Society takes that kind of thing very seriously."

"Yeah right," I replied. "Who's going to listen to me? I'm persona non grata around here."

Graham shrugged. "So, what's new? You still working for Chase or did you finally wise up?"

"I'm sort of in hiatus."

"What are you doing for him anyway?"

I hesitated. "I signed a non-disclosure agreement so I can't say much. But I do have a favor to ask."

"What's that?"

I reached into my pocket and closed my fingers around the hard, sharp object. No one else knew about it but me. Not the doctor who examined my wounds a few hours ago. Not Chase. Not even Beverly.

Extending my hand, I opened my fingers. "Have you ever seen something like this before?"

He took the tooth and examined it. A frown spread across his face. "Where did you find this?"

"Never mind that. Do you recognize it?"

Graham stood up. Wobbling slightly, he retrieved a book from the bookshelf and scanned it. "I thought so," he said at last. "Here it is."

He placed the book on the desk and flipped it around to face me. Leaning in, I noticed a photo of a tooth that looked quite similar to the one I'd found. My eyes drifted to the caption and I felt my heart skip a beat.

"It's an alligator tooth," Graham said. "The American alligator to be exact. And a massive one too from the looks of it."

"But that's impossible."

Graham settled back into his chair. "I answered your question. Now, you answer mine. Where'd you find it?"

"In a sewer tunnel."

"I thought I smelled something rancid in here."

"I guess one shower wasn't enough to erase the stench."

Graham grimaced. "You guessed right. So, are you going to tell me what the hell is going on here or not?"

"I haven't seen an alligator if that's what you're wondering. But the tooth did come from a sewer tunnel."

"That doesn't necessarily mean anything. Maybe someone flushed it down a toilet for some reason. Hell, if you looked closely enough, I'd bet you'd find all sorts of strange shit in those sewers."

"Could an alligator even survive in the sewers?" I asked. "I mean, I've heard the stories but I always considered them urban legends."

"There was one gator back in 1935. Some folks found it in a Harlem sewer. But if my memory is correct, it didn't actually live in that sewer. It escaped and took refuge in it. By the time it was discovered, the reptile had nearly starved and frozen to death. I can recall a few other discoveries since then. But most of those alligators were small, maybe a foot or two long."

He tipped his head back, deep in thought. "I also recall hearing about a guy named Teddy May. They used to call him King of the Sewers. He achieved some fame in the 1940s and 1950s for his supposed exploits under New York. He once claimed to have led a sewer safari to wipe out an alligator colony. Of course, Teddy was renowned for his tall tales so who really knows for sure?"

I thought for a second. "You've hunted alligators before. Do you think one could survive in Manhattan's sewer system?"

"Well now, that's a tough question to answer. Our cold winter climate isn't really conducive to an alligator. The sewers would give it some degree of warmth but I don't know if they could provide enough food."

"What if it, uh, ate people?"

He gave me a questioning look. "Well, gators are man-eaters, no question about that."

Did that explain it? Were Kolen, Adcock, and the others attacked and consumed by a hungry alligator? The thought made me nauseous. "So a gator could survive on humans alone?"

"Not without being noticed."

"What other food could it find in New York?"

"Rodents." He tapped his jaw. "Pets. Fish too. But it would have to get outside to find them."

His last few words rang a bell. "I remember reading a story in the New York Times about some guy who fished for carp in the basement of his building."

"That's a bunch of nonsense."

"Assume that it's not for a moment. Where would the fish come from?"

He sighed. "You've spent a lot of time researching New Amsterdam. Well, back then the rest of Manhattan looked quite different as well. Dozens of streams and brooks carved their way across the landscape. I couldn't name them all. In fact, I'm not even sure all of them had names. But I remember a few. For example, Minetta Brook cut across what we now know as Greenwich Village and emptied into the Hudson. Supposedly, it was great trout fishing."

"How about in midtown? What rivers ran through that area?"

Graham rose to his feet again and dragged himself to another bookshelf. He rummaged around for a moment before pulling out a large, colorful map. "Back in 1860, a civil engineer named Egbert Viele began tracing the remains of Manhattan's original waterways. This map, the Viele Map, is the result of his efforts."

Graham spread the map across his desk. "Viele's primary concern was disease. He wanted to provide drainage for active springs covered up by construction. These days, engineers use it to avoid building on top of groundwater."

Leaning over, I examined the map. Three separate streams ran southeast, intersecting around 42nd Street and 3rd Avenue. From there, the combined stream ran all the way to the East River.

I pointed at them. "What happened to these waterways?"

"They got pushed underground to make way for new construction. But they didn't go away. They're still flowing under the surface, fed by recurring springs. When the tide changes, they even wreak some havoc from time to time."

"And yet you don't think fish still live in them?"

"Fish don't live underground. If a stream ran through a pond, I suppose a fish could get sucked into the current. But otherwise, it just doesn't happen."

"What about cave fish? Don't they live underground?"

He looked thoughtful. "Good point. Still, for a population of fish to self-sustain under Manhattan, it would need some way to access food derived from photosynthesis. Either that or someone would have to feed them."

"But it's possible, right?"

"Unlikely. But possible."

An alligator under Manhattan. The very idea seemed fanciful. And yet, between the tooth and the corpses, it was the only explanation that fit the facts.

"Are you going to hunt it?" Graham asked.

"Hunt what?"

"I'm not an idiot, Cy. You obviously think an alligator is living in the sewers and eating people. So, what are you going to do about it?"

I shook my head. "My role's over. I'm just curious, that's all."

"Do you really think a gator's down there?"

I stood up. "I don't know for sure. But something's down there. Something evil. And it needs to be stopped."

Chapter 20

My brow furrowed as I attempted to recall that once-familiar odor of fresh barbecue. My breathing slowed and my senses stirred.

I flashed back three years ago. I saw the litter on the sidewalk, the flowerboxes hanging from windows above. I heard the occasional screeching of tires, the chirping of birds. But try as I might, my nose just wouldn't cooperate. The best I could manage to gin up was a dull, lifeless memory.

My lip curled in annoyance. That aroma had remained locked in my brain for the last three years. But now, I felt it slipping away.

It was frustrating yet comforting. I'd miss the memory. But if good memories could fade, perhaps bad ones could as well. Maybe someday I'd forget my sins. Maybe I'd forget all that transpired three years ago. Maybe I'd even forget the last few days.

Maybe.

Twenty-four hours had passed since I'd first set foot in New York. Twenty-four long sleepless hours. My limbs felt tired and my legs demanded rest. My body ran on fumes, yet my mind remained crystal clear.

I shuffled the facts in my brain, examining them over and over again. Hartek's treasure. The mysterious homeless man. The alligator attacks. The diseased colony. Something connected them all. Something that continued to escape me.

But what?

Strong winds whipped down the block. The surging rainfall switched directions, drenching my torso. Never in my life had I seen a more ferocious storm. Even time itself couldn't weaken it. If anything, the rain had grown stronger since I'd arrived in Manhattan. Ancient civilizations would've considered it a sign from above.

I considered it a sign to get indoors.

As I neared the intersection, I caught glimpses of morning traffic. Lines of cars, bumper to bumper, ran as far as I could see. I noticed furious faces, staring straight ahead. Clenched hands wrapped around steering wheels. Mouths working a mile a minute, spitting anger into Bluetooth devices.

My mind drifted to Kolen. Did an alligator really kill him? It seemed so unlikely and yet I couldn't think of any other explanation that fit the facts.

I swallowed as I recalled his dead body. Saliva burnt my throat like battery acid. Quickly, I put him out of my mind.

I turned at the corner and started to walk down 78th Street. Despite the heavy cloud cover, I could see the familiar apartment building. My eyes lifted toward her window, second from the left and four stories above ground. It shone brightly.

A sudden gust of wind blasted into my side. My body tipped. Fighting hard, I managed to regain my balance without a spill.

I glanced upward. Storm clouds churned in the sky. The tempest seemed to worsen by the minute.

I started walking again. My boots stomped across the slippery pavement, sending small puddles of water flying into the air. After reaching the exterior of her building, I stepped underneath the overhang.

Cupping my hands around my eyes, I peered through the doors. A small lobby sat on the other side of the glass. Although nothing fancy, it appeared clean and well kept. A dark brown rug covered the floor, its color and texture hiding any traces of wet, muddy boots. Off to one side, I saw a wall of mailboxes, a set of crooked stairs, and an elevator.

A list of names with corresponding buttons was mounted on the wall next to me. I ran my finger down the list to Apartment 4H and read the name.

D. Blair.

I pressed the appropriate button. A faint buzzing noise hissed from the wall, followed by static.

"Who is it?"

I took a deep breath. "It's Cy," I replied into the metal speaker. "Cy Reed."

Silence followed. After a few seconds, I tried again. "Can we talk for a few minutes?"

More silence followed.

Finally, she coughed. "I don't have time for this right now."

"I can come back later."

"I won't have time then either."

"I understand. Say the word and I'll never contact you again."

Once again, silence fell over the area. As I waited for her answer, I stared hard at the door, as if my gaze could somehow cause it to magically open.

"Cy?"

The faraway voice lacked static and seemed to come from above. Venturing out from underneath the overhang, I saw the silhouette of a face looking down at me. I squinted, trying to peer between the raindrops, but her features were impossible to distinguish.

"I'm here," I called back.

"Why?"

"I wanted to clear the air."

"That makes one of us."

"Well, for what it's worth, I owe you an apology. I was a jerk to leave the way I did. You deserved better."

Lightning flashed across the sky and I caught a tiny glimpse of her face. It looked blank. But I could sense the emotional struggle just underneath the surface.

"You never said goodbye."

My mind flashed back to that fateful night. I remembered walking into her apartment, pretending that nothing had changed. We talked. We ate. We slept together.

Late that evening, I snuck out of her room, packed my bag, and left New York. Just like that, my life changed forever.

"You left me in the middle of the night." Her voice changed. "You didn't even have the guts to tell me to my face."

"It seemed like the easiest —"

"Well, it wasn't," she said, practically yelling now. "You never said a word to me. You just left me this lousy note."

She reached her hands out of the window. I saw a spark and a flash of light. A brief flame erupted into the dark sky.

As the ashes drifted toward me, Diane turned away. The glass slammed down to the sill and I suddenly felt very cold. Shoving my hands into my pockets, I watched her window for a few seconds, searching for her silhouette.

But it never appeared.

I backed away from the building. Then I turned and retraced my steps. I crossed slabs of concrete, feeling numb both inside and out.

Thunder crashed across the sky and the rain picked up speed. Hunching down, I struggled through the stormy weather.

I decided to make one more stop at ShadowFire's headquarters. Despite Beverly's threat about yanking my payment, I needed to tell them about the alligator. Once I did that, I'd leave Manhattan.

This time for good.

A loud pop deafened me.

And then, everything went black.

I looked around. All nearby artificial lights had been extinguished. It looked like a power outage. And judging by the blocks of dark buildings in all directions, it was a massive one.

Seconds passed and I became aware of another light, a smaller one and far more distant. My eyes drifted to the sky. High above, I saw the sun's rays peeking through the thick cloud cover. It was beautiful, breathtaking even.

There was something strange in the air. I could sense it. It made me feel small, but at the same time, free.

The sound of rain splattering against the sidewalk disappeared. I no longer tasted salt in the air. One by one, my senses faded away until only my eyesight remained.

And as I stared at the wonders of nature, something changed within me. I couldn't leave New York, not yet. Last time I faced adversity, I'd tucked tail and ran away. I'd spent the last three years running. And all I had to show for it was a trainload of guilt and endless bouts of anxiety.

I didn't want to run any longer, not from New York, not from Diane, not from anything else. I needed to make peace with my past. I needed to take charge of my future.

Abruptly, a thought hit my brain. It happened so fast that I never even saw it coming. And after it passed, I finally understood.

I adjusted my direction, steering myself back toward the subway tunnels. I just hoped Beverly had left them unlocked. I needed to gather proof before I went to her and Chase. And I needed to do it fast.

If my theory was correct, the Grim Reaper wasn't done yet.

And that meant that there was more death to come.

Lots of death.

Chapter 21

Sidling up to the wall, I took a quick peek into the layup yard. The space was dark and muted. In the dim light offered by a small, crackling fire, I saw a single shadow. It was large and shaped just like the giant I'd fought the previous night.

Terrific. Just what I need, another round with that monster.

The giant swept across the yard and back again, evidently keeping watch over the area. As my eyes adjusted to the quality of light, I noticed a second person. He seemed to come out of nowhere, a fact I found intriguing. The man walked a couple of yards and disappeared into the far end of the layup yard.

It made sense that the colony lived in that part of the space. The layout provided them with more protection from prying eyes. Fortunately for me, it also made the near end of the yard vulnerable to infiltration.

I continued to observe the near end of the yard for the next couple of minutes. Eventually, a petite woman strode into my line of sight. She glided toward the back wall. As she walked, she pumped her arms, waving a plastic bottle back and forth in the process.

Abruptly, she disappeared into thin air.

Two minutes later, she reemerged. Adopting a swift pace, she walked across the ground, still swinging the same bottle. Moments later, she vanished into the other half of the layup yard.

I turned my attention back to the giant. I timed his movements as he trooped back and forth, in and out of sight, over and over again. After memorizing the pattern, I ducked into the layup yard and flattened myself on the ground. I waited for him to run through his pattern again before standing up. Then I darted toward the back wall.

I heard footsteps as I moved and I turned my head for just a moment.

My foot caught on something.

My arms splayed to the side.

My body tipped.

I fought to keep my balance.

Abruptly, I crashed to the ground with a jarring thud, my gun rattling hard against the concrete. I sucked in a mouthful of air as the giant wheeled around and stared in my direction.

Shit.

Quickly, I rose to a knee and raised a hand in front of my face. "Sorry," I said in an overly deep tone. "My fault."

The giant stared at me and I felt like a kid caught shoplifting. My eyes drifted to the obstacle on the floor.

My chest tightened.

It was a body, newly dead.

Steeling myself, I stood up. I was in too deep to back out now. Confidently, I strode toward the back wall.

I felt the giant's eyes blazing a hole in the back of my head.

I kept walking.

As I neared my destination, I shot a quick glance over my shoulder. The giant had returned to his marching.

I was in the clear.

Letting out a deep sigh, I looked at the ground. I saw plastic tubs full of silverware and chipped plates, piles of unused blankets, and stacks of dog-eared paperback books.

I expanded my search, casting my eyes over the immediate area, seeing more tubs, empty water bottles, a decorative sheet hanging from the wall, stacks of cans...

My eyes shifted back to the sheet on the wall. Besides graffiti, the layup yard lacked decorations of any kind. So why was a single sheet hanging there?

I walked over to it. Something that sounded like white noise caused my ears to perk. I listened to it for a few moments. Then I pulled the sheet aside.

The mouth of a corridor yawned before me.

I stepped into it, let the sheet fall back into place, and found myself in a cramped makeshift area. Turning on my flashlight, I examined the roughly shaped walls and ceiling. The numerous marks and gouges looked manmade and fairly recent.

Shifting my light forward, I headed into the tunnel, descending steeply into the ground. As I walked, the white noise deepened and grew in volume. The tunnel expanded as well, growing wider and wider.

Suddenly, the ground disappeared beneath my foot. Bone chilling water engulfed my leg, threatening to drag it away. Immediately, I yanked it out of the current. Stepping back, I shifted my beam toward the water.

What I saw took my breath away. It lacked romance and style but there was no mistaking the water that rushed through the small cavern.

It was a river.

An underground river.

My heart pounded as I knelt down and jammed my arm into the water. I stretched as far as I could, but the bottom eluded me. Although bested by urban development long ago, the river had survived and perhaps even thrived deep underground.

Shifting positions, I flattened myself next to the waterway. I couldn't measure it completely, but the stream seemed wide and deep. Then images of Kolen flooded my mind. It didn't take much imagination to picture an alligator floating nearby. I jerked my arm from the water.

As I stood up, my beam reflected off something in the corner of the cavern. Leaning down, I discovered an empty water bottle wedged into the bedrock. Unless I missed my guess, the colony used the river as a water source.

Some enterprising person had dug out the tunnel to access it. But who? Ghost? Providing a supply of fresh water might explain the intense loyalty his people seemed to feel toward him.

Picking up the bottle, I scooped it into the water and filled it to the brim. Then I capped it and stuck it inside my satchel.

As I turned to leave, I swiftly organized the relevant events in my brain.

Fred Jenson, the mysterious homeless man, pawning a bar of Nazi gold.

The alligator attacks.

The strange disease afflicting the colony.

I wasn't sure about the first event, but the river was definitely at the physical center of the other two events. I shifted the facts around and reorganized them again. But no matter which way I looked at them, I kept coming back to one inescapable conclusion.

Something besides the alligator was flowing through the river.

Something that hadn't been there a few weeks earlier.

Something deadly.

Chapter 22

As I pulled back the sheet that separated the tunnel from the layup yard, I saw something disturbing.

Very disturbing.

Five people from the colony stood in a semicircle, surrounding me. One by one, they crossed their arms and adopted defiant looks. The giant stepped forward.

But before he could reach me, a hand touched his side. He paused to glare at me. Then he stepped out of the way.

Ghost walked past him and stopped directly in front of me. "I thought I told you to leave."

"It must've slipped my mind."

"I doubt that."

"When did you notice me anyways?"

Ghost patted the giant on the shoulder. "Fritz here recognized you from the moment you entered our home. He summoned the rest of us."

I eyed the giant. "Pretty cowardly, Fritz. What's the matter? Couldn't handle me by yourself?"

He didn't say a word. But the glare etched across his face spoke volumes about his feelings for me.

Ghost cleared his throat. "Listen to me very carefully. I don't like you. My people don't like you. The only reason you're still alive is because I haven't given the order to kill you yet. Do you understand?"

I shrugged. "Sure."

"Now, I want answers. If you provide them, everything will be fine. If you don't, then we're going to have problems. Do you understand that?"

I nodded.

"Why did you come back here? Aren't you afraid of the infection?"

"You're not infected. At least, I don't think you are. I need to run some tests to be sure."

"Yesterday, you were looking for someone who tried to pawn a gold bar." He gave me a suspicious look. "Now, you claim to be studying our sickness. Which one is it?"

I decided to level with him. "Both. A few weeks back, a homeless man named Fred Jenson attempted to pawn a gold bar dating back to World War II. He was last seen escaping into a nearby subway station. My employer sent out search teams to find him. One of those teams vanished under mysterious circumstances. I was hired to find the team and if possible, Jenson as well. I don't know anything about Jenson yet but I believe the team's disappearance is related to the problems your colony is experiencing."

"Keep talking."

"It's the river. I think it's poisoned."

He frowned. "Is that right?"

"Late last night, my partner and I found four bodies. Two of them belonged to the search team. I think the other two are the people you lost recently. Peter and Mary."

He clenched his fists. "You're lying."

"I wish I was. But like it or not, something killed them in the Lexington Avenue tunnel and dragged them through a series of natural crevices into the sewer system. And then, that something ate them."

Whispers and murmurs started to circulate among the others. But one hard look from Ghost shut them up again.

He turned back to face me. "If that's the case, then what exactly ate them?"

"I found a tooth. An alligator tooth."

The colony members burst into frantic whispers and discussions. Ghost gave them another hard look, but this time, they didn't stop.

Annoyed, he wheeled around again. "Alligators in the sewers? That's just an urban legend."

"First, it's not confined to the sewers. At the very least, the gator was capable of accessing the subway system. And second, it's not impossible. It's reality."

"How would a gator get down here anyway?"

I shrugged. "It doesn't matter. All that matters right now is that it appears to be snacking on people. And that means one of two things. First, we might be dealing with an alligator that's developed a taste for human flesh. Or second, the alligator turned to humans after an interruption in its food supply."

"Food supply? What food supply? There's no food in these tunnels."

"But there is food in the river," I replied. "Up until a few weeks ago, I think the alligator survived on fish from the waterway. Then something happened to the water. Something big. In the aftermath, the fish were poisoned. The gator's food supply dried up. So, it ventured out into other tunnels, searching for sustenance."

"And you think that whatever poisoned the fish also poisoned us?"

"It makes sense. After all, your colony uses the river as a water source."

"What's the poison?"

"If I had to guess, I'd bet on industrial waste. But without testing, it's impossible to know for sure."

I took the bottle I'd found in the tunnel out of my satchel. "That's why I gathered this water. I'm going to take it back to the surface and get it tested."

"Give me the bottle."

"Why?"

"Just give me the bottle."

I handed it to him.

He unscrewed the top. Before I could stop him, he poured the liquid down his throat. Afterward, he tossed it on the ground. "It tastes fine to me."

"You don't understand. Just because you can't taste poison doesn't mean it isn't there."

"No, you don't understand. I've had enough of your lies. Now, get out of my yard. And this time, stay away. If you come back, I won't be responsible for what happens to you."

"There's an alligator loose around here." My fists shook with anger. "And your water's most likely poisoned. You need to take your colony and get out of these tunnels before you're all dead."

"We're not going anywhere."

"My employer's wealthy and connected. He can fix everything. We'll bring in the CDC. We'll evacuate all of you to a private hospital where you can undergo tests and receive treatment.

Ghost got in my face. "I already told you, we're not going anywhere."

Fury burned within me. Reaching out, I grabbed him by the shirt collar. "Damn it, Ghost, your people are sick. If they stay here, they'll die."

He pushed me away. "We're not leaving."

"Stop drinking the water then. Let the toxins flush their way out of your systems."

"No."

I stared at him for a moment. Then, I turned my attention to the others. "You don't have to listen to him," I said loudly. "You can come with me if you want. I'll take you to the surface, find help for you."

No one budged.

Ghost flashed me a triumphant look. "We're a family. And nothing you do is going to tear us apart. Now, leave."

I forced my way out of the semicircle and walked out of the layup yard. Why'd I even bother trying to help him and his colony? All it had brought me were threats and aggravation.

Halfway out of the area, I snuck a glimpse to the side. During my previous visit, I hadn't gotten a chance to examine the living situation. But now that it lay sprawled out before me, I knew I'd never forget it.

A couple of men and women, clearly emaciated, sat in small circles, sipping water from dirty plastic bottles and gnawing on bits of garbage. Little boys and girls, their eyes dull and lifeless, sat on ripped and tattered mattress pads and sleeping bags. They played quietly, without energy. I felt ill just looking at them.

As I walked out of the layup yard, I considered my next move. I could return to the surface and seek out Chase and Beverly. I could relay my suspicions about the river.

But Beverly's threat still rang loudly in my mind. And without hard evidence, I doubted they'd listen to me. Even if they did, it would take time to find them, convince them, and organize a rescue effort.

Time I didn't have.

Time the colony didn't have.

But I didn't have a choice. The colony needed help, whether they wanted it or not. And I was the only one who could give it to them.

Chapter 23

Upon returning to the subway tunnels, I noticed a troubling development. The thin layer of water that covered the track bed had doubled over the last hour. Since it was only ankle deep, I wasn't in danger of drowning anytime soon. However, since it covered the third rail, it was more than deep enough to kill me.

I didn't know for sure if electricity still fed into the third rail, but I didn't want to find out the hard way. Looking around, I spotted thin concrete ledges on both sides of the tunnel. They were shoulder-high and stretched outward as far as I could see.

I clambered onto the nearest ledge. As I steadied myself, I started to wonder if I was making a mistake.

But I couldn't force the colony to stop drinking from the river. And I didn't have enough evidence to convince Chase of my theory. As I saw it, that left me with one move.

I needed to find proof.

And to do that, I needed to access the river. If I could find another route to it, I could empty one of my bottles of store-bought water and gather a sample. Then I could take the stuff to Chase to get it tested.

It seemed like a reasonable strategy. I'd gotten a good look at the river's direction during my visit. I also held an image of Viele's map in my memory.

Then again, although I could trace the river's course in my head, only certain parts of it would be reachable from existing tunnels. And the chances of actually accessing the waterways seemed remote at best.

Halting, I closed my eyes. I took a deep breath and held it, forcing everything out of my mind.

As my questions and doubts faded away, an image of the Viele map formed in my head. First, I saw the green expanse, layered with small rocks and wavy lines. Next, other lines traced up and down the map, forming a grid of city blocks. Finally, thin, curvy blue lines materialized. Those were the lines that mattered the most. They represented Manhattan's original waterways.

Three streams stood out above the others. They originated in a small section of midtown. From their separate origins, they flowed southeast before combining into one stream. That stream drifted farther southeast before pouring into the East River.

I recalled the locations of every subway tunnel in the area. Unfortunately, there were only four overlapping points with the waterways. Two of those points were positioned along the Lexington Avenue Line. The third point was a small stretch of the IRT Flushing Line, specifically the tunnel between Grand Central Terminal and Fifth Avenue. The final point was the area encompassed by the 42nd Street Shuttle Line.

Since I was already in the appropriate tunnel, I started by checking the two spots on the IRT Lexington Avenue line. As I walked to the first point on my mental map, I swung my flashlight beam across the expanse. The tunnel looked totally ordinary. Tall metal pillars, buried within a thick concrete wall, separated two sets of tracks while simultaneously supporting the ceiling. Letters and symbols, painted white, stood as a small memorial to the sandhogs, or underground construction workers, who once operated in the area. On the opposite side of the tunnel, my flashlight illuminated a row of rusty pipes that lined the wall.

It didn't take me long to decide I was wasting my time. There wasn't a single opening or fracture in the area.

Giving up, I used a series of maintenance tunnels to transfer to the IRT Flushing line. It took me another twenty minutes to walk up and down both sides of that tunnel.

Seeing nothing, I walked back to the Lexington Avenue Line and headed toward the 42nd Street Shuttle Line. As I strode forward, I kept one eye on the concrete ledge at my feet and the other on the tunnel. The tracks, including the third rail, were now completely covered with water. Although I couldn't see sparks or other signs of electricity, I still didn't want to take any chances.

I heard a splash. Reeling to the side, I pointed my light through the tunnel and waited, breathing heavily.

But nothing emerged.

An eerie feeling came over me. What if the alligator spotted me? What if it was hunting me? By the time I saw it, I'd already be within striking distance, with mere seconds to defend myself.

I shoved the thought out of my mind. If electricity continued to flow into the third rail, anything trying to follow me would suffer the consequences. And if it didn't, the ledge offered me several feet of protection from anything on the track bed.

As I walked down the first leg of the 42nd Street Shuttle's long, twisting tunnel, my thoughts flipped back to Ghost and his colony. Something about our most recent meeting bothered me. It wasn't the animosity between us. Nor was it the overriding tension in the room. It was something smaller, something I couldn't quite put my finger on.

A soft whooshing noise pierced the stale tunnel air. I froze in place, not moving a muscle.

Pipes hissed.

Water lapped gently against the tracks.

A full minute passed.

Then I heard it again.

It seemed to come from the direction of the wall. Gently, I placed my ear against the cold concrete.

I heard nothing.

I waited a few seconds.

Still nothing.

I continued to wait.

Then the whooshing noise echoed softly in my ear, sounding close yet far away at the same time.

I frowned. The noise, whatever it was, had definitely originated from the wall. It didn't sound like a subway train, not that it mattered since they weren't running anyway. And to the best of my knowledge, there were no maintenance shafts in the immediate area.

It didn't make sense. Other than bedrock, there was nothing on the other side of that wall. And yet the whooshing noise persisted as if air circulated around a large space.

Curious, I looked around. I realized that the portion of concrete on which I stood appeared newer and thicker than the rest of the ledge.

Bending over, I examined the surface. I saw a very thin, jagged crack. Using my flashlight, I followed its path. The crack ran across the length of the ledge and then started up the wall. After a few feet, it turned at a right angle and cut across another section of concrete. Then, it drifted down again, cutting a second crack through the ledge.

Near the second crack, I spotted something etched in the wall. I pointed my flashlight at the distinct marks. They appeared to form a skull and two crossed pickaxes, designed in a similar manner to that of the skull and crossbones.

A couple of lines were carved out of the wall, surrounding the design. An idea hit me. Reaching out, I placed my thumb against the etching.

And pushed.

The design depressed, acting like a button.

Something clicked.

The ground rumbled.

I stumbled as the ledge shifted. Leaning down, I clutched it for support. A cloud of dust filled the air, blinding me. I coughed, hacking out a handful of the particles.

As the dust cleared, I raised my flashlight. My heart began to pound.

Save for a few feet at the top and bottom, the entire wall had shifted inward, like a door on hinges.

Shifting my beam, I illuminated a hidden corridor, ten-feet deep and five-feet in diameter. It was dusty and dry, with the bottom part of the wall acting as a barrier against the rising water.

It can't be...Hartek's treasure?

The possibility shot through my brain. Of course, it was just a possibility. In fact, the more I thought about it, the more I realized that there were plenty of other explanations, none of which involved lost Nazi gold.

Still, I wavered for a few seconds, debating my options. Part of me wanted to find Chase. If Hartek's gold bars did reside on the other end of the corridor, Chase deserved to be there to see them. The other part of me felt compelled to gather evidence...and satisfy my curiosity.

That other part won easily.

I leapt off the ledge. Landing lightly in the passageway, I heard another click and swung around.

The wall slammed shut behind me.

My body tensed.

I'm trapped.

I lifted my light and examined the wall. Then I tried to shove it. But it didn't move an inch. After a few attempts, I turned to the side to search for a lever or another button.

In the process, my beam illuminated the dark abyss. All thoughts of my predicament instantly vanished.

A sizeable room, shrouded in dust, lay on the other side of a short passageway. In the dull glow provided by my flashlight, I could see large tables, chairs, beakers, tubes, and strange-looking apparatuses.

I twisted my light, examining every inch of the room.

Then I froze.

A sense of horror arose within me.

A corpse lay on the floor, positioned partially in front of the tunnel. I could see the rotting flesh…the dried blood…the holes.

It was the body of a dead man.

A man riddled with bullet holes.

A man who'd been murdered.

Part III

THE BELL

Chapter 24

Questions bounced through my mind like ping-pong balls. The room looked like an old laboratory. But what was a laboratory doing buried under the city streets, behind a false wall? Who was the dead person in the lab? Who killed him?

And why?

I didn't have a single answer. But I knew one thing for certain. I wasn't going to find any standing in that passageway.

I studied the area around me. The passageway consisted of smooth concrete walls. The laboratory itself appeared to be constructed from bricks, painted grey. No matter where I looked, I didn't see any cracks or signs of disrepair. Whoever built the lab and connecting tunnel had built them to last.

I strode into the laboratory. A cloud of thick dust burst from the floor. It swiftly devoured my flashlight beam. Coughing, I waved my arms, brushing away the annoying particles. The edges of a nearby desk, covered with a heap of unorganized papers, came into view.

Secluded from society? Check.

Messy beyond belief? Check.

Yup, these people were definitely scientists.

I saw scattered equipment among the papers, including test tubes, rubber stoppers, pipettes, and clamps. Three framed pictures sat at the back of the desk. Toward the front, I noticed a small calendar.

The date read March 6, 1976.

It hit me like a bombshell. Had the laboratory really sat untouched all of this time?

More questions poured into my brain. Who built the lab? What was its purpose? And why was it connected to the subway system?

I walked toward the west wall and pointed my beam at the ground, illuminating the corpse of a young man. He wore a lab coat and pants, punctuated with bloody bullet holes. What remained of his mouth lolled open, revealing a blackish interior. His eyes stared at me, seeing everything and nothing at the same time.

Carefully, I stepped around him. At the corner, I noticed a small hole at the bottom of the wall. A pile of bricks lay in a heap next to it. It looked like someone had started a repair job but never got a chance to finish it.

The dust seemed to gather around me as I walked past the corner. My flashlight dimmed.

On the south wall, I saw a metallic door built into the concrete. I tried the knob. It creaked open, revealing a neat, manmade corridor behind it. I entered and stopped next to a pile of rubble.

The corridor seemed long enough to stretch across the street to the buildings that faced Grand Central Terminal. Perhaps the laboratory was originally connected to the basement of one of those buildings. At some point, the corridor collapsed, sealing the laboratory behind a wall of crushed rock and concrete.

But why did no one come to recover the dead body?

The answer hit me immediately. Most likely, the lab was built and maintained in absolute secrecy. After the man was killed, no one alive would've known where to look for him.

No one except the killer.

I headed back into the laboratory and closed the door. As I turned around, I tripped on something and stumbled.

Rotating my head, I saw what I'd tripped over.

I grimaced.

Another corpse.

This one belonged to a young woman, or what was left of her anyway. Her head had been ripped in half as if someone shot off her skull at close range. Her body, covered in a bloodstained lab coat, lay awkwardly on the ground. A pair of glasses, attached to her shriveled neck by a thin chain, lay smashed at her side.

My chest tied itself in knots as I stared at her pathetic form. I wondered about her friends and family. What happened to them? Were they still looking for their lost loved one? It angered me just to think about it.

I started walking again, this time at a slower pace. I swung my flashlight in wide arcs to avoid another stumble.

After I finished trekking around the room, I returned to the desk and looked at the photos. One face stood out in particular. It belonged to a lopsided man, attired in a cheap suit. His nose was too big for his wrinkled face. His eyes looked large and baggy. Yet for all his imperfections, he carried a certain aura about him that caused him to stand out above the other faces.

I recognized him instantly.

Karl Hartek.

I tried to fit the information into place. I knew that Hartek worked as a Nazi physicist during World War II. After coming to America, he could've used the gold bars supplied by ODESSA to build the laboratory and continue his work. Maybe Jenson stumbled onto the lab, found a leftover gold bar, and tried to pawn it.

The story explained everything and nothing at the same time. More questions came to mind.

What was Hartek working on? Why had he hidden it deep underground? Who had invaded his lab and murdered the other scientists? And what happened to him? Why wasn't his body in the lab along with the others?

I shifted the flashlight to my other hand. In the process, my beam lit up a strange contraption.

I walked over and studied it. Several metal bars were secured to the concrete ceiling. Other bars led straight down to the floor, forming a sort of metal cage. Every couple of inches, I saw metallic struts attached to the bars, providing ample reinforcement. Thick chains hung loosely from the structure.

As I followed the bars to the ceiling, I spotted something odd. I leaned into the structure and looked up. Without exception, every single one of the reinforcement bolts had been completely sheared off. It was awe-inspiring. Nothing less than an abrupt, extremely powerful force could've caused such damage.

The longer I stood in the structure's presence, the edgier I felt. I'd never seen anything like it before. It looked like some sort of rigging designed to support a massive object. However, the object was missing. Did that explain the murders? Did someone kill the scientists to steal the object? Or was it still in the lab?

I looked around, searching for something that would fit into the rigging. Near the northwest corner, close to where I spotted the bricks, I noticed a humongous, black cylinder. It lay tipped on its side, as if someone had knocked it over.

I walked over to the heavy cylinder and knelt down. It had crashed to the ground with a ton of force, cracking the cement in the process.

As I moved my beam across its dented surface, I heard a faint dripping noise. I realized that the cylinder was filled with some sort of liquid. Liquid that was slowly seeping into the cracked cement.

This isn't the object missing from the rigging.

It's a chemical container.

And right now, it's leaking those chemicals into the cement…

And into the river.

Chapter 25

As I heaved the massive cylinder back to a standing position, I felt distinctly uneasy. I'd located and removed the source of the poison that plagued the river. However, I sensed that the room's darkest secrets remained concealed from my eyes.

I stared at the cylinder. Part of me wanted to return to the surface and alert Chase. The other part of me felt drawn to the laboratory. I didn't want to leave it, not without finding more answers to my endless questions.

Turning around, I let my flashlight's beam linger on the male corpse. He and the woman were nobody special, just two nameless people who'd died before I was even born. Yet, their stories needed to be told.

They deserved to be told.

I knew that poking around the room could destroy valuable evidence. Evidence that could help the police locate the killers. If I was going to search it, I needed to take precautions.

I removed a pair of worn leather gloves from my satchel and donned them. Then I walked over to the male corpse, fished in his pockets, and withdrew a wallet.

For a few seconds, I stared at the lumpy old billfold.

Is this just a wallet?

Or is it Pandora's box?

Shutting away my doubts, I flipped it open and removed a driver's license. I scanned it quickly, noting that the man's name was Jason Hatch

Cook. The dull color photo showed a serious-looking fellow with thin brown hair and jocular cheeks.

After returning it to his pocket, I looked toward the female corpse. A few feet past her, I spotted a small fabric handbag lying on a table. I searched it and found her wallet. According to the license, her name was Gretchen Janet Topper. The accompanying photo depicted a studious girl with short black hair and large glasses.

A sense of frustration set in as I returned the wallet to her purse. I knew the names of the two assistants, but little else. So far, I'd found nothing that indicated the laboratory's true purpose.

I walked back to Hartek's desk and studied the chaos that engulfed it. The papers were barely readable, covered with equations and half-thoughts, many of which were crossed-out, rewritten, and crossed out again. It would take a team of geniuses months to organize it all. I didn't have that much time. I needed to find something I could understand and I needed to find it fast.

I sat down and counted seven drawers, three on either side and one in the middle. I began rummaging through them, unveiling a treasure trove of pens, pencils, glue, staples, and other office supplies. In the third drawer, I found a stack of half-used writing pads. My eyes flitted to the desk, taking another look at the piles of loose-leaf papers. Their tops were crimped and ripped.

Nice detective work, Sherlock. It looks like you cracked the case of the missing paper source.

The next drawer was more helpful. It contained a stack of letters, fragile to the touch and covered with lines of faded ink. I scanned the text, reading words like *mit, auch,* and *für*. I knew enough to recognize them as German. As I returned the letters to the drawer, something fell out of the pile and clattered to the ground. Reaching down, I picked up a small gold key. It looked important.

The fifth drawer revealed nothing of interest. The sixth drawer seemed no different. It held a few personal items. A toothbrush and a quarter tube of toothpaste. Batteries. Glasses case. Small jar of peanut butter.

I quickly lost interest. But as I reached for the knob, I saw something glimmering in the corner.

It was a small, circular metal badge. The outermost ring depicted a gold wreath, exquisitely carved out of some kind of metal. A white ring was next, followed by a red one. Inside the red ring, I saw two sets of tarnished golden letters. One set, which ran across the top of the ring, read *National-Sozialistische*. The second set, situated along the bottom of the ring, read *D.A.P.*

They would've been meaningless to me if not for the symbol in the center of the badge. It stood out like a beacon of horror, colored black with gold trim.

It's a swastika.

The symbol of the Nazis.

I stared at the badge for a few seconds. I already knew that Hartek held a membership in the Nazi Party. But why had he continued to hold onto the badge after Germany's unconditional surrender?

I stuck the badge into my pocket and closed the drawer.

Six down. One to go.

I grabbed hold of the last knob and pulled it.

It didn't move.

Puzzled, I tried again. And again, it didn't budge. I pushed the chair away and knelt on the ground. My flashlight quickly picked up the reason for the stuck drawer.

A tiny keyhole stuck out from the side of the desk. As I stared at it, I felt the weight of the gold key in my hand.

I inserted the key into the lock and it clicked. Pulling the drawer open, I peered inside.

It was empty, save for a single, small book. The fine brown leather cover looked aged and worn. The edges of the pages were soiled and cut unevenly. A thick black band ran vertically around the bulging book, keeping it sealed.

I touched the oiled leather and lifted it up. Although the book was smaller than a standard paperback novel, it weighed twice as much in my hands. Wasting no time, I peeled off the stretchy black band and opened it up.

Tiny, scribbled sections of English text, mathematical equations, scientific formulas, and the occasional hand drawn picture covered the book's interior. Dates written across the tops of the pages indicated it was some sort of journal. I paged through it, passing numerous terms.

Liquid nitrogen. Electricity. Torsion. Die Glocke.

As I looked through more pages, I caught glimpses of a large bell and a structure that looked a little bit like Stonehenge. I stopped on a page. The bottom left hand quarter showed the large bell hanging from a rigging. My forehead tightened. It was the same rigging I'd seen on the other side of the laboratory.

I read a couple of paragraphs at the bottom of the page.

...die Glocke's field effects continue to puzzle me. During this morning's tests, we left several plants unprotected. Within an hour, all of them began decaying at incredible rates. In addition, Sam continues to complain of a metallic taste and persistent skin pricks that began shortly after last week's experiments.

All in all though, today's work showed significant promise. I firmly believe that I am on my way to unlocking the secrets of die Glocke. However, I must admit that it continues to frighten me. Am I doing God's work? Or the work of something else?

My palms felt sweaty as I closed the book and replaced the strap. What was *die Glocke*? What happened to it?

And most importantly, why was Hartek afraid of it?

Chapter 26

Soft banging noises interrupted my concentration.

My ears perked.

A few seconds passed.

I cocked my head to the side.

Then I heard another banging noise.

I shoved the journal inside my satchel and relocked the drawer, leaving the key in place.

I jogged out into the corridor and stopped in front of the wall that separated me from the 42nd Street Shuttle Line. Leaning my ear against it, I heard more noises, different ones this time.

Buzzing.

Cutting.

Pounding.

It sounded like somebody was building a house on the other side of the wall. Cupping my hands around my mouth, I bellowed as loudly as my lungs would allow. "Can you hear me?"

I put my ear back to the wall. The noises continued without pause.

I turned my attention to the wall itself. Using my beam, I scanned it for a lever or a button or anything out of the ordinary.

Nothing.

I expanded my search. But no matter where I looked, the wall appeared flat and unadorned.

Frustrated, I braced myself and rammed my shoulder into the concrete. Pain shot through my upper body. I turned the flashlight back to the wall and studied it.

Nothing.

It hadn't budged an inch.

Lowering my shoulder again, I drove it back into the wall. A stinging soreness ripped through my body. But still, the concrete surface refused to move.

Rearing back, I smashed my shoulder into the wall again and again. My mind started to slip away. I couldn't think. I couldn't see. I couldn't feel pain.

Six straight times I drove my shoulder into the wall.

Six times.

And yet, nothing.

I paused for a moment, panting. The situation didn't call for brute strength. It called for intelligence.

I expanded my search to the nearby walls. I scoured the concrete on one side of the passageway and then on the other.

Finally, I saw something that brought a weary grin to my face.

A skull and pickaxes.

The symbol was small and etched out of concrete above my head. I stared at it for a few seconds. What did it mean?

I pushed the center of the etching. It resisted my pressure for a few seconds. Then, it slowly depressed into the concrete.

The wall clicked.

The ground rumbled.

Dust shot into the air.

I heard slight scraping as the door opened toward me. Intense relief formed in the pit of my stomach.

Bright light burst into the hidden passageway. I shielded my eyes, stepped forward, and looked out onto the non-pedestrian track that connected the 42nd Street Shuttle Line to the Lexington Avenue Line. Amazement crept through me, twisting my facial features into knots.

No more than two hours had passed since I'd first entered the laboratory. And in that brief amount of time, the subway tunnel had undergone an astounding transformation.

Overhead fixtures shone blinding light down on the space, eliminating all signs of darkness. Temporary concrete dams blocked both ends of the tunnel. The track bed, once covered with nearly a foot of water, had been completely drained thanks to two separate pump hoses. Battery-operated fans whirred, drying the tunnel's last remnants of water.

Directly in front of me, a recently constructed twenty-foot long temporary platform, built from thick wood planks and other materials, rose into the air. It appeared to line up with the concrete ledge, creating a sizeable elevated workspace. Three workers knelt on the platform with their backs to me, examining a couple of handheld hammer drills.

Slightly dazed, I looked around. My eyes caught a glimpse of Beverly Ginger standing off to the side, just beneath the platform. She wore slim-fitting cargo pants, a tank top, and a hardhat. Two women and a man surrounded her and they appeared to be engaged in a heated conversation.

I walked onto the platform and knelt down. "Fancy seeing you here."

Beverly froze. Then, she waved the others away and ever so slowly, peered up at me. "What are you doing here?"

"I should be asking you the same question. You told me you were going to abandon your search. Well, wait until you see –"

"You shouldn't be here."

Something in her voice gave me pause. "What do you mean?"

"You have to get out of here. Don't ask questions. Just go."

"But…"

A new voice sounded. One I recognized.

One I despised.

"How are you, Cyclone?"

I shifted my glance. Ryan Standish stood several feet away on the platform. He wore a hardhat and a cocky expression on his face.

I went numb. It didn't make any sense. He didn't work for ShadowFire. He didn't know Beverly.

All of a sudden, I realized that the cacique retrieval job in Colombia had been a set-up. From the very beginning, Chase, Standish, and Beverly had conspired to manipulate me. But for what purpose?

Lights flashed in my eyes. A severe headache raged inside my skull. I tried to keep my emotions from raging out of control. "I'm fine," I replied. "I'm surprised to see you here. I guess ShadowFire doesn't believe in hiring standards."

He stepped forward. "I'm the one who should be surprised. Beverly said you snuck out of town."

Instinctively, I stepped backward, vaguely aware I was reentering the passageway. "Yeah, well, sorry to disappoint you."

Standish stopped at the mouth of the passageway and leaned up against the concrete wall. "Oh I'm not disappointed. In fact, I'm thrilled."

He looked over my shoulder into the laboratory. Then, he smiled. "You've done good work down here, Cy. Great work even. I'm impressed. Really, there's only one more thing I need you to do."

"What's that?"

Suddenly, his hands flew to his belt, a blur of speed and force.

He yanked out a gun and pointed it in my direction.

"Die," he said in a cold tone. "I need you to die."

Chapter 27

Stall!

The thought raced through my mind, like a runaway subway car. I needed to buy time.

Time to think, time to strategize.

Time to curse my stupidity.

I should've known something was wrong. But now, thanks to my lousy instincts, I stood in the front half of the sealed-off laboratory. Standish's large, burly form occupied the passageway, blocking the only exit. Nothing but floor rested between us. There was no place to hide. No cover.

Nothing.

I thought about reaching for my weapons. But Standish's gun caused me to rethink that strategy. The moment I moved, I knew he'd kill me.

"I always knew you were an asshole," I said. "I just never figured you for a corporate asshole."

He laughed. "During the Iraq War, Jack Chase realized he could pad his profit margin by appropriating things from local museums and archaeological sites. He needed someone to manage his various digs and fence his artifacts. So, he hired me. We've been working together ever since."

"A match made in hell."

"Call it what you like. But it's been a big success."

"So, when Chase found out about the Nazi gold, he hired you to find it."

A slow smile spread across Standish's face. "That's just the consolation prize. I'm after something else."

I took a stab in the dark. *"Die Glocke?"*

"Very impressive. How do you know about it?"

"Lucky guess," I replied. "That explains why you needed me. You're not a treasure hunter. Heck, you're not even an archaeologist. You'd never have found this place on your own."

His face darkened. "Kolen and Adcock worked for me, although they didn't know it at the time. After they vanished, we searched every inch of these tunnels for them. When they failed to turn up, Chase decided to bring in outside help."

"In other words, he lost confidence in you and decided to bring in a real expert."

"Actually, you were my choice. I knew you'd studied the tunnel system and your experience as a treasure hunter seemed useful. But Chase was wary. He'd already lost two people to his little venture. He didn't want to risk losing more and bringing on unwanted publicity. So, he insisted on a test."

"Which I passed with flying colors."

Facts and memories spiraled through my head, as I sought to understand the situation. But without organization, I found myself more confused than ever. Shifting gears, I began to establish a timeline.

People broke into Hartek's laboratory in 1976. They murdered the two scientists and stole a large bell-shaped object, known as *die Glocke*.

I flashed forward to the present. Somehow, the large cylinder in the laboratory toppled over, spilling unknown chemicals into an underground river. The poisoned water injured or killed members of the colony as well as the fish that inhabited the waterway. An alligator subsequently emerged, looking for food.

Around the same time, Jenson attempted to pawn a bar of Nazi gold but fled before he could be questioned. The story got back to Chase. Shortly after, the Chairman of the MTA died an untimely death, allowing Chase to take temporary control of the system.

He hired Standish to find the trove. Standish, in turn, hired Kolen and Adcock. The alligator attacked and killed Kolen and Adcock, among others. Then Chase hired me and staged his phony lockout to give me breathing room.

Three things struck me as important. First, Jenson. It seemed probable that he set the entire chain of events in motion. He must've entered the laboratory, stolen a gold bar from somewhere, and accidentally knocked over the cylinder.

Second, Chase was a lying, manipulative, driven bastard. Most likely, he'd killed the former MTA Chairman to carry out his plan. Who knew what other crimes he'd committed as well?

And third, Standish indicated that *die Glocke*, and not the gold bars, was his main priority. Why? What made it so important?

"You did well," Standish admitted. "Without you, we might not have found those bodies. The chemicals we discovered on the remains matched up perfectly with what we knew Hartek stored in his laboratory. It didn't take long to realize there was an underground river at work."

"And that led you here." I frowned. "If I had to guess, I'd say that Chase knew about the laboratory for a long time. A very long time. He just didn't know where to find it. Is that why he joined the MTA's board in the first place? So he could keep an eye out for it?"

Standish shrugged and I saw a bored look in his eyes.

My time was almost up.

I scanned the room, making observations. The laboratory was quite dark, despite the light fixtures in the other tunnel. The closest large object was the desk, which stood several feet away. Most importantly, Standish was alone, with no signs of immediate backup.

"So, tell me," I said casually. "How do you like being at Chase's beck and call? Do you even think for yourself anymore?"

His eyes burned with hatred.

"You're a joke," I continued. "Nothing but a yes-man with a gun. If you weren't so pathetic, I'd almost feel sorry for you."

"Shut up."

I grinned, throwing even more kindling on the fire. "And the worst part is, you know I'm right. You owe everything to Chase. Without him, you're nothing."

His face clenched and wavered. He struggled to keep his gun hand steady but it refused to cooperate.

Steeling my body, I prepared to leap toward the desk.

"Ryan!"

The shout, which originated from outside the passageway, caught me off guard. I froze for a split second and by the time I realized what had happened, Standish's gun was steady again.

The light coming from the subway system dimmed and a shadow flitted across the room. A second person, a woman I didn't recognize, emerged from the passageway.

"What?" Standish asked.

"I just wanted to make sure everything was okay. I heard the shouting from outside."

"I'm fine."

"Do you want me to take care of him for you?"

"Oh no, Cyclone's all mine."

A small smile crossed his face.

Suddenly, distant gunfire crackled through the air.

All traces of light vanished.

I heard shouts and screams. Scuffling. Running footsteps. People crashing into things. People crashing into each other.

I dove behind the desk. As I removed my pistol, I felt the pain in my head resurge. Ignoring it, I scanned the room, trying to pick out Standish and the woman.

I heard scraping sounds to my left. Rotating my body, I fired three shots into the darkness. A feminine yelp followed and then a thud.

Gunfire spat right back at me and I took cover behind the desk. I knelt there for a minute, breathing softly. My thoughts briefly turned to the sounds emanating from the subway tunnel.

What's going on out there?

I didn't wait to find out. Lowering my head, I began crawling across the room. I moved quietly, like a slithering snake.

A wooden table leg appeared in front of my face and I pulled up, barely avoiding a noisy collision. I paused for a moment, taking stock of the situation.

Part of me wanted to fight Standish. Yet, I was outnumbered and outgunned. Even if I managed to defeat him, Beverly and the others would kill me the moment I emerged from the laboratory.

I needed to escape. And the chaos outside provided me with the necessary distraction.

That is, assuming it lasted long enough.

Cautiously, I reached up and felt around the table. My fingers closed around something. It felt like the purse I'd searched earlier.

I launched it across the room. A moment later, it smashed against the concrete floor, bounced, and skidded. I cringed. It was supposed to sound like something falling off a table due to a sudden jostle. Instead, it sounded like a diversion.

A poor diversion.

An easily traced diversion.

An idea popped into my brain. Immediately, I slid across the floor to the southwest corner. Upon reaching the purse, I hung a right and headed straight along the wall.

I gained confidence as I approached the passageway. No doubt Standish heard the noise, guessed it was a diversion, and acted accordingly. The last thing he'd expect was for me to head toward the diversion.

But as I neared the passageway, I saw a shadow looming in front of the opening. All along, I'd assumed that Standish was reacting to my actions. Instead, he'd merely positioned himself in front of the only exit, knowing that eventually, I'd have to come to him.

Before I could stop myself, a frustrated grunt escaped my lips. Standish turned his head. Jumping to my feet, I hurled myself at him. His gun hand shifted in my direction. I chopped down on it and the weapon dropped to the ground.

His fist slammed into my jaw with the force of a jackhammer. My vision blurred and I saw colors around the edges. My headache returned with a vengeance and I knew I didn't have long before I experienced another incident.

Ducking under his arm, I swept his leg and he fell on his back. Before he could recover, I sprinted through the passageway.

As I exited into the subway tunnel, I saw darkness, interspersed with frantic movements.

"Cy."

The familiar, feminine voice rang in my ears like a discordant note. Spinning to the side, I pushed Beverly against the wall and placed my arm against her windpipe. "Why the hell did you do this to me?"

"We don't have time for this," she gasped. "I knocked out the lights and fired a few bullets. They're confused now, but it won't take long before they've got this area back under lock and key."

"That was you?"

She nodded.

It only took me a second to decide. She'd ordered me to leave Manhattan in the first place. And now that I found myself in trouble, she'd come to my aid. It wasn't enough to make up for her role in the whole affair.

But it's a start.

I removed my arm from her neck. "Which way?"

"Follow me."

Crouching down, I followed her through the tunnel. At the end, she hoisted herself onto the concrete ledge and angled north, heading along the Lexington Avenue Line.

I followed suit and as I darted after her, I heard the lapping of water below me. It sounded deeper than I remembered.

My emotions roiled. My headache worsened. My sense of balance diminished. Gritting my teeth, I forged on, determined to put as much distance as possible between Standish and us.

Subway stations and maintenance tunnels blurred as we raced north. My headache spread until it encompassed my entire body. My vision clouded over in endless colors, leaving me nearly blind.

I heard a dull rushing noise. I wasn't sure if it was my imagination or something else. Either way, it sounded familiar. Familiar and intense.

Stumbling, I fell onto the ledge, scraping my hands on the concrete.

Beverly swiveled around. "What's wrong?"

"I'm fine," I mumbled. "Just another one of these damn episodes."

"Do you hear that?"

"It sounds like water."

"More like a flood."

I looked down. Despite the colorful blurriness, I saw several feet of water churning through the bottom of the tunnel. It looked like a canal, albeit one with serious water flow issues. The sight of it stunned me into silence.

"We should get to a platform." My words slurred at the end of my sentence. I felt my muscles give way.

I never saw it coming. Abruptly, a wall of water ripped into my body, sweeping me right off the ledge.

I toppled toward the track bed.

The third rail.

I hit the water.

My brain exploded into colors.

And then I lost consciousness.

Chapter 28

As he stalked across the laboratory, Standish cursed his stupidity. He'd made a foolish mistake by not killing Cyclone Reed. And very shortly, he'd have to answer for it.

He forced himself to look on the bright side of things. The hidden laboratory, missing for over thirty years, had finally come to light. And Reed's escape wasn't really his fault. The blame belonged to that turncoat, Beverly Ginger.

He stopped and turned in a circle. After two hours of work, the laboratory had been completely transformed. Yellow caution tape wound around the room, forming walking lanes and blocking off areas of interest. Light fixtures hung from the ceiling, covering the space in a bright glow. Masked workers concentrated on the two corpses, examining them carefully. Later the corpses would be bagged and toted to the surface for more tests.

Meanwhile, two photographers roamed the room, taking pictures of every detail. Other workers followed them around, carefully securing and bagging all items for later examination. A third set of workers followed the second set, vacuuming and sweeping up the mounds of dust.

A small smile crossed his face. The operation was neat and well organized. If the room held answers, he would uncover them.

"Hello, Ryan."

As Standish turned around, he felt his stomach muscles clench. "Hi, Jack. Was it difficult getting down here?"

Chase shrugged. "I've been through worse."

"I'll bet."

"I saw some of my people are wounded. What happened?"

"Cyclone happened. He just showed up out of nowhere. I was about to kill him when all hell broke loose. Someone turned out the lights and fired a few bullets. In the confusion, Cyclone escaped."

"Who helped him?"

"Beverly Ginger."

Chase frowned. "Are you sure?"

"Some of the workers noticed her fiddling with the lights. And at least one person saw her and Cyclone running away."

"Where are they now?"

"Our guys are tracking them through the tunnels. It shouldn't take long to find them."

"For your sake, I hope you're right."

Standish felt a twinge of annoyance.

"So, where is it?" Chase continued. "Where's *die Glocke*?"

"I'm not sure."

"How can you not be sure? It looks like a bell, a giant bell. Six feet tall. Four feet wide. Even a moron would recognize it."

"I know what it looks like." Standish glared at him. "It's not here."

"Are you certain?"

"I've been in this lab for over two hours now. If *die Glocke* was here, I would've seen it."

Chase's face tightened and lines emerged. Standish felt the man's eyes lingering on him. He suddenly felt uncomfortable and his hands started to shake. Taking a deep breath, he hiked across the room and stopped in front of the strange metal rigging.

"We may not have *die Glocke*," he called out. "But we have its holding structure."

Chase walked over to join him. "That's definitely the right size and shape."

Standish stepped back and took a long look at the rigging. His eyes swept across its surface, looking for anything that might hint at *die Glocke's* current whereabouts.

The floor underneath the rigging was swept clean of debris and dust. As such, he could see that the concrete was heavily smeared and cracked in multiple places. It was an impressive sight and told him everything he needed to know about *die Glocke's* power.

"This doesn't make sense," Chase said. "Where could it have gone?"

"Don't know. But I'll find it."

"You'd better find it."

"There's another option though."

"Is that right?"

Standish waved his hand at the desk. "We found those papers. They might contain Hartek's blueprints for *die Glocke*."

Chase studied his face. "It sounds promising. But you're hiding something from me. What is it?"

Standish sighed. "One of your scientists already looked through them. He told me that for the most part, they contain unreadable gibberish and strange equations. He might be able to decipher them. But it will take time."

"Did you find a journal?"

"Journal?"

Chase nodded. "Back in 1976, my contact told me that Hartek recorded his discoveries and breakthroughs in a journal. It was his life's work, contained in the covers of a small leather book. If we find it, we might be able to use it to duplicate Hartek's research."

"We haven't found it yet."

Chase walked over to the desk and began searching drawers. At first, he merely shifted through their contents. But his movements became increasingly frantic.

Standish watched his actions with distaste. A controlled environment, strong organization, and smart, educated decisions. That was the formula for success. Ultimately, Chase's haphazard search would only make things harder on everyone.

Chase pulled out the top drawer on the right hand side. He flipped it over, dumped its contents on the floor and scanned them with his steely eyes.

Breathing heavily, he yanked out the second drawer and repeated the process. Then he grabbed the last drawer and tried to jerk it out of the desk. It didn't move.

Looking to the side, he noticed the key in the lock. After turning it, he removed the drawer and started to flip it over. Then he stopped. His face turned bright red.

Standish watched as the drawer dropped to the ground, crashing against the mess of papers and trinkets. Leaning over, he took a closer look. It was empty except for a thick layer of dust. However, in the very center of the drawer, was a dust-free space. It was about the size of a small paperback book.

The size of a journal.

"It must've been Cyclone," Standish said. "He probably found the journal and took it."

"I suggest you find him then. Find him and kill him."

Chapter 29

Get up. Get up already!

My inner voice screamed at my brain. I tried to blink. Where the hell was I? What happened?

I struggled to lift my head off a cold smooth surface. But a wave of dizziness struck me with the force of a thunderbolt and my skull crashed back with a thud.

The sound sickened me. Nausea took root in my stomach. Desperately, I tried to focus my mind on something else, anything else.

Bits and pieces of memories drifted through my brain. I snatched them out of the air, doing my best to stop them from floating away for good. But the recollections were vague and disconnected.

Mouthfuls of stagnant water.

The thudding of footsteps.

A sniff of cigar smoke.

I rewound my mind, searching for my last complete memory. I pictured the laboratory, the dead scientists, Standish's arrival, and Beverly's rescue. I recalled running and the sudden wave cresting through the tunnel. But from that moment on, everything was a blur.

I wanted to pass out, to forget the pain in my head. But that wasn't an option. I probed my aching body. No wounds. And my weapons seemed to be in place as well.

It was a small miracle. But a miracle nonetheless.

I sensed light to my left. I blinked and saw a fuzzy, nearby orb. Slowly, my vision cleared and I recognized it as my flashlight.

Following the beam, I saw Beverly lying next to me, still as a corpse. I scrambled to her side and checked for a pulse.

Nothing. My stomach churned.

I checked it again.

Several agonizing seconds passed.

Then I felt it, beating faintly.

Exhaling, I looked around. I knelt on a concrete island located between two sets of subway tracks.

How in the world did I get here?

My eyes searched the cavernous tunnel. A massive river of dirty, oily water floated on both sides of me. The current was slow, almost languid, and carried a garbage dump's worth of plastic bags, ripped clothing, and candy wrappers.

The ever-present concrete ledges poked out from either side of the tunnel, maybe twenty feet away. Graffiti of varying quality adorned the walls, providing some color to an otherwise bleak setting. An outdated video camera, covered in cobwebs and dust, stuck out from the western wall. I doubted it even worked.

But no matter where I turned my head, I saw no signs of life. Well, to be more accurate, there were no signs of people. Life, however, was plentiful.

It was also creepy.

Cockroaches crept their way up a pillar to my side. Frightened rodents scurried across the concrete island, squealing and slipping under my boots. Pigeons flew back and forth above me, like vultures circling their meal. I felt queasy just looking at them.

Leaning down, I shook Beverly hard.

She didn't move.

Gently, I slapped her face.

Still no movement.

I slapped her harder.

This time, her eyes fluttered open and brightened in recognition.

Abruptly, a rat ran over her chest. Caught off guard, she scurried backward and looked around, wild-eyed. "Where are we?"

"I don't know. But we're surrounded by water, so the only way we're going to find out is by taking a swim."

She made a face. "Just what I hoped for…another dip in New York's cesspool."

"Thanks," I said after a moment. "You saved my life."

She shrugged. "I'm the one who put you in danger in the first place. And anyway, I should be thanking you. You kept me from drowning."

"I thought you pulled us out of the water."

"That wasn't me."

"Then who…?"

"Honestly, I don't remember. I hit my head when I fell into the water. I guess we can safely say that there's no electricity running through the third rail."

"A good thing too."

"Let's get out of here."

I shook my head. "Not so fast."

"What's wrong?"

"Since I met you, I've been manipulated, Tasered, and kidnapped. I found my friend's dead body and searched for an alligator that shouldn't exist. Now, I'm running for my life in the middle of a closed subway system. So do me a favor and tell me something. Just what the hell is going on around here?"

"You're right," she admitted. "I owe you an explanation. Unfortunately, I'm short on facts. Jack and Ryan kept me in the dark most of the time."

"You must know something."

"For over three decades, Jack has searched for something called *die Glocke*. It's his obsession. I don't know much about it. But I do know that it's some sort of weapon. And not just any weapon. It's a strange, horrific weapon capable of killing thousands of people. He swears it will revolutionize warfare."

"It's over thirty years old. How revolutionary can it be?"

"It's rated Priority Alpha. Only a handful of ShadowFire projects have ever received that ranking. Jack has directed every available resource to finding and recovering *die Glocke*. He'll kill anyone who gets in his way as well as anyone who's outlived his usefulness."

"Like me?"

"Like you. Jack needed you to help him find the laboratory. Once you succeeded, you became expendable."

"Is that why you cut me loose?"

She nodded. "After we found the dead bodies, I knew we were on the right track. I had to tell Jack but as soon as I did, I knew he'd kill you."

"I don't get you." I shook my head. "You tried to keep me out of harm's way but continued to help search for a weapon that could harm thousands of others. What gives?"

"I wasn't just trying to find *die Glocke*. I was trying to destroy it."

"Why?"

"For the last few years, I've helped ShadowFire wage war across the globe. No matter what, I've always convinced myself that the good we did outweighed the bad. And part of me still believes that. But *die Glocke* changed everything, including Jack. All of a sudden, he started seeing the world in an entirely different way. It's as if he's on the verge of gaining untold power. Power that he intends to wield against his enemies. And if *die Glocke* is as deadly as I think, well, I can't allow him to have it."

"Sounds risky. What if you found it but couldn't destroy it in time?"

"I knew he'd find it with or without me. Better that I help him and maybe give myself a chance to blow it up."

"I guess you're not as heartless as I thought."

"Thanks…I think."

I thought for a second. "Okay, I assume you know about the alligator and the underground river?"

She nodded. "When we crawled through the bedrock tunnel, I heard running water. I knew right then there was an underground river in the vicinity. And when I saw the bodies in the sewer, I realized we were dealing with an alligator attack. I took some tissue samples while your back was turned. Tests showed the presence of several metal compounds including significant traces of thorium dioxide and beryllia, or beryllium oxide."

"Thorium dioxide? But that means that the water is…"

"Yes," she said. "It's radioactive."

"How radioactive?"

"The traces are small. Too small to cause much damage as long as exposure is kept fairly short."

"Any idea why those particular chemicals were used?"

"Unfortunately, no. Thorium dioxide can be used as a nuclear fuel. It's also a stabilizer for arc welding, electron tubes, and aircraft engines. Beryllia is utilized in rocket engines and semiconductors."

She brushed her hair from her face. "Our people found other chemicals as well, including heavy doses of mercury in its purest form. Mercury is far more common in industrial usage, although I don't know why Hartek used it."

"That explains the so-called disease that ravaged the colony," I said thoughtfully. "It's mercury poisoning. I saw an outbreak of it while working a hunt in Japan. The symptoms are a good fit with what we're seeing here. Discoloration and shedding of skin, loss of hair and teeth, brain damage, even death."

"And the radiation would only add to their troubles. If consumed in small, consistent doses, it would weaken their immune systems and cause vomiting and loss of appetite, among other things."

"Those chemicals might explain the alligator attacks too. The gator could've lived off fish that somehow survived in the river. The mercury would've killed off large amounts of the fish and contaminated the rest, stunting their growth and damaging their gills. Eventually, the gator would've faced a food shortage."

Beverly nodded. "It makes sense."

"What's our next step?"

"Your next step is to leave town."

"What? Why?"

"Well, first your face looks like it just went a few rounds with a gorilla. And second, it's far too dangerous down here for a civilian."

"You can't go back to Chase." My eyes tightened. "He'll know you helped me escape."

"I'm not going back to him. I'll watch him from a distance. When he finds *die Glocke*, I'll make my move."

"I'm coming with you."

"No you're not."

"Three years ago, I started running and I've been running ever since. Well, I'm tired of running. It's brought me nothing but problems. So, like it or not, I'm coming with you."

A thought flashed across my brain. Kneeling down, I removed my satchel and felt around inside. My fingers closed around leather and I withdrew the book from the bag.

"What's that?" Beverly asked.

"A journal. Karl Hartek's journal."

I opened it up and examined the pages. The water had caused some damage but large portions of the journal remained readable. Grimly, I closed it and placed it back in my satchel. Somehow, I knew that Standish would come looking for it.

And when he does, I'll be ready.

Beverly sighed. "Okay. You can stick with me for now."

"What's our next move?"

"We go back to the laboratory. Maybe we can figure out a way to eavesdrop on the operation."

"Sounds good. But first, we have to make a pit stop. We need to help Ghost and the colony. That is, if it's not too late."

Chapter 30

Something clicked in my brain as I retrieved my flashlight. My chest loosened and for the first time in many months, I felt lighter on my feet. I couldn't explain the feeling. Didn't even want to. I just didn't want to lose it.

Standing up again, I doused my beam. "We're south of the layup yard." I pointed to the other end of the tunnel. "Unless I miss my guess, we need to go that way."

"Before we do, should we, I don't know, test the water again?"

"What for?"

"Electricity."

"We fell in once and we're still alive. Chase must've disabled it."

"But maybe he turned it back on."

She had a point, but I wasn't in the mood for logic. Placing my palm on the ground, I hopped off the platform.

Moments later, my lower half plunged into the water. The cold, swirling liquid shocked me to my core and I felt my teeth chattering. "We're good to go."

Quickly, I waded to the western concrete ledge and climbed onto it. Then I helped Beverly clamber up behind me.

Questions peppered my brain as I paced down the narrow ledge. What was *die Glocke*? And why did Chase want to find it so badly?

I shivered involuntarily as water dripped from my sopping wet clothes. In the back of my mind, I knew I needed to get dry and warm. But the never-ending barrage of questions easily overwhelmed those thoughts.

Were they searching for us? And if so, were we making a mistake by staying in the tunnels?

I was drowning in unanswered questions. Reluctantly, I threw up a wall in my mind. Further speculation was pointless. I needed to get to the layup yard and get Ghost and his colony to safety. After that, I could worry about everything else.

I hurried forward. Soon, we passed the 28th Street station followed by the 33rd Street station. Shifting direction, we jogged toward the yard.

A short while later, the ledge forked, heading off in two different directions. I selected my path and picked up my pace. As we drew closer to the yard, I increased my focus. Every detail from the surrounding area caught my attention.

Small waves of shimmering, grimy water.

A trashcan, filled with free Metro newspapers, balled-up Kleenex, and soda cans.

Coughing and sounds of movement.

I dodged around some I-beams and caught a glimpse of the yard. It looked dry, thanks to a makeshift barrier that someone had constructed out of rotten wood and other scrounged materials.

Stepping over the barrier, I entered the layup yard. My muscles tightened. My breath caught in my throat.

Bodies were everywhere.

"What's wrong? Why are we stopping?" Beverly stepped around me. "Oh my God. What happened...?"

The stench of blood and death hovered in the air. Turning on my flashlight, I wandered into the yard. The beam illuminated faces. Faces I'd barely known.

Faces I'd never forget.

I spotted movement and headed for it.

"Didn't I...didn't I tell you to go away?"

I shivered as I knelt down next to the Ghost. The yard was like an icebox. I peeled back his shirt. It only took me a moment to realize that his wounds were fatal. "What happened?" I asked.

"Help me up."

I helped him into a sitting position. As I propped him against the nearest wall, he shot me a determined scowl.

"They...they're after *die Glocke*."

"You know about *die Glocke*?"

"Of course I do...don't you know who I am?"

A tingling sensation rose in my chest. "You're Fred Jenson, aren't you?"

"Damn straight. Never should've tried to pawn that gold bar."

"Why'd you do it?"

"We were in rough shape and needed food, medicine. God, I was stupid. Should've just forced everyone to go to the hospital. But no, my ego was too big for that. Thought I could handle everything by myself."

"That's not important now. We need to get you to the surface."

He pushed away my arms. "I'm not going anywhere. My time's short. So, level with me. What are you? Army? FBI?"

"I'm an archaeologist. Well, I used to be one anyways."

He chuckled, then coughed, spitting up blood. "Well, doesn't that just beat all? How'd you get roped into this anyway?"

"A man named Jack Chase hired me. He runs a military outfit named ShadowFire. I imagine his people are the ones who shot you."

His face darkened. "I see."

I noticed a glimmer of recognition in his eyes. "Do you know him?"

"Yes," he replied after a moment.

"How?"

"What's it matter?"

"I want to stop him."

"I know what you want from me. But I can't talk about it. They swore me to secrecy, said it was the only way to keep *die Glocke* from falling into the wrong hands. Kept my word for over thirty years and I'm not going to break it now."

"Maybe that worked before," I said. "But Chase and his men are searching these tunnels for *die Glocke*. It's only a matter of time before they find it."

He gave me a long look. "You need to hear a story. It's not…"

Suddenly, he coughed, wheezing for air. I slapped him on the back. He sounded horrible and I knew that his time was near.

"…my story," he continued. It's…it's compiled from scraps I picked up from the Sand Demons. Back in 1976."

"The Sand Demons?"

Sweat poured from his forehead. "I'll…I'll get to them. But first I need to tell you about the war. A Nazi physicist named Hartek…a real brainy guy…he worked at some top-secret facility."

"I found his laboratory. Apparently, you did too, since you recovered one of his gold bars." I reached into my pocket and removed the badge. "This was in his desk."

"That's the…"

He gasped, spitting blood all over himself. My heart wrenched as he lapsed into another coughing fit. His fate was sealed. There was nothing I could do to help him. The only question that remained was whether or not he would finish his story in time.

"Stay with me," I said. "You were talking about the badge."

"It's a…a Golden Party Badge. Given to the original Nazi Party members. Hartek…he wasn't one of them. He got his because of *die Glocke*."

"What is *die Glocke*?"

"The Bell."

"The Bell?"

"*Die Glocke*…is…German for the Bell."

I recalled the bell-shaped object from Hartek's journal. "What can you tell me about it?"

"Saw it only once. Looked like…like a bell. A big bell."

"What did it do?"

"I…"

His eyes closed. I tried to speak but my mouth was dry. My hands grabbed his shoulders and shook him vigorously.

Hold on Ghost…just a little longer…

His eyes fluttered open. "I…the Bell…don't know what it did." He swallowed. "Some kind of particle accelerator I think. The Nazi's…they called it a *wunderwaffe*."

"*Wunderwaffe?*"

"Wonder weapon. To turn around the war. Fortunately, they ran out of…out of time. SS bastards didn't want the Allies getting the technology. Murdered over sixty scientists."

"But Hartek survived."

He nodded. "SS spared him. His Bell…it was going to help them build a Fourth Reich. But our guys got to Hartek first. Brought him here. He slipped away a few years later…built a lab to continue his research…in secret. Hired a couple of kids…Cook. Gretchen. And Rictor…Sam Rictor."

"There were only two bodies in the lab."

"Rictor betrayed Hartek." Jenson coughed and his voice became scratchy. "Killed the two kids. Kidnapped Hartek with his two brothers. They…they…stole the Bell. Planned to sell it to the highest bidder…Jack Chase. Sand Demons…they found out about it. And they…"

His eyes closed. Gritting my teeth, I shook him again.

His lids opened ever so slightly. "What…?"

"The Sand Demons. You were just about to tell me about the Sand Demons."

"The Sand Demons. They were sandhogs...subway miners. They liked Hartek, even helped build his lab. They learned...about Rictor. Came to the rescue...."

"What happened to Hartek?" I asked. "And where's the Bell? Did they destroy it?"

Jenson's voice suddenly grew feeble. "Didn't destroy it...couldn't destroy it...don't know why. Sand Demons put the Bell into the *Omega*...there's a tunnel although it doesn't look that way. Oh, and don't forget the gold...it's the foundation...the foundation of Hartek's..."

His eyes closed.

His raspy breathing slowed, then stopped.

I shook him violently.

But he never awakened.

Chapter 31

"Is he...?"

I nodded. "He's dead."

Beverly paused a few seconds. "What do you think?"

"Jenson mentioned that the Bell was some sort of primitive particle accelerator. Does that sound familiar to you?"

"No."

"He also talked about some group called the Sand Demons. And there was something about the Bell being in the *Omega*. And a tunnel that didn't look that way. I don't know. Maybe he was just delirious."

"Let's assume that's not the case." She scrunched up her forehead in thought. "So, a third assistant named Rictor decided to steal the Bell and sell it to Jack. Obviously, he wouldn't want Jack to steal it out from under him. So, he kept the laboratory's location a secret."

I stood up. "That's right. Then Rictor killed the other assistants and took the Bell with the help of his brothers. But before he could sell it, the Sand Demons intervened. That explains why Chase never got his hands on the Bell. The Sand Demons stole it."

"And did what with it?"

I shrugged. "Who knows? Unfortunately, that's when Jenson started babbling."

"Did you catch what he said about not being able to destroy the Bell?"

I heard the edge in her voice. "Maybe he misspoke. After all, that's when he started to get delirious. Anyways, it's a moot point unless we actually find the Bell. And unfortunately, we're no closer now than when we started."

"What about that journal you found? Maybe it can tell us where the Sand Demons took the Bell."

"It's nothing but observations and equations. Anyways, Hartek left the journal behind. So, even if he knew where the Bell went, he never got a chance to write it down."

"What do you think happened to Hartek?"

"We know that Rictor kidnapped him," I replied. "As to what happened afterward, well, I have no idea."

She sighed. "We're out of leads. I say we go back to the tunnels and keep an eye on Jack."

I stood still for a few seconds, mulling over our options. Finally, I cleared my throat. "Maybe it's time we went to the police."

"If you do, you'll end up with a bullet in the back of your head. Jack's untouchable. Believe me, I should know."

I looked around the yard, seeing the sad, still corpses and the meager possessions scattered about the space. My gaze lingered on Jenson. It struck me that he seemed to have a troubled past, one which drove him to become a hermit. He existed outside the mainstream. Respectable people shunned him. In short, he was like me, post-Explorer's Society.

The Explorer's Society was as much a part of me as my college education, my days as an urban archaeologist, and my memories. But I was now an outsider to its hallowed halls, something I doubted would ever change.

I knew I could never fully return to that world. The past three years had seen to that. I was a different person now, irrevocably changed in ways I had barely begun to contemplate.

Yet, I could never fully leave that world behind either. It was too much a part of my past, too much a part of me. Regardless of where fate led me, I would always have one foot within the Explorer's Society and one foot outside it.

As I mulled over our situation, my mind suddenly focused. I knew what I had to do. I needed to stop thinking like a respectable urban archaeologist and start thinking like a treasure hunter.

"You follow Chase and his people," I said. "I'm going to the surface."

"You're leaving town?"

"No. But we need more information. Chase spent over thirty years searching for the Bell. If we can get our hands on his files, maybe we'll be able to match it up with Jenson's ramblings."

"His files?" She laughed. "And how exactly do you plan to pull that miracle off?"

"I'm going to visit ShadowFire's headquarters."

"You'll die before you get through the front door."

I grinned. "Who said anything about the front door?"

Chapter 32

It wasn't the tallest building in Manhattan, not even close. But as I stared up at the towering urban precipice, it looked as if it rose into the heavens themselves.

Rain swirled above my head, soaking my bloodied and mud-caked clothing. I was so damn tired of rain. Tired of Manhattan.

Tired of everything.

Lowering my eyes, I looked around. The sidewalks were clear and the streets were mostly empty, thanks to the storm and the late hour.

Thunder cracked. Lightning ripped across the sky.

It jolted me into action. I sprinted across the street and leapt over a metal railing that separated the sidewalk from the building. As I banged into the wall, my fingers closed around a slippery concrete windowsill.

Kicking my feet against a small, granite block, I struggled to gain traction. But my fingers started to slip.

I dug my fingertips into the windowsill, halting my descent. Pain raced through my hands and I screamed silently. Swiftly, I hoisted my body into a crouching position and jammed myself into the window frame.

I leaned out and slowly traced the building as it lifted into the dark clouds, before vanishing from sight. Scaling the structure was reckless, even dangerous. And climbing it without equipment was downright suicidal.

No ropes. No camming devices. No sky hooks.

Nothing.

Still, I wasn't unprepared. I knew how to free-climb a mountain. On the other hand, there was something wildly different about free-climbing an industrial mountain. Especially one engulfed with rain and surrounded by powerful winds.

My eyes drifted up and down the skyscraper, mapping out a path. A direct approach looked impossible. Flat granite blocks, thick columns, and smallish windows stood between the top floor and me.

Fortunately, urban cliffs abounded off to the side. I saw window ledges, frames, decorative piping, and ornamental outcroppings. Plenty of opportunities for hand and footholds.

Crouching on the sill, I rubbed my sore fingers. Then I carefully edged out of the frame and grabbed hold of a protruding brick. I pulled my feet onto another brick, keeping two points of contact between the building and myself.

I started to climb.

I moved hard and fast, doing my best to ignore the howling winds and drenching sheets of rain. My fingers and toes danced from bricks to vents to pipes to windowsills. It wasn't pretty and it wasn't precise but slowly, very slowly, I ascended the building.

I caught a brief rest at the fourth floor and then again at the sixth floor. Feeling renewed, I headed out again, eager to finish the climb. Eager to at last fully understand the Bell.

Rain soaked my body as I worked my way up a piece of piping to an outcropping. I lifted myself onto it and edged my way toward another pipe.

Suddenly, I heard a crack.

Something crumbled under my foot.

I slipped.

My hands flailed out, looking for something, anything.

Nothing.

Air rushed into my ears.

I felt myself falling.

I thrust my hands at the building and my fingers brushed against a hard surface. I flexed them, forming claws.

Horrible pain shot through my hands.

My body jolted to a halt.

I looked up. My fingers were stiff and extended, wrapped around the edge of a windowsill.

A gust of wind slammed into me. Gritting my teeth, I switched every ounce of strength I possessed into my fingers.

But the wind continued to attack me. My fingers began to weaken. Desperately, I swung my legs to both sides, feeling around with my boots.

Nothing.

Wait. Back there…what's that?

My left toe returned to the wall. It caught hold of something. I couldn't see it, but I had no other choice. My fingers were about to give way.

I braced myself against the toehold.

My exhausted fingers wrenched themselves open.

I waited for the inevitable plunge.

But it never happened.

Exhaling, I flexed my fingers a few times. They hurt like hell. I wanted to give them a rest. But first, I needed to get to safety.

Gently, I placed my hands back on the sill. Then I dragged myself upward. After a little maneuvering, I slid into the frame and took a quick look at my hands. They were a mangled, aching mess. I wanted nothing more than to just hunker down for a few minutes and give them a chance to heal.

But then I heard noises.

Footsteps.

They were coming toward me. My eyes shot to the window and I realized there was no shade or blinds. I was exposed.

Totally exposed.

I rose to my feet, and leaned out the window frame. My eyes drifted to the sky. The rain fell faster. The wind continued to push and pull at me with ease.

Jumping up, I grabbed hold of an old air conditioning unit. Pain rushed back into my fingers and it took all my willpower to keep them clenched around the piece of machinery.

I pulled myself out of sight and climbed into another sill. A small part of me wanted to quit, to just climb in the nearest window and hope I could find another way to the top floor. But I immediately disregarded the idea. Between guards and alarms, I knew I'd never make it.

I continued to climb. The wind picked up speed until I could hear nothing else. It slammed against my arms and legs, threatening to rip me from the building. My limbs grew increasingly numb to the point that they stopped hurting. I could no longer feel my fingers or my toes.

And still I climbed.

After what seemed like forever, the dark clouds split overhead. The top floor materialized as if it were the cornerstone of some ancient, forbidden city.

My adrenaline kicked in and I doubled my climbing speed until finally, at long last, I reached the top floor.

As I lifted myself into the last window frame, I felt something in my head. It didn't feel like one of my incidents though. Instead, it seemed more like a dizzy spell. I wasn't surprised. My body was exhausted and I'd lost some blood during the climb.

Maybe too much blood.

I took a moment to peer through the glass. But the shade was drawn and it was dark inside. I tried to lift the window but it didn't move.

I unsheathed my machete. My raw, peeling fingers stung as they wrapped around the handle.

Leaning back, I jabbed the machete at the window. Glass shattered, bits and pieces of it digging into my arm. Wincing, I withdrew the blade and stabbed the window several times, breaking out a large hole.

I reached inside the window, unlocked it, and lifted it up. Quickly, I crawled through the frame and hopped down onto the floor.

My head spun and I leaned against the wall for support. My eyes cast about the space. A bolt of excitement shot through me.

I was in Chase's office.

And I was alone.

As I rested, I looked around the room. It was exactly the same as I remembered it. A clean desk, an antique desk lamp, a bookshelf, a mini-fridge, a few chairs, and a couple of paintings on the walls comprised its contents. But although it hadn't changed, somehow it still felt different.

I stumbled across the hardwood floor, leaving a trail of blood in my wake. Stopping behind the desk, I rummaged through its contents. Like the desktop, the drawers were neatly organized. Finding nothing inside, I turned around and examined the bookshelf.

Hundreds of thin binders, labeled in neat black lettering, filled the shelves. I selected one at random and opened it up. The first page indicated that the book summarized the cleanup of an oil spill during the Persian Gulf War. I returned it to the shelf.

For the most part, Chase seemed like a neat, orderly person, albeit one prone to fits of insanity. With that in mind, I started at the beginning of the binders and systematically searched through them by date.

I passed through two dozen binders before I came across one labeled, "Operation *Die Glocke*."

My tired fingers shook as I retrieved it from the bookcase. The binder was old and worn. It looked like it had been read dozens if not hundreds of times. I sagged into Chase's chair and took my flashlight out of my satchel.

I read page after page, record after record. And soon, the entire story began to emerge in front of my fatigued eyes.

Sam Rictor was indeed a traitor. He'd reached out to ShadowFire, which was still in its infancy at that time, with an offer to sell them the Bell. Based on some sort of sample or demonstration, Chase offered to pay him a million dollars upfront with five million more upon delivery.

I flipped back and forth a couple of pages. A description of the Bell and its purpose was absent from the binder. I wondered if I was looking at whitewashed records, designed to protect Chase in the event of a raid.

I flipped another page. My eyes widened. The page didn't have anything to do with the Bell. Instead, a photograph of a subway car was taped to the top of the paper. Underneath it, a box of text provided all sorts of information such as year built, conductor controls, and propulsion.

I studied the photograph. The subway car was unlike any I'd seen of that era. In fact, I'd never seen anything like it in my entire life. It wasn't covered with graffiti and faded, peeling paint. Instead, it was sleek and painted silver. On the side, tall black letters spelled out a word.

Omega.

Jenson mentioned something called the Omega. Maybe he wasn't delirious after all.

I flipped another page and continued to read. Soon, the importance of the *Omega* became clear. After Rictor disappeared, Chase started a massive investigation to find him. In the process, he discovered that Rictor secured the *Omega* on the evening of March 6, 1976, presumably as a transport vehicle to move the Bell out of the lab.

I flipped more pages. The final notations were handwritten and confusing. From what I could gather, the *Omega*, along with Rictor and the Bell, had vanished completely into thin air.

Abruptly, the door opened.

Apprehension crept over me, oozing its way through my veins. The light flicked on. Holding my breath, I whirled around and found myself staring into familiar eyes.

Standish.

He strolled into the room. "Well, well, well. It looks like I won't have to track you down after all. I can just kill you right here."

Chapter 33

Standish reached to his waist and removed a 9 mm.

The gun rose, pointed in my direction.

His finger tightened on the trigger.

"Hold it," I said loudly. "You don't want to do that."

Suddenly, Jack Chase walked into the room, surrounded by shadows. He looked bony, wiry, and tired. He wore a well-tailored black suit, a dark blue tie and white gloves over his hands. He looked similar to the last time I'd seen him with every inch of his body, save for his face, covered with clothing.

Immediately, he pulled out his Smith & Wesson. "Cyclone? How the hell did you get in here?"

"Never mind that. Tell your goon to lower his gun."

"Or what?"

"Or you'll never get Hartek's journal."

"Ryan," Chase said sharply. "Do as he says."

Standish's eyes bulged. "He's lying, Jack."

"I'm not lying. I hid the journal. If you kill me, you'll never find it."

Chase shrugged. "I'll play along. For now. Stand up and remove your weapons. Place them on the desk."

Thunder crashed. Out of the corner of my eyes, I saw a bolt of lightning shoot across the sky. Raindrops poured through the broken window. A small puddle formed on the floor and swiftly grew in size.

I'd convinced Beverly to wait for me in the tunnels until I finished in ShadowFire's headquarters. We were supposed to meet later that evening. That meant she wasn't following Chase or Standish.

Which meant I was on my own.

I paused for a moment, debating my chances of grabbing my pistol and blasting holes right through their foreheads. But no matter which way I ran the scenario in my mind, it always ended the same way…with me bleeding out on the floor.

Standing up, I took my gun from my holster and tossed it carelessly on the desk. "Happy?"

"The machete too. And put everything into your bag."

I did as he requested, stuffing my weapons into the satchel and placing it on the desk.

"Ryan," Chase said. "Get the bag."

"Don't be an idiot, Jack. Just let me kill him now and be done with it."

"Not yet."

"But…"

"But nothing. Get his bag. Then pat him down and make sure he doesn't have the journal on him. Afterward, I need you to leave us alone for a few minutes."

"Jack…"

"Now."

Standish clenched his jaw in fury. But he moved toward me anyway, keeping his 9 mm trained on my forehead. Upon reaching the desk, he retrieved my bag.

"Spread your legs and bend over," he said. "And place your palms on the desk."

I obliged. His hands swept across my legs, feeling every inch of them. I glanced over my shoulder. "Could you hurry this up? The grown-ups have to talk."

The butt of his gun crashed into my forehead. I winced and fell to a knee, feeling blood trickle down my face. Another wave of dizziness came over me. But again, I didn't notice any headaches or discoloration in my vision. I was so used to battling episodes while under stress that I found myself thrown off-balance by their absences.

As the dizziness vanished, I saw Standish striding toward the door, my bag in his hands. "Hold onto that for me," I called out. "I'll be coming for it real soon."

Standish didn't bother to respond. Instead, he walked out the door and slammed it shut behind him. The entire room rattled slightly but one noise rose above the rest. It sounded like trembling glass.

But it wasn't coming from the broken window. It was coming from the side of the room. Immediately, I recalled the case full of antique guns.

There were dozens of ways I could attempt to smash the glass. However, Chase was armed. Retrieving a gun under such circumstances would prove nearly impossible. And even if I got my hands on one, there was a strong chance it wouldn't be loaded.

I lifted myself into Chase's chair and propped my legs on the desk. "Is this really the most comfortable chair you could afford? Because…"

"I see you've been doing some reading."

I glanced at the Operation *Die Glocke* binder. "Yeah, it's an interesting story actually. It's about this guy named Jack Chase. He struck a deal to buy a weapon but ended up paying a million dollars for nothing. The weapon slipped through his fingers and the rest of the world lived a happy ending."

"That remains to be seen."

"Why did Rictor go to you anyways? Why didn't he just offer to sell the Bell to the U.S. military?"

Chase shrugged. "Well, he didn't invent it so it wasn't his to give away. And if he tried to sell it to the military, they might've detained him and forced him to turn it over, free of charge. He couldn't take that chance. You see, Rictor liked living the good life and spent himself into heavy debt. He needed cash and he needed it fast. I was his only option."

I doubted he knew about the Sand Demons. And I wasn't about to fill him in. "Looks like he found a third option. He took the Bell and ran, along with a million dollars of your money."

Chase frowned. "I must admit I'm surprised to see you. I figured you'd flee the city. Why'd you come here anyway?"

"Answers."

"Did you find them?"

"Some."

A curious expression came over his visage. "How'd you beat my security? No one's ever made it past them."

"That's because you never pissed off a guy who knew how to climb."

Chase glanced toward the broken window. I followed his line of sight and stared at the puddle of water. It seemed to ooze toward the desk with an almost magnetic attraction.

"Impressive," he remarked. "Perhaps after this is over, we can find some common ground. I could use someone with your skill set."

"Sorry. I don't work for assholes."

He smiled thinly. "Well, let's do business. You have something I want. If you give it to me now, I'll let you go."

"Do you really think I'm that stupid?"

"I have no reason to kill you. All I want is your cooperation."

"As soon as you get what you want, I'm dead. You can't afford to let me live."

"Don't flatter yourself." He laughed. "You're nothing but a pesky fly. I'm wealthy, powerful, and connected. I employ thousands of people and have influence with hundreds of politicians and bureaucrats. When I'm accused of crimes, people jump to my defense, even in the face of overwhelming evidence. And you? You're nobody. You have no money. No job. No influence. Your former peers consider you a disgrace and a crackpot. I have nothing to fear from you. It would be a waste of my time to kill you."

"Have you ever considered becoming a psychotherapist?"

"Where's Hartek's journal?"

"Beverly has it."

His features hardened. "I see."

"If you let me go, I'll get it for you."

"I have a counteroffer. If you tell me where to find it, no one gets hurt. If not, I'll take matters into my own hands. With a snap of my fingers, my people will scour every inch of this city."

"You'll never find her."

"They won't be looking for her. They'll be looking for Diane Blair."

A jolt of electricity shot through my body, lighting my joints on fire. "I don't know her."

"Of course you do. Ryan followed you both times you went to see her."

"If you hurt her…"

"I won't hurt her," he replied. "As long as you give me the journal."

My mind raced, clicking through strategies. I couldn't let him hurt Diane. At the same time, I wasn't about to give him the keys to the Bell. I needed a third option of my own. "Okay. I'll get it for you."

He shook his head. "You're a good liar. Good, but not great."

"Well, we can't all be perfect."

Chase walked forward, sloshing through the thin layer of water that surrounded the desk. He stared at me through cold, dark eyes. "Tell me where to find the journal. I won't ask again."

"Go to hell."

I don't know if it was from loss of blood or sheer exhaustion, but I never saw it coming. I felt a sharp jab as his fist slammed into my head.

The chair tipped over and the back of my skull crashed against the hardwood floor. My vision grew foggy and I almost passed out. But the sight of a steel-toed boot hurtling toward my head kept me awake.

I rolled. The heavy boot smashed into the floor, barely missing my ear. I hopped to my feet and limped around the desk, backing away from him. His strength and speed had caught me by surprise.

I didn't intend to let it happen again.

Chase's left fist flew through the air. But this time I was ready. I parried the blow and grabbed his wrist. With a quick yank, I sent him hurtling toward the wall.

He spun to the side in mid-air. His heels hit the wall, he compressed his body, and launched at me like a Hellfire missile.

His fist punched my face at the precise moment his body crashed into mine. The combined impact drove me backward and I fell to the ground.

As he rose to his feet, I felt warm blood pouring from my forehead. He was tearing me apart, turning my face into hamburger meat.

He stood up, smoothed the wrinkles out of his clothing and stared at me with contempt. "Where's the journal?"

Slowly, I rose to my feet and wiped the blood from my face. "Half your life," I said. "You've spent half your life searching for the Bell. Was it worth it?"

"Of course it was worth it. The Bell is the future of weapons technology. Its value is immeasurable."

"The future? The thing's over thirty years old."

He laughed. "You don't know what the Bell is, do you?"

I backed around the desk, keeping a corner between him and me. I needed time to think of an escape plan. The window and the door were the only exits. Unfortunately, I doubted my body could handle another climb. At the same time, Standish stood outside the door, guarding it. "It's a particle accelerator," I replied. "Hartek probably used it to create some useless material. What was his deal anyways? Just another scientist gone mad?"

"Hartek wasn't a scientist. He was an alchemist, the last of his kind, yet decades ahead of the world. And yes, the Bell is a particle accelerator. But it's not just any particle accelerator. Hartek used it to subject a mercury-based fuel to tremendous amounts of electricity and torsion. Eventually, he created Red Mercury."

"What's that?"

Chase considered me for a moment. "It's a superheavy element on the Island of Stability. While similar substances decay in a matter of seconds, Red Mercury has a half life of one hundred and fifty-five days."

I shrugged. "So what?"

He clucked his tongue, clearly annoyed at my ignorance. "So, Red Mercury is a super-dense form of exotic matter. It's nearly indestructible. But when subjected to extreme pressure, it undergoes a chemical reaction that releases an enormous amount of heat energy."

"Sounds like a blast at a barbecue."

"The amount of energy released is sufficient to replace the fission-based primary in a fusion bomb."

My heart beat faster. "Wait, are you saying…?"

"Indeed I am. Once I have the Bell, I'll be able to produce an endless supply of Red Mercury, which will allow me to build hydrogen bombs without going through the costly and tedious process of gathering and enriching uranium."

He smiled. "In other words, in a few short hours, I'll be the world's newest nuclear power."

Chapter 34

The truth crashed into my mind, sending it spinning in a dozen different directions. "You're lying."

"Why would I lie?"

I suddenly felt very tired. I'd lost a lot of blood during the last hour. I just hoped I had enough left in me to keep from passing out. "But how…?"

"The Bell originated from the *Uranverein*. It…"

"The *Uranverein*?"

"The Nazi nuclear energy project." He took a step toward me. "When it became clear that Germany was doomed, the SS dismantled the Bell and murdered all of the scientists and technicians associated with it. But they spared Hartek, seeing him as a valuable asset for the inevitable rise of the Fourth Reich. Later, they entrusted him with Nazi spoils via ODESSA."

I stepped back. "Come to think of it, I've heard of Red Mercury. Back in the 1990s, there were all sorts of reports about it. But it was developed by the Soviet Union, not the Nazis."

"The reports started much earlier than that – 1976 to be exact." He frowned. "After Rictor vanished, I suspected a double-cross. I did everything I could to find him. When that failed, I leaked the existence of Red Mercury to the media, hoping to smoke him out. Unfortunately, it didn't work."

"How do you know Red Mercury even exists? What if Rictor made the whole thing up just to get a payout?"

"Do you really think I'm stupid enough to buy something without proof?"

A wave of dizziness hit me and I grabbed the desk to steady myself.

"Frankly, yes."

He sneered. "Rictor gave me a sample of Red Mercury during our first meeting. Tests confirmed that it generated sufficient amounts of energy to explode a hydrogen bomb. After it decayed, my best scientists spent years trying to recreate it. But without the Bell, nuclear weapons are beyond my capabilities."

"Along with any hope for sanity."

Chase ignored me. "Theoretically, it's not difficult to build a nuclear weapon. The U.S. Army proved that in 1964. They secretly hired two physics professors to design an atomic bomb using only public information. In just two years, those professors had developed the blueprints for a Hiroshima-sized weapon that could be built in a normal machine shop."

His eyes tensed. Then, his hand reached to his collar and scratched his neck. I caught a glimpse of a large ugly welt underneath his shirt's fine fabric.

"Just blueprints?" I asked.

"Even with a working design, an atomic bomb was out of their reach. They lacked the appropriate fissionable materials. Specifically, Uranium-235 or Plutonium-239. That's the secret of non-proliferation efforts. While the knowledge to build a bomb is available, the materials are nearly impossible to procure. Red Mercury will change that."

"And in the process, put nuclear weapons in the hands of terrorists." I shook my head. "Are you crazy?"

"I'm not crazy. I'm a businessman who sees an opportunity. For over sixty years, a small club of elite states has held a monopoly on nuclear arms. They've fought hard to maintain that monopoly, even going to war in some cases. And yet, they refuse to give up their own weapons."

"There hasn't been a nuclear attack since 1945. I'd say that's the only thing that matters."

"That's because you're an American."

"Takes one to know one."

His lip curled. "I might live here, but I'm not an American. Since the end of World War II, this nation has waged countless wars across the globe. Korea, Vietnam, the Dominican Republic, Nicaragua, Panama, and nations throughout the Middle East have all faced the wrath of the American empire. And do you know why? Because they lacked a nuclear deterrent."

He stepped forward and I took another step back. "You've got a lot of nerve complaining about wars," I replied, "considering that your entire business model revolves around them."

"Obviously, your small mind can't see the big picture. I didn't start ShadowFire to prolong wars. I did it to help bring them to an end, with as little blood and chaos as possible. But my efforts have failed to address the big picture. Red Mercury will change that. It will end war on this planet."

"How? By wiping out the human population?"

"By raising the cost of war to an unacceptable level. With Red Mercury, even the most backward countries can own nuclear weapons."

I circled around the desk and back toward the window. The giant puddle covered one half of the entire floor and was slowly seeping over to the other side of the room. In a few minutes, it would be totally flooded. "And of course, you'll earn a tidy profit in the process. Since Red Mercury decays quickly, nations will be forced to keep buying it from you."

He shrugged. "Global deterrence comes at a price."

"You know damn well that deterrence requires rational leaders who know how to make good decisions. Does that sound even remotely similar to any politician you've ever known?"

"Any nation that chooses to use Red Mercury without just cause will find its supply cut off. That alone will keep leaders in check."

"Your plan only works if all nations buy your product. What if that doesn't happen?"

"It will," he promised. "Red Mercury will be a godsend to leaders throughout the world. For the first time, they'll have the ability to defend against an American invasion."

Chase had an answer for every objection I could muster. He was utterly convincing and yet, I wasn't convinced. "Every nation that buys Red Mercury will insist on a demonstration. Imagine over a hundred hydrogen bombs exploding at the same time. Nuclear winter is a foregone conclusion."

"I'm way ahead of you. There will be just one demonstration. A very visible one that will be impossible to miss."

"Oh?"

"I'm going to detonate a hydrogen bomb in New York City." He said it easily, as if he were ordering lunch at a sandwich shop.

My body tensed. "You're crazy."

"Hardly."

I clenched my fists. "You're going to kill innocent people if you do that. Why not just detonate it underground or over the ocean?"

"America needs to pay for its crimes. And it's only fitting the country that dropped the first nuclear weapon suffer the fallout from the last one."

"What do you have against this country anyways?"

Chase grabbed both side of his silk shirt and yanked. It burst open, revealing a disgusting mass of scars, welts, and discoloration.

Bile rose in my throat. "What the hell happened to you?"

"August 6, 1945." His voice took on a harsh, bitter edge. "The Enola Gay dropped Little Boy on Hiroshima. Eighty thousand civilians died instantly. Thousands more perished afterward, due to injuries and radiation fallout."

"You were there? But that's impossible. You told me your father was an American soldier who died while you were an infant. You said you wanted justice for him."

"My father was an American soldier. He was also a prisoner of war. The Japanese kept him in Hiroshima, along with at least eleven others, as a deterrent to prevent American bombings. Somehow, a Geisha girl found her way into his cell. She gave birth to me. But the politicians didn't care about any of that. The deterrent, if you will, wasn't large enough."

"Killing innocent Americans won't bring back your dad."

"Even today, most Americans glorify Little Boy for saving lives. They don't even realize that the atomic bombs were completely unnecessary. They weren't the last bombs of World War II." He glared at me. "They were the first bombs of the Cold War, with no other purpose than to scare the Soviet Union. Americans are fools who deserve to feel the pain that they've brought to the rest of the world. I plan to give them a taste of their own medicine and in the process, bring about the end of war."

Feverishly, my brain considered my choices. The window was a non-starter. My only option was to take out Chase and then do my best to get past Standish. But between my injuries and loss of blood, I wasn't sure I was up to the task.

I stared into his eyes. "War begets war. If you blow up a bomb in New York City, you'll merely unleash more hell upon the earth."

"That's enough talking," Chase said. "I need Hartek's journal. I hope you'll give it to me because you understand that I'm doing the right thing. If not, I'll be forced to kidnap Diane. How much torture do you think you'll allow her to endure before you tell me where to find the book?"

His feet shifted positions, causing light splashes in the giant puddle.

My mind flashed back to the subway. To the industrial river flowing through the trackbed.

To the third rail.

Leaping forward, my hand grabbed the desk lamp.

Startled, he shifted his gun toward me.

I smashed the lamp onto the ground and leapt away from the water. It exploded and sparks shot across the floor, lighting up the dark space.

As Chase scrambled onto the desk, I darted across the room. At the door, I turned and shot him a quick glance.

He glared at me. "You're dead."

I smiled grimly as I barreled into the next room.

No, I'm not. Not yet anyways

Chapter 35

The metal door caught as I crashed through it. I heard Standish shout. Lowering my shoulder, I shoved it with all of my might.

Abruptly, it gave way and I burst into the reception area. Out of the corner of my eye, I saw Standish collapse in a heap on the floor. I'd bought myself a few seconds. It wasn't much.

But it would have to do.

I whipped my head to the left. The double glass doors came into view, as did the hard chairs, the framed articles and pictures, the side tables, and the stacks of military-themed magazines.

Not a single damned weapon.

My head revolved to the right so fast my vision blurred. More framed articles and pictures. A small water cooler. A single-serving coffee machine on a table. A swivel chair. The receptionist's desk.

Something glinted in the overhead light.

My hand shot to the desk. My fingers closed around the textured grip and I ripped the gun from my satchel.

I wheeled around and pointed it directly at Standish's heart. He lay sideways, one elbow balanced on the floor, the other poised loosely in the air. His tense hands were wrapped around his 9 mm. His eyes peered out from behind the sight.

"Ryan," screamed Chase from the other room. "Don't shoot him. We need him."

Standish's eyes tightened. "Drop the gun."

"You first."

"I'll shoot."

"No you won't." I intensified my gaze. "But I will."

"Ryan," Chase yelled again. "Don't –"

Standish growled. "Shut up, Jack."

For ten seconds, we stood there, neither of us moving an inch. We were like two statues in some sort of bizarre museum exhibit…quiet, unyielding, and deadly.

I still felt dizzy from loss of blood. But despite everything, I still hadn't experienced a stabbing headache or a sudden burst of strange colors. What did that mean? Was I finally putting my PTSD behind me?

My muscles grew tense and my mind focused on the task at hand. I couldn't afford to waste time. I needed to get out of that room and fast.

Keeping his gun leveled with my eyes, Standish slowly rose to his feet. "I don't care what Jack says. If you don't put that gun down, I'll kill you."

"Is that right? Am I just another obstacle on your way to mass murder?"

"What are you talking about?"

He looked genuinely confused. I decided to press the point. "Chase told me about his plans for Red Mercury. I knew you were cold-blooded, but a nuclear attack on Manhattan? That's insane."

He laughed. "We're not attacking anyone. We're going to make a mint selling the stuff. But that's as far as it goes."

I grinned knowingly. "You might want to have a talk with Chase. It seems he's been keeping secrets from you."

Standish didn't blink.

Keeping the pistol trained on him, my right hand reached to the desk and felt around until my fingers touched my satchel. I grabbed it and hoisted it over my shoulder.

I strode to the front of the desk, edged my way around it, and slowly started backing toward the hallway.

"I'm not joking," Standish said. "I'll kill you."

"You shoot me, I shoot you."

"I'll do it. I swear to God I'll do it."

My chest tightened as I walked backward. Was he bluffing? Or would he follow through on his threat?

I continued to walk backward until I bumped up against the clouded glass doors. I pushed my way through them and into the corridor. Seconds later, the clouded glass doors swung shut, shielding me from sight. A wave of relief swept over me.

But it didn't last.

Keeping my gun pointed at the door, I pressed the elevator call button. As the gears worked, my thoughts turned to the next step. Undoubtedly, there were guards in the lobby. How would I get by them?

The doors opened and I ran into the elevator car. As it descended toward the lobby, I tried to formulate a plan. But I quickly discarded all of my ideas due to lack of information. There were just too many variables to consider.

I plastered my back against the wall next to the door. It wasn't the ideal position to stage a gunfight, but at least it gave me some cover.

My body jolted as the elevator jerked to a halt. I stood still for a moment, feeling blood and sweat drip down my face. I tried to remain patient, but the elevator car remained absolutely still.

Reaching over, I pressed the Down button.

The car didn't move.

I waited a few seconds and then pressed it again.

Still no movement.

Abruptly, the elevator jerked and started to glide along its rails.

My heart started to pound against my chest.

The elevator wasn't going down…it was going up.

Chapter 36

The elevator car ignored me as I repeatedly slammed my finger against the Down button. Instead, it continued to creep upward at about half speed, slowly returning me to the one place I didn't want to go.

Back to the top floor.

Back to Standish. Back to Chase.

Back to danger.

I examined the control panel. But besides the Up and Down buttons, the only other object within reach was a small black phone.

Suddenly, it rang.

I froze in place.

It rang again.

I picked it up. "Hello?"

"Nice try, Cyclone," Chase said. "But I'm afraid your luck's run out. We'll see you soon."

"Can I get a rain check?"

The dial tone buzzed in my ear.

I returned the phone to its cradle. Chase sounded confident, cocky even. I got the sense that it wasn't just him waiting for me. With my luck, he'd probably called for additional support via a back staircase or something.

Suppressing my annoyance, I returned my attention to the control panel.

Removing my machete from the satchel, I rammed it into the small space between the wall and the panel. It took a few seconds for me to pry it open.

I was greeted by a dizzying array of wires and switches. I fiddled with them for a few seconds, trying to understand the complicated network at my fingertips. But I knew I'd never figure it out in time.

Stepping back, I raised the machete and stabbed it into the panel. The blade swooped through the air, shearing the wires and destroying the switches.

The lights evaporated.

The humming noise stopped.

And then, the elevator car ground to a halt.

Triumph surged through me. But it melted away quickly. Twenty stories still separated me from the lobby.

I hadn't stopped the inevitable.

I'd merely delayed it.

My eyes swept the space, searching for options. To the right of the now-dark overhead light, I noticed something that looked like an access panel. Climbing around in an elevator shaft didn't sound like a good time. And between my sore, exhausted body and torn, bloody hands, I wasn't even sure I could handle it.

But anything was better than waiting around for the welcoming party.

I returned the machete to its sheath and leapt into the air. My hand banged against the metal panel. It lifted an inch and slammed shut again.

As I dropped back to the floor, I looked up in frustration. The overhead panel was locked. I reached for my flashlight to take a closer look.

Light blazed from above. Squinting, I shielded my eyes.

What the hell…?

The phone rang.

I grabbed it without looking. "Can't this wait? I'm a little busy in here."

"Watch this."

The elevator jerked again.

Then it started to rise.

Chase's voice spat into my ear. "Now, you listen to me, asshole. That was your last…"

I hung up on him.

As I turned back to the overhead panel, I felt my stomach tying itself into knots. Obviously, the elevator car was hooked up to a backup power source somewhere. On the bright side, I was only rising at a quarter of the original speed.

But I was still rising.

I jumped up again, smashing my fist into the panel. Again, it only budged an inch. However, this time I managed to catch a glimpse of the lock's position.

Grabbing my gun, I took aim at the panel.

As I prepared to fire, a brief vision of a bullet bouncing around inside the elevator crossed my mind. Pushing it away, I gritted my teeth.

No time for doubts.

I fired. The blast reverberated in the elevator as the lock exploded into smithereens. I steeled myself and waited for the telltale sound of bouncing metal. But silence followed. After a few seconds, I released my breath.

Wasting no time, I returned the gun to its holster. Then I bent down and jumped again. My fist crashed into the access panel. It flew out of the way, revealing a wide gap.

I landed back in the elevator car. Crouching low, I jumped again. My fingers wrapped around the sharp metallic edges of the hole. Wincing, I flexed my arms and slowly pulled myself up.

Moments later, I scrambled onto the roof of the elevator car. It quivered slightly and although it seemed secure, I couldn't help but wonder when it received its last inspection.

I knelt next to the crosshead and took the opportunity to study the elevator shaft. Each corner contained two metal beams, which ran the length of the shaft. Thin metal fencing, interspersed with long blocks of wood, ran in a continuous loop behind the beams. Between two of the beams, I saw a substantial counterweight, slowly dropping to the ground.

My eyes followed a pair of thick hoist cables to a pulley positioned at the top of the shaft.

"I see him!"

A glint of light caught my eye as the unfamiliar voice rumbled down from above.

I heard a burst.

A breeze shot by my side.

Abruptly, a torrent of gunfire rained down upon me. I scrambled back to the hole and dropped head first into the elevator car.

The gunfire ceased but it didn't matter.

I was screwed.

Completely, utterly screwed.

The elevator car was hauling me to my eventual grave and my long-shot attempt to escape had been thwarted. In frustration, I slammed my foot on the floor.

It moved.

Not much, but it still moved. I kneeled and studied the area. A thin patch of carpet covered the car's entire floor. Taking out my machete, I began hacking away at it.

The blade quickly exposed a depressed compartment. Inside it, I saw a second access panel, locked with a small padlock. I fired my gun at the panel. Metal exploded as the bullet ripped through the lock and left a steaming hole in its wake. Leaning down, I unlatched the panel and opened it up.

Below, I saw a couple of cables vanishing into a deep, dark abyss.

Why can't I just use the stairs like everyone else?

I sat and dangled my legs out of the elevator car. They wrapped around the cable and I carefully lowered myself into the shaft. Then I began to climb downward.

My frustration began to seep through as I worked my way down the cable. For every foot I descended, the elevator seemed to pull me another two feet into the air. I felt like a damn iceberg.

The elevator slammed to a halt. I snuck a glimpse upward. I'd managed to separate myself from the car. Unfortunately, I wasn't out of shooting range.

Far from it.

I heard angry shouts. A few moments passed. Then a thin light poked through the car and into the dark shaft. It swept from one side to the other. As it fell onto me, it stopped.

Then it clicked off.

I looked at the gigantic counterweight, but it was too far away to reach. Shifting my gaze, I realized that the thin shaft offered nothing in the way of hiding spots or cover.

Bracing myself, I loosened my grip and slid down the cable. The metal strands sliced through my raw skin. My blood splattered all over the shaft.

Blocking out the pain, I peeked upward.

I saw no light.

I heard no gunfire.

See you later, suckers.

But the farther I slid, the more doubt I felt. The shaft was thin and wide open and I was climbing down the centermost cable. I might as well have been hiding in front of a bulls-eye.

A motor whirred to life and the cable jerked to the side. Caught by surprise, I halted for a split second. But to my horror, I continued to descend.

Chase wasn't going to shoot me.

He was going to crush me.

Some people die having sex with a beautiful woman. But not me. I get to be smashed like a bug on the bottom of someone's shoe.

I loosened my grip further. My hands stung as I dropped down the shaft. Soon they felt like they were on fire and I could almost smell the smoke wafting from the cable. But still, I felt the car bearing down on me. I was moving fast, but not fast enough.

As I slid down the cable, I kept my eyes glued to the bottom of the shaft. At first, I saw only darkness. But soon, the bottom appeared.

It looked like a mixture of metal blocks and rails. I slid down another few feet. Then with about ten feet to go, I released the cable.

Bending my knees on impact, I absorbed some of the blow. But the landing still jarred me to my core and my right leg began to throb uncontrollably. Shaking it off, I hobbled over to the elevator doors.

My hands stretched out, gripping their edges. I pulled with all my strength.

And they didn't budge an inch.

As the whirring noise grew louder, I looked up. The elevator soared down at me at an incredible clip. My gaze shot to the open access panel. If I positioned myself under it, I could reenter the car and...

Metal slammed against metal.

And suddenly, the access panel was closed.

There was nowhere to hide. The elevator was freshly pressed to the rails, leaving just a few inches of room on all sides. I had no more than thirty seconds before it landed on top of me.

Thirty seconds until it crushed me.

Thirty seconds until I died.

I twisted back to the doors. My hand flew to my belt, extracting my machete. Rearing back, I stabbed it at the thin opening. It slid in a little bit but when I tried to maneuver it, the blade slipped out again.

I felt the elevator car looming above me.

Fifteen seconds until impact.

Balancing myself, I reared back again and stabbed my machete at the crack. This time, it neatly slid into the space.

I pulled hard and the doors opened an inch or two. Jamming my hand inside the space, I lifted myself onto a small platform.

Ten seconds.

I struggled to pull the doors open.

Five seconds.

Four seconds.

Three seconds.

The doors opened a foot. I dove through them and rolled. As they slammed shut behind me, I heard the elevator car settle into its berth.

Standing up, I shoved the machete into my sheath and sprinted across the lobby.

I heard a dinging noise followed by the sound of angry shouts. Ignoring them, I grabbed my pistol and took aim at the glass doors separating me from the streets.

I squeezed the trigger. The glass cracked as bullets collided with its smooth surface. Ducking my head, I leapt forward.

As I soared through the doors, they shattered into a million pieces. I felt a surge of adrenaline.

I was exhausted. I was bleeding like a stuck pig. And I was sore as hell.

But I was alive.

Sorry, Reaper. Maybe next time.

Chapter 37

Rain stung my neck and shoulders as my momentum carried me onto the sidewalk. I didn't want to do a face plant but there was no time to tuck and roll. With no other alternative, I curved my legs downward and bent my knees, hoping to somehow land on my feet.

My right leg crunched on impact and I heard a pop. Somehow, I managed to kick off the sidewalk, tuck my head, and roll.

As I stood up again, my leg buckled underneath me. Gritting my teeth, I tried to run through the pain but came up limping. It didn't feel broken. But that didn't improve my mood.

Suddenly, I couldn't breathe. My lungs gasped for air but my throat refused to abide. Dimly, I became aware of a thin, wiry arm. It wrapped around my neck and started to squeeze the life out of me.

"Remember me?"

It took me a moment to place the harsh voice whispering into my ear. Then, I recalled the Town Car that picked me up at the airport.

"Walker?" I gasped.

"In the flesh."

The driver? I escaped that hellhole only to get caught by Chase's personal driver? That's just embarrassing.

I struggled to escape. "You don't know what you're doing."

"Do you know how much trouble you got me in? I was just doing my job, minding my business. Next thing, I know you're running away and I'm getting my ass reamed out."

"It wasn't…"

His arm muscle tightened. "Mr. Chase docked me a month's pay for that little stunt of yours. Now, it's your turn to suffer."

I clawed at his arm but it didn't budge. Blinking my eyes, I saw Chase, Standish, and several guards running toward me.

I gulped in a few breaths of air and gathered my strength. Abruptly, I pushed out with my good leg. Stumbling backward, I fell.

With a jolt, I collided with Walker. He collided with the sidewalk.

The grip around my neck loosened.

Gasping for air, I spun around. Walker lay crumpled on the ground next to his Lincoln Town Car. I reached into his pocket and removed a ring of five keys.

Car keys.

Sorry, Walker. You're about to get docked another month's pay.

As I stood up, I glanced over my shoulder. Chase, Standish, and the others were almost at the doors. I began ramming the keys into the lock.

I tried one key.

And then another.

A loud pop filled the air. Instinctively, I ducked. The driver's side window exploded, sending shards of glass flying into my face.

I dove headfirst through the broken window. Jagged edges slashed my sides, drawing blood. They hurt like hell.

I slid into the footwell beneath the steering wheel, praying that the sides held up to the firestorm. Reaching up, I placed the third key into the ignition. It didn't fit.

Tiny pings flicked against my back as bullets dented the door.

I tried the fourth key.

No dice.

Pounding footsteps caught my attention. They were close and getting closer. That meant one thing. Chase and his men were closing in for a direct shot.

A kill shot.

My fingers trembled as I stuck the fifth key into the ignition. Unbelievably, it slid in. Quickly, I turned it.

But it didn't move.

Desperately, I jiggled it and tried again.

This time, it turned. The engine roared to life. Releasing the emergency brake, I stomped on the gas.

As the car shot forward, I climbed out of the footwell, keeping one foot on the accelerator and one hand on the steering wheel.

The rear window exploded. Shards of glass sailed through the car's interior, embedding deep into the fabric.

I ducked my head and then looked in the rear view mirror. Chase and Standish stood in the center of the street, flanked by three other men.

Pressing down on the accelerator, I spun the wheel, sending the Town Car lurching onto another street. I let out a long breath.

Well, that could've gone better.

At least I was free. But even as that welcome thought passed through my brain, another disturbing one popped up to take its place. Chase was way too motivated to stop now. He wouldn't give up until he had his hands on Hartek's journal. And since I'd escaped, he'd turn his attention to the one person he knew could get me to give it up.

Diane.

The Town Car hit a puddle and skidded. For a few seconds, I nearly lost control of the vehicle. But I managed to slide through the turn.

It was hard to believe that I still cared for Diane after all of these years. Maybe it was just a passing phase. Maybe not. Either way, even thinking about her brought a smile to my face. That had to count for something.

Keeping one bleeding, aching hand on the wheel, I felt around the immediate area, searching for a phone. Finding nothing, I opened the glove compartment and rummaged through its contents. Still, no phone.

I turned my attention back to the street. A phone wouldn't have helped much anyway. It's not like I had her phone number. And after what Beverly told me about Chase's influence, calling the police seemed like a fool's errand.

Three minutes. As far as I could figure, that was the length of time it would take me to reach Diane's apartment. It would take another few minutes to convince her to come with me. If that failed, I'd drag her out by her hair.

Caveman-style.

Thanks to the late hour, lockout-related traffic was limited and the streets were largely clear. I drove as fast as I dared on the soaked, mist-covered streets.

The Town Car hit another puddle. Tapping the brakes, I gripped the wheel to maneuver my way out of the slide.

My body jerked like a puppet on strings. The engine cut off and the air bag deployed, smashing into my face with a vengeance.

Clouds filled my brain and I felt my tongue loll out of my mouth. Somehow, I managed to squeeze my hand toward my side.

Grabbing the machete, I punctured the bag. It deflated a bit and I used the opportunity to poke a few more holes in it. After a few deep breaths, I returned the machete to its sheath and pressed down on the bag, driving the rest of the air out.

Sluggishly, I stared out the window. The front of the Town Car was completely crushed up against a streetlight. The light hung loosely in the air, bent at a crazy forty-five degree angle.

Glad I'm not paying for that.

I turned the ignition off, then on. But the engine stayed quiet. I frowned and tried again. Still, the engine failed to sputter to life.

I tried yet again.

Nothing.

Cursing, I slammed my hand against the steering wheel.

Can this day get any worse?

I forced the door open into a roaring wind. Rain flew at me from an almost horizontal direction. It was like an endless cloud of bullets, attacking my arms and splattering against my face.

I extracted myself from the wreck. Pain in my chest spread slowly through the rest of my body. Each breath that passed through my lungs brought with it excruciating agony.

Looking around, I got my bearings. Then I began hobbling in the direction of Diane's apartment.

The powerful rain brought me more misery and after just a few steps, I was already sick of it. Picking up my pace, I started jogging. Soon, I was half-running, half-limping.

At half-speed of course.

I don't know how long I ran. But by the time I stumbled around the corner of Diane's street, I could barely move. My body ached and my right leg felt like it might fall off at any second.

But all that was forgotten the moment I glimpsed the light in her apartment. It drifted down to the street, blazing a path through the darkness.

I'd made it.

And then I saw the Land Rover.

It was parked just outside her building, smoke rising from the exhaust.

Abruptly, Diane emerged. Two large figures propelled her out of the apartment building and onto the sidewalk. After shoving her into the Land Rover's backseat, they climbed in after her.

As the vehicle zoomed toward me, I felt the sudden urge to grab hold of my pistol and start firing away. But I couldn't risk hurting her.

I ducked into the shadows. As the car sped past me, I caught a glimpse inside the rear window. Diane sat inside, flanked by the two men. The image of her livid, yet alarmed visage seared itself onto my brain.

A moment later, the vehicle hurtled around the corner and she was gone, swallowed up into the night.

Chapter 38

Why'd you drive so carelessly?
Why didn't you run faster?
Why, why, why?

Twenty minutes later, I stumbled down the street. Twenty minutes since I'd left 78th Street and 2nd Avenue. Twenty minutes since Chase's men kidnapped Diane.

Ordinarily, I would've covered the distance to 116th Street and Frederick Douglass Boulevard in forty-five minutes. Thirty-five minutes tops. But despite the pounding rain and my aching body, wave after wave of furious thoughts spurred me on.

At the corner of West 116th, I turned and walked past a few empty storefronts and a fried chicken restaurant. Stopping in front of the 116th Street station, I took a few seconds to stretch my rubbery, tired legs.

The station served the IND 8th Avenue Line and thus wasn't directly connected to the layup yard or Hartek's laboratory. I could still access those areas via maintenance tunnels and other shortcuts. Still, I found myself wishing I'd chosen a different place to re-enter the tunnels. Preferably, somewhere I could accidentally run into Chase's guys.

And beat the crap out of them.

A hand gripped my shoulder. I wheeled around, fists cocked.

"Whoa, boy," Beverly said with a grin. "No need for violence."

"I'm not so sure about that."

"What happened to your forehead? It looks like someone beat you with a cheese grater."

"That's good to hear. It feels a lot worse than that."

"I take it Jack didn't appreciate your visit."

"Oh, he appreciated it all right. In fact, he appreciated it so much he decided to return the favor with a little visit of his own…to an old friend of mine."

"Who?"

"Diane Blair. We used to be close."

"Is she…?"

"She's alive, at least for now."

Beverly led me down a small set of stairs into the 116th Street Station. As she fumbled with the gate, my anger resurged. Diane didn't deserve this. She just happened to know the wrong person at the wrong time.

Why does everyone I care about end up getting hurt? What am I? The human equivalent of a broken mirror?

Beverly opened the gate and let me through. Then she closed it and walked down the stairs, joining me in the station's interior. "Sorry about your friend. I should've suspected that Jack would go after someone you knew."

"Not your fault. You didn't kidnap her."

"Well, how do we get her back?"

I thought for a second. "Chase wants Hartek's journal. That's the whole reason he kidnapped her in the first place. He's hoping to pressure me into handing it over."

"We're not trading. Even if the book were useless, I still wouldn't trade it to him. The instant he gets his hands on it, he doesn't need us anymore. We become liabilities."

"Agreed. Anyways, I'm not letting him get his hands on the Bell. Hartek didn't exactly build a giant coffee maker in that lab of his. He built a machine that could generate a fuel called Red Mercury."

"A fuel for what?"

"Hydrogen bombs," I replied. "Chase wants to recreate Hartek's research and sell Red Mercury across the globe."

She gasped. "Are you serious?"

"It gets worse." I gritted my teeth. "In order to prove that Red Mercury works, he's going to detonate a hydrogen bomb in the middle of Manhattan."

She stared at me.

"What can I say?" I held out my hands, palms up. "He's got a shitload of anger left over from the Hiroshima bombing…and the scars to prove it."

"We have to stop him."

"First, we need to rescue Diane."

She shook her head. "Chase has the numbers and the firepower to beat back any attack we could manage. And besides, we don't even know where he's keeping her."

I frowned. "We can't trade for her and we can't rescue her. We can't trust the police and I'm betting the same goes for the military. So, what the hell can we do?"

"I wish I knew."

I thought for a second. "Where's Hartek's journal?"

She shrugged off her bag and groped around inside of it. "Here you go." She handed me the book. "What are you going to do with it?"

I set the journal on the ground and opened it to a random page. Then I removed a chunk of flint from my satchel and extracted my machete from its sheath.

"You're going to burn it? Are you sure that's a good idea?"

I nodded. "We don't need it. And I'm not willing to let Chase get his hands on Hartek's research."

As I placed the back of the blade against the rock, I felt a hint of trepidation. Throughout history, people had destroyed artifacts for the greater good. When Bishop Diego de Landa staged his Inquisition of the Yucatán Mayans in 1562, he thought he was saving their souls. But centuries later, archaeologists cursed his name for burning forty irreplaceable codices as well as the rest of that civilization's rich history.

What made me different than the Bishop? Would future archaeologists curse my name? After all, Hartek's journal could shed new light on the Nazi's atomic weapons program.

But the treasure hunter in me disagreed.

Strongly.

The journal was no ordinary artifact. Its very existence could enable the creation of the Bell and Red Mercury. It could be used to destroy lives.

It could be used to set the world aflame.

My mind wrestled itself for a minute or two. But I was unable to fully reconcile the differences between my archaeologist and treasure hunter sides. They were both part of me, even as they stood in stark opposition to each other. Like it or not, eternal inner conflict was my fate.

I looked at Beverly. Her solemn expression told me that something was on her mind. "Last chance," I said. "Any reason we should keep it around?"

She furrowed her brow. "Maybe."

"Maybe?"

"Remember what Jenson told us? He said the Sand Demons couldn't or wouldn't destroy the Bell."

I shrugged. "So?"

"So, if it's the former, maybe we should keep the journal around. If we find the Bell, the journal might help us figure out a way to destroy it."

I exhaled loudly. A single brush against the flint would send tiny sparks hurtling toward the journal, igniting it instantly. Tiny, golden flames would lick the air, adding light to the dim station. It would take just a moment. And then, I could forget all about Hartek's journal.

Do it. Do it already.

With a deep sigh, I shoved the machete back into the sheath. As I picked up the book, I glanced at Beverly. "We'll keep it. For now."

She nodded. "So now what?"

"Chase is searching for us. There's no question about that. But he's not the type to place his eggs in a single basket."

"You mean he might go after the Bell itself?"

"Exactly. And if he finds it before us, he'll kill Diane and half the city of New York. Our best bet is to beat him to the Bell and destroy it. Then we'll figure out a way to rescue Diane."

"But how are we going to find the Bell?

"Jenson told me Rictor used the *Omega* to remove it. According to Chase's files, the *Omega* was a subway car."

"That only tells us how he removed the Bell. It tells us nothing about where he took it, let alone what the Sand Demons did with it."

I stared at the ground, trying to focus. Every little movement caught my attention. The slightest sounds perked my ears. But my mind wandered. I knew I was missing something. I ran the facts through my brain.

Rictor stole the Bell. He placed it into the Omega. The Sand Demons stole it. They, along with the Omega, vanished.

So, where did they go?

I thought about Jenson's final words. *There's a tunnel although it doesn't look that way.*

What tunnel? What was he trying to tell me?

Then it hit me.

"The Sand Demons never removed it," I said slowly. "It's still here. The Bell and the *Omega* are still in these tunnels."

Chapter 39

Chase rose to his feet, picked up the Smith & Wesson Victory Model from his desk, and aimed at Standish's forehead. "Tell me why I shouldn't kill you right now."

"Put the gun away, Jack. This is ridiculous."

"You let Cyclone escape."

"None of this would've been a problem if you'd left the guards in the lobby. Calling them up your personal elevator was foolish."

Chase breathed rapidly through his nose, so rapidly that he thought he might snort flames out of it. "Watch your tongue. You're stepping on dangerous ground here."

"I knew something like this would happen." Standish shook his head. "Cyclone is like an annoying gnat. He just won't go away. You should've let me kill him while I had the chance. Why the hell did you want to have a private chat with him anyway?"

Chase slammed his other hand down on the desk. "He's the only person who knows where to find that damn journal," he shouted. "I thought I could talk him into turning it over to us."

Standish lifted an eyebrow. "I guess you were wrong. And while we're on the subject, Cyclone told me something strange. He said that you were planning a nuclear attack on Manhattan."

"Why in the blazes would I do that?"

"I'm just repeating what he told me."

"Did it ever cross your idiotic mind that he was trying to weaken your resolve? That if he put a few doubts in your mind, you'd crumble?"

Standish shrugged.

"Of course not." Chase sneered. "Otherwise, you wouldn't have let him escape."

"It wasn't my fault."

Chase placed his gun back on his desk and happened to catch a glimpse of the broken lamp in his trashcan. Anger roared through him and he broke into trembles. He'd always prided himself on his ability to overcome anyone, no matter how big or powerful. His entire sense of self was wrapped up in his ability to dissect people, to ascertain their weaknesses, and to exploit them on the field of battle.

And then, this disgraced urban archaeologist…this treasure hunter…this nobody…had entered his life. When he looked into Reed's eyes, he thought he saw a man at the edge of his limits. He thought he saw a man looking for a way out. And so he offered one in exchange for Hartek's journal. It was a bogus offer of course. There was no way in hell he'd have let Reed survive.

But now, Chase realized the error. Reed wouldn't accept a deal. He wouldn't let limits constrain him. Even worse, he was reckless, daring, creative, and unrelenting. In short, Reed was a major threat.

A threat to ruin everything.

Deep down, Chase blamed himself. It was his inability to judge Reed's character that allowed the man to get the best of him on his own turf. It was a humiliating defeat. He wanted to forget it, but knew that would never happen. It would linger on, under the surface, like some kind of festering wound.

In a way, that was a good thing. The next time he saw Reed, he'd be prepared. Next time, there would be no chatter. No deals. Next time, there would be only death.

Chase sat down. "Let's talk about something else. What's the latest on Ms. Blair?"

"Our people took charge of her a few hours ago. She's currently being held in the Jersey City facility."

"How did she handle the extraction?"

"Not well," Standish admitted. "She put up quite a fight. Even took a cheap shot at one of our guys with a frying pan. The poor bastard's got a black eye the size of a pancake."

"Sounds like everyone's having a bad day today."

"When it rains, it pours."

"Still, it's good news. With her under our control, we have some negotiating leverage with Cyclone."

"We have to face facts." Standish crossed his arms. "The journal's gone. No doubt he destroyed it the first chance he got."

Chase frowned. "If that's the case, it's over thirty years of work down the drain."

"I think you're forgetting something."

"What's that?"

"Cyclone didn't break into your office just for kicks. He had a reason for coming here."

Chase glanced at his desk and saw the Operation *Die Glocke* binder. He began thumbing through it. "You think Cyclone's looking for Hartek's original Bell?"

"I wouldn't put it past him."

"But where would he look? My men combed the world for years looking for Rictor and his brothers. They never found a thing."

"That's because they didn't think like treasure hunters."

Chase stared at him. "What do you mean?"

"Treasure hunters know that when the pressure's on, thieves don't always take their loot with them. Sometimes, they leave it behind."

"You mean like pirates burying chests of gold?"

Standish glanced at the picture of the *Omega*. "That's exactly what I mean. Now, you told me that Rictor removed the Bell with a subway car. What happened to that car?"

Chase shrugged. "We never found it. We figured that they scrubbed the train and dumped it off in one of the yards."

Standish stood up. "Call your men together. We need to search every inch of those tunnels. Unless I miss my guess, they didn't get rid of the train. They hid it."

Chapter 40

Mixed emotions swirled within me as I maneuvered my way across the thin concrete ledge. The idea of locating a long-lost subway car, buried deep under Manhattan, carried with it a certain romanticism I found difficult to resist. It was every treasure hunter's dream, the underground equivalent of finding a sunken ship or a forgotten city.

My cause seemed worthy. Destroying the Bell would save lives. But every second I spent searching for it was another second I didn't spend trying to find Diane.

I knew Chase wouldn't kill Diane until he obtained either the Bell or the journal. I couldn't let either of those things happen. I needed to destroy them both. Then I'd rescue her.

But what if something happens to her first?

Ignoring the thought, I continued to press on through the tunnel. I couldn't afford to doubt myself. Not now.

It was early morning, yet I didn't feel rested. I lacked sleep and still suffered from my injuries. But I was too restless to recuperate. I needed to work. I needed to search the Lexington Avenue Line for signs of a hidden tunnel.

I glanced over my shoulder. Beverly walked behind me, her eyes locked on the ground. She looked tired. I didn't blame her.

Earlier that morning, we'd taken a roundabout path following the Eighth Avenue Line to the Sixth Avenue Line. After another long walk, we popped out around the Broadway–Lafayette Street station, transferred to the Lexington Avenue tracks, and began walking uptown.

It was a long, exhausting walk. I just hoped it paid dividends.

Suddenly, the ledge cracked under my foot. Small chunks of concrete broke loose and fell into the track bed, sending ripples through the quiet water. I stumbled about clumsily for a second before regaining my balance.

"Nice moves," Beverly said. "Did you ever consider a career on Broadway?"

"Well sure. But I could never contain my talents to one city. I prefer to spread my awkwardness as far as possible."

She chuckled. "Are you sure we're looking in the right place?"

"Jenson knew where to find Hartek's laboratory. That means he most likely saw the Bell being loaded onto the *Omega*. I'm betting the Sand Demons arrived at the same time. After they seized the train, Jenson started following them."

"But why would they take it this way?"

I sensed the doubt in her voice. "Necessity. As they left the lab, the only tracks available to them were the southbound ones."

She shrugged. "They could've veered off somewhere or even taken it farther south, all the way into Brooklyn."

"Maybe. But remember, Jenson followed them on foot. And I doubt he could've kept pace with the *Omega* for more than a mile or so. As I see it, that makes our search area the southbound tracks between Grand Central Terminal and Union Square."

After more walking, we passed through the Union Square station. My eyes scanned the area for signs of Jenson's tunnel. For a couple of blocks, I saw nothing but ordinary walls, occasionally covered in subway script or graffiti.

But a few minutes later, I noticed something interesting. "See that?"

She followed my pointing finger. "See what?"

"The eastern wall continues in a straight line. But the western wall gradually slants farther and farther to the west."

"I see what you mean. The tunnel gets wider."

"Only temporarily. Farther ahead, the western wall returns to its original heading."

"It's not a perfect line. So what?"

"So the enlarged space allows the tracks to split."

I lowered myself into the water and waded over to the area. As I turned around, I found myself staring at a concrete wall, notched in such a way that it looked like a sealed, bell-shaped tunnel entrance.

Great. I'm seeing bells everywhere.

"This thing is called a bellmouth," I said. "Someone planned to build a connecting tunnel here once upon a time."

"Too bad they didn't actually do it."

"Maybe they did. It's possible that a tunnel existed here some thirty to forty years ago. The Sand Demons could've steered the *Omega* inside it and then sealed off the tunnel to make it look like an ordinary bellmouth."

Reaching into my satchel, I removed my flashlight and studied the wall. I allowed my hands to drift over its surface, noting each fissure and crevice.

"What do you think?" She gave me a puzzled look. "Is this it?"

I removed my hand. "I don't think so. The concrete's color and consistency match that of the rest of the wall. This bellmouth hasn't changed since the original construction of the tunnel."

I marked the position in my mind and then climbed back onto the ledge. If we failed to find any other bellmouths in the rest of the tunnel, we could always return and give it a closer look.

We continued to walk, passing the 23rd Street station and then the 28th Street station. And as we drew closer to Grand Central Terminal, I began to wonder if I was making a mistake.

There's a tunnel although it doesn't look that way.

Jenson had been half out of his mind when he told me that. And slurring too. I couldn't even be sure I'd understood him correctly.

After another two blocks, I saw the western wall branching out again. I walked a little farther and then lowered myself back into the flooded trackbed.

I traced my beam around the space. This bellmouth looked different from the other one. The sealed concrete surface was cleaner and less marked than the surrounding walls.

I sloshed over to the bellmouth and removed my machete. Carefully, I knocked the end against the concrete. It banged softly and then reverberated in the air for a couple of seconds before fading away.

Beverly arched an eyebrow. "It sounds hollow."

I shifted my light back and forth across the surface. Then I noticed something etched into the bottom, right hand corner of the wall, just beneath the water line.

I leaned down and studied the marks.

A skull.

Two pickaxes, the tools of the sandhog.

The symbol of the Sand Demons.

A smile creased my face. It was time go to hunting.

Train hunting.

Chapter 41

Reaching out, I pressed the skull and pickaxes symbol.

But it failed to depress.

I pressed again but it refused to budge. I tried another few times before finally giving up. The door-opening mechanism had seemingly been disabled.

Lowering my shoulder, I drove it into the wall. I heard a soft thud. My shoulder started to hurt.

As I yanked myself away from the wall, tiny pieces of concrete came with me, leaving a small gap in their wake.

"Maybe we should look at the rest of the tunnel first," Beverly said. "I'd hate to see you injure yourself trying to find something that's not here."

"It's here." I jabbed a thumb at the wall. "You can see the concrete for yourself. This section's different."

She sighed. "I guess I'm not sold on your theory. How could the Sand Demons just cover up a side tunnel? Wouldn't other people notice that it suddenly disappeared?"

"If there's a tunnel behind this wall, it's nothing special. Most likely, it was only partly excavated and never used. The kind of tunnel that wouldn't attract much attention."

She knelt down and felt around in the water. "I don't feel any tracks leading to the wall."

"If you were trying to eliminate all evidence of a tunnel, would you leave the tracks behind?"

She removed a knife from her waistband. "Good point."

For the next ten minutes, Beverly and I hacked at the bellmouth with ferocity. Her knife and my machete moved like perpetual motion devices, swinging forward and backward, forward and backward. It was almost hypnotic.

Soon, a small, jagged gap formed in front of me. I pushed on, my attention solely focused on widening the hole. I swung over and over again, until my arms began to ache and the scabs on my fingers started to bleed all over again.

My mind began to drift. I thought about Diane. I thought about Beverly. I thought about the alligator. I thought about Standish. I thought about Chase and his long search for the Bell. I was so deep in thought that I barely noticed what was going on around me.

Abruptly, my machete sliced through the wall. The boundary collapsed in a heap of rock and I stumbled forward. Dust curled into the air, blanketing everything. Particles stung my eyes and slipped into my throat. But I refused to turn my head. Instead, I peered through the dust cloud. I saw a small tunnel, lined with rusted tracks.

But that was it.

There was no *Omega*.

No Bell.

Nothing.

It was empty. Completely, utterly empty.

Chapter 42

Two hours and all I've got to show for it is an empty tunnel.

Exhaling, I stood up and stared into the small, dark space. I clenched my jaw so hard it hurt. I felt irritated. Annoyed.

Downright pissed-off.

I'd wasted two hours locating and unearthing the hidden passage. Two, long, tiring hours. It was an utter waste of time.

"Well, what are you waiting for?" Beverly glanced at me. "Let's check it out."

"Maybe you didn't notice, but it's empty."

"But the fact that it even exists tells me that you were right all along. At some point, this passage contained the *Omega*. And the Bell."

"A lot of good that does us now."

"We might find some clues inside. Clues that could lead us to the Bell's final resting place."

"I doubt it."

She shook her head. "I get it. You feel like you wasted your time. But feeling sorry for yourself isn't going to get us anywhere."

Before I could respond, she stepped over the crumbled cement and vanished into the small passage.

I was wrong and I knew it. Coupled with Jenson's statement, the passage's existence constituted significant proof. And the skull and pickaxe button, even though it didn't open the wall, was impossible to ignore.

I walked over to the bellmouth and climbed into the passage. The bright glow of my flashlight illuminated the space. It was about the same height as the main tunnel and about two-thirds its width. However, while the Lexington Avenue Line ran for miles, the passage only penetrated about a hundred feet into the bedrock.

As my frustration ebbed, I found myself fascinated by the passage. But something about it also bothered me. Kneeling down, I examined the trackbed. Piles of gravel separated long planks of dark wood. Two metal rails ran across the boards, extending the length of the tunnel. Overall, the configuration looked normal for a typical subway tunnel. There was just one difference.

One big difference.

"No third rail," I remarked.

"Maybe the Sand Demons removed it after they disconnected the tracks from the main tunnel."

I nodded slowly. "You're probably right."

"Let's back up for a second. What happened here?"

I shrugged. "It looks pretty cut and dried to me. The Sand Demons once stored the *Omega* in here. Now it's missing."

"But why is it missing? Did someone else take it?"

I shone my flashlight to the side of the passage, casting light upon several armfuls of wadded up material. "Maybe." Walking over to the pile, I noticed that a thin concrete-like substance covered one side of the material. "Or maybe the Sand Demons only used this passage as a temporary storage area. Once the coast was clear, they moved the *Omega* to a permanent location."

"But why would they go to all that trouble?"

I thought for a moment. "They originally planned to wall it up in here. But then Jenson showed up. They didn't like him knowing about the Bell's location. So, the first chance they got, they hid it somewhere else."

We lapsed into silence. For the next few minutes, I scoured the space, searching for evidence that could lead us to the *Omega*. Unfortunately, I didn't see much in the way of clues.

But I pressed on, passing by discarded tools, a workbench, and building supplies. It wasn't until I reached the far end of the passage that I found something interesting.

The flashlight illuminated a couple of gouges in the wall. My heart skipped a beat. "Beverly. Come over here."

She appeared at my side. "What's up?"

"Take a look at this drawing."

"My God." Her voice became hushed. "It's a map. A detailed map of Manhattan."

"And it's accurate. Right down to the block."

She pointed at the wall. "That deep line, the one on the east side, is probably the Lexington Avenue Line. But I don't recognize the other one that connects to it."

I stared at the map. A single line began at the southern tip of the island and extended north to Union Square. From there, it branched out into two lines, one of which continued straight up the east side while the other one angled to the west before traveling up the west side.

"Actually, I don't think it is the Lexington Line." I traced my finger along the map. "It travels straight up Park Avenue. The Lexington Line, for the most part, runs to the east of this one."

"So, the Sand Demons made a mistake."

"The rest of the map is accurate. Why would they mess up the subway tunnels? Heck, they worked down here."

"Well, I…"

Her voice trailed off. I stared into her face for a second, waiting for her to finish. But she just stood still.

"Are you okay?" I asked.

She lifted a finger and pointed it toward the mouth of the passage. I shifted, following her lead.

Then I froze.

Something was moving south just outside the tunnel.

Something big.

Something alive.

My feet pounded against the trackbed. Simultaneously, my hand flew to my holster, yanking out my pistol. I hadn't caught a full look at it yet, but I knew what was out there.

And I was going to kill it.

At the front of the tunnel, I vaulted over the broken concrete wall, landing on top of a pile of debris. My flashlight shifted to the flooded trackbed.

And then I saw it.

The brownish-green mass was over twelve feet long. Its body was thick and scaly. It moved in crazed fashion, twisting and thrashing about from one side of the tunnel to the next.

"Good lord," Beverly whispered. "It's huge."

Adrenaline completely consumed me. All I could think about was the horror the beast had unleashed upon the city.

Upon Javier Kolen.

I aimed my gun into the darkness, trying to target its head.

"Don't be a fool," Beverly hissed. "If you fire that thing, Jack will hear it."

My finger tightened around the trigger. "It needs to die."

Suddenly, the alligator reared upward. The movement was so fast I didn't have time to react.

Its head turned toward me and I saw its eyes. They were red as blood, yet dark as night. As I stared into them, I felt like I was looking into the soul of the devil himself.

The gator lunged at me. My instincts took over and I dove to the south. As I rolled through the water, I seized the machete from my waist with my free hand.

I rose to my feet. The gigantic alligator was just a few feet away. I backed up, trying to get some breathing room.

It followed me.

I backed up farther. It continued to follow me, gnashing its teeth in the process. Looking down, I studied the small puny objects in my hands.

I'm going to need some bigger weapons.

Suddenly, it lunged at me.

I thrust my machete at its head.

But nothing happened.

Abruptly, the alligator reared to the side. As I watched it struggle, I realized that thick ropes were wrapped around its neck and attached to long sticks. My eyes traced the sticks back to their origins and for the first time, I noticed numerous shadows in the darkness.

Chase's guys. This just gets better and better.

But as the seconds passed, I began to doubt my initial impression. The shadows were quiet and still. They didn't try to kill or capture me. They just seemed to watch me.

I heard frantic whispers from Beverly, imploring me to return to the relative safety of the passage. But the alligator dominated my focus.

My pistol lifted into the air.

I took careful aim.

"Stop right there."

Startled, I turned to the side and saw a man pointing a shotgun in my direction. A thick cigar dripped from his lips, its end burning a reddish hole in the darkness.

He was a walking contradiction. He stood tall, yet hunched over. His body was strong, yet withered. He stared at me with a face that was at once both handsome and haggard. He looked a little like a former professional wrestler who'd fallen on hard times.

Very hard times.

But one look into his menacing, angry eyes told me that he wasn't the sort of man to be overlooked.

"That thing's a killer," I replied angrily. "It deserves to die."

He chewed on the cigar. "I know she's a killer. That's the whole point."

"I…"

"If I were you, I'd shut up. You've got ten guns trained on you as we speak."

I glanced at the shadows and then back at him. "What do you want?"

"I want you to get out of the way."

Slowly, I maneuvered away from the man and the alligator. After reaching the passage, I climbed back over the crumbled concrete. As I joined Beverly, the other shadows started walking south through the tunnel, propelling the gator ahead of them.

The man kept his shotgun aimed at me. As the others vanished into the darkness, he slowly edged away, following their path. "Leave these tunnels now. And don't ever come back."

"I'm not leaving," I replied. "Not yet. Not until I find something."

He stopped and chomped his cigar for a moment. "I know why you're here. And I know what you hope to find. So, let me give you a piece of advice. Stop looking. If you don't, you'll die."

Chapter 43

What the hell was that? Some kind of urban alligator wrestling league?

I exhaled deeply through my nose. My body sagged and I realized that I'd been holding my breath for over a minute.

A strong whiff of smoke caught my attention. I turned it over in my mind, trying to place it. It seemed familiar yet distant.

I glanced at Beverly. "That's definitely not something you see every day."

"Wow," she muttered. "I mean, wow. At first, I thought it was a trick of the light but...wow."

I sniffed again. "Do you smell that?"

She didn't respond. Glancing over, I saw that her head poked out of the passage with her face turned south.

"Did you hear me?"

She withdrew her head. "That's the biggest alligator I've ever seen. It must've been..."

"Just pay attention to me for a second. Do you recognize that smell?"

"Smoke," she said after a minute. "It's cigar smoke."

"My thoughts exactly. I smelled the same thing after we woke up on that island. I guess we know who kept us from drowning."

"I wouldn't mail your thank-you cards just yet. That is, unless you want to shower your appreciation on a bunch of murderers."

"Murderers?"

"In case you didn't notice, they seemed awfully familiar with that gator."

"How does that make them murderers?"

"They don't want to kill it. Otherwise, they would've already done so. Maybe it's their pet."

"No one keeps an alligator as a pet."

I looked out into the main tunnel again, but the alligator and its wranglers were long gone. Why were they keeping the gator alive? Did they know about it before it started to attack people? And most importantly, where did they intend to take it?

Turning around, I headed for the rear of the passage. Stopping just short of the wall, I knelt down. The beam from my flashlight illuminated the carved map of Manhattan. The deeply etched lines that ran across its surface captured my attention. I traced their path, beginning in Battery Park City and extending north. At Union Square, I studied the line as it branched into two separate lines. One continued past Central Park to East Harlem while the other one veered off to the west before turning north again.

Seeing nothing, I leaned in closer and shifted my beam backward, following the lines back to Battery Park. When I reached Union Square, where the two lines joined, I noticed a bit of tiny lettering carved out beneath the space.

"Beach's Tunnel," I read aloud. "Beach. You don't suppose it refers to Alfred Ely Beach?"

"Who?"

"I studied him while researching these tunnels." I rubbed my jaw, deep in thought. "He was an inventor of some renown. In 1869, he unveiled an invention that shocked the world…New York City's first subway tunnel."

"You know way too much about these tunnels."

"Maybe. Or maybe you just know too little."

She glanced at the map. "Do the lines match his work?"

"I'm afraid not. Beach's tunnel was short, more a curiosity than an actual means of transportation. It started on Warren Street, and curved around Broadway, eventually reaching Murray Street. All told, it ran three hundred feet with a nine foot diameter."

"Did it use a third rail?"

I shook my head. "The tunnel was a giant pneumatic tube. A large rotary fan blew a railcar from one end to the other. Then, the fan was reversed, sucking it back to the original station."

She smiled. "Its hard to imagine New York before subway tunnels."

"It was a nightmare. Streetcars and carriages raced down crowded streets at reckless speeds. You can imagine the number of accidents. So, after London opened its subway in 1863, New Yorkers started clamoring for one too."

"And Beach got the honor to build it?"

"He did it on the sly," I replied. "Back then, Boss Tweed ruled Manhattan like a king. Beach knew Tweed would never give him a chance, especially since Tweed got kickbacks from the streetcars. So, he got a permit to build a pneumatic mail tube under Broadway. But instead of a skinny tube, he constructed one big enough to fit his subway car."

"That's pretty ingenious." Beverly tied back her hair. "He probably figured that public approval would force Tweed's hand."

"That was his plan. People lined up around the block just to get a glimpse of it. The New York Herald called it Aladdin's Cave, and marveled at how people could miraculously transport from one end of the tunnel to the other."

"Tweed must've blown a gasket."

"Tweed was an opportunist. He tried to capitalize on the invention. But he wasn't Beach's only enemy. The Astors and a whole bunch of rich folks were petrified that subway tunnels would undermine their properties. Beach didn't stand a chance. By the time he got the political go-ahead, popular support had waned and the Panic of 1873 had dried up funding sources."

"What happened to the tunnel?" she asked.

"Beach closed it up and it was lost for almost forty years. Transit workers rediscovered it in 1912. The tunnel and wooden train were still intact, as was the tunneling shield. Unfortunately however, the workers dismantled the whole thing."

She sighed, frustration evident in her tone. "Good story, but a waste of time."

I looked at the map, between the lines that represented Warren and Broadway streets. "You know, this part here looks a little like the original tunnel. As I recall, it didn't run straight with Broadway. It was angled to the east, just like this line."

"Who cares?"

"Beach did everything to avoid government interference." I rubbed my jaw. "He wasn't the type to let a bunch of politicians stand in his way."

"I still don't see…"

"What if Beach got frustrated with the politics and decided to expand his original tunnel, counting on public opinion to force New York's hand?"

"Then why didn't he ever make it public?"

I shrugged. "Maybe he ran out of funding. Maybe the project turned out to be an embarrassing boondoggle. Or maybe he worried that New York would punish him for building tunnels without permission."

"I don't know." Her voice turned skeptical. "If you're right, why was it never discovered?"

"Maybe workers just never stumbled on it. After all, if Beach expanded his original tube according to these lines, it would've drifted away from the modern subway system."

"But you're forgetting those other workers from 1912," she countered. "If Beach built a tunnel that extended throughout Manhattan, they would've found it."

"Not necessarily." I felt a surge of excitement. "When they blasted their way into Beach's tunnel, they could've triggered a cave-in that blocked any extension from view. It's also possible that Beach left the original walls of the demonstration tunnel in place. He might've worked behind them to keep the extension a secret."

"I don't know. It seems like a long shot."

"But you have to admit, if an extension actually exists, it would make an excellent place to hide the *Omega*. The chances of someone finding it by accident are slim to nothing."

"Maybe. But it's still a long shot."

My flashlight caught sight of an etching on the map. It looked a lot like a microscopic X. "Some long shots are worth the risk."

"You actually want to do this? You actually want to search for a tunnel that might not even exist?"

"I don't want to search for it. I want to find it.

Chapter 44

Diane's face appeared in my mind as I strode south through the Lexington Avenue tunnel. I felt guilty I wasn't searching for her. But on a deeper level, I also felt something else.

Turmoil.

Diane served as a painful reminder of all I'd given up while trying to escape my inner demons. A part of me regretted leaving New York, leaving her. But at the same time, I wouldn't have traded the last three years of my life for anything in the world. I'd hunted for treasure, made a few friends, and helped out many others. I knew I couldn't leave that behind me. If only there was a way to take the good things from my former life and meld them into my new one.

But that was impossible. My two worlds were different from each other. Diane was different. Her attachment to the ideals of archaeology conflicted with my chosen profession. No amount of prodding would change that part of her.

At the Union Square platform, Beverly touched my shoulder. "What's the closest station to Beach's demonstration tunnel? Spring Street?"

"Canal Street's a better approximation. We'll start there and work our way north."

"Not south?"

I shook my head. "The X on the map was north of Canal Street."

"But that might represent the *Omega*'s final resting place. If the map is accurate, then the expansion should extend both north and south from the original tunnel."

"Honestly, I doubt Beach built his tunnel to the south. You have to remember that he caused a massive stir with his original tunnel. The public would shrug if he merely added on a few blocks south to Battery Park. The only way to make a splash, to really raise the stakes, was to build a tunnel that dwarfed his old one. And to do that, he'd have to go north."

"How long do you think it would've taken him to expand the tunnel as far as say, Union Square?"

"It took him fifty-eight days to build his original tunnel."

She frowned. "At that pace, it would've taken him a year to build out six blocks. There's no way he could've expanded the tunnel across Manhattan."

"Nice try, bright eyes. Much of that time was spent building the station, the system, and the railcar. Expansion would've gone much faster. And anyways, he didn't need to build the entire system to get attention. He just needed to prove underground transportation was feasible and that he was the man to do it."

"I still say this is crazy."

Pipes banged nearby. I strode past them before looking in Beverly's direction. "We're searching for a three-decade-old device that can be used to build a hydrogen bomb. We're racing the head of a respectable PMC to find that device. Oh, and there's a group of strange men wandering around here with a giant alligator. And you think a lost subway system is crazy?"

"Yes."

"Well, then bear with me for a little bit. If I'm wrong, you get to say you told me so."

"It's a deal. By the way, as long as we're walking in this direction, shouldn't we look for this lost subway system of yours?"

I shot her a grin. "I've been looking for it ever since we started walking. Haven't you?"

She returned my grin with a sheepish one of her own. "Uh, no."

"Well then, less talking, more looking."

We walked a little farther. Soon, another bellmouth appeared out of the darkness.

"Want to check it out?" she asked. "Or should I?"

"Don't waste your time."

"What do you mean? The other tunnel was behind a bellmouth."

"If Beach actually built his expansion, it pre-existed this tunnel. So, we won't find a bellmouth this time."

"What should I look for then?"

"The Sand Demons would've needed a way to access Beach's tunnel from this one. I'm guessing they created their own hole. So look for concrete that's a different color or texture than the surrounding walls."

Beverly turned and without another word, continued to walk south. As I followed her lead, I kept my beam focused on the east wall. I saw a couple of places where the concrete texture or color appeared to change. But upon closer inspection, these anomalies proved to be nothing more than tricks of the light.

At the Canal Street platform, I leapt off the ledge and sloshed my way through the water. After climbing up on the opposite ledge, I began to retrace my path.

The tunnel was almost silent and I could hear the faintest of noises as we walked north.

Skittering claws.

Beverly's soft footsteps.

Hissing noises.

My ears perked. I stopped and lifted my face to the ceiling, listening carefully.

I heard gurgling water. Making as little noise as possible, I slid off of the ledge and back into the cool water.

I stepped onto the trackbed and my boots gripped the hard, wooden ties that supported the metal tracks. Following my ears, I cut a path through the water, heading north. Soon, the tunnel dipped and the water got deeper, extending all the way to my thighs. But my gaze stayed firmly locked on the submerged western wall, right where it met the ground.

I nearly missed it. But just as my flashlight passed over a section of concrete, I saw a tiny bubble. Immediately, I flipped my wrist back an inch and examined the area.

I saw another bubble.

And then another.

Leaning in close, I spotted more bubbles. They seemed to emit from the wall itself, rising gently before barely breaking the surface.

Expanding my search, I noticed a strange object beneath the dark, cloudy water. It poked out of the loose track ballast like a worm out of the ground. I bent down and pointed my light at it.

It looked like a long metal nail.

I plunged my hand into the cold, flowing liquid. My fingers wrapped around the head of the nail and I yanked.

It held for a moment and then slid out of the ballast. As I pulled it above surface, gravel slipped into the former hole, erasing all evidence of it.

"What's that?"

"It's a rail spike," I replied. "It's used to connect tracks to each another."

"Is it important?"

"Maybe. But it could also be a discarded leftover."

I dropped the spike and placed my hand against the wall. It felt smooth and cold, yet electric to my touch.

Pointing my flashlight at the surface, I worked my way south, an inch at a time. I was looking for something specific. Something indisputable. Something that, beyond a shadow of a doubt, would connect the wall to the Sand Demons.

Come on you bastards. Where'd you leave it this time?

My beam fell upon an etching at the bottom of the wall, just above the water level. Its lines were deep and straight, the product of powerful, controlled hands. My insides lit up like a Christmas tree.

One skull.

Two pickaxes.

The symbol of the Sand Demons.

I studied it in silence. Each time I saw it, I felt increased curiosity about it. It reminded me of something else. Not just the skull and crossbones either.

It reminded me of a secret society.

Reaching into the water, I touched the design, feeling its grooves and cuts. Gently, I pushed it.

The button depressed and the wall clicked.

A gurgling noise caught my attention. Tilting my head, I tried to locate its origin.

"The wall..."

Beverly's voice, quiet yet screaming with excitement, broke my concentration. Looking to the side, I noticed a long, straight crack in the concrete. I pushed it and it swung inward, like a well-oiled door.

Water from the trackbed whooshed away from my feet and vanished through the opening. A musty breeze coursed through the crack and swept into my face. It smelled like the inside of a car.

A used car that stank of mothballs and mildew.

Sticking my flashlight through the crack, I peered into the space. The beam shook slightly in my hand as it penetrated the dark recesses in front of me.

"What do you see?"

"It's a tunnel." My voice sounded hollow to my ears. "We found a tunnel."

As Beverly slid off the ledge and walked over to join me, I stared into the cavernous space. The tunnel was large and roughly cut. It angled steeply downhill and at the moment, was covered with running water.

Exhilaration seeped through my veins. But all that was instantly forgotten as another thought crossed my mind.

Somewhere ahead, the *Omega* and the Bell were waiting for us. But if Beverly and I could find them, so could Chase.

His face appeared in my mind and for a few seconds I stared into his unblinking eyes. Somehow I knew that within the next twenty-four hours, one of us would kill the other.

PART IV

ALADDIN'S CAVE

Chapter 45

As I strode into the tunnel, alarm bells clanged in my head. Puzzled, I stopped and examined the space.

Okay, brain, I'm listening. What are you trying to tell me?

At about thirteen feet tall and ten feet wide, the tunnel was large, yet far smaller than a normal subway tunnel. It took me a few seconds to decide whether the *Omega* could fit within its walls. It seemed possible, but it would've been a tight squeeze.

My eyes lingered on the walls and I found myself intrigued by them. They were roughly hewn and colored a charcoal black, quite dissimilar in appearance from a typical New York subway wall.

I walked over to the nearest one, my boots splashing through the running water, and touched the surface. It felt cold, sharp, and pockmarked. I removed my finger and examined it.

It was covered in black dust. The walls weren't constructed from artificial materials. They were the original bedrock.

So the Sand Demons hadn't bothered to pour concrete. The more I thought about it, the less surprising it seemed. The Sand Demons didn't need to build a permanent structure. They just needed a way to move the *Omega* into Beach's secret system.

Something clicked at the mouth of the tunnel.

My free hand grabbed my gun and I spun to the side.

Beverly turned around. "Feeling a little jumpy?"

"Of course not." I deliberately poured on the sarcasm. "It's not like people are trying to kill us or anything."

As I stuffed the pistol back into the holster, I noticed that water no longer ran at my feet. Glancing up again, I saw that the mouth of the tunnel was blocked. "Did you close that wall?"

"I gave us privacy," she replied indignantly. "The last thing we need is Jack stumbling in here."

"Did you check to see if there's a way to reopen it?"

"Not exactly."

"It sounds like you really thought this through."

"Well, I…"

I shook my head. "Forget it. Just forget it."

I swung my beam to the ground and moved a couple of yards into the tunnel. I could see that the floor, like the walls, consisted of bedrock. Across its uneven, soaked surface ran a single set of tracks, with chunks of extra wood used to level them out. They wouldn't pass inspection, but they looked more than capable of managing the weight of a single subway car.

I maneuvered my light, confirming the absence of a third rail. Then I knelt down and examined one of the metal tracks. Although heavily smudged, it still looked almost brand new.

"What was that about?"

I glanced up and saw Beverly looking down at me. Her face expressed disapproval.

Vehement disapproval.

My defense mechanism instantly kicked into gear. "You were careless. If we can't reopen that wall, we'll die in here."

"What else was I supposed to do? Leave it open? In case you didn't notice, this tunnel is right off the Lexington Avenue Line. A deaf, dumb, and blind man couldn't miss it."

"You should've checked with me before you closed it."

"I did what I thought was best."

"And potentially made a mistake in the process." My chest tensed up. "Unfortunately, we can't afford to make mistakes. Chase has Diane and he and Standish want to kill us. Plus, there's a bunch of maniacs running around with an alligator on a leash."

"You're blowing this out of proportion."

"Am I? Because last time I checked, it's not just our lives on the line. Chase wants to detonate a hydrogen bomb in this city. Thousands, maybe millions could die if we mess up."

"I know all that. That's why I closed the wall in the first place."

I exhaled. "You're right. Don't mind me. I'm just spouting off some steam."

She arched an eyebrow. "Is this just about the wall? Or is something else bothering you?"

"Yeah, this tunnel."

"What about it?"

"That's just the problem. I can't figure it out."

"Walk me through it. Maybe I can help."

I rotated my torso so that I faced away from the tunnel mouth. My beam penetrated for about fifty yards before giving way to the darkness. "I don't know. It's probably nothing. Let's keep moving. I'll walk up the left side of the tunnel. You take the right. If you see something out of the ordinary, don't keep it to yourself."

I slipped to the left of the tracks and cautiously began walking through the tunnel. Despite my nagging concern, I couldn't help but feel astonished by it. The Sand Demons must've slaved away for weeks, quietly carving it out of the bedrock.

As we traveled farther across the chewed-up landscape, I started to move my light a little more frequently. I couldn't escape the feeling that there was something off about the tunnel. Something wrong.

Something that could kill us.

Beverly cleared her throat. "Take a look at that."

I pointed my light through the tunnel and sucked in a mouthful of air. A wall loomed in front of us. "Well, how about that? It looks like another dead-end."

"What's that stuff on it?"

I squinted. "Whatever it is, it's bright. There must be a reflective surface mounted on the bedrock."

"But why?"

"Don't know."

Beverly resumed walking but I stood still. The nagging feeling returned. It was much louder now, practically screaming at me to slow down, to watch my step. Reluctantly, I shifted my flashlight from left to right and then from down to up.

I'm imagining things. Why would anyone…?

My beam caught a strange glint of light originating from the ceiling. Tilting my head, I noticed a couple of old wires strung along the bedrock. I followed them with my eyes as they veered to the sides of the tunnel and then plunged to the floor.

There weren't any light fixtures in the vicinity. There wasn't even anything remotely electrical for that matter. So, what purpose did the wires serve?

The ceiling rumbled.

"It's a trap," I shouted. "Run."

My gaze shot to the right and I saw Beverly stumble.

With a thunderous explosion, rock blasted into the air.

I veered to the side and crossed the tracks. Yanking Beverly to her feet, I shoved her with all my might.

A large weight crushed me.

Terrible pain shot through my body.

And then, all was quiet.

Chapter 46

I inhaled a mouthful of dirty water and choked. My oxygen-starved brain panicked. My lungs worked, trying to suck in air. But instead, I choked on more water. I tried to move but something heavy held me down.

"Cy, where are you?"

Who's that? And where the hell am I?

My brain felt sluggish and dull. My head felt like it had been repeatedly dunked in a swimming pool. I just wanted to drift off to sleep. But something told me that if I slipped into unconsciousness, I'd never return.

I felt the weight on my back. It pressed my body firmly into bedrock and wet wood. Maneuvering my arms, I placed my palms on the ground and pushed upward, thrusting my chest an inch off the ground.

Fresh air poured into my burning lungs. My mind crystallized. I was in the makeshift tunnel. I was searching for the *Omega*. I was…

"If you hear me, make some noise."

It was Beverly and her tone sounded desperate. I heard frantic movement as if she were scooping away rocks and debris.

I opened my mouth to respond but my voice box refused to listen to my brain. Before I could take charge of it, my strength gave out and I plunged back into the icy, muddy liquid.

My nose slammed into rock. Blood from my face oozed into the water. I tried to shout but merely swallowed more of the nasty sludge. Opening my eyes, I realized that my face was positioned over a water-filled crevice. I attempted to twist my head to the side but my mouth still failed to clear the water.

I noticed a thin shaft of light. It passed over me and quickly vanished. As darkness returned, I realized that I was no longer holding my flashlight. And since I couldn't see a second beam, I assumed it was no longer working.

I propped myself on my hands for a second time. Then I pushed up, lifting my haunches a few inches off the ground. This time, I slid my legs forward and curled them up underneath me.

I couldn't quite reach the air. My brain felt foggy and my mind seemed to be floating away.

Desperately, I tried to lift my head out of the water. But the heavy weight on my back cut me off.

I steeled myself.

Then I burst upward.

Air entered my lungs and I gasped. The heavy weight on my back shifted. With one final twist, I managed to shake it off of me.

A heavy rock crashed onto the ground next to me with a loud booming noise. A bright beam poked at my eyes. Lifting my hands, I shielded my face. "You can put that away now. I'm here."

The light shifted and Beverly's face materialized out of the darkness. She smiled. "Nice of you to finally show up."

Slowly, I extracted my legs from under a few chunks of bedrock. "You can't get rid of me that easily."

"I'll try harder next time. By the way, thanks."

"For what?"

"For saving my life."

"No prob—"

"Then again, if you'd seen the explosives in the first place, you wouldn't have had to save my life."

I feigned shock. "Wait, you're blaming this on me?"

She laughed. "Well, I'm certainly not going to blame myself."

Before I could respond, she pointed at something beyond me. "Whoever set those explosives meant business."

"What do…?" My sentence trailed off as I twisted around. A mountain of crushed rock reached almost to the ceiling, separating us from the Lexington Avenue Line.

"Lucky break," I said. "Hell, I'm amazed the whole street didn't cave in on us."

"Luck had nothing to do with it."

"Oh?"

"I know about explosives. And whoever planted the ones in here knew their stuff. They were designed to cause a small, controlled cave-in with no impact on the surface above."

I nodded. Then I glanced at her leg. "It looks like you've got a nasty cut."

"It was just fine until some jerk came along and shoved me onto the ground."

"You're just grumpy because you owe me one."

I checked my body for injuries. While I saw plenty of cuts and bruises, none of them seemed overly serious.

After brushing myself off, I reached down and felt along the ground. My fingers bumped into my flashlight. Carefully, I withdrew it from the pile and tried to turn it on. To my surprise, it lit up, casting a dim glow upon the bedrock.

I clambered off the rock pile, ignoring my protesting muscles. I was tempted to call for a brief rest but all that changed when my beam fell upon the wall at the end of the tunnel.

It twinkled brightly, casting additional beams in hundreds of different directions. As my eyes grew accustomed to the light, I realized that the wall wasn't the end of the tunnel.

It was part of an entirely separate tunnel.

A perpendicular tube connected to the one in which we stood, forming a T-intersection. Keeping an eye out for explosives, I strode forward and stopped at the point where the two tunnels intersected each other.

I shone my light about the new tube in both directions, marveling at the spectacle before me. It wasn't gigantic, maybe two feet taller and five feet wider than the current one. But it was unlike any tunnel I'd ever seen. There were no signs of crumbling concrete or ugly metallic beams. In fact, the entire passageway looked like it belonged in an art museum.

It was almost perfectly cylindrical except for a deep, smooth groove carved out of the red-bricked floor. Arching beams, painted bright red, sprouted out of the ground and ran across the ceiling before returning to the ground again. Brightly colored, ornate tiling covered the walls.

My remaining doubts melted away. Still, I could scarcely believe that I was looking at an abandoned subway tunnel constructed decades before the rest of the system. But it wasn't just any tunnel.

It was Alfred Ely Beach's lost subway system.

My eyes drifted to the one unsightly structure in the area. On either side of the groove, metal tracks ran to the north as far as I could see. They looked exactly like the tracks from the other tunnel.

It was most likely the work of the Sand Demons. They installed the tracks to transport the *Omega* farther into Beach's system. I frowned as I examined their addition. It was a little like drawing a smiley face on a Norman Rockwell.

Nice going, Sand Demons. Way to ruin a masterpiece.

Beverly joined me and for five minutes, we just stared at the uplifting piece of art masquerading as a subway tunnel.

Finally, she broke the silence. "Why do you suppose the Sand Demons set up that trap? Why didn't they just seal off the tunnel after they moved the *Omega* in here?"

I shrugged. "Flexibility? Maybe they wanted to keep their options open in case they needed to move it again."

She frowned. "I wonder if they knew about its true purpose. They sure seemed hell bent on keeping it hidden."

"I don't know." I stepped into the tunnel. "But I do know one thing. If there was one booby-trap, there'll be more. And if we're not careful, the next one could be our last."

Chapter 47

As the tunnel's visual impact faded, my nerves began to tingle. I knew that the *Omega* and its lethal cargo weren't far away. Yet, I was short on time and even shorter on patience.

"Just so I'm clear," Beverly said. "This is Beach's work right?"

"Undoubtedly. I saw some drawings of his demonstration tunnel a few years back. They looked a lot like this one, albeit on a different scale."

"Different scale?"

"The demonstration tunnel was just nine feet in diameter." I looked up. "This one pushes fifteen feet."

She frowned. "That doesn't help."

I shrugged. "You asked, I told."

"I don't need measurements. I need actionable intelligence, something that can help us find the *Omega*."

She took a step backward. "Is all of this from Beach's original design? Or was some of it added by the Sand Demons?"

I pointed to the nearest wall. "Those rails are definitely Beach's. They're running rails, designed to hold the wheels of his subway car."

"Beach put his wheels on the side of his car?"

I nodded. "It gave him extra stability of motion."

I pointed to the four-foot groove at the floor of the tunnel. "That bar is Beach's brake rail. When the driver applied the brakes, the car's weight would come down on its brake shoes. In turn, they would slide on the rail, causing the car to stop."

She pointed at the metal bars lying on either side of the groove. "What about those? They stick out like a sore thumb."

"They're typical subway tracks." I kicked one of them. "And since they connect to the other tracks, I think it's safe to assume they were used to transport the *Omega*. But there's no third rail."

"Didn't you say this was a pneumatic tunnel? Maybe the Sand Demons used compressed air to propel the *Omega*."

"I don't see how. The *Omega* weighed a ton. And its shape wouldn't have created a seal with this tunnel."

"Then how did it get past this point?"

My eyes traced the path of the tracks as they curved out of the makeshift tunnel and into the pneumatic one. "Gravity."

"Gravity?"

"From the moment we left the Lexington Avenue Line, we've been walking downward. The Sand Demons could've steered the *Omega* onto the tracks and let her roll."

"I suppose it's possible. Of course, these tracks can't go downhill forever."

"Maybe not. But by the time the *Omega* hit an incline, it would've already built up some momentum."

"I don't know. Like you said, the *Omega* was heavy. It would need a –"

I held up a hand, cutting her off. "You wanted actionable intelligence. I gave it to you. Now, we can sit around and debate this all day or we can find out with our own eyes. I say we do the latter."

I started walking north. A short while later, the tunnel opened up and I entered a large underground room. I halted and flicked my beam across the space. The light revealed decorative columns, an angled ceiling, and a partly tiled floor. The room remained unfinished. And yet, it still managed to radiate luxury and style.

"Nice digs," Beverly remarked. "You know, with a little sweat, we could turn this place into an apartment complex."

"Great idea. And without that nasty sun poking around, vampires would be lining up around the block to rent it."

She smiled that dazzling smile of hers. For the first time in awhile, I got a good look at her. Her face was smudged with grime. Her damp tank top clung to her sleek body, showing me everything and nothing at the same time.

Damn, you're hot.

She pointed across the room. "That looks like a platform. What do you make of those markings on the other side of it?"

"Indentations for another tunnel. Probably one going south."

"That makes sense. Those other markings could be plans for a staircase."

She stopped and looked around for a second. "Okay, so we can be pretty sure this is a platform. But if that's the case, how did Beach intend to move a car once it stopped here? I don't see fans anywhere."

"He probably hid a steam engine and blower somewhere inside the tunnel. As long as the car stopped before the platform, it would be easy to get it moving again."

"Yeah, that's great, except for one little thing." She put her hands on her hips. "It couldn't stay in the tunnel. Passengers needed to, you know, exit and enter the car."

"You're assuming that the only way to exit a car is through the sides. And you know what happens when you assume."

"I end up being right?"

"Not this time." I grinned. "I bet Beach intended his cars to continue all the way into the next tube before stopping. Doors in the rear allowed folks to exit and enter. Then the fans started and it continued on its way."

Walking past the platform, I continued to the next tube. Pins and needles poked my skin, keeping me in a constant state of anticipation.

After passing a few half-finished stations, we arrived at another, larger station. Markings on the wall indicated space for no less than three additional tubes. One of them would've run parallel to the one in which we stood. The other two looked like they were intended to branch off to the west.

"We're near Union Square," I said. "This must be where Beach planned to split his system into two lines, one to cover the East Side and one to cover the West Side.

"It looks like he never got a chance to build out the western tunnels."

I shrugged. "I'm not complaining. Fewer places to search."

We walked for another thirty minutes, passing a couple more half-finished stations along the way. Finally, we branched out into another wide-open area. However, this area looked quite different than the one under Union Square.

Two tubes? What were you up to, Beach?

"Interesting," Beverly remarked. "This is the first time we've seen a second tube. Up until now, it's been only markings. Beach must've drilled his uptown tube first and then swung back to drill the downtown one."

I shifted my light from side to side, illuminating the two separate tubes. One of them, blocked by a large metal grating, continued straight ahead. The other tube veered off to the west. Strangely enough, the metal tracks at our feet followed suit.

I glanced at the other side of the platform. "Maybe not. See those markings on the wall? They look like plans for another tube."

"Three tubes?" She cocked her head, confused. "Why would Beach plan for three tubes?"

"Maybe he planned to build another branch."

"But wouldn't he build four tubes then?"

"Yes." *You should've built four tubes, Beach. So why didn't you?*

I walked over to the two existing tubes and quickly studied them. Other than the grating, they looked identical. I shone my light into their recesses but was unable to see anything of interest.

"Which way do you want to go?" Beverly asked.

My ear caught a noise. Putting my head up against the grating, I listened closely. It sounded like water lapping against some sort of hard surface. "Let's go this way."

"But the tracks go the other way."

"Someone blocked this one off for a reason." My gaze hardened. "And I want to know why."

With Beverly's help, I untied a couple of long, metal wires that held the grating shut. Then I flicked my light into the tube and proceeded forward.

As I headed into it, it began to morph before my eyes. First, the paint on the bricks gave way. Then, the bricks themselves disappeared, leaving just a crumbling passageway chiseled through the rock.

Abruptly, I walked into a natural grotto. A deep, ten foot wide river cut across the floor in front of me. Its water flowed rapidly to the east, crashing loudly against the rear wall in the process.

Is this the same river as before? Or a new one altogether?

"Cy..."

Ignoring Beverly, I strode forward and stopped next to the river. "Beach didn't know about the water. His tunneling shield must've broken right into this cavern. That explains the extra tube. He built it to circumvent the river."

"Cy..."

I turned around. "What's wrong?"

Her eyes were wide, her face frozen in a mask of fear. I followed her gaze to the far end of the grotto.

Something rose upward, out of the water, like some kind of demon from hell.

The alligator's eyes burned red. They showed no concern. No emotion. Nothing but pure animalistic instincts.

Like how to kill.

And how to eat.

Chapter 48

More than thirty years of anger and angst. Thirty years with nothing to show for his troubles. Thirty years.

It was a long time to wait.

Jack Chase climbed over the broken wall and stepped into the passage. He'd spent half his life seeking the *Omega* and the Bell inside it. The search had cost him much...his health, his wealth, perhaps even his mental state.

For years, the Bell eluded his grasp. He'd scoured the world, paid off private investigators, and even leaked the existence of Red Mercury to the press. But none of it worked.

And then, in the blink of an eye, decades of secrets began to unravel. For the first time in thirty years, he knew he was on the right trail. The realization thrilled him.

But someone kept his excitement in check. Someone named Cyclone Reed. First, the bastard had turned Beverly against him. And now, Reed threatened to derail all of his plans. The very thought of failing so close to the end caused Chase's stomach to churn.

Chase couldn't help but admire the man. In just a few days, Reed managed to make more progress toward finding the Bell than generations of ShadowFire's finest minds ever did.

But underneath that admiration, Chase felt a searing, intense hatred toward Reed. Reed was, after all, supposed to be just a little part of a gigantic project. But thanks to a little luck and incredible resourcefulness, he now threatened to destroy everything.

Chase grimaced. He hated thinking of himself as a follower. And yet, Reed continued to stay well ahead of him. The man had already discovered the underground river and penetrated Hartek's laboratory. Now, it looked like Reed had tracked the *Omega* to the passage as well.

His nonstop success was exacerbating. Maddening.

Infuriating.

Chase clenched his fists. Rotating his body, he took his time examining the interior of the passage.

Temporary light fixtures had been installed on the ceiling, sending fresh light to all corners of the room. A set of rusted metal tracks ran through the center of the space. On one end of the tracks lay a device consisting of two large subway wheels that held up a small piece of wood. Pencil markings on the wood indicated that the existing tracks were perfectly spaced to accommodate the *Omega*'s specifications.

Chase walked to the far end of the passage. Portable lights, positioned on the ground, shone brightly on the wall. The beams provided extra depth to the etch marks. Chase examined the strange map of Manhattan. His mind raced, trying to understand its purpose.

"Your engineers completed their analysis. The lines on that map don't correspond with any existing tunnel system, subway or otherwise."

Standish's voice rolled into Chase's ears. Chase didn't turn around, choosing instead to keep his attention focused on the map. "Did they run cross-patterns? Maybe we're looking at a combination of different types of tunnels."

"Some tunnels and pipes are close to the lines and some even intersect them. But nothing follows those routes for more than a few yards."

"Maybe it's a false lead. Cyclone could've drawn it to throw us off the trail."

"It's possible." Standish shrugged. "But unlikely. The detail is stunning. It would've taken hours, if not days to complete. If Cyclone wanted to mislead us, he could've chosen a much simpler, easier way to do it."

"Are we sure that he didn't find the *Omega* in here? Maybe he discovered it and moved it."

"Without a third rail?"

"Okay, so he didn't move it. Can we at least prove conclusively that the *Omega* was stored in here?"

"Not conclusively. But it's a safe bet. The engineers told me the tracks were barely used. However, pressure marks indicate that something heavy once sat on them."

"So where'd the *Omega* go?"

Standish thought for a second. "Well, it seems clear that it was stashed in here at one point. And since Red Mercury never appeared on the global market, I doubt it was ever taken to the surface. No, I'm betting that it's still down here somewhere."

"So you think they dug out a new tunnel."

"More likely, they stuck to their pattern. They found an existing, out-of-service tunnel and exploited it."

"How do you think we should proceed?"

"Our best chance to is to locate Cyclone and Beverly. If anyone has the knowledge to find the *Omega*, it's them."

Chase sighed. "I don't like it. I agree with you. But I don't like it."

"We have one other ace up our sleeve."

"What do you mean?"

Standish walked toward the mouth of the passage and disappeared. A few moments later, he returned to the hole with Diane's struggling body in his arms. He climbed into the room, walked across the tracks, and dumped her on the ground. "Cyclone has something we want." Standish grinned. "We have something he wants."

Leaning down, Chase removed Diane's blindfold and gag.

She blinked and stared at him for a few seconds. "Who are you?"

Her gaze shifted to Standish. Her eyes popped open. "Ryan? What are you –?"

"Be quiet," Standish said harshly. "Otherwise, your chances of survival go way down."

Chase crossed his arms. "What can you tell us about Cyclone Reed?"

"Don't know him."

"Don't lie to us." Standish growled. "I saw you guys at the Explorer's Society. I even followed him to your apartment."

"You're mistaken."

Chase felt his anger grow. He wanted to slap her right across her pretty mouth. But he kept his temper under lock and key. "Ryan, please leave us for a moment."

Standish shrugged and walked to the mouth of the tunnel. He stepped over the broken wall and disappeared from view.

Chase looked at Diane. "I don't like having my time wasted. If you can't help me, I don't need you. And that means you're expendable. Do you understand?"

Her face softened and Chase smirked to himself. He'd broken her.

Suddenly, she leaned back.

Her head flew forward.

Spittle landed all over Chase's face.

Chase felt his heart darken and his self-control vaporize. His arm shot out and his powerful fingers wrapped around her neck. She choked and struggled but was no match for his strength.

He wrenched her to the side and smashed her up against the wall. "If you ever do something like that again…"

She gasped for air. "Go to hell."

His hand flew to his waist and he removed a long knife. He brandished it for a second and then brought it close to her stomach.

"Jack!"

Chase didn't move a muscle. "I told you to leave us alone, Ryan."

Standish peered into the tunnel. "Your engineers found something that you need to see. They uncovered an 1873 proposal for something called the Beach Pneumatic Transit route. It's an almost perfect match with the map."

"Thank you, Ryan. I'll join you in a minute."

As Standish left the passage, Chase felt a surge of triumph. He stared into Diane's eyes, enjoying the mixture of horror and powerlessness he saw. Abruptly, he whipped his hand to the side. She doubled over in shock and pain.

Chase slid his bloody knife back into its scabbard as he watched her collapse on the ground. She would live.

But not for long.

Chapter 49

"Get out of there!"

Vaguely, I heard Beverly's shout. But I couldn't move. I stood frozen to the spot, utterly hypnotized by what I saw in the gator's eyes.

I was in danger. I knew that.

But everything seemed to move so slowly, so sluggishly. Try as I might, I couldn't jerk myself into action.

The alligator pulled itself onto the shore. It stayed there for a few seconds, half-in, half-out of the roiling river.

Water sprayed on my face.

My brain suddenly awoke. My hand reached to my waist as the alligator lunged at me.

Grabbing my machete, I stabbed it at the beast.

The gator roared as the blade penetrated its thick skin. Its tail whipped to the side, striking me with tremendous force.

I crashed into the western wall and fell to the ground in a heap. My mind clouded. My body hurt everywhere. I didn't want to get up. I just wanted to lie there. I wanted to let go of my pain and drift off to sleep. Maybe then, the nightmare would end.

Get up, you bastard. Keep fighting!

I tried to ignore the voice in my brain but it wouldn't stop screaming at me. My head lifted off the rocky, uneven ground and I saw the alligator turn toward me. My gaze flew past its scaly face, its large jaw, and its gigantic teeth, all the way to the back of its head, to its eyes.

Adrenaline surged through me. I planted my hands on the rough ground and pushed myself to a kneeling position. My body protested but I shouted it down.

Loud bursts of gunfire filled the grotto. Out of the corner of my eye, I saw Beverly crouching low, moving toward me. Her gun, angled to the side, recoiled abruptly with another ear-splitting blast.

"We've got to get out of here," she called out. "Can you move?"

I spit out some blood and worked my mouth. "I…"

The alligator paused. Its jaw dropped and for a moment, I almost expected it to roar.

Suddenly, it lashed forward like a bolt of lightning. Before I knew what was happening, its humongous body vanished into the carved out tunnel.

I looked around.

My stomach shot up to my chest.

Beverly lay on the ground, unmoving.

I ran to her side. Her eyes were closed, her face covered with blood. Kneeling down, I felt her pulse. It was beating but not at a normal pace.

She looked hurt. Badly hurt. I didn't want to move her. But I didn't have much of a choice. I shook her shoulders. "Wake up."

She groaned and shifted away from me. I pulled her back and clapped my hands above her face.

She groaned and started to flail about, looking for something to grab, to help her to her feet. Grasping her hand, I hoisted her to a standing position.

"You all right?" I asked.

"What do you think?"

Abruptly, the alligator poked its head out of the tunnel. Its body jerked with every movement yet remained utterly smooth. My eyes burned as I watched its tough, leathery body slide toward us, leaving a trail of water and soft mud in its wake.

I felt a strange sense of excitement. Thanks to generations of explorers and the rise of satellite technology, the world often felt like it lacked mystery. And yet, here I was staring at a giant alligator in the middle of a lost subway system, far beneath the earth's surface.

I remained in total awe of the beast's size, strength, and speed. I'd never seen anything like it and I feared what it could do to me.

And to Beverly.

As I stared at it, I felt my emotions change. My anticipation and awe slowly melted away. The alligator was an incredible breathtaking specimen. And it was a powerful, dangerous hunter that had earned the right to be feared.

But I felt none of those things as it faced me. I felt only contempt.

Cold, hard contempt.

You killed my friend. Now, I'm going to kill you, you son of a bitch.

I yanked the pistol out of my holster. "Get to safety."

Before Beverly could argue, I sprinted forward. The beast cast a wary eye in my direction. It slipped backward a foot and angled its neck toward me.

I squeezed the trigger as I ran. The alligator was so damn big that I couldn't have missed it if I'd tried. But I wasn't looking to hit it just anywhere.

I wanted it to feel pain.

The gun unleashed a barrage of bullets into the air. They sailed forward, twisting toward the ferocious gator. Some bullets found their mark. Others bounced off the tough hide like arrows off a shield. The alligator thrashed about but seemed more angry than hurt by my attack.

That is, until I fired the last bullet in my magazine. It cut through the air like a homing missile, slicing right through the monster's jaw. Bits of rubbery brown flesh flew through the air, splattering onto the ground. A moment later, the bullet spiraled out the other end of the gator's face and burrowed its way into the wall.

The beast slammed backward and to the side, bashing its head against the far wall. It gnashed its teeth, trying to open and close its mouth. But one end of its jaw hung grotesquely in the air, refusing to operate.

Its tail shot out again and I tripped.

My pistol clattered to the ground.

Thrusting forward, I dove onto the beast's slimy body. I tried to stab it with my machete, but it was moving too fast. My other hand scrabbled for purchase before finally latching onto a hard scale.

The gator convulsed and thrashed from side to side, repeatedly smashing into the grotto's walls. I struggled to maintain my grip but with each blow, my hand weakened.

Crap. How do I get myself into these situations?

The beast whipped downward and next thing I knew, my free hand was clutching at air. The gator shook violently and my legs spilled off of the side of its body.

Lifting my machete, I plunged it at the gator. It slashed through the air and I held my breath.

But the blade missed its mark, sailing harmlessly to the side.

A glancing collision stunned me and tore the machete out of my hand. I landed back first on the sharp, jagged edges of chewed-up bedrock. Looking around, I saw Beverly shifting her aim, trying to shoot the gator without shooting me.

My eyes fell on my gun. I reached for it with one hand and grabbed a spare magazine with the other.

But the beast whipped around and loomed before me, casting a gigantic shadow in the dim light afforded by my fallen flashlight. I stared into its bright red eyes. It was ready to strike.

There was no time to grab my gun. No time to dodge. No time to run.

Just time to die.

The gator's head shot toward me. It moved so fast that I didn't even have time to lift my hands to my face.

Suddenly, loud, harsh bursts punctuated the grotto. The alligator reared to the side and then backward.

Taking advantage of the opportunity, I grabbed my machete and gun from the ground. Then I rolled to the other end of the cavern and loaded the pistol.

My eyes stayed locked on the beast as it slid backward. Then, without warning, it lunged into the river. With a tremendous splash, it disappeared from sight.

I watched the water for a full minute, waiting for the monster to reemerge.

But it never did.

Finally, I turned away from the river and looked toward the mouth of the unfinished tunnel. My jaw dropped. Ten heavily armed men stood in a tight semi-circle. Their hardened faces, covered with impassive expressions, revealed little.

A man stepped forward. He carried a shotgun. A thin column of smoke trailed out of the barrow. I recognized him as the man I'd spoken with back at the passage.

The gator wrangler.

Although his best days were behind him, his body remained burly and powerful. His eyes, menacing and furious, studied me carefully. "I told you to leave these tunnels."

I shrugged. "Yeah, well, I should've warned you. I've never been one to follow orders."

"It's going to cost you. Drop your weapons."

"No."

Light clacks sounded in unison as nine other guns swung in my direction.

The man took a cigar out of his pocket and stuck it in his mouth. "Put them down, you live. If not, you die. It's your choice."

I looked at Beverly. She looked back at me with confusion etched across her face. Then she shrugged.

Grunting in frustration, I set my pistol and machete on the ground.

The man took a second to light his cigar. Afterward, he directed me to stand aside while he retrieved my weapons. "Start walking," he said harshly. "And don't try anything. Or I'll kill you myself."

With no other recourse, I followed a few of the other men back through the dark tunnel.

See you later, frying pan. Fire, here I come.

Chapter 50

I marched through the tube, my brainpower split between the battle I'd just fought and the one that was coming. I knew I'd never forget the alligator. But if there was one thing that could give me temporary amnesia, it was a confrontation with the men who seemed to control the beast.

I slowed my pace until I was walking next to Beverly. She hobbled slightly. And although her soot-covered face lacked expression, I could see the tension lines around her jaw every time she placed her weight on her injured leg.

"How bad is it?" I asked quietly.

"I can walk."

The barrel of a gun jabbed into my shoulder blades. "No talking."

It was the alligator wrangler. I shot him a glance. "What should I call you?"

"Cap. Cap Cartwright."

"Cap? Are you serious? That's not even a real name."

"I'm not sure a guy named Cyclone should be making fun of other people's names."

"How do you know my name?"

"How do you think?"

I thought quickly. "You searched me after saving us from the flooded trackbed. I don't carry a driver's ID but you could've gotten it from a half dozen other things in my satchel."

"Very good."

"Where are we going?"

"You'll find out."

We marched all the way back to the partially built station. We paused for a few seconds as Cartwright closed over the grating and reattached the wires that held it in place. Then he led us toward the second northbound tube, the one we never got a chance to explore. But instead of turning into the tunnel, we marched right past it.

I lifted my chin. "Just where are you taking us anyways?"

Cartwright ignored me and continued walking. At the westernmost end of the platform, he knelt down in front of the wall.

A few moments passed. And then, as if by magic, it jerked open. I caught a glimpse of a small, dimly lit corridor. I barely had time to appreciate the workmanship before I was prodded into it.

I examined the walls as I entered the tight space. They were made of bedrock and lacked a concrete cover. We followed the corridor in a twisting, turning path. On the way, we passed by a couple of side corridors. Eventually, I lost my sense of direction, which evoked a small feeling of panic deep in my gut. I could handle underground passages, but getting lost in one wasn't my idea of a good time.

I wanted to say something, to ask about the tunnel system, to gain assurance that we, in fact, weren't lost at all. But my head told me to keep quiet. Less ruckus meant boredom for Cartwright and his men. Eventually, they'd let down their guard.

Then I'd strike.

We passed through a couple of additional corridors. As we walked past one particular section of wall, I noticed a jutting piece of bedrock.

A very familiar jutting piece of bedrock.

How nice. They're leading us in circles.

The thought irritated me. Why were we walking in circles anyway? Was it to keep us from escaping? Was Cartwright trying to mess with our heads? Or was it something much, much worse?

Are we lost?

We continued walking, following Cartwright through the labyrinth of passages. With every passing second, I grew increasingly stir-crazy. My pent-up emotions clamored at the gate.

We took a sudden right and crossed through a short corridor. At the end, Cartwright opened a door. Bright light filled my eyes. Half-blinded, I stumbled through it.

I looked around. We stood in the middle of a large room. A gigantic piece of machinery poked through one of the walls. A long metal shaft connected it to the opposing wall.

Through spotty vision, I examined the rest of the room. It was an intriguing area, outfitted like a hunting cabin. Seven beds were pushed up against the eastern wall with a couple of additional cots stacked neatly in the corner. There were a few dressers, a bookshelf, and even a small kitchen.

"Nice place you got here," I said. "Rat-infested to be sure but not bad."

Cartwright looked at me. "You've got a smart mouth."

"And here I was worried that I had a stupid mouth."

"Why are you here?"

"I'm looking for a place to live. New York real estate prices are ridiculous. Still, I think I can do better than this place."

He lifted his shotgun and pointed it at my head. "One last time. Tell me why you're here."

My brain cleared and I had a moment of understanding. "Wait a second. You're…all of you, you're the Sand Demons, aren't you?"

He grunted, but lowered the gun a few inches. "Will you just answer the damn question already?"

"Who are you guys anyways? Some kind of secret society?"

"No."

"But I saw the skull and pickaxes. The secret doors with the push-button mechanisms."

"Tricks of the trade."

"So, you're just a bunch of ex-sandhogs living underground?"

"That about sums it up. Now, for the last time, I want you to tell me why you're here."

I hesitated as my brain reeled through a couple of possible answers. He must've seen it in my eyes.

"I think I know why," he said. "But I need to know for certain. I don't care for violence but if you refuse to talk…"

I didn't like him, but Cartwright seemed like a straight shooter. I decided to take a chance. "We're looking for the *Omega*. If you know where to find it, you need to take us there right now."

"And why would I do that?"

"We don't have time for this."

"Make time," he growled.

"It's got a device stored inside. Something called *die Glocke* or, if you will, the Bell."

He swallowed. "So you do know."

"Of course I know. And I also know that you and the rest of your goons here have the *Omega*."

"Why do you want this Bell so badly?"

It was a good question, one that touched a lot of trigger points for me. But I decided to go with the most obvious response. "Whoever controls the Bell becomes an instant nuclear power."

He shook his head. "Why would you want such a thing?"

"I want to destroy it."

He gave me a long, close look. "You're assuming that it can be destroyed."

Beverly cleared her throat. "We have Hartek's journal."

"What journal?"

I reached into my satchel and withdrew the small book. "You probably didn't give this a second look when you searched my stuff. But it's a record of Hartek's work. Assuming you haven't done so already, we might be able to use it to dismantle the Bell."

He eyed the journal suspiciously. "What makes you think I want to do that?"

"You stole the Bell over thirty years ago. You and the rest of the Sand Demons kept it out of the public eye all this time. I'm guessing you want to get rid of it just as much as we do. Now, let's get moving. We need to see the Bell if we're going to figure out how to destroy it."

"If there's something to destroy around here, we'll handle it."

"Yeah, you've doing a great job of that," I retorted. "Over thirty years and you've got nothing to show for it."

"That's enough."

"Let me tell you something else. Right now, a man named Jack Chase and his private army are scouring these tunnels for the Bell. Now, he's on your doorstep. And if he finds it, he'll unleash hell upon the earth."

"You're lying."

I stared him straight in the eye. "Do I look like I'm lying?"

"It's impossible." He shook his head. "No one's ever breached our defenses."

"We did. And if we can find these tunnels, so can Chase."

"How do I know I can trust you?"

"I don't care if you believe me or not. But at least prepare yourselves for Chase. He's coming, whether you like it or not."

Cartwright considered me for a moment. Then he glanced over my shoulder again. "Put your guns down."

One of the Sand Demons cleared his throat. "But, Cap –"

"Do as you're told."

I heard soft metallic noises as the Sand Demons holstered their weapons. I nodded in appreciation at Cartwright. "Do you have a contingency plan in case Chase arrives before we destroy the Bell?"

He gave me a dirty look. "Did you see a third rail in any of the tubes? Of course not. This place is our contingency plan, you moron."

"Then take us to the *Omega*. Maybe we can destroy the Bell before he gets here."

Cartwright stared into my eyes, carefully evaluating my every move. "First things first. You need to see something. Walk toward that door."

"But –"

"Not another word. I still don't know if I can trust you. So, if you want to see the Bell, do as I say. Otherwise, I'll shoot you dead where you stand."

Chapter 51

I felt tension flowing through me as I stepped through the door. But it wasn't external.

It was internal.

I'd been so caught up in getting my way that I hadn't stopped to consider things from Cartwright's point of view. He and the Sand Demons had risked their lives to acquire the *Omega*. And then they'd spent more than thirty years watching over it and the Bell.

Thirty years.

I let that number sink into my brain. It was an astounding level of commitment and dedication. Despite Cartwright's contention, the Sand Demons reminded me more and more of a secret society. Brought together by friendship, a single fateful day back in 1976 had melded them into a determined, unified force.

When considered from that angle, Cartwright's attitude made perfect sense. He and other sandhogs had spent decades protecting a secret, one that could irrevocably change the world. But it went even deeper than that. The Bell was the glue that linked the Sand Demons together. It gave them a purpose beyond their normal lives. He wouldn't just give up its location on a whim.

I glanced at Beverly. Her attention was directed at the ground. I looked over my shoulder at Cartwright. He returned my look with a stern one of his own.

Since no one seemed interested in talking, I started to think about other things. My mind drifted to a question, one that had plagued me for some time.

Why did they steal the Bell in the first place?

"Turn left."

I angled my footsteps in line with Cartwright's instructions. But my brain remained focused on the question at hand. The answer seemed obvious. The Sand Demons stole the Bell to keep Chase from getting it.

But why? And furthermore, why had they hidden it away in a maze of underground tunnels rather than turned it over to the authorities?

I mulled it over in my mind. Maybe the sandhogs were pacifists. Maybe they, like myself, just wanted to keep the Bell from hurting anyone. But if that was the case, why hadn't they dismantled it? Was it true that the Bell couldn't be destroyed?

That's impossible.

Isn't it?

Plagued by questions I couldn't answer, I forced my mind to switch gears. Ultimately, none of those things mattered unless I could get my hands on the Bell. But to do that, I'd have to earn Cartwright's trust.

"Turn right."

I complied, leading our group through yet another passageway. If I was going to earn his trust, I needed to get him talking. I needed to build a connection to him. "How did you find this place anyways? I ran a dig down here a few years back and I had no idea something like this even existed."

He didn't respond. Frustrated, I sorted through my mind for another question. "Well, how –?"

"Research." He interrupted me. "And a whole lot of luck."

It wasn't much of an olive branch, but I seized it anyway. "So you didn't just stumble on it one day. You guys deliberately looked for it."

"Don't you ever stop asking questions?"

"Nope."

He grunted in annoyance as he directed us down a different tunnel. "Me and the Sand Demons, we were different than the other sandhogs. For them, the tunnels were just a place to work. But for us, they were our lives. While everyone else hit the bars after quitting time, we stayed down here, exploring the underground."

"I get it. I used to be an urban archaeologist. There's just something about the underground that's addictive. It's raw, real. More real than what's above ground."

"Save your sucking up for someone else. That crap won't work on me."

He seemed eager to talk. But his guard remained up. I decided to provoke him a little bit. "You talk a good game. People like you always do. But I'm willing to bet you didn't do a damn thing to find this place. Admit it. You and your friends got wasted one night and stumbled onto it, probably fell flat on your faces in the process."

"We worked our butts off to find this place."

I laughed. "And you think I'm just going to take your word for it?"

He glared at me. "While you were still a nightmare in your mother's eyes, we were exploring every nook of this city. I can't even count how many speakeasies, cellars, and crypts we discovered over the years."

"Some guys chased skirts, you chased the past." I felt admiration toward him, tempered by pity. "Frankly, I think you would've been happier if you just got yourself a girlfriend."

He shot me a contemptuous look. "We originally set our sites on Alfred Ely Beach's demonstration tube. But it had been destroyed. A few years later, I got my hands on some of his papers. I found a couple of maps and plans related to a new subway tube."

"And that led you here?"

He nodded. "For three straight days, my buddies and I chipped away at the cement. Eventually, we discovered a small natural crevice in the bedrock. When we looked through it, we knew there was a manmade tunnel on the other side. We hollowed out a space to crawl through the bedrock. And when I finally set foot in here, well, it was the greatest day of my life."

"Who cares?" Beverly's tone turned exasperated. "Can we move on to something more interesting? Namely, how the hell did you get involved in this mess?"

Cartwright looked at her and then looked away. I took the opportunity to glance at Beverly. She shot me a wink and a crafty smile.

Cartwright grumbled quietly for a couple of seconds. I sensed his internal struggle. He wanted to talk, but felt guilty doing so. I knew we could break him, but we needed to keep applying pressure. If we played our cards right, he'd open up to us. If not, he'd shut down for good.

"Yeah," I said. "What happened that day? Wrong place, wrong time?"

"How much do you know about what happened down here?" he asked.

"Just about everything." I shrugged. "We know about Hartek's laboratory, Rictor stealing the Bell, and the *Omega*. What we don't know is your side of the story."

"Rictor's brothers were friends of ours. We met Rictor and Hartek through them and they also became good friends. When Hartek needed help building his lab, we agreed to do it. And when he needed something delivered, we'd make the arrangements and handle it."

Beverly kicked a pebble. "Did you know what he was doing at the time?"

"Only that he was building some kind of device. One day, I overheard a conversation between Rictor's brothers. They planned to kill Hartek and seize his invention. They said it was some kind of nuclear weapon."

"Did you warn Hartek?"

"We were too late. By the time we reached the laboratory, Rictor had already killed the other assistants, kidnapped Hartek, and stolen the Bell. We ventured back into the tunnel and covered the tracks with debris. When they stopped, we opened fire."

"On your own friends?"

He paused and his eyes grew distant. "We wanted to rescue Hartek. He'd been tied up in a burlap bag and moved into the *Omega*. But during the fight, Rictor shot him. After it was over, Hartek used his dying breaths to tell me about the Bell, about Red Mercury."

"What exactly did he tell you?"

"After he came to America, he spent decades researching and testing the Bell in secrecy, hoping to discover at least one peaceful purpose for it. He never wanted to add another weapon to the world. He saw enough pain and suffering during the war to last a lifetime."

"Are you sure?" I asked. "I found an old Nazi badge in his desk."

"He used to carry that around with him. He said it was to remind him of the horrors of war."

Beverly coughed. "Did he tell you that the Bell couldn't be destroyed?"

"He warned us not to play with it." Cartwright's face hardened. "It's a nuclear device in its own right. Unless dismantled properly, it'll explode."

I lifted an eyebrow. "Well, that's not exactly good news. But why'd you stay down here all this time? Why didn't you just abandon it?"

"He told us one other thing before he died. He said we needed to keep operating the Bell or it would explode. Every one hundred and fifty-five days, we remove the decayed Red Mercury particles and refuel the Bell with a special mixture."

"What's in the mixture?" Beverly asked.

"Gold, mercury, and a few other things. Fortunately, we've never had to make it from scratch. We're still using some of the fuel we got from his lab."

I walked around a bend. "So, after Hartek died, you sealed up his laboratory and started to hide the *Omega* in a side tunnel. But when Fred Jenson showed up, you knew you had to move it. You'd already cut out a small tunnel to Beach's system. So you just needed to expand it. Am I right?"

"One hundred percent." He sounded impressed. "How'd you know about Jenson?"

"We met him. Just before Chase killed him."

"I'm sorry to hear that. Jenson was a good man. We ran into him from time to time. To the best of my knowledge, he never told anyone where we had hid the *Omega*."

"There's one thing I don't understand." Beverly adopted an accusatory tone. "I know why you sealed up the lab. But couldn't you have at least returned the bodies to the surface? Did you ever consider the pain their families must've felt?"

"It was Hartek's final wish. He wanted us to seal off everything, bury all traces of him and his work. I don't know if it was the right decision, but I listened to him all the same."

I stopped as I entered a small room. There was nowhere else to go. I examined the space. It was covered with dirt. Chunks of stone stuck out in seven areas. My heart raced as I saw etching upon the stones. They weren't ordinary stones.

They were gravestones.

I whirled around and looked at Cartwright. He returned my stare with cold, calculating eyes. I needed to buy time. "One more thing. What's the deal with that alligator?"

"We found her in here some time ago. She was a lot smaller then. We didn't know what to with her so we blocked up the tube with the grating and kept her as a pet. To feed her, we poured fish into the river. As she got bigger, she got meaner. I guess you could say she's become our guard dog."

"Let's cut the small talk." Beverly placed her hands on her hips. "We know why you brought us here. And you're making a mistake. We're on the same side. If you kill us, you're throwing away valuable allies."

"I'm not going to kill you. I brought you here to show you something. Do you see those graves?"

I nodded.

"Three are for Rictor and his brothers. Three more are for Sand Demons who died in the gunfight. The big one belongs to Hartek."

I knelt down next to Hartek's tombstone and quickly read the engraving. It was just his name, date of birth, and date of death. There was no inscription or flowery sentiment. But I still sensed the passion that the Sand Demons felt toward the man.

"I want you two to understand something," Cartwright said. "We've taken a vow to keep the Bell hidden until we can find a way to destroy it. We'd sooner die than give it up to anyone else. So, I'm sorry. You're not going to see it, not today, not ever."

I'm going to end this, Hartek. One way or the other, I'm going to find your Bell and destroy it.

Distorted, splattering noises erupted from the room's entrance. They bounced off the walls and were distorted even further. But I recognized them all the same.

Gunshots.

Chapter 52

I sensed two presences as I raced through the passageways, hot on Cartwright's heels.

Standish.

Chase.

They're here. They're in the damn control room.

My blood curdled as screams filled the air. Part of me knew I was listening to the death throes of the Sand Demons. Part of me tried to deny my ears.

I roared around a curve at top speed. On one level, it was practical. Cartwright flew through the corridors like a 747. If I lost him, I might never find him again. But on another level, it was entirely emotional. The faster we moved, the sooner we'd find survivors and rescue them. The sooner we'd stop Chase and Standish.

The sooner I'd rescue Diane.

But speed came at a price.

I winced as sounds exploded all around us. Gasps of breath. Boots pounding on the bedrock. The occasional splash of water. Pumping arms, brushing up against clothes.

We were making noise.

Lots of noise.

I knew we needed to slow down. Caution, not haste, was the safest way to proceed. The smart action was to reach out, grab Cartwright's shoulder, and wrench him to a halt.

But I just kept running.

Soon, the screams died away and the passageway returned to relative silence. After a few more turns, Cartwright tilted his face in my direction. "Our bunker's just ahead and to the right. We'll be there any minute now."

I looked at my holster, which hung over his shoulder. "Give me my weapons."

"No."

Suddenly, I heard light murmuring.

Someone was close.

Very close.

Reaching out, I grabbed Cartwright's shirt and yanked. He stumbled backward and spun into the wall. As he fell to the floor, I reached out and snagged my holster before it could hit the ground.

I reattached the holster. Cartwright groaned and lifted up his arm. His shirt was in tatters and the whole right side of his body was scraped up. "What the hell is wrong with you?"

Beverly reared up behind me. Ignoring Cartwright, I shot her a quick glance. "Did you hear that?"

As she nodded, Cartwright rose to his feet. Leaning over, he jabbed a thick finger into my chest. "Listen here, asshole…"

I didn't have time to listen to his nonsense. Rearing back, I slammed my fist into his stomach. His eyes bulged and a wheeze escaped his lips. Then he dropped back to the ground and rolled around in agony, groaning softly.

Leaning down, I retrieved my machete from his waistband. "Keep quiet," I whispered. "Or there's another one of those waiting for you."

"Why'd you –?"

"Because something's not right. Now shut up and let me listen." My pulse raced and my breath came out in short, quick bursts. I could barely hear myself think, let alone any nearby murmuring. I itched to move, but stayed in one place, forcing myself to listen. Irritation rose within me. One moment, my instincts told me to run while my brain urged me to stop. The next minute, my instincts led me to stand still while my brain told me to do the opposite.

Why can't you guys get on the same page for once?

Gradually, my labored breathing began to slow and with it, my pulse. I closed my eyes. My concentration increased. My senses heightened.

I heard voices, some masculine, some feminine. But from where?

I rotated in a small circle. The walls played tricks on my ears but I felt reasonably certain the voices originated from the southwest. Tilting my head in that direction, I listened carefully.

But try as I might, I was unable to distinguish individual words. It was just one big mess. Giving up, I turned to Beverly. "Did you catch anything?"

"Just jumbled words."

I looked at Cartwright. "Sorry about that. I couldn't afford you making any noise."

He glared at me.

"We've got voices coming from the southwest. Is that where your bunker is located?"

"Go to hell."

"Chase might be in there." I returned his glare. "If so, the others are already dead."

"Then, I'm wasting my time here. I need to get to the Bell."

"It's nice to know you care about your friends."

His eyes tightened. "I care about them just fine. But I made a vow to keep the Bell safe and nothing's going to stop me from doing that."

"Fine," Beverly said. "But take us to your bunker first."

Cartwright pushed himself to his feet, led us all the way down to the end of the corridor, and then opened a small door.

I looked inside, seeing a dark, four-foot tall passage.

"This leads to an air flue." He lowered his voice. "Beach planned to use it to filter compressed air into the tunnel to propel his subway car. If you follow the path around, you'll see a slab of metal. Pull it aside and you'll be able to peek into the bunker without anyone noticing."

"Thanks."

He gave me a hard look. "We'll meet again, Cyclone. Count on it. But for now, you're on your own."

I watched as he slid by Beverly and disappeared into the tube. Then, I ducked my head and entered the short, dark passage. Keeping low, I followed it around in a winding path for about a hundred feet.

Finally, I stopped in front of a small piece of metal. Dousing my flashlight, I quietly cracked it open a quarter of an inch.

I peered into the next room and saw about a dozen people milling around. It looked perfectly ordinary, similar to how we'd left it. And yet, it was totally different. The faces had changed, the weapons were fiercer, and the expressions lacked emotion.

I switched my gaze to the floor and swallowed.

Hard.

Ten bodies lay in a heap against one side of the bunker, bloodied and unmoving. Their frozen expressions told me everything I needed to know.

The Sand Demons were dead.

My gaze swept the room. It passed by the soldiers. It passed by the row of beds, which were covered in gore. Finally, I saw them.

They sat on one of the empty beds. Standish appeared to be writing something on a sketchpad. Chase held his gun, unwavering, off to the side.

I reached for my pistol. Two bullets. That's all it would take. With two bullets I could end their lives, end my misery.

And then I saw her.

She sat on the floor with her head sagging to her chest. She appeared to be bleeding heavily from the stomach and looked near death. To make matters worse, Chase's gun pointed directly at her chest.

Fury poured into my brain, cutting off my sense of logic. I wanted to kill Chase for what he'd done to Diane.

I wanted to kill them all.

My fingers clenched the grip of the gun but I left it in the holster. I couldn't let my emotions get the better of me. The instant I fired my weapon, hell would rain down on us. Beverly and I would die instantly. Diane, if she didn't perish in the crossfire, would die shortly afterward.

I glanced back at Beverly. She stood behind my shoulder, peering through the small crack afforded by the slab of metal. "Seen enough?" I mouthed.

She nodded and stepped away.

Gently, I pushed the slab back into place. Then I followed Beverly back through the flue.

Once we were out of earshot, I took a deep breath. "We need to rescue her."

"Don't you ever get tired of playing underdog?"

"It's the American way."

"I know those people. They're some of Jack's best soldiers. We can't beat them, especially not with just two of us."

"We don't have a choice," I replied. "She needs our help. She's dying."

"There's always a choice. And right now, the smart thing is to wait for our opportunity."

"You just want to sit here and do nothing?"

She shook her head. "We've got two things going for us. First, we know where to find them but they don't know where to find us. And second, we know what they want."

"The Bell."

"I say we go and destroy the thing before it hurts anyone. Then, we set a trap for them. In the confusion, we'll grab your friend and run for it."

"How the hell are we going to do that? I thought you said we didn't stand a chance against them."

"We don't. But we can't stage an effective fight here. If I know Jack, he's itching to find us. We might as well make sure that when he does, the advantage is ours. Because the instant he sees us, he won't let up until he's dead…or we are."

Chapter 53

Doubt wrapped its icy fingers around my heart as I darted through the passageway. I didn't like leaving Diane behind. It felt wrong.

Completely, utterly wrong.

You're doing the right thing.

I repeated that mantra over and over again in my head. Part of me knew Beverly was right. We didn't stand a chance in a fair fight. We needed to regroup at the *Omega* and destroy the Bell. Then we could marshal our resources and strike at our enemies in an unconventional fashion.

But no matter how many times I tried to convince myself we were doing the right thing, it didn't help. I still felt guilty.

Guilty as hell.

As I rounded the corner, I squinted. To find the *Omega*, we first needed to find Cartwright. Unfortunately, he had a lead on us. Even worse, we didn't know how to navigate the maze of passages.

To make matters worse, once we caught up with him, there was no assurance he'd take us to the *Omega*. In many ways, that task seemed even more daunting than the first one.

I turned at a corner and hustled through a short passageway. At the next corner, I took the turn too quickly. My feet slipped and my hands reached out to brace myself.

It worked, but not enough.

My forehead slammed into the bedrock.

I saw stars. Lifting my hand, I touched my forehead. It felt sticky, gooey. Shifting my light, I studied my fingers and saw smears of fresh blood on them.

Beverly halted behind me. I swung around and faced her. "How bad is it?"

"I suppose it could be worse." She grimaced. "But not much."

I felt sticky liquid pouring down my face. "Damn it."

"You reopened a cut. If you give it some time…"

"We don't have time."

I noticed an annoying slur in my voice. It bothered me. Destroying the Bell and rescuing Diane would prove difficult even under the best of circumstances. Losing a lot of blood might ruin our already infinitesimal chance of succeeding.

I turned away from her worried eyes. Pointing my flashlight at the ground, I quickly studied the tunnel that branched off to my left. It looked perfectly ordinary.

Twisting back to the right, I directed my beam down the tunnel and saw bits of mud and wet partial footprints on the bedrock.

I followed them. For the next ninety seconds, I led Beverly down a series of corridors, doing my best to follow the trail. But with every second, it faded.

Blood dripped into my eye. Blinking awkwardly, I swatted it away like a gnat. So far, the wound on my forehead had failed to clot. If I continued to lose blood at my current pace, I wouldn't have to worry about passing out.

I'd be dead.

I pressed my right palm against my forehead, hoping to quell my blood loss. But my vision dimmed and I began to wonder how much longer I could keep running. Gritting my teeth, I kicked it up a notch and darted through a short, winding passage.

At the end of it, I heard a light shuffling noise. Turning the corner, I saw a silhouette in front of me. It paused for a moment. Then it spun around, pointing a shotgun in our direction.

"It's us," I hissed. "Don't shoot."

As the silhouette lowered its weapon, I jogged over. I halted next to him and bent down, breathing hard, doing my best not to vomit all over the place. I felt horrible.

After a moment, I looked up and saw Cartwright's dark, angry eyes.

He flinched. "What the hell happened to your face?"

Lifting a hand, I signaled that I needed a few seconds. Then I stripped off my satchel and shirt. I flopped down on the bedrock, barely noticing its sharp edges. Bunching up the shirt, I pressed it hard against my forehead and began to count slowly in my head.

"Why are you here?"

I opened my mouth to respond. Immediately, a queasy feeling hit my stomach and I doubled over in pain.

"We're looking for you," Beverly said. "We want to help."

"I don't need your help."

"You have no electricity, no third rail. As I see it, you've got no way of moving the *Omega*."

"I'll stop them."

To my surprise, my body started to move. My knee jerked under me and then planted on the rock. My sore, scratched palms shifted, one to the wall and the other to the ground. Next thing I knew, I was standing up and struggling to put my shirt back on.

Cartwright shook his head. "You're in no shape to go anywhere. Why don't you just stay down like a normal person?"

My feet wobbled under my heavy body and my mind felt sluggish. But when I spoke, my voice ripped through the air like a jackhammer. "I'm not going anywhere. I'm done running."

He turned around. In the dim glow afforded by my light, I saw uncertainty in his eyes. "My friends…?"

I shook my head. "They didn't make it."

"If you hadn't followed me down here…"

"Then Chase would've found you anyways." I swallowed thickly. "What's done is done. All that matters now is destroying the Bell."

He shook his head. "I already told you. That's impossible."

Beverly rolled her eyes. "So, what's your plan? Sit on top of it with your shotgun?"

"I'll think of something."

"We have Hartek's journal," she reminded him.

He hesitated. "You realize that this isn't going to end well."

My gaze grew hard. "Yes it will."

He looked closely in my eyes. "What aren't you telling me?"

"Excuse me?"

"I can see it in your face. There's something else going on here, something beyond the Bell."

I took a deep breath. "Chase is holding a friend of mine hostage."

"Your lover?"

Out of the corner of my eye, I noticed Beverly looking very hard in my direction. I shook my head. "Just a friend."

"How do I know you won't try to trade the Bell for her life?"

"Even if I wanted to do it, it wouldn't work. He'd just kill all of us and take the Bell anyways."

Cartwright emitted an annoyed sigh. I sensed his internal strife. Abruptly, he turned around and started walking.

I raised an eyebrow at Beverly. She shrugged in return.

I started to follow him through the corridor. We walked for a minute, passing an intriguing metal door along the way.

Suddenly, he stopped. I stepped to the side to avoid bumping into him. Then I looked over his shoulder. "Really? A dead end? When are you going to stop wasting time?"

He didn't say a word. Instead, he bent down and felt along the bottom of the bedrock wall. His finger pressed something.

I heard a soft crack. The wall shifted open. Turning my beam toward it, I saw a giant room.

It was filled with many things but one object stood out above all the others. As my light glinted off its smooth, metallic exterior, I felt staggered to the core.

"My God," Beverly whispered. "Oh my God."

Despite nearly forty years of inactivity, the giant metal monster appeared sleek and polished. My flashlight traced its silver side, illuminating a single word painted in black one-foot high letters. My hand trembled as I read the word.

Omega.

Part V

THE RACE

Chapter 54

Cartwright shoved his hand into my face. Startled, I glanced to the right. "What's your problem?"

He pointed a finger at the ground. Following it, I spotted a tripwire running just past the open wall.

"Stay here," he growled. "I need to disable the explosives."

"You put explosives next to the Bell?" Beverly made a face. "Doesn't that seem a little, you know, dumb?"

"Just enough to blow up this entranceway," he replied. "But the tremors wouldn't reach the Bell. Anyway, the *Omega*'s a powerful beast. Nothing's going to pierce her shell."

"What is this place?"

"The end of the line. According to his notes, Beach got tired of fighting with the politicians. He knew they'd never let him run his system in peace, so he just stopped work and abandoned everything."

So, that's why he never went public.

Cartwright stepped carefully through the wall. After he disappeared off to the side, I shifted my flashlight toward the open space.

"Do you see anything we can use?" Beverly asked.

"Not yet. It looks like the other stations we passed through. Just larger and –"

"And what?"

My eyes bugged out. "And you have to see it to believe it. There's a marble fountain. Chandeliers hanging from the ceiling. Windows, fake ones, with velvet curtains. A giant fish tank. Hell, there's even a grand piano."

I stepped to the side and she squeezed into the void. For a moment, we stared silently into the station. Then she whistled. "Wow. You have to hand it to Beach…the guy sure had style."

I felt dizzy. I touched my forehead again. It felt tacky, the kind of slight stickiness one experienced when stepping on dried, spilt beer. Gently, I swept my hand across my head, checking myself for other wounds.

Finding nothing, I shifted my focus to the rest of the room. We stood just outside the western end of the station. To my right, a circular tube entered the room, carrying with it the familiar groove as well as the metal tracks. Beach's groove continued north, ending at a large pile of debris and trash. The Sand Demons' tracks drifted off to the east, ending abruptly near the middle of the room.

The *Omega* rested on those tracks. If it hadn't been facing the wrong way, it would've looked ready to leave the station. Unfortunately, without a third rail, that wasn't going to happen anytime soon.

The hairs on my arms stood on end. Although it initially seemed wide open, the station suddenly felt closed off and isolated. And although everything had seemed so exciting moments earlier, it now felt ghostly and still.

Cartwright reappeared in front of us. "We're all clear."

I walked into the station and took a deep breath, inhaling the aroma of dust, trash, and electricity. They were familiar smells but somehow they seemed different. I took another sniff. This time, the odors seemed more muted and indistinguishable.

That's strange…

I didn't know what was wrong but I found it unsettling. It felt like I'd lost control of my faculties.

"Are you going to set up the explosives again?" Beverly asked. "They might come in handy against Jack and his guys."

Cartwright pressed a button, closing the wall behind us and gave her a withering look. "Of course."

"Are there any others in here that we should avoid?"

"As long as you stay around the *Omega*, you'll be fine."

"Where are your other traps?" I asked.

He jabbed a thumb at the large circular tube. "There's just one more in the vicinity but it's a big one. It's set up in there, just outside the station. Hopefully we won't have to use it."

"Did you block off this station?"

He nodded. "We sealed the tube off with one of our doors. It's just a piece of metal covered with a thin layer of bedrock. If we're lucky, Chase will think he's hit a dead-end and turn around. If not, well…"

"Disable the bomb."

He gave me a funny look. "I made a solemn vow to keep the Bell safe. I'll do whatever it takes to accomplish that."

I clenched my fists. "Diane's out there. If Chase brings her through that way…"

"Not my problem."

"Then, what about the people on the streets above us? Don't you care about them?"

"They won't feel it." He crossed his arms. "The bedrock will cut off any impact long before it reaches the surface."

I felt my face grow red. I started to step forward but a small, delicate hand cut me off.

Beverly looked at me. "Cool it."

I gestured at Cartwright. "Why don't you talk to him? He's the one who—"

"I'm talking to you. We need to focus on what matters here. And before we do anything, we need to destroy the Bell."

I exhaled a few times then walked past Cartwright. As I crossed the station, I felt my anger boiling inside of me. I wanted it to consume me. Reluctantly, I shoved it aside instead.

The pile of debris and trash at the end of the groove caught my attention for a second time. It lay against the north wall, directly in front of some large markings. I could see the exact spot where Beach had planned to continue his tubes but ended up halting construction instead.

For some reason, it filled me with hope. Maybe it was the area's untapped potential. Maybe it was the unexploited resources that we might find within the debris. Either way, it was the first real positive feeling I'd felt since seeing the *Omega*. I stowed it away deep inside, knowing I might need it later.

I stopped next to the *Omega*. Three sets of wide doors were spread out in front of me. The two sets in the rear were closed while the one in the front was wide open.

It was a beautiful car, free of rust and dust. It looked like the Sand Demons had taken good care of her over the years.

I saw a couple of long thick power cables nearby. They rose off the ground and disappeared through a tiny crack in the rearmost window. Shifting my gaze, I tried to follow them, but thick blankets on the inside kept me from seeing the car's interior.

Lifting my hand, I brushed it against the siding. Shivers ran down my spine. I could almost feel the history and pain that the car had brought on all those who'd touched it. Rictor and his brothers killed the lab assistants while using the *Omega* to steal the Bell. They themselves, along with Hartek, died when Cartwright hijacked it. The Sand Demons then spent the best years of their lives living like hermits, watching over the car, always wondering if someone was about to steal it from them.

Am I the next to fall under the curse? Or will I break the cycle?

I walked to the front of the car. Holding my breath, I boarded the *Omega*, as if that act would somehow ward off its curse. But my effort didn't last long. As I strode into the interior, I exhaled loudly.

The seats were punctured with small holes and splattered with bloodstains. Closing my eyes, I could almost picture the gunfight between the Rictors and the Sand Demons.

I turned my attention to the back half of the subway car. A wide thick blanket hung from the ceiling, cutting off my view into the rear portion.

I knew Beverly was behind me, but I could no longer feel her presence. The blanket dominated my attention. While unremarkable on its own, it carried heavy symbolism for me.

It was the last remaining barrier between the Bell and me.

I walked over to it. As I grasped its coarse edge, I wondered what secrets I'd find on the other side. Would the Bell look the same as I'd imagined it? Could we destroy it?

I pulled the blanket out of the way. My beam lifted, casting into the space.

I froze.

The flashlight fell from my fingertips. It bounced on the floor and rolled. I felt a sudden reverence as if I stood before the Almighty Himself.

"Oh my God," Beverly whispered. "Is it…?"

"It's not touching the ground," I replied dumbly. "The damn thing's floating. It's floating in mid-air."

Chapter 55

My brain wrestled with my eyes as I stared at the large floating object in front of me. I couldn't comprehend the thing, couldn't rationalize it. And yet, I knew my eyes weren't lying.

My wildest impulses rose to the forefront, eager to accept the miracle at face value. But my analytical side slammed them to a halt. Adopting, a cold, methodical viewpoint, I began to study the object in earnest.

It was quite similar to the drawings I'd seen in Hartek's journal. Shaped like a bell, it measured about six feet tall and four feet at its widest point. Its outer surface appeared to be constructed from some sort of brownish-colored metal. More than a dozen ring-shaped attachments sprouted out from various places along the metal exterior. At first glance, they looked like part of a suspension mechanism, used to hoist the Bell into the air. But another look at the free-floating object stopped that theory cold in its tracks.

Although the Bell stood perfectly still, it seemed to have a life of its own. It crackled slightly and emanated the occasional spark of electricity. I heard faint buzzing and hissing noises that when combined, sounded a bit like a large beehive.

Twisting my head, I searched for invisible wires or some sort of platform that might explain the Bell's defiance of the law of gravity. After a brief search, I noticed the high-voltage electrical cables I'd seen outside the *Omega*. They poured in through an open window and branched off, disappearing into numerous ports on all sides of the Bell. At first, they seemed like a promising explanation to the mystery. But almost immediately, I realized that the cables were slack and not supporting a single pound. If anything, their presence actually added weight to the Bell.

I recalled the rigging installed in Hartek's laboratory. At the time, I'd thought it was designed to keep the Bell off the ground for the purpose of experimentation. Now, it struck me that its real purpose might've been to keep the Bell from floating away.

I shook my head, trying to make sense of it. Clearly, the object weighed a ton. So, how was it able to hover in the air like that with no visible means of support?

"When I first laid eyes on that thing, Hartek called it the Ark. He told me that God himself lived inside of it."

Glancing over my shoulder, I saw Cartwright standing behind us. His face appeared flushed and he looked harried. But I caught a wistful, childlike flash in his eyes. Despite more than three decades, it was clear the Bell's magic hadn't diminished for the grizzled old Sand Demon.

"More like the Devil," I replied. "How's it able to stay afloat?"

"I don't know. My friends and I knew everything there was to know about subway systems. But we weren't scientists."

Beverly waved her hand to the side. "What do those cables do?"

"I don't know that either. But Hartek warned us to keep it operational at all times to avoid an explosion. And part of keeping it operational is maintaining a constant flow of electricity."

"Where do you steal your power from anyways?" I lifted an eyebrow. "Somehow, I doubt you're paying your own electric bill."

"All of these tunnels are wired for power. Years ago, we modified Beach's electrical systems to fit our needs. Then we hooked everything up to the underground power lines that run above us. I won't go into the details but there's very little chance that our, uh, adjustments will ever be noticed. And if they were discovered by some fluke chance, no one could ever trace them down here."

"What about power outages?"

He shrugged. "The Bell can last several hours without power. In any event, we have numerous back-up options at our disposal."

"You spent a lot of time and energy protecting this thing."

"We didn't exactly have a choice," he replied tightly. "It was either that or risk an explosion. It wasn't easy, I can tell you that much. There were some moments, especially early on, where I thought we'd fail. But somehow, we always found a way to keep the Bell operating."

"But how can you be sure Hartek wasn't just delirious?" I asked incredulously. "What if he meant to tell you something else? For all you know, you wasted over thirty years of your lives for nothing."

"Don't you think we debated that a million times?" His voice grew angry. "Of course not, since you already have all the answers. Well, here's a news flash for you. We never knew anything about the Bell. So, we did the best we could. And we must've done something right since the damn thing hasn't blown up yet."

I looked back at the Bell. No matter how hard I tried, my brain refused to accept it. Sure, it was real. I could see that with my own two eyes. But it was also irrational, even impossible. In order to square it with my own sense of reality I needed an explanation. Scientific, supernatural, a trick of the eyes, anything.

Anything but the unknown.

Turning around, I slipped between Beverly and Cartwright. Then, I walked past the blanket and through the aisle. After exiting the *Omega*, I turned left and began walking. I followed the tracks to where they joined the groove and then, all the way to the mouth of the tube.

I stopped just short of the entrance and peered inside. I couldn't see the explosives, but I knew they weren't far away.

Kneeling down, I touched the tracks. They seemed to be in good shape. Unfortunately, without electricity they were useless to us.

I look around and noticed a small air flue, similar to the one connected to the bunker. Unfortunately, the *Omega* was top-heavy. Even if we figured out a way to seal it with the tube, I doubted that anything less than a gale force wind could budge it.

I heard faint footsteps coming from the *Omega*. Standing up again, I joined the others just outside its cold, metallic body.

I kicked my shoe at the tracks. "Do these things connect with the other ones on the other side of your fake wall?"

Cartwright shook his head. "We pulled up the tracks to make it look like a dead end."

"Do you really think that'll fool Chase?"

He shrugged. "Probably not."

I thought for a second. "So even if we got the *Omega* working, we don't have the tracks to ride it out of here."

"That's right. Not that it matters since we don't have a third rail."

"Can we move the Bell?" Beverly asked.

"Move it where? The side tunnels are too small. The only exit big enough is the tube and you can bet those guys are out there waiting for us." Cartwright paused. "Face it, there's no way out of here."

Beverly nodded. "So let's forget about that then. We should come up with a plan to deal with Chase when he arrives. Then we need to figure out a way to destroy the Bell."

I turned around. The station was mostly open space with few hiding spots. The only real cover consisted of the *Omega* and the pile of debris on top of the groove. Since they were both on the north end of the station, they could prove helpful when the time came to stage a defense.

Regardless, once Chase breached the tube, I knew it was only a matter of time. I already knew exactly how it would play out. We'd pick off a few of his men as they stormed into the station. In return, he'd threaten to kill Diane. We'd either surrender and die or fight and die.

Why didn't I make out a will before I came down here? Although it's not like I actually own anything.

My eyes swung back to the giant pile of debris. I couldn't believe how high it stretched. "What's all that stuff anyways?"

Before he could respond, I hiked over to the pile and began pulling aside empty boxes and rags. I uncovered a flat, shiny, metallic surface.

"That's Beach's car," Cartwright said. "It's not his original car. That one was smaller and made of wood. This one was built for these tunnels. It's the reason we positioned our tracks the way we did. When we coasted the *Omega* into this room, we didn't want it to crash into the car."

I wiped sweat off my forehead. "I say we focus on setting up our escape plan first. Then we'll work on dismantling the Bell."

Cartwright frowned. "Haven't you been listening to me? Escape is impossible. The tracks aren't connected and the third rail is disabled. We'd literally have to push the *Omega* out of the station."

"I'm not talking about escaping in the *Omega*," I replied. "I'm talking about escaping in Beach's car."

Chapter 56

"You're out of your mind." Cartwright sneered. "That thing hasn't been moved in over a century. Let me repeat that for you. A damn century."

"Have you ever tried to move it?"

"Of course not."

"Then how do you know for certain?"

"Because it's over a hundred years old."

"I saw an air flue near the entrance of the tunnel. Is the necessary equipment inside of it?"

He sighed. "There's a blower and an engine if I remember correctly, but there's zero chance that either of them still works."

"They might."

"Of course they might. You would know. After all, you've been down here for what, a couple of hours? Who cares about my three decades when we've got Cyclone Reed in the vicinity?"

I shook my head. "This isn't about you."

"Let me put this a different way," he retorted. "I once had a television set. Nothing special. Black-and-white and cheap. But it lasted me a decade. By the time it ran its course, I found myself looking at color sets of all different shapes and sizes and qualities. Ten years is an eternity in terms of technology. Do you really think that a hundred-and-forty year old system that was never fully operational still works today?"

"If the technology worked then, it might work now."

"Technology wears out."

"Only parts wear out. Take your example. I bet you used your television set every day, for a couple of hours at a time. Normal wear and tear eventually took its toll. That's not the case here. As you said, the blower and engine haven't been used for over a century."

Cartwright turned his back and stalked away in a huff. I glanced over at Beverly for help. But instead, I found myself staring at another doubtful face.

"It sounds a bit crazy," she said.

"It's worth a try."

"Maybe we should just start working on the Bell."

"If we stay here, we'll die. Our only chance is to find a way to escape."

"The priority is destroying the Bell."

"You know as well as I do it's going to take time to figure that out. Hell, I read most of Hartek's journal and I barely understood half of it."

She shook her head. "Let's assume you're not crazy. After we get the Bell into Beach's subway car, where do we take it?"

"Out of these tunnels. We can take it back into the Lexington Avenue Line and out through one of the closed-off stations. With a little luck, we'll find a place to hide it. Then you and Cartwright can figure out how to dismantle it while I go after Diane."

"Aren't you forgetting that little explosion earlier today? There's now a rock pile standing between us and the other tunnels. We can't get past it, not without a bulldozer anyway."

"Cartwright's got explosives. If worse comes to worst, we can try to blow up the rock pile and escape into the dust."

She frowned. "There are just so many variables to consider. We don't know if the car's brakes will work. We might zip right into the connecting tunnel and crash into the rock pile."

Cartwright spun around, a crazy gleam in his eyes. "You can talk all you want, but it doesn't make a difference. These tubes are ancient and unfinished to boot. Beach's subway car sat here for all of that time, gathering dust. Frankly, I have doubts that it was ever even tested."

I gave him a determined look. "Is the Bell safe to move?"

"For a few hours, tops. If we don't plug it in after that, all bets are off."

"Beach's car looks like it can hold a nearly airtight seal with the pneumatic tube." I studied the ground. "The groove's in good shape although the metal rails might pose a problem. Still, we've got an air flue, blower, and engine. Everything we need is right here. We just have to get it all to work."

Cartwright shrugged. "It's impossible."

"There's only one way to know for sure."

I walked over to the west wall. After checking to make sure that it was clear of explosives, I pressed the button. The bedrock clicked and yawned opened.

As I entered the maintenance tunnel, I hung a left and walked back to where I'd seen the other door. I stopped outside and twisted the knob. It opened easily. Extending my flashlight, I peered into a stuffy room. It was nearly identical to the one that now held the slain bodies of the Sand Demons.

I shone my light around the room, allowing it to linger on the blower and the metallic shaft.

Cartwright appeared behind me. "It looks in good shape," I said. "You helped to hook up the power lines to the Bell. You must know something about this stuff."

He placed his gnarled hand on the blower. "I'll try. No promises, but I'll try. However, you need to understand something. Even if I get the blower to work, the metal tracks will act as friction. It'll take a miracle to overcome them."

"Unfortunately, we don't have a choice." I gave him a hard look. "If we don't get Beach's subway car to work, we're dead."

Chapter 57

What the hell are you doing?

As I stepped out of the mechanical room and back into the maintenance tunnels, doubts flooded my head. And by the time I reached the station, those doubts had grown into a full-blown crisis of confidence.

My plan involved taking the equivalent of a small hydrogen bomb, hauling it into a one hundred and forty-year-old subway car, and then transporting it via a technology that was ordinarily used to deliver mail. The whole thing was ludicrous and I would've laughed if the stakes weren't so damn high.

I jogged across the station and boarded the *Omega*. As I passed through the aisle, I saw traces of dried blood and grime. The *Omega*'s cursed history immediately came to mind.

I'm stuck in an underground subway station with ShadowFire on my tail and nowhere to go. I don't have to worry about a curse. I'm already cursed.

I tossed the blanket aside and gazed upon the Bell. It continued to float in mid-air, undeterred by the impossibility of it all. Shaking my head, I walked to the right of the wide-open space and stopped in front of the two metal doors.

Holding my breath, I grasped the rubber edge on the nearest door and pulled. To my surprise, it opened easily.

As I opened the other door, I heard a loud thump. Taking out my flashlight, I pointed it across the station at Beach's car. I didn't see anything.

Suddenly, a resounding smash pierced the air. I shifted my beam and saw a large wooden crate on the ground. Looking up, I noticed Beverly standing on the roof of the car. She bent down, momentarily disappearing from view. Seconds later, a short metal beam hurtled through the air, crashing against the bedrock.

I scrambled out of the *Omega* and sprinted over to her. "Stop that."

She peered over the edge. "What?"

"You're making too much noise."

"I was just trying to –"

"Forget it. Look, I need a favor. There's a door in the rear of this thing. Can you get it open for me?"

"But what about all of this debris? The car won't fit in the tube unless we get rid of it."

"The Bell's the priority. After we move it, we can focus on everything else."

She nodded. "Help me down."

Beverly knelt on the car's roof and lowered herself off the edge. I grabbed her waist. As she let go, I scooped her into my arms. I stood still for a second, cradling her.

She gave me a sly look. "Admit it. This is the most fun you've had in days."

Shifting my arms, I propped her unceremoniously on her feet. "That's not saying much."

She grinned. "Say what you want but we both know you enjoyed that."

"The only thing I'm going to enjoy is watching you open that door."

I jogged back to the *Omega*. Once inside, I walked around the Bell, examining it from every angle. The particle accelerator buzzed at me, like a swarm of angry bees ready to attack. Tentatively, I reached out to touch it.

The bell vibrated as my finger approached its surface. It struck me that my action was foolhardy at best, suicidal at worst. But despite my better judgment, I couldn't help myself.

At the last second, I saw something poking out of the Bell. Shifting my hand, I managed to steer my fingers away from the surface. Instead, they closed around a high-voltage cable.

Cartwright said this thing could last without electricity for a few hours. Let's hope he wasn't exaggerating.

Closing my eyes, I took a deep breath. Abruptly, I yanked the cable out of the socket.

The Bell hissed angrily at me.

But after a moment, the noise died down. And as more moments passed, it seemed to grow quieter and calmer. Emboldened, I quickly removed the other cables.

There could be no more stalling. It was now or never. I touched the Bell's metal surface. Instantly, a small jolt of electricity flowed through me. My mind cleared. I felt a strange sensation in the base of my skull. The experience only lasted a second. But I knew I'd never forget it.

I looked at the Bell, not knowing what to expect. Part of me thought it would remain motionless to my touch since it obviously weighed a lot. Another part of me figured it would move like a balloon since it floated in the air with ease.

I shoved it.

How about that? Wrong on both counts.

It moved. Not far, but it still moved. Yet, it wasn't weightless. In fact, it felt surprisingly heavy to me, as if my touch temporarily brought the strange object back into the real world.

I pushed it downward. It moved in that direction before floating up again to its original position. Crouching down, I pushed it upward. It moved a few inches before drifting back down again. It was completely, utterly bizarre. The Bell seemed to sit on some kind of imaginary shelf. And yet, it still managed to maintain its mass. How was that even possible?

I desperately wanted to understand it, but that would have to wait. I pushed my body against the Bell and slowly maneuvered it out of the

Omega. Hopping down to the ground, I directed it toward Beach's pneumatic car. As I got closer, Beverly stared at me, wide-eyed.

"Did you get the door open?" I called out as loudly as I dared.

"Sure did. Do you need help?"

I stifled a fake yawn with one hand while propelling the Bell forward with the other. "I think I can handle it."

"Show-off."

Looking past her, I studied the car. The garbage that covered its rear had been stripped away, revealing a set of two small doors. A new potential problem formed in my head. "Is the opening wide enough?"

She jogged over to the Bell and eyed it. Then she returned to the doors and studied them for a moment. "Honestly, I'm not sure. It's going to be close."

I pushed the Bell all the way to the rear of the pneumatic car. As I neared it, I snuck a peek. The space was larger than I'd initially thought but not by much. Beverly was right. It would be a tight squeeze, if indeed it fit at all.

She joined me and together, we pushed the Bell forward. Abruptly, metal scratched on metal. I jolted as the Bell bumped into something.

"You've got to be kidding me," she grumbled. "Of all the lousy..."

"We're hitting there." I pointed to the top right corner. "Let's try pulling it down."

Reaching up, we directed the Bell downward. It dropped a few inches. Before it could settle, I shoved it into the car. It came to a halt a few feet into the interior before slowly drifting upward again.

"Should we reconnect the cables?"

I shook my head. "We have more important things to do."

"Aren't you worried about an explosion?"

"That won't happen for a few hours. We'll get the cables from the *Omega* and put them in here. But after that, we need to work on our escape plan."

We spent the next few minutes detaching the cables and piling them into the pneumatic car.

Afterward, Beverly cleared her throat. "What now?"

"We need to finish clearing off the car," I replied. "But first, we should focus on removing the explosives from the tunnel."

"I can do that."

"How? By blowing yourself up?"

She shrugged. "I'm trained to handle unexploded ordinance."

"Really?"

"Sort of."

My ears perked. The air started to crackle with tension. Swiftly, I made my way to the mouth of the pneumatic tube.

"…your guess…"

"…up. The tracks…"

The voices were faint but they were audible.

And close by.

I looked at Beverly. "They're here," I whispered. "Clear away the explosives and make it fast."

"What are you going to do?"

"I'm going to check on Cap."

I ran back into the access tunnels and headed for the maintenance room. Inside, I found Cartwright lying on the ground underneath the engine.

"How's it going?" I asked.

He looked up at me, his face covered with sweat and grease. "It's not," he grunted. "I barely understand what I'm looking at here."

"Well, you're going to need a steep learning curve. We've got company."

"I need more time."

"I'll see what I can do."

I sprinted back to the station and saw Beverly kneeling on the ground, playing with wires. She looked at me. "What did he say?"

I grabbed a long piece of loose wire from the ground and examined it for a moment. "He needs more time."

"He doesn't have more time."

"He needs it and we have to give it to him. I've got an idea. If it works, we've got a chance."

"If not?"

"Well, then it's been nice knowing you."

Chapter 58

Although cool on the outside, my insides broiled. I shifted my footing, trying to get comfortable.

It didn't work.

I stood just outside the pneumatic tube, slightly off to the side. My position mattered. When Chase penetrated the wall, he needed to see me. But he also needed to see the *Omega*.

The noise level outside the tube increased and I heard scuffling noises. It wouldn't be long before they found the Sand Demons' symbol and opened the door. Frankly, I preferred it that way. I was tired of waiting for the inevitable.

Gradually, I got my restlessness under control and expelled it to the far corners of my body. It was still there, just beneath the surface. Still, that was the best I could do given the circumstances.

Will Chase believe me? Or call my bluff?

The next few minutes would determine the future. Not just for me, not just for my friends, but for New York and perhaps, the rest of the world as well. It was all so simple, yet so complicated at the same time. I could count the possible outcomes on one hand, but predicting the most likely one was impossible.

How would it all end? Would I buy enough time to escape with the Bell? Could I manage to do it without causing harm to Diane? Could I rescue her?

Or would I die and in the process, enable Chase to recover one of the deadliest inventions in the history of mankind?

I directed my flashlight at the small, hunk of plastic in my hand. It looked real enough, but it, along with the wires that extended from it, was just a prop. I twisted to the side and followed the wires as they trailed across the floor. My beam finally settled on Beverly. She stood next to the *Omega*, leaning into the interior.

After a few moments, Beverly removed her head from the *Omega*. She caught my eye and flashed me a thumbs-up.

I heard a soft sliding noise. I spun around just in time to see the bedrock door open. Quickly, I stepped into the tube and leaned against the wall, adopting a casual pose.

Dust cleared. Chase materialized before me. He stood on the opposite end of the tube, arms crossed. His eyes reflected ecstasy as he stared over my shoulder and took in the *Omega*.

Chop off the snake's head and the body will die.

My hand reached for my pistol. I wanted to shoot him right in his cleanly shaven face. But somehow, I managed to stay in control. The moment I opened fire, it would be open season on me, Diane, and everyone else. Even if I managed to kill him, I doubted his soldiers would stop shooting until we were dead.

Shifting position, I deliberately drew his attention.

His eyes flitted toward me. His expression changed, reflecting a mixture of surprise and suspicion. "Cyclone," he said in a booming voice. "I can't say I'm not surprised."

"Me neither. I've been one step ahead of you this entire time."

Chase strode toward me. I considered doing the same and meeting him in the middle of the tube. While it was essential for him to see the *Omega*, I didn't want him to know about Beach's pneumatic car just yet.

But he stopped after a few steps. His expression changed again, morphing into one of amusement. He snapped his fingers.

One of his guards marched forward, pushing Diane ahead of him. She looked weak and pale. But she was alive and I was determined to keep her that way.

I turned back to Chase. "We want to make a deal."

He chuckled. Reaching for his jacket, he withdrew his Smith & Wesson Victory Model. "It's too late for that."

This was it, the moment of truth. I lifted my hand into the air. His eyes shifted to the hunk of plastic in my fingers and the long wires that trailed away from it.

"I don't think so," I replied. "If you want to live, put your gun away."

"Why would I do that?"

"Because if you don't, I'll use this device to blow up the Bell. You may have survived Hiroshima. But there's no way in hell you'll survive this."

Chapter 59

Chase pointed his gun at me and I held my breath.

Then his hand wavered.

And in that brief moment, I saw a spark of uncertainty in his eyes.

Standish stepped forward, next to Chase. He folded his powerful arms across his chest and shot me an amused look. "You're not fooling anyone."

"Go ahead then," I retorted. "Shoot me. Shoot me and see what happens."

Standish looked at Chase. "You heard him, Jack. Shoot him and be done with it."

I held up my hand, displaying the plastic hunk. "This thing here is hooked up to explosives. Those explosives are currently sitting in the *Omega*, surrounding the Bell. So, if you shoot me, I press this button. They blow up, followed by the Bell, followed by, well, everything."

"That wouldn't do anything but make a big mess." Chase frowned. "The Bell is nothing more than a particle accelerator."

"As we stand here, the Bell is creating Red Mercury."

"I don't believe you."

"It needs to be in operation at all times." I narrowed my gaze. "Otherwise it loses stability and becomes explosive. And since the Bell is always working, there's always a small amount of Red Mercury inside."

Standish glanced at Chase. "Don't listen to this crap. He's lying."

"Maybe I am," I said. "But are you willing to risk your life to find out?"

Chase gave me a skeptical look. "What do you know about explosives?"

"Nothing. But your old friend Beverly, well, she knows all about them. And she assures me that the moment I press this button, this whole place blows up."

Chase pointed his gun at my face. "Then I guess I'd better shoot you quick."

"Beverly's in the *Omega*. If you shoot me before I reach the button, she'll just blow the explosives manually."

"I want to talk to her."

"Too bad she doesn't feel the same."

"Beverly!" he shouted.

Glancing back, I saw her stick her head out from inside the subway car. "Did I hear my name?"

"This has gone far enough."

"I don't work for you." Her voice stiffened. "Not anymore. Now do us all a favor and listen to Cy. No one needs to die today."

As she vanished back into the *Omega*, Standish shook his head. "You're a liar. A damn good one maybe, but still a liar. A couple of ounces of Red Mercury wouldn't just kill us. It would kill everyone above us as well. And I know for a fact you could never do that."

He was right, of course. There was no way in hell I'd ever kill innocent people. But if they didn't believe my threat, then I was as good as dead. "Why not? If I don't do it, your boss will."

"He's lying," Chase said. "Just like I told you he would."

"No, I'm not."

Standish sneered. "I'd believe Jack over you any day of the week."

I glanced at Chase. "You told me before you didn't want to kill me. Is that still true?"

"Of course."

Liar.

"Then, look at it this way. You want the Bell. You want it so badly that you've spent the better part of your life searching for it. I'm not looking to be a hero. I just want Diane back and safe passage out of these tunnels. If you agree to those terms, you'll have your Bell in a matter of minutes."

Chase hesitated. Then he lowered his gun.

Standish shot him an angry look. "Are you really listening to this crap?"

Chase snapped his fingers. Instantly, the guard pushed Diane forward.

He shoved her to her knees. Repositioning himself, he pointed his gun at her head. "Put the detonator down. And do it slowly. Then I need my little traitor friend to exit the *Omega*."

I did my best not to look at Diane. But I couldn't completely avoid those pained blue eyes.

I'd expected the situation, prepared for it even. But as I stared deep into her eyes, surging anger threatened to overwhelm me.

I breathed deeply. After a moment, the surge dulled. My mind crystallized. Backing down wasn't an option. Although it would buy Diane a few seconds, I'd lose all my leverage. We were in a standoff and if I blinked, my entire side would die.

"Go ahead and shoot her," I said. "But if you do, I press the button."

"You have five seconds. Five…"

My face twisted defiantly.

"Four."

"Three."

An unwelcome thought crossed my mind. We were locked in a lethal standoff and as far as Chase was concerned, the explosives were like a gun with a single bullet. The moment I used them, the standoff ended and everyone lost. Knowing that, he might decide to murder Diane, assuming I still wouldn't detonate the Bell.

"Two…"

Panic gripped my chest. What if he shot her?

"One…"

I steeled myself and glared into his eyes.

"Zero."

Chase didn't move a muscle.

Neither did I.

With an annoyed grunt, he pushed Diane onto the floor.

Relief swept over me. "Are we done with this nonsense? I'd like to get on with our deal."

"What do you propose?"

"You leave Diane with me. Then you wait outside for five minutes. After that, this room and everything in it is yours."

"How do I know you won't use the time to set a trap for me?"

"We have nothing to gain from fighting. That's a battle we won't win. I just want to take my friends and leave."

Standish gave me an amazed look. "You're just going to walk right by us?"

"Of course not. There's a maze of maintenance tunnels connected to this station. We'll leave through one of them."

"How do I know you won't detonate the explosives once you're gone?" Chase asked.

"And blow ourselves up too? I'm a little crazy but I'm not suicidal. I just want out of here. And I want to take my friends with me."

Chase stared at me. Then, he nodded. "You've got five minutes. After that, we're coming in with guns drawn, explosives or not."

"Fair enough."

Chase glanced down at Diane. Before I could react, he reared back and kicked her in the head. Her face distorted to one side and blood splattered onto my clothes.

I started for him but he lifted the gun again. "You've got five minutes," he said. "Use them wisely."

Seething with anger, I watched him back away and leave the tube. Moments later, the door slid to a close.

Leaning down, I checked Diane.

Her eyes fluttered and looked up at me. "I should've known you had something to do with this."

"I didn't mean –"

"Look, I don't know what this is all about," she whispered in a pained tone. "But that man's insane. He'll never let us escape."

"I know."

"Then, what's your plan?"

"Let me put it like this. The easy part is over. The hard part comes next."

Chapter 60

As I helped Diane out of the tube, I felt fireworks shooting off inside me. She was in even worse shape than I thought. Her face was pale and dripping with sweat. Her clothes were unkempt and covered with dirt and blood. She clutched her stomach as she walked as if she were having gastrointestinal problems. Unfortunately, I knew it was far more serious than that, given the sheer amount of dried blood caked on her shirt.

At the end of the tube, I heard a soft pop followed by a choking noise. A sudden gust of wind bowled into me, bringing with it a lungful of musty, dusty air. I coughed. Clearly, Cartwright was making progress.

But was he making enough of it?

We hustled over to Beach's car and I helped Diane into the rear. Then I ran to the opposite end, away from the Bell.

"I finished clearing off the debris," Beverly said. "How is she?"

"If we get her to a doctor, she'll live. But she doesn't have much time."

"Did they buy your bluff?"

"They're confused but it won't take Chase long to get his act together."

"Do we have the five minutes?"

"We'll be lucky if we get two."

She put her hands on the back of the pneumatic car and began to push with all of her strength. I joined her and after twenty seconds of backbreaking effort, we managed to get Beach's old car moving.

At first, it took all our combined strength just to move it an inch. The second inch was a little simpler and the third one was even easier.

Ever so slowly, we pushed the car along the groove toward the open tube. Despite its heavy weight and old age, it slid at a smooth and silent pace.

I saw shifting shadows out of the corner of my eye. They moved swiftly and silently, barely making a disturbance in the station. Four of them stole out of the tube and angled themselves toward the *Omega*.

Undoubtedly, they worked for Chase. They must've snuck into the tube before the door closed over. Since they were professional soldiers, I knew that they were equipped for the situation. Night-vision goggles were an absolute certainty. I just hoped that they weren't paying too much attention to the slow-moving pneumatic car.

I eased myself out of the line of sight and continued to push against the car as hard as I could. Things were about to get ugly. Real ugly. And once that happened, all bets were off.

Suddenly, the station exploded into flames. The ground rumbled and a mighty boom pierced the air. A shock wave barreled into me and I fell to the ground. Looking up, I saw chunks of metal flying in all directions, slamming into the bedrock walls with chilling force.

As I rose to my feet, a burst of smoke spread out from the mangled wreckage of the *Omega*, blanketing everything in sight. Squinting, I saw four bodies lying on the ground, writhing in pain. They were still alive.

But I doubted they would last for long.

I might have been lying about the gadget. But I sure as hell wasn't lying about putting explosives in the Omega.

Angry and confused shouts, muffled by distance, filled the air. The explosion would force Chase to reconsider his options. But it wouldn't be long before he tried again.

There was no point in keeping quiet any longer. Grunting, I threw my shoulder into Beach's subway car and heaved. With Beverly's help, it slowly began to move again.

We pushed it all the way to the mouth of the tube. It screeched as its bottom scraped lightly against the Sand Demons' metal tracks.

I glanced at Beverly. "Get in there. And keep the door on the other side closed as long as possible. Whatever happens, don't let Chase and his men into the car."

As she vanished into the interior, I stepped back and quickly examined the tube. The metal rails would present a problem. I just hoped the car could handle them.

"Cap," I called out. "Tell me you're done."

I heard a metallic cough and then gears churning. Another strong gust of wind blasted out of the air flue and caught me right in the face. It blew me straight back into the car, which started to move. For a moment, I imagined myself glued to the back of it, racing through the tunnel at top speed.

But the wind quickly died off and I fell to the ground, gasping for air. My eyes burned from the dust particles and it took me a few seconds to blink them away. As my vision cleared, I saw a shadow emerge from the open wall that connected the station to the passages.

My body tensed.

My hand slipped to my holster.

I grabbed hold of the pistol and watched as the figure darted toward me. As Cartwright's face came into view, I breathed a sigh of relief.

"We're ready to roll," he announced. "At least I hope we are. Just so you know, this is the craziest thing I've ever done."

"Crazier than stealing the Bell and guarding it for over three decades?"

"Well, okay. Second craziest thing."

I hopped into the car, catching a glimpse of Beverly in the process. She knelt on the other end, arms tense, both hands grasping the doorknob. Spinning around, I offered my hand to Cartwright.

He jogged over to the west side of the tube and opened a control box. Then he turned around and looked at me. "The instant I pull this lever, the air's going to burst out of here like nothing you've ever felt. So grab hold of me and then shut the door as quickly as you can."

"Let me do it."

"No, I –"

Loud blasts filled the air and reverberated against the bedrock walls.

Time slowed down.

Horror filled my gut.

Cartwright stumbled and fell to a knee.

I saw the blood, the bullet holes.

Kneeling down, I peered into the dimly lit station and saw a single moving shadow in the vicinity of the *Omega*. It was struggling to rise to its feet. I felt a rush of anger. Grabbing my gun, I squeezed the trigger a few times. The shadow dropped like a stone, wriggling in pain.

I looked back at Cartwright. Shaking all over, he stood up and hobbled to the wall. He gave me a tired smile. "I'm done, Cy," he wheezed. "Take good care of her."

"Cap, wait…"

He fell against the box. His hand pushed the lever. I tried to jump out to help him, but a sudden burst of wind sent me sailing back into the car's interior. As I scrambled to my feet, I felt the car floor shuddering and realized we were already shooting through the tube.

I struggled to the rear of the car and slammed the door shut. Then I looked through the small window and watched as Cartwright's lifeless body slid to the ground and vanished into the darkness.

Chapter 61

As we thundered through the tube, I felt a moment of odd serenity. For more than thirty years, Cartwright lived a troubled life, full of anxiety, stress, and paranoia. He'd dedicated every ounce of his soul to protecting something he barely understood for reasons he couldn't fully explain. And now, after all that time, he'd found peace at last.

Don't get sappy. You know damn well that eternal peace is just a nice way of saying he's dead. And there's no waking up from that.

"I can see the next station," Beverly called out. "And still no sign of them."

I spun around. Diane sat hunched on the floor in the middle of the car. Her face looked grim yet determined. Beyond her, Beverly pointed a flashlight out the far window.

"Are you sure?" I asked.

"I think I would've noticed if something splattered in front of me."

She paused. "I hate to bring this up now, but what happens when we hit the next station?"

"What do you mean?"

"Does this thing have brakes? Or will we just shoot on through?"

"I don't know," I admitted. "But if it stops, we're in trouble."

Beverly lowered her flashlight and edged her body to the side, taking cover next to the door. Mere seconds separated us from the next station. Seconds that could bring salvation.

Or disaster.

As I nervously fingered my gun, I ran the possible scenarios through my head. As long as the car continued to head south, we were safe. If it ground to a halt while in the present tube, we'd have two options. Flee back to the north or stay in the railcar and defend the door. In the worst-case scenario, we'd stop in the middle of the station. From that position, escape would be impossible and we'd be flanked on either side by Chase's forces.

A loud screeching noise punctured the silence. My fingers tightened around my pistol as bright lights blazed through the side windows.

Abruptly, the car slid completely out of the tube and into the station. Glancing out the back window, I saw a dozen silhouettes gathered around the tube's mouth. They remained immobile as we passed by them. Squinting, I saw the shock registered on their visages.

My gaze landed on the tallest person in the crowd and although I couldn't discern his face, I knew it was Standish. There was no mistaking his giant frame, his broad shoulders, and his commanding presence. To his left, I saw the shorter silhouette of Chase.

I felt no intimidation, no fear as I stared at them. Nothing but cold, silent rage filled my soul. One way or another, a day of reckoning was coming. They would pay for their crimes.

The subway car bumped and I felt a surge of adrenaline. The car skidded into the next tube, slowing down in the process. I steeled myself, preparing for the worst.

I heard a rush of air. Beach's car jolted.

Then it accelerated and we raced through the next tube.

"What happened?" Beverly asked.

"The pneumatic system." I grinned. "When Cartwright fixed the first fan and turned it on, he must've turned the entire system on with it."

Diane's weak and halting voice spoke out. "Do either of you have another gun?"

I glanced at her. She looked even paler than I remembered. "Nope."

"Do you even know how to use one?"

Beverly's voice sounded skeptical and I didn't blame her. To the best of my knowledge, Diane had never fired a gun in her life.

But she seemed to gain energy at the question. "Of course not," Diane replied. "Why would someone like me know how to fire a gun, right?"

"I didn't mean –"

"Save it. Do you have another gun or no?"

Beverly glanced at me and then turned back to Diane. Her hand reached to her belt. Removing a pistol, she twisted it around and offered the handle to Diane. "Don't make me regret this."

As Beverly walked away, I jogged over to join Diane. Her eyes shimmered under my flashlight and I saw both fear and fortitude within them. Gently, I reached for her shirt.

She slapped my hand away. "I'm glad you find me attractive, but this is no time to mess around."

"I need to look at your wound."

"I know. And you don't have to worry about me. I'm fine."

"Like hell you are. Now are you going to lift up your shirt or do I have to tear it off you?"

She sighed. Then she slowly wiggled her bloodstained shirt up a few inches. Exhaling, I stared at the long, gaping wound across her belly. It was a nasty cut, oozing with blood and puss.

Standard medical procedures – cleaning it, removing the dead flesh, and dressing it – were outside the realm of possibility. Makeshift medicine would have to suffice until I could get her to a hospital.

Lifting my arms, I stripped off my tattered, bloody shirt. After tearing it into pieces, I tied the strips tightly around her body, enclosing the wound.

Diane looked at me. "Can I ask you a question?"

"Of course."

"What did you get me into?"

"You wouldn't believe me if I told you."

"At this point, I'll believe just about anything."

"Oh yeah? Would you –"

The subway car lurched. My body launched into the air and I slammed into something cold and hard. Dazed, I crumpled to the floor. I was hurt but alive.

I just hoped I wasn't the only one.

I peeled my sore body off the floor and rose painfully to my knees. Fishing around for a few seconds, I managed to locate my flashlight. As I switched it on, a dim glow covered the interior of the car.

The Bell, which had stopped my movement, rested directly in front of the double doors. Beverly knelt on its left side, head in hands. I noticed a bit of blood dripping from her skull.

I shook my head, trying to free myself from my mental fog. "Are you okay?"

Beverly nodded. "What happened?"

"We hit something."

I looked around for Diane and spotted her lying on the ground, feet splayed out across the floor. "How about you?" I asked. "Are you all right?"

"I've been better."

I stood up. "I hate to rush everyone, but we can't stay here. We need to move before Chase arrives."

Diane pointed at the Bell. "We're leaving that thing, right?"

"No. It's coming with us."

"Why? What is it anyway?"

"You wouldn't believe me if I told you."

"Try me."

"It's a particle accelerator." I took a deep breath. "It creates a substance called Red Mercury which can be used to fuel hydrogen bombs."

Her eyes grew wide. "Forget I asked. How are we supposed to move it? It's got to weigh a couple hundred pounds at least."

I winked at Beverly. Then, I bent down and put my hands under the lip of the Bell. "I'm sure I can manage it."

My grin vanished as I found myself struggling to lift the Bell off the car's floor. Finally, it lifted into the air for a few seconds. Oddly, it had gained significant weight since being unplugged. I found it curious.

And troubling.

"Nice trick," Diane said. "What's it made out of?"

I shrugged my shoulders, deliberately removing my hands from under the Bell in the process. "Who knows?"

Her jaw dropped as the Bell remained floating in the air. Quickly, I opened the doors. Then, I pushed the Bell out of the car and into the tube. Looking around, I noticed that one of the running rails had cracked, presumably under the weight of Beach's subway car.

I reached up and helped Diane out of the car. Her face looked flushed and she seemed to move with more energy.

"How…?"

"Don't ask." I shook my head. "I don't have the slightest idea."

Beverly hopped out of the car. "There's no lock on the other door. And unfortunately, there's nothing to barricade it with either."

"What if we shoot out one of the seats and use it to block the knob?"

"Honestly, I think we're better off saving our ammo. By the time we finished setting it up, they'd be right on top of us."

"We don't have enough time." The realization hit me hard. "Without the car, we'll never escape with the Bell. We need to destroy it."

"How do we destroy it?" Diane asked.

I pulled Hartek's journal out of my satchel. "Hopefully, this will tell us. I'll push the Bell forward to give us some more breathing room. I need one of you to read this book and figure out a solution."

Beverly shook her head. "You're our best chance. You've read far more of that book than either of us. You read, we'll push."

I didn't like it. It made sense but I still didn't like it. I looked at Diane. "How's your stomach?"

"I'll manage."

Glancing back at Beverly, I shrugged. "Let's get to it then."

Beverly and Diane threw their combined weight behind the Bell. Soon, it started to shift forward through the tube. Although it still floated, its growing weight was cause for concern. What happened when it finally fell victim to gravity?

As the two women pushed the Bell, I focused my attention on Hartek's journal. I flipped through page after page, scanning them with my flashlight, searching for clues.

Red Mercury is a superconductor.

I stopped on the page and quickly read the surrounding notes. I saw something about a property called the Meissner effect. I flipped a page and read some more. Although I didn't understand everything, it appeared that the Bell's anti-gravity properties were due to Red Mercury itself, which was subjected to extremely low temperatures and manipulated with magnets inside the Bell.

I read more. It seemed that when the Red Mercury and magnets moved together, they started to both attract and repel each other. The magnets, which were positioned above the Red Mercury, levitated. As they rose, the Red Mercury rose with it.

I turned it over in my mind, trying to understand the inner workings of the particle accelerator. I was so caught up in my thoughts that I almost missed the sound of splashing water.

But as it grew louder, it grabbed my attention. I realized we were nearing the giant alligator's home.

My ears perked. Pounding footsteps. And they were running toward us.

Not now! I need more time!

Stuffing the journal under my arm, I leaned my back into the Bell and helped push it through the tube. Fifty feet separated us from the next station.

But it was a temporary refuge at best. We couldn't stay ahead of them forever, especially not with the Bell gaining weight with every passing second.

We lumbered into the station. Something whizzed over my head and slammed into the opposite wall. Immediately, I veered to the side, pushing the Bell away from the tube's mouth.

Beverly turned and fired a few shots over her shoulder. The footsteps retreated.

I looked around, trying to formulate a plan. We couldn't reach the opposite tunnel, not without stepping in the path of gunfire again. And the station itself offered no means of protection.

My eyes crossed the space. We needed to destroy the Bell and escape. But how?

A crazy idea popped into my head.

Immediately, I spun to the side of the Bell and shoved it across the station. The abandoned tube lay in front of us, its metal grating warning us away.

By entering it, we could buy ourselves a few seconds. And if I could figure out how, we could destroy the Bell and escape into the underground river. It wasn't a great option.

But it was the only option.

There was nowhere else to go.

Nowhere but back into the monster's lair.

Chapter 62

"Are you out of your mind?" Beverly shot me an amazed look. "We can't go in there."

Grunting, I turned around and shoved my back against the Bell. It felt strangely warm against my bare skin. "We don't have a choice."

"There's always a choice."

"Not this time."

"We can hole up in the corner," she said. "Use the Bell as a shield. With a little bit of luck…"

"We're as good as dead if we stay in here." Sweat poured down my face. "And you know it as well as I do. We'd be cornered with no means of escape."

"We'll be cornered in there too."

I grinned at her.

She frowned. "Wait, you're not thinking…"

"I hope you know how to swim."

"I do. Unfortunately, so do alligators."

"Hopefully, it's somewhere else. We're going to figure out a way to destroy this thing and escape into the water. With any luck, it'll take us clear out to the East River."

"I swear to God this is the worst plan I've ever heard."

Out of the corner of my eye, I saw Diane limp to the grating and begin fiddling with the metal wires. A few seconds later, metal screeched against metal.

As the grating creaked open, Beverly slid to the side and helped direct the Bell toward the abandoned tube. We passed through the gate and Diane hobbled in behind us. I heard a light swinging noise followed by soft rattling. Moments later, her silhouette appeared at my side.

"I retied the wires," she whispered. "As tightly as I could. It should give us another minute or so. Now get back to that book. I'll push from here."

I had to give her credit. When Chase arrived in the station, he'd find it empty. Between the closed grating and the darkness of the other tube, it would take him a few extra seconds to realize where we'd gone. If we were really fortunate, he might even divide his forces in order to search both tubes.

As she took my place, I grabbed Hartek's book from under my arm. Silence fell over the tunnel and I began to read. But my mind drifted and I had trouble concentrating.

The Bell was many things to many people. It was a particle accelerator to Hartek. An object of reverence and fear to the Sand Demons. A tool of revenge for Chase.

It could create Red Mercury. Red Mercury, of course, had its own multiple identities. It was a superheavy metal. A ballotechnic explosive. A superconductor.

But that last identity was collapsing before my eyes. With every passing second, the Bell appeared to sink closer to the ground. I guessed that it was only a matter of minutes before it touched the bedrock.

As I flipped through the pages, it became increasingly apparent to me that Red Mercury's superconductivity was not only the key to the Bell's anti-gravity properties.

It was the key to everything. Red Mercury first became dangerous when it entered a superconductive state. But since it existed as a superconductor within the Bell, I knew that wasn't enough to cause an explosion.

So, how did it become a superconductor in the first place? And what triggered it to detonate?

"Cyclone!"

Chase's voice roared through the passageway. I sensed his rage, his hatred. He was close.

I couldn't let him have the Bell. But I didn't have the slightest idea how to destroy it. A vague notion came rushing into my brain. The underground river was deep and its current was powerful. Even better, it ran at an angle, descending steeply into the earth. If I could get the Bell into its clutches, it might drag the particle accelerator far below ground. When it inevitably exploded, the additional space and bedrock that separated the Bell from the surface could save lives.

Of course, that assumed that the river led deep underground. In which case, Beverly, Diane, and I were royally screwed.

"Enough with this nonsense, Cyclone," Chase shouted. "This is a waste of time and energy. Leave the Bell and your weapons behind. Come out here and I promise I'll let you live."

Beverly glanced at me, her face glistening with sweat. "You know he's lying, right?"

"Yup."

It wouldn't have mattered to me if he'd been telling the truth. I wasn't about to run away. Not again. Not ever again.

For three long years, I'd been haunted by those poor souls who'd died under my watch. I'd tortured myself. I'd given up everything and everyone I'd held dear to me. I'd left home, undergone a career change, and pledged myself to doing good works.

But as I looked back on that time, I no longer saw myself as someone who sacrificed or sought forgiveness. Instead, I saw someone who ran away from his past. I supposed that was the reason for my recurring PTSD episodes. And the fact that I hadn't experienced one since I'd stopping running only bolstered my theory.

I needed to stop the Bell from hurting anyone ever again. Then I needed to figure out a way to save Beverly and Diane. If I could accomplish those two things, maybe I could finally put my guilt to rest. Maybe, just maybe, the nightmares would end.

This time for good.

Assuming I live that long.

"I see the river," Beverly announced breathlessly. "It's about twenty feet away. No sign of the gator."

At least one thing had gone our way. Now, we just had to get the Bell into the water and hope the current carried it underground. Then we could swim after it and hope for the best.

It wasn't much of a plan but it was better than nothing.

"Stop. Don't take another step."

I froze. A strong beam illuminated my body, casting my shadow onto the ground. Turning around, I saw Chase. He stood twenty feet away, the Smith & Wesson in his hand.

No.

Not now.

I could hear the gushing water of the river behind me. It sounded like it was just several feet away. We'd come so close.

Only to fail at the last moment.

I shoved the journal discretely into my satchel. Two soldiers stepped forward and quickly disarmed us, throwing our weapons in a small pile on the ground. Then they steered us toward the western wall. As my body was shoved into the bedrock, Chase walked forward.

He stopped in front of the Bell and studied it for a moment. His trembling fingers rose into the air and caressed its side. The Bell appeared to flinch at his touch. Silently, it dropped another eighth of an inch closer to the ground.

Chase glanced at me with awe written across his face. "How is it floating like that?"

I shrugged. "Magic?"

"Very funny, Cyclone. Now, before I let you go, is there anything else I should know about it?"

You prick. You know you've got no intention of letting us leave. You just want to know everything we do before you kill us.

Diane cleared her throat. "There is one thing you might want to know. This Bell of yours is about to blow up."

I seized the moment. "She's right. It's highly unstable. And when it explodes, it's taking all of us with it."

"I've had enough of your lies."

"I'm not lying. Why do you think we were running this way in the first place? We were going to force the Bell into the water and hope that the current dragged it deep underground."

Chase nodded. "Okay, I believe you."

"You do?"

He pointed at the Bell. "See those ports? Those are for high-voltage cables. My guess is that electricity keeps it stable. Am I right?"

One hundred percent.

"No," I lied. "Nothing will keep it stable. Our only option is to reduce the explosion's impact."

Chase studied me for a moment and then turned to a few soldiers behind him. "We need power now. I want four of you to move the Bell into the station and load it onto our cart. The rest of you return to that wrecked car and gather those high-voltage cables. Get this thing stabilized before it explodes."

I heard scuffling as the soldiers started to move. A small part of me said to just give up. If Chase's men managed to repower the Bell, it would save lives, at least temporarily. On the other hand, once he repowered the Bell, he'd have a permanent supply of Red Mercury. And I already knew what he planned to do with it.

I was outnumbered, unarmed, and with my back literally against a wall. I couldn't run anymore. I couldn't do anything.

My head started to hurt. Bright colors appeared in my field of vision. My emotions surged.

I glanced to the side and my eyes lingered on Beverly's face. Her eyes were bright and full of fire. I shifted my gaze to Diane. Despite the loss of blood, she looked confident and determined. I looked back at Chase. The departing soldiers momentarily diverted his attention.

I felt stabbing pains in my head. My body started to go limp. I was about to pass out, a fate from which I'd never awaken.

It was now or never.

With a mighty battle cry, I leapt toward Chase. My body smashed into his. Instantly, my headache vanished. My emotions focused. My vision returned.

His hand slammed into the wet bedrock and he dropped his weapon. Gunfire reverberated from all directions as we rolled toward the water. We tussled for a moment but as I leaned over to punch him in the face, something caught my attention.

Two beady eyes rose out of the river and turned to look at me. Then more eyes popped up and did the same thing.

It was the alligator.

And it wasn't alone.

Chapter 63

The largest pair of eyes twitched as they examined me. I remained frozen, poised above Chase, fist cocked at the ready. Behind me all activity had ceased. I heard no footsteps. No scuffling noises. No words. I heard nothing but heaving chests.

Nothing but quiet terror.

A creepy inkling spread through my body. I was the prey. And the gator was sizing me up.

Bubbles churned and fizzed. The gators weren't thrashing about so it struck me that something was going on just beneath the river's surface.

I blinked.

My skin prickled.

Something had changed in the last second. I was sure of it. The largest eyes loomed before mine, seeming bigger and…

Wait. They don't look bigger.

They are bigger.

My heart froze. With no apparent movement, the gator had drifted close to the bedrock shore. In less than a second, it would be within striking distance.

I rolled to the south, taking Chase with me.

Water roiled as the gator charged out of the river. Powerful jaws snapped at my skull. I sensed the gnashing teeth. I felt the breeze and smelled the creature's foul breath.

As I continued to roll, I sensed the gator veering off to the side. Then I heard the sickening crunch of sharp teeth plunging into flesh and bone. Bloodcurdling cries erupted, bouncing off the bedrock walls and into my ears.

Shoving Chase out of the way, I leapt to my feet. My head spun to the side. The gator's jaws were clamped around a leg. Vigorously, the beast shook it back and forth, dragging a shadowy person along with it. It was one of Chase's soldiers.

And she looked terrified.

I sensed more movement coming from the river and twisted my head in that direction. All of a sudden, six smaller alligators stormed ashore. They moved in unison like a well-trained army. They moved with purpose.

They moved to kill.

Sparks of light punctuated the air. Loud bursts of gunfire deafened me. Smoke curled to the ceiling and dissipated. New smoke rose to replace it. And yet, the gators kept coming. I was smack in the middle of a damn war, surrounded by two sides fighting over the right to kill me.

A fist slammed into my back. My pain sensors erupted and I sank to my knees. Calloused hands grabbed my neck and yanked. I toppled backward and fell onto the bedrock.

Chase gave me a caustic look. "When I'm done with you even the gators won't touch you."

He grabbed something from the ground. His hand shot into the air. As it plunged toward me, I caught a glint of metal.

I screamed as a sharp blade stabbed into my side. Scalding heat raced through my body. Glancing down, I noticed my own machete penetrating my flesh just above my hip.

Abruptly, Chase's hand wrenched it out of my body. Fierce stinging pain shot down my side and I nearly passed out.

The searing pain shifted to my head. My entire scalp felt as if it were on fire. I blinked. Through blurry eyes, I saw the gators grow smaller.

I blinked again, thinking that it was a trick of light. But no, they were indeed shrinking.

My boots jerked across the bedrock. The pain in my scalp intensified. I felt Chase's powerful fingers dragging me backward.

By my hair.

I twisted to the side and rolled. He lost his balance and nearly stumbled on top of me. But at the last second, he let go of his grip. The throbbing in my scalp vanished.

Chase grabbed onto the wall for support. I rose to my knees and dove at him. My arm smashed into the back of his left leg. It collapsed and he fell to the ground. A cry of anguish emitted from his lips, rising above the din of gunfire, shouts, and alligator teeth grinding on bone.

Snaking under his right arm, I grabbed hold of it, isolating it from the rest of his body. I chopped at his hand but he refused to drop the machete.

I stood up, forcing him to rise with me. Then I yanked him around in circles, keeping him off balance.

One time around.

Two times around.

His hand opened.

The machete clattered to the bedrock.

I stopped suddenly, catching him off balance. Lowering my shoulder, I slammed it into his chest and drove him into the wall. He shook off the blow and shoved me away.

Twisting my body, I grabbed the machete. But Chase's fist caught me on the shoulder before I could swing it at him. I stumbled north, forging an awkward path between two mid-sized gators. Out of the corner of my eye, I saw Diane and Beverly, back to back, warding off Standish and some of Chase's men. Beverly fought fiercely, using her forearms as vicious clubs. Diane, while lacking Beverly's training, seemed to hold her own amongst the chaos.

I crashed into the Bell. My skin crunched into the metal surface and I tripped over its lip, landing hard on the ground.

Despite my collision with it, the Bell barely moved. If anything, it had drifted closer to the ground rather than toward the river. I examined it for a second. It seemed to be perspiring.

This can't be good.

"Get up."

Chase's scream sounded nearly inhuman. I tried to respond, but I could barely move. I glanced behind me.

Chase marched toward me. He moved with ferocity, twitching with adrenaline. But it was the gun dangling from his right hand that dominated my attention.

I spat out some blood. "Screw you."

To his right, a gator thrashed about on the ground. Two soldiers stood several yards away, pumping vast amounts of lead into its body. Chase walked by the gator and squeezed the trigger of his Smith & Wesson. It recoiled with a loud blast and a thin column of smoke wafted out of the barrel. The gator collapsed to the bedrock and ceased to move.

As he strode past the dead beast, my gaze fixed upon his face. I thought about Kolen and Adcock, Jenson and his colony, Cartwright and the Sand Demons.

I didn't care what he did to me. What pissed me off was what he'd done to everybody else. But what really drove me to the edge of insanity was what I knew he would do if I failed to stop him. Not just to me. Not just to Beverly and Diane. But to thousands, if not millions of innocent people. I felt anger pouring through my body. It turned into fury and my fury turned into raw energy.

I started to roll over. But then I caught a glimpse of the Bell's underside. A long stationary shaft ran from the top of the device to the bottom. Two drums, one on top of the other, were positioned at the top half of the shaft. Dripping with condensation, they counter-rotated slowly, emitting a soft-pitched buzzing noise in the process.

Toward the bottom half of the shaft, I saw a partially cracked door with a big thermos inside of it. Something crystallized inside my head. I still didn't understand how the Bell worked. However, I knew that it produced a continuous supply of Red Mercury, which acted as a superconductor. And as I stared at the cracked door, I realized that, more likely than not, I was staring directly at the stuff.

Rictor removed some of the Red Mercury to give to Chase and that didn't blow up the Bell. What if I do the same? Will the device explode?

Only one way to find out.

Sticking my machete under the Bell, I jabbed it at the thermos. My blade bounced off harmlessly. Clenching my fist, I jabbed it again and again. Eventually, I poked a few holes in it and a razor-thin line of powder began to seep out.

Grabbing some of the powder, I palmed it. Then, I rolled onto my stomach and lifted myself to my knees.

Chase strode right up to me and stopped. Just beyond him, I saw the giant alligator lumbering toward us. A plan formed in my brain and I readied the powder. If I threw it in his face at the exact moment the gator arrived, Chase wouldn't have a chance.

"See you in the next life, Cyclone."

As the gun leveled at my face, I realized my plan wouldn't work. The gator was still a few yards away. The powder was at my side, clutched in my fingers.

Jumping up, I knocked his gun hand into the air. As I did so, I released the powder and it flew toward the river.

Chase and I struggled over the gun. I knocked it from his grasp. It fell to the ground and he shoved me toward the river.

As he stooped for his gun, I saw my pistol. My fingers closed around it. There was no time to think, only time to react. Raising the gun, I pointed it into the air. But before I could fire, the drifting cloud of Red Mercury sparked.

And then, the whole damn place went up in flames.

Chapter 64

A fireball formed over the river, sucking oxygen out of my lungs. The ground rumbled. The bedrock walls imploded.

Small slabs of rock hurtled in all directions, some smashing harmlessly into the walls. Others crashed into the gators. Still others knocked people down like bowling pins.

I focused my attention on the river. It seemed almost alive, shuddering and frothing angrily. I edged away, unsure of what to expect.

A jet of water exploded through the western wall. It slammed into the waterway, turning the seething river into white water rapids.

A loud bursting noise filled the air. The water level started to sink. Leaning closer, I saw a long, deep crack forming at the bottom of the rapids. It sucked the river into it, like bathwater running down a drain.

The gator paused in mid-step. Chase stood rooted to the spot. Both seemed to recognize that something bad was about to happen.

Something really bad.

I looked past Chase and saw Diane and Beverly ten yards away. They were staring at me and pointing. They appeared to be yelling, but I couldn't make out the words.

My eyes shifted and I saw others looking at me. I swung around. Abruptly, the bottom of the riverbed crumbled away. My eyes widened as the river vanished. Next thing I knew I was standing next to a gigantic natural chasm.

Water gushed from the west, cascading into the hole. The torrent crashed thunderously against an invisible bottom, somewhere far beneath me. It was like the underground version of Niagara Falls.

And I was standing right next to it.

The Bell was still my primary concern. At any moment, it could explode, turning the current destruction into a citywide nightmare.

Remove the rest of the Red Mercury? Or shove it into the chasm?

As I stared at the Bell, which still floated several inches above the bedrock, I weighed my options. Somehow, the exposed Red Mercury had self-detonated, albeit at a relatively small level. Removing the rest of it all at once could cause a catastrophic explosion.

On the other hand, if I shoved the Bell over the chasm, it would eventually fall to the bottom. It would explode, that much seemed certain. But the reduced amount of Red Mercury along with the extra distance from the surface could limit its reach. Even better, it would be difficult, if not impossible to recover the Bell from the bottom of the hole.

I made up my mind. Turning away from the chasm, I took up position behind the Bell. I leaned my shoulder against it, feeling its lukewarm, wet surface against my skin. I pushed it with all my might.

"Cyclone."

I ducked just as Chase's fist sailed through the air. His hand slammed into the side of the Bell. Despite the mayhem that surrounded me, I heard a light ping emanate from the object.

He howled and shook his hand vigorously.

"It's over," I said. "You lost. Now help me get this thing over the chasm before it kills us all."

"This isn't over, not by a long shot."

He tackled me to the bedrock. The ceiling above my head began to tremble. A collapse seemed imminent.

My eyes locked on his and I saw the insanity that plagued his soul. He was beyond reason, beyond help.

I elbowed him in the side and rolled back to the Bell. And that was when I got my second look at its interior. The drums vibrated but barely turned. The thermos of Red Mercury, now punctured, emitted a strange smoke.

I turned it over in my mind, quickly comparing my observations to everything I'd read in the journal. But I kept getting distracted by a single question.

Why does it need a constant source of electricity?

Ever since I'd unplugged it, the Bell had changed. It gained weight. It started to emit strange condensation. It no longer felt cold to the touch.

I remembered something from the journal. It talked about the process of creating a superconductor. One of the steps involved temperature. Words flashed before my eyes.

Liquid nitrogen.

Torsion.

My brain lit up like a Christmas tree. It was so obvious that I couldn't believe I hadn't figured it out already.

Red Mercury was a superconductor and thus, required supercooling. That was the purpose of the liquid nitrogen. Most likely, it was stored in the central shaft.

Chase jumped on top of me and rained blows down on my face. As I covered up, protecting myself, I pictured the Bell in my head. Fuel poured into the counter-rotating drums. They spun at top-speed, causing the molecules to undergo torsion. The resulting substance, Red Mercury, was collected in the thermos.

By removing the electricity, the liquid nitrogen apparatus had stopped working. As a result, the Red Mercury gradually lost its superconductivity. And that, I was willing to bet, was what caused it to become explosive.

I lifted my knees, throwing Chase off-balance and snapped an elbow at his jaw. It smashed against his face and I heard a tiny pop.

As he slipped to the side, I reached a hand underneath the Bell. I wasn't one hundred certain that I was doing the right thing, maybe not even fifty percent. But I was out of options. Chase wasn't going to allow me time to push it into the chasm. That left me with just one move.

I grabbed hold of the thermos. Doubts appeared in my mind, but I brushed them away. Everything I saw in Hartek's journal indicated that Red Mercury became a dangerous substance upon reaching a superconductive state. However, it only became volatile when it lost superconductivity. And based on the relatively minor detonation I'd observed, I was willing to bet that one other factor played a role in the substance's explosive power.

Concentration.

If my theory was correct, it wasn't the Red Mercury losing superconductivity that I needed to worry about. It was a ton of Red Mercury particles losing superconductivity while still bottled up tightly within the Bell.

Bracing myself, I yanked the thermos and it popped out of the Bell.

I bit my tongue as the Bell slammed to the earth, crushing my arm under it. I heard a crack but it sounded like it came from the bedrock instead of from my bones. Still, it hurt so badly, I could barely think.

Clearing my mind, I lifted my hand and smashed the thermos against the bedrock. I heard it crack and felt the glassy substance disintegrate in my fingers. A single thought rose in my brain.

I'm still alive.

The Red Mercury hadn't exploded. Yet. But I didn't have time to enjoy my brief triumph. Through hazy vision, I saw Chase step over me. His face was twisted with rage.

I chuckled despite the pain. "I hate to have to tell you this. But I think I broke it."

I spotted movement out of the corner of my eye. It was Beverly, running toward me. But it wasn't just her. There was something else.

Something big.

Something mean.

Something deadly.

Chase shoved his face into mine. "Where's Hartek's journal?"

I reached into my satchel and removed the book. "You mean this?"

Before he could stop me, I launched it into the air. It arced gently before falling unceremoniously into the chasm.

His face tightened and he lifted his gun.

I yanked my pinned arm as hard as I could. The bedrock scraped off a layer of flesh as I dragged the limb partway out from under the Bell. But once my wrist reached the lip, I couldn't move it any farther.

Chase pointed the gun at my head.

I looked at the alligator. It raced at me, its damaged jaw hanging open in grotesque fashion.

It was close, almost within striking distance of my head.

Why don't you go after someone else for a change, you asshole?

I grabbed my machete with my free hand. In one smooth movement, I sliced it at the alligator.

It flinched.

Diverted slightly, the beast plowed into the Bell, bashing its head into the metal surface.

The particle accelerator wobbled. An ear-splitting noise filled the area. The ground shifted under my body. The bedrock surface splintered.

Abruptly, it disintegrated beneath me.

Then, the huge Bell was gone along with the gator, both swallowed up by the yawning chasm.

Chase blinked, overcome by shock. Shaking his head, he pointed the gun at me again. Vaguely, I saw Beverly closing in on him. But she'd never make it in time.

I realized that my newly freed hand still clutched a handful of Red Mercury and broken glass. I launched it at Chase. The dust flew upward. Recoiling in fear, he backpedaled toward the hole.

He fell.

"Cyclone!" His scream echoed in the collapsing space.

And then he was gone, swallowed up by the chasm.

Chapter 65

Chase was dead.

The alligators were dead.

The Red Mercury was dissipated, the Bell and Hartek's journal lost in the chasm.

I felt a measure of grim satisfaction as the ground rumbled beneath me. I was bound to die, but at least I'd done some good first. Maybe eternal slumber wasn't such a bad thing after all.

Get up, idiot. You're not dying today.

With a loud groan, I rolled toward my injured arm. But it protested, sending shooting pain down my side.

I flopped onto my back again and stared at the ceiling. The blackish, jagged bedrock shuddered and heaved uncontrollably. It looked ready to collapse at any second.

Small hands grasped hold of my shoulders and lifted me into a sitting position. Then, they propelled me upward.

"If we ever get out of here, promise me you'll lose some weight."

I looked over my shoulder. Beverly stared back at me, her face a mixture of mirth and tension. "It's not me that's the problem," I joked. "It's all these damn muscles."

As I gained my footing, she pushed me against the wall for added support. Small chunks of rock crumbled away at my touch, falling all around me, leaving trails of dust in their wake.

"Are you okay?" she asked.

"I'll be fine."

I looked around. The war had ceased. Several gators lay on the ground, still and lifeless. Bloodied bodies were heaped about the bedrock. The sight of so much death took my breath away.

"Where's everyone?" I asked.

"You're looking at most of them. Some died, others ran for it."

"What about Diane? Is she okay?"

To my surprise, her face twisted. For a split-second, I detected disappointment in her eyes. Then, in an instant, it vanished. "She's fine. So am I by the way."

"I didn't mean –"

"She's wounded pretty badly. If we're going to save her life, we need to get her to a hospital now."

I nodded at the bodies. "It looks like we're missing someone. What happened to Standish?"

"I'm right here."

I followed the voice. Standish stood at the mouth of the tube, leaning against one side of it. His face was directed at the chasm and I thought I saw a wistful look in his eyes.

I stepped toward him. He slid into the center of the tube, blocking my path.

"Get out of the way."

"That's not happening," he replied.

"We don't have to die here."

"Yes we do."

I glared at him. He was a large, powerful man. But I saw none of that. All I saw was a man who'd helped to kill Jenson and Cartwright. A man who wanted to kill me.

If he succeeded, he'd surely murder Diane and Beverly as well. I'd spent the last three years regretting my inability to save others. Three years of inner pain.

Three years of an endless nightmare.

I leapt at him. He socked me in the jaw and I flew back into the grotto. I landed on my back and skidded a few feet along the bedrock. Beverly reached for him, but he shoved her aside with ease. Then he ran at me.

I saw my machete lying on the ground. Picking it up, I rose to my feet. But before I could swing it, Standish's body crunched into my chest.

As he propelled me backward, I looked over my shoulder. The chasm was just a few feet away. In mere seconds, the ground would disappear and both of us would tumble to our doom.

With a savage cry, I slashed the machete through the air, implanting it several inches into a gap in the crumbling bedrock wall. As Standish pushed me farther, my feet left the ground. A wall of water slammed into me and then, I was dangling over the chasm, utterly engulfed by the raging waterfall.

My body hurt like hell but I hung on anyway. Through the torrent, I saw Beverly running toward me. Diane limped along behind her.

I felt heavy. Glancing down, I saw Standish holding onto my waist. He looked up, staring at me with insanity in his eyes. "Let go, damn you," he shouted. "Let go!"

He wrenched his body. His fingers clawed at me. My right hand loosened then slipped off the handle. My left fingers began to weaken.

I was seconds away from death.

My gaze hardened. I pulled back my right arm and swung.

I swung with every ounce of passion I could muster. I swung for the colony. I swung for the Sand Demons.

I swung for myself.

My fist smashed into his jaw. His head flew backward. He lost his grip. As I watched, he tumbled end over end into the bottomless chasm.

My body sagged with relief.

Suddenly, the machete moved. I turned toward the wall.

It moved again.

Reaching up, I scrabbled for a grip. But the onrushing water thwarted my efforts.

Fingers enclosed around my waist. They were smaller than Standish's, yet larger in number. I felt myself dragged away from the chasm, the machete still stuck in my left hand.

I fell to the ground. My eyes focused and I saw Beverly and Diane leaning over me.

Diane shook her head. "Can't you do anything the easy way?"

Her tone was filled with annoyance, but I saw the smile etched across her face.

I grinned. "That's just not my style."

With their help, I rose to my feet. As I retrieved my pistol, I heard loud shuddering noises. Then a large bedrock slab broke off from the ceiling and crashed onto the ground.

As if on cue, the western wall burst into pieces, sending hundreds of pounds of rock hurtling into the grotto. It seemed to start a chain reaction and the entire area along with the tube began to implode.

Beverly shot me a look. "I guess we wore out our welcome."

"I think that happened a few hours ago."

She took off running. I pushed Diane in front of me and then raced after them, driven by the sound of crashing rock.

In a few minutes, we reached the intersection leading to the main subway system. As I darted into the connecting tunnel, I stole one last glance over my shoulder. The entire collection of tubes was rapidly vanishing under a mountain of broken bedrock. Memories of the last few days flashed through my brain, but one face stayed prominent. It was a face that belonged to a man I'd never met. And yet, I felt like I knew him all the same.

"Sorry, Alfred," I said quietly. "You built one hell of a subway system."

EPILOGUE

HARTEK'S CACHE

September 15

"Are you sure you're up for this?"

Diane narrowed her eyes. "I should be asking you that question. You're the one with his arm in a sling."

I walked to the edge of the platform. It was well after midnight. Other than a few college kids, the area was empty.

I stopped next to the wall and waited for Diane to join me. After nearly a week in the hospital, she looked like a whole new woman. Her face exhibited a rosy complexion and the spark in her eyes had returned with a vengeance.

After she joined me, I looked both ways and then hopped down to the tracks. Setting a course due south, I led her down the Lexington Avenue Line.

The track bed was dry. And thanks to Chase's unexplained disappearance, temporary control over the MTA had fallen into new hands. Those new hands saw fit to settle affairs with the labor unions. It was just a temporary settlement of course. As Chase's memory faded into oblivion, I had no doubt that negotiations and conflicts would begin anew.

But for the time being, the lockout was over. And that meant a return to normalcy of a sort. Subway trains flew through the tunnels on a semi-regular basis. City traffic decreased to pre-lockout levels. Foot traffic also declined as large numbers of people stopped walking to work and instead, returned to the relative comfort and speed of the subway system.

Even the rain finally came to an end.

Of course, there was still the small matter of the recent earthquake. Just a few days earlier, a rash of buildings, primarily situated in the midtown area, experienced strange ground shifts. It was nothing serious of course, since steel pilings supported the buildings in that area. Engineers and architects were investigating the phenomenon but so far, hadn't announced an explanation.

I wasn't worried. It would take a lot of digging to unearth Beach's tubes, even more to excavate the Bell. And I doubted that would happen anytime soon.

"So, you couldn't get in touch with Beverly huh?"

I shook my head. "Nope."

"She just left?"

"That's right."

"Strange. Very strange."

Agreed. Where are you, Beverly?

After escaping Beach's subway system, she'd vanished. I never even saw her leave. One minute she stood right next to me.

The next minute, she was gone.

While Diane recovered in the hospital, I searched the entire island of Manhattan for her. I even staked out ShadowFire's headquarters. But I never found her.

Although she never mentioned it, I knew the reason for her disappearance. I saw it in her stormy violet eyes back in the tunnels.

She knew I had feelings for Diane, feelings that were too complicated to dismiss. But what she didn't realize was that my feelings for her were just as strong and just as complicated.

Diane was beautiful, loyal, accomplished, graceful, and driven. She lived her life by a firm moral code, which I begrudgingly admired. She was everything the archaeologist in me desired in a lady.

Beverly was similar in many ways, yet different in so many others. She was sexy as all hell, endowed with a daredevil's spirit, and mysterious to boot. Coupled with her unbridled passion, she was everything the treasure hunter inside of me wanted in a woman.

How do you choose between two sides of yourself?

As I turned to follow the 42nd Street Shuttle's non-pedestrian track, I peeked over my shoulder. Diane flashed me a winning smile. She was so much. But was she enough? Would anything ever be enough to satisfy my conflicting personas? Or was I doomed to walk the earth alone, always caught between two worlds, part of both, but belonging to neither?

I stopped in the middle of the tunnel. I heard clanging machinery and hissing pipes. But there were no signs of life.

I looked at the smooth, slightly discolored wall. It was closed, revealing no sign of the hidden door.

Diane halted next to me. "I don't see anything."

"You will in a minute," I replied. "Chase must've covered up Hartek's laboratory after he realized that the Bell wasn't inside."

I hoisted myself onto the concrete ledge and walked across it until I reached a crack. On the other side, the surface changed. It looked newer and thicker than the rest of the ledge.

Kneeling down, I felt along the wall. My fingers brushed up against the etching of a skull and two crossed pickaxes. Placing my thumb against the symbol, I pushed.

The button depressed. I heard a click and the ground started to rumble. I grabbed onto the wall as the ledge shifted inward, revealing the hidden corridor.

Taking out my flashlight, I slid into the space. I held my breath, preparing myself for the stench of death.

Instead, I was greeted with a strong odor of disinfectant. Surprised, I shone my light around in all directions. The bodies were gone as were most of the lab's materials. The room was now empty, save for some scattered bricks in the corner.

I grunted in disappointment. "Well, if there was anything here, it's gone now."

"What were you hoping to find?"

"Gold. Nazi gold. According to Chase, Karl Hartek was entrusted with a supply of gold bars from ODESSA. I figured we might find them here."

"Always the treasure hunter." She shook her head but there was a small smile on her face. Then, her expression changed to one of puzzlement. "Why did you think it would be in here?"

"Something Jenson said to me before he died. He said, 'Don't forget the gold…it's the foundation…the foundation of Hartek's…'"

"Hartek's what?"

I shrugged. "I thought I'd find the answer in here."

"Did he use gold in the Bell?"

I nodded. "Its fuel consisted of a liquid formulation of gold and mercury. When the Sand Demons captured the Bell, they found a supply of the stuff, which they used to refuel it over the years."

"So maybe that's all he meant." She gave me a thoughtful look. "Maybe he was just trying to tell you that the gold was used as fuel, or if you will, the foundation of the Bell."

"Maybe. Maybe not."

I replayed the conversation over and over in my mind. His wording struck me as rather strange. Why would he use the term foundation?

Unless...

Swiveling to the side, I saw a small pile in the northwest corner of the room. I marched over and knelt down. My flashlight illuminated a couple of bricks, sending brilliant rays of light cascading in a million directions. I shielded my eyes and leaned in close.

My heart began to race. "These aren't ordinary bricks."

I picked up one of them. It weighed a ton. Brushing off the powdery surface, I saw a picture of a bird perched atop a wreath that held the Nazi symbol. Silently, I read the lettering.

Deutsche Reichsbank. 1 kilo. Feingold. 999.9.

I glanced at the wall. If my memory was correct, the entire surface had previously consisted of brick. But now, many of those bricks appeared to be missing.

Confused, I started to put the heavy brick back on the ground. But my eye caught some tiny scratches. Leaning down, I saw a few lines of text.

If you found this, then you know I was already here. I need to apologize. I lied to you. I can't explain it now, but the Bell was never my main priority. I was after these bars, from the very first day we met.

I know you have feelings for her. When you sort them out, come find me if you want. All you need is this bar. It and the others are not what they appear to be. Until we meet again...B.G.

Her words slammed into me like a subway train. I couldn't help but feel betrayed. Beverly had returned to the laboratory and stolen what remained of Hartek's gold. But what did her cryptic message mean? And why had she been after the gold in the first place? For its value? Or some other reason?

I didn't understand it. But as I looked back at Diane, I wasn't sure that I even cared. Maybe she was enough for me. Maybe not.

Either way, I intended to find out.

Reaching over, I gently touched her face. Then, I guided her lips to mine and we kissed. Electric shocks ran through my brain and I forgot everything around me.

Everything but her.

"What are you doing?" she whispered.

"Making up for lost time."

"You've been gone for three years, you know."

I grinned as I guided her onto the floor. "Well, I guess we've got a lot of catching up to do."

About the Author

David Meyer is an adventurer and first-time author. Whether hunting for pirate treasure or exploring ancient Pre-Columbian ruins, his love of mystery inspires him to seek answers to the unknown. As the *Guerrilla Explorer*, he writes regularly about lost treasure, historical mysteries, forgotten lands, and strange cryptids at http://www.GuerrillaExplorer.com/.

Printed in Great Britain
by Amazon.co.uk, Ltd.,
Marston Gate.